LIGHTNING RISING

Book 1 of The Shadow Wars Series

Kristin Satterfield

Warden Bear Press

Summary: Forced from her home Sally Brown, Loran must learn quickly how to hide in plain sight at Kent Wood. Though with war on the horizon, it could be harder than she expected.

[1. Dystopian- Fiction 2. Science Fiction]

Paperback: ISBN-13: 979-8-9869306-0-2

Kindel: ISBN-13: 979-8-9869306-1-9

Ebook(Epub): ISBN-13: 979-8-9869306-2-6

Hardback: ISBN-13: 979-8-9869306-3-3

Audio: ISBN-13: 979-8-9869306-4-0

First edition 2023 Printed in U.S.A

THIS BOOK STARTED BACK in 2012 and it's hard to believe it's finally here in my hands years later. It feels like a dream. I couldn't have done this without all the amazing people in my life that have been beside me along the way.

To the man who has stood beside with through this process. I'm not sure I could have done this without your support. The long nights and hectic days were easier with you beside me reminding me of all that is good. Thank you so much for putting up with my excitement, worry, and late-night brainstorming sessions. I love you, James.

To my number one fan, Kathryn Bogar. I love you. You have been there with me from the first draft giving me input and fangirling with me along the way. The truth is many aspects of this story were inspired by you and I hope you love the finished product as much as I do. I can't wait to keep sharing ideas with you for years to come.

To my amazing parents Leigh and Joe Bogar. To think after all this time, we are here. I would have never become the writer I am today if you all hadn't believed in me. When others said I couldn't, you told me I could. When they doubted me, you pushed and stood beside me. Whether it was long walks talking about ideas or simple grammar edits, I always knew I could count on you all. Thank you for your love, I love you both!

To my amazing editors:

S.D Howard, you have been a God-send in my life. It is thanks to you that this story reached its full potential. You knew how to help me voice ideas that have been in my head for years and put them on paper. I can't thank you enough.

Cheyenne Van L. thank you so much for all your work. You have been patient with me when I'm sure I've been hectic, and you have ensured my book is smoother. Thank you so much for all you have done.

To my beta reader Kate Tomlinson. Thank you for all your input it really allowed me insight into my readers and what I needed to move forward with. I hope you enjoy the final work as much as you enjoyed its predecessor. Don't worry I kept some of your favorite scenes in the bonus content.

To my author community. The truth of the matter is I wouldn't be here today without all of you. Through your amazing support, both financial and emotional, I have been able to push through and make it to this point. I hope this book and its series are all you hoped for and more when you put your faith in me. I look forward to sharing this journey with all of you!

Jack Satterfield   Ann and Gary Wooley   Rachel Langdon   Mike Dillard   Arwyn Nyx   Monica Cook   Daria A Kotys-Schwartz   Joshua Dillard   Julie Steinbrenner   Sarah Thomas   Regan Voit   Ashley Cowan   Kate Tomlinson   Caereen Allen   Ginger Barnhart   Anthony Ennis   Linda D'Andrea   Debra Bryson   Eric Koester   Elizabeth Noble   Sarah Silverstein   Ben Henderson   Donna Westwood   Elijah Monroe   bathsheba45   Rachel Jacobs   Alicia Magee   Pablo Rodriguez   Rebecca Blandin   Chase Owen   Adele Thomas   Jenny & David Larsen   June Weiss   Susan Michele Riffe   Betty Pilcher   Megan Fier   Krista Rietema   Laura Highsmith   Cindy Alvarez   Megan Flake   Laura De Young   Judy Liu   Matthew Kleberger   Jim Stanczak   Dana Lee Haines   Paul Yevcak   Janet L Townsend   David Morrison

Joe Bogar   Russ and Cyndy Hoover   Kathryn Bogar   Lisa Stern   Stephen Howard   Mark and Stephanie Hamilton

PROLOGUE

"My Love,

I know this story will be hard to hear. It was hard to live, but I think it's time I shared it. There aren't many of us left that lived through it. The rivalries, the war, the end of it all.

Sometimes I look back on our school days and wonder what we were thinking. Did any of it really matter? I know it felt like it did. We really weren't that different, despite our reputations.

Sally Brown, the school for the creative and athletic. Whatever your passion might be, they could bring it to life.

Kent Wood was for the brilliant. The world never saw students more intelligent than those who graduated from its hallowed halls.

Sandy Village was for the strong. Trained from birth for combat, the students were willing to fight for what they wanted—no matter the cost.

The Falcons knew how to cultivate the kind of heart, but don't mistake kindness for weakness. Any of them could slit your throat without a blink of an eye.

Trident was the place for the brave and loyal. When they were on your side, you knew you had an ally for life.

Water High was as ruthless as they were cunning. Never make a deal with a Water student—you won't be on the winning side.

Michel Thomas valued only the wise. *Though schools weren't supposed to kick students out, they would if you couldn't meet their standards.*

Though I didn't get along with any of the other schools, Kent Wood was always the worst in my eyes. It took my parents forcing my transfer to realize everything wasn't all I thought it was. Sure, they were as stuck up as I expected, though not as bad as Water High. I mean those students were a different breed...

I'm getting off track.

My story starts when I transferred. Things were quite different then, the schools in constant turmoil, the MEDs still in their infancy, and The Picking.... Well, that was its own thing....

There is just so much to tell, and I'm not sure how much time I have left. I want you to know it all. How I met your father. When we fell in love. Our betrayal at your uncle's hands."

"Wait, Grandpa, what does GG mean: uncle's betrayal?" The voice of a young boy broke through the sound of the hologram's speakers. "Uncle Mike could never hurt a fly!"

An elderly man reached over to pause the recording. "Of course, not little one, she's not talking about Mike. You must remember this was originally recorded for your dad."

"That really doesn't explain much. How does this have to do anything with my assignment on the event in the 20s? Or The Founding Group?" the boy whined.

"You asked me my story because I used to know them all. Your grandma knew them better though. Her story is theirs as well," the old man said patiently.

"There is no way you knew them all."

"No, it's true. We once considered them family, but that was a long time ago, before the war. Now do you want to argue more, or should I continue? Your grandma's story is not a short one."

The boy sat down, properly chastised. "Sorry, Grandpa. Continue."

"Thank you." He flipped the small disk in front of them back on and the image of a middle-aged woman, covered in scars, flickered to life in the middle of the large study.

"Let's start at the beginning.

The atmosphere in the car was unusually tense for a dinner out with my parents...."

Chapter 1

Me: *Have you ever wanted your favorite meal so bad that you were willing to be arrested for it?*

My fingers flew across the Holo-screen of my PortMed.

7:19 p.m.

Chris: *Nope. Never.*

Chris's reply was almost instant, and I scoffed.

7:20 p.m.

Me: *Me neither.*

"Loran, dear, what are you up to?"

My head snapped up as Mother's question broke the mostly silent atmosphere of the car.

"Nothing, Mother," I replied, quickly swiping away from the screen, smiling brightly up at her as it disappeared into the silver band on my left wrist.

"You are on that Portable Communication and Medical Device too often," she said with a hint of disdain.

I let out an exhausted sigh. "It's called a PortMed, Mother. All of that is just way too much to say. It's like calling the MEDs: Medical Express Devices."

Mother hummed in the back of her throat as she raised a single, perfectly groomed eyebrow, leaning back in her chair and crossing her tight-covered legs. Father let out a soft chuckle next to her as he flipped the map on the car's Holo-screen closed.

"Now, my dear, be nice; it's a special occasion, let the girl enjoy her time off." He placed a gentle hand on her leg, teasing the ends of her skirt with his large fingers.

With another hum, Mother slapped his hand away, crossing her arms and turning her head away from him.

"You are far too lenient on her," she chastised, but the smile tugging on her red lips and the mirth in her deep green eyes countered the sharpness of her tone.

"What is the occasion, anyway?" I asked, crossing my own white tight-covered legs and leaning forward. I steepled my blue-painted fingernails.

"Why, the end of your last term as a high school junior of course!" Mother said, not looking my way.

"Uh-huh," I countered, raising my eyebrow, and watching as my parents shot a quick nervous glance at each other. "You have never celebrated the end of any of my years before."

"Well, this year is quite special, is it not?" Father said with a tight smile that made the freckles on his cheeks, so like my own, squish. "After all this time, next year you will be a Paired Woman."

I felt my PortMed squeeze as my anxiety spiked. Almost immediately, my racing heart calmed as the MEDs took effect, releasing whatever chemicals where needed to balance me.

"The Picking, how could I forget." The sarcasm in my voice made Mother glare.

"You should be excited for—"

"I'll only be happy if I end up with Chris," I interrupted her as the car took a sharp left and my seat adjusted under me to counter the motion.

"I've told you time and time again—"

"Oh, we're here!" It was Father who interrupted Mother as the car pulled up in front of the restaurant. Unease settled in as Mother dropped the issue without a fuss.

The black-tinted windows of the car dissolved, revealing the majestic entrance before us. A valet walked our way along the velvet red carpet, his suit as immaculate as his manners as he opened the car door.

Father exited first, buttoning his suit jacket. The expensive black silk complemented his tan skin. He reached down extending his hand to Mother. She took it. Her blood-red nails shone in the overhead canopy light as she gripped his hand. In a swift motion, he pulled her up, her golden dress, bright against her pale skin, flowing around her with the movement.

After assuring she was settled on her six-inch heels, he turned to me. I took a deep breath, adjusting the long sleeves of my deep blue dress to cover my Silver PortMed before I accepted. His large hand encompassed mine, my skin standing out only slightly lighter than his as he pulled me up. Gracefully, as I was taught, I glided forward on my heels.

With a bow, the valet tapped instructions on the side of the car, and it hovered away to park.

I watched him, waiting until he turned and offered me his arm. Resting my hand in the crook of his elbow, I flipped my wavy brown hair back with the other. The blue-tipped ends of my hair complemented the black-bricked building before me as they flew backward.

Father took the lead, Mother on his arm as they headed to the golden door.

Following, I nodded my head in thanks to the girl who opened it for us.

The restaurant was filled with the soft melody of the grand piano in the farthest right corner. The mouthwatering smell of high-end food wafted from the small kitchen in front of us. Ten small tables filled the u-shaped space, their black legs contrasting against white marble tiles.

The three other parties didn't turn, our entrance unimportant in their eyes. A stern glare from Mother accompanied my scoff. I checked once again that my silver PortMed was covered as the valet pulled out my chair and I sat.

"Welcome to La Perle. We are honored to have you, Mr. and Mrs. Black." A tall, wiry man in a chef's uniform walked up to our table, an enormous smile on his face.

"Chef Martenz, it is an honor to be here," Father said with a slight bow of his head. "To enjoy the food of a ten Michelin-starred chef is a dream of ours."

Chef Martenz beamed. "Yes, two years running; here's hoping for 2122 next year, no?"

"Oh yes," Mother agreed. "I have no doubt you will receive another soon."

"Well, I wouldn't be here if it hadn't been for your family's generous recommendation. Tonight is on the house."

Father sputtered. "Oh, you don't have to."

"Nonsense. Now I have been quite rude ignoring this beautiful young lady here." Chef Martenz turned to me, holding out his hand.

I was careful to place my right one in it.

He brought it to his lips, kissing it before letting go. "Who might you be, dear?"

"This is our daughter, Loran." Father's voice was filled with pride, and I felt myself blushing.

"It is very nice to meet you, sir," I said with my best manners, bowing my head. "I am honored to be here."

"Oh my, I have heard about your beautiful child. The rumors don't do her justice. It is *my* honor to meet you," he countered, and my blush grew.

"Yes, we are here to celebrate the beginning of her final year," Mother said.

Chef Martenz brightened, fiddling with the thin gold Mate Necklace around his neck. "Ah yes, The Picking. Such fond memories," he reminisced. "Well then, it is quite a special occasion. I know just the course for you. Please settle in, your food will be out soon!" His deep bow drew the eyes of the other occupants in the room before he disappeared.

"Why are we really here?" I hissed in a whisper as a few of the fairer ladies began gossiping behind their hands.

Mother shot them a pursed smile as she hissed back at me, "Behave." Louder, she said, "I am so glad your tutors agreed to give you the night off to be with us. I have missed you so, dear."

The whispers grew to a subtle roar before they were silenced by one sharp look from Father's gray-blue eyes.

My PortMed squeezed as my unease grew. I felt calm again as the MEDs took effect, releasing whatever was needed to settle my nerves, then inspected my parents. It had been a long time since they expected me to play the tutored student act in public. They were up to something.

"Why yes, I am so very grateful," I replied, my voice light and airy as I forced myself to play the part. "It has been too long." Father's hand upon mine as he reached across the table was comforting.

"Please fill us in on what you learned this year," he said.

I did as requested, editing the information to sound as though each class was tailored to me. Our food arrived soon after. I ate with my best table manners, responding where needed as my parents spoke about work and the future. The duck melted in my mouth as Mother fiddled with the intricate gold Mate Necklace laying along her collarbone. Thin branching lines split from a central chain, like the tops of a tree, each ending in a tiny gem, none of them alike. I eyed Father's complimentary band, the thick chains housing a single gem inside each loop.

"And that is why we think it would be best if you joined us," Mother said.

There was a pregnant pause as I tried to remember what they had been talking about. "I am sorry, Mother, it seems I missed something. Could you repeat that?" I asked as I fiddled with the tasseled ends of my dress. As she shot me a disappointed look, I gave her my best smile.

"I was saying, dear, that your father and I think it would be best if you joined us on our move to California." She repeated through clenched teeth. "We both think it could benefit you to see more of the world before you graduate."

My blood turned cold.

"Your move to District Seven," I clarified.

"Yes, of course. Where else?" she snapped.

Father placed a hand upon hers, glancing at the other tables as he did.

"You can't be serious." I dropped all pretense as I hissed under my breath, leaning forward.

"Manners," Mother hissed back.

"You're talking about Kent Wood."

Father's hand on mine reminded me of our audience.

With a forced smile, I continued lowly, "Now I see why you brought me here. You wanted an audience to witness my death sentence."

"Now, Loran, behave." Father's tone was soft, but the edge in his eyes had me clamping my mouth shut. "We are doing no such thing."

I let out a barked laugh, not caring as a lady across the way gasped. "Oh, really Father? Then what would you call sending me straight into the heart of my rival school?"

Mother hissed, and I straighten as the waiter returned to our table with dessert. We thanked her with gentle smiles before turning to our food.

As the piano crescendoed, Mother whispered, "You are eighteen and almost a Paired Woman. You need to learn to let go of such childish things."

"I'm not being childish. It's simply a fact. The moment I step onto the Knights' campus, I will certainly lose my head." I could feel my hysteria growing.

"You will listen to your mother and stop at once. She was kind enough to think of you in this time and suggest you join us," Father snapped.

The air grew cold as my heart broke. Father hadn't snapped at me in many years. I cast my eyes down to my dessert. Their green-gray reflection stared back at me from the silver dining plate, wet with tears.

"I'm sorry," Father said sometime later, placing a gentle hand upon mine as I put down my spoon. Mother did the same beside him. Their twin Mate Tattoos flashed at me on their ring fingers, complementing their necklaces. "I should not have raised my voice. We are just worried about you, my little bear." His soft tone gave me the strength to look up at him.

"I don't want to go," I pleaded.

They exchanged a look.

"Listen, dear, the simple fact is Sally Brown is no longer the best place for you." Mother's tone was soft as she rubbed my hand. "Your ranking has been slipping. It will not be long before you fall into the third tier."

I stiffened. "You do realize that's not a bad rank to have, right?" I countered.

"For everyone else, sure, but you are our daughter, and as such you will be nothing but the best," Father said with certainty.

"Your father is right. Before this last year, you were on your way to the top. What happened?"

The image of a white, twisted root flashed before my eyes before I forced it down. "Nothing," I ground out.

"And that is exactly my point," Mother continued. "Your school is obviously to blame for this slip. To be honest, we should have made the move sooner; after all Kent Wood is known for its academics. But things have been so busy in the office."

I ground my teeth, feeling my PortMed squeeze, but not receiving any relief as my anger grew.

"You don't know what you're talking about. Sally Brown is the best school in the districts!" Mother's grip was sharp, and I lowered my volume, glancing around to make sure no one heard me. One of the tables was vacating the room, and I watched as the young boy in the middle of their party flounced forward. His golden PortMed shone brightly in the light. I glanced back to make sure my dim silver one was still hidden before I continued. "You know, if you felt this way the whole time, you could have actually sent me to a private school or hired those tutors you are so fond of flaunting."

"You know why we did not," Mother said. "You need to experience what life is like for all the other children of the country, not just the select few. You have many years ahead of you to rub elbows with the cotton heads and all that. The connections you make now, though, those are the ones that will truly matter."

I opened my mouth to argue when a waiter approached our table.

"Chef Martenz wishes for me to make sure all has been to your liking tonight?"

Mother nodded, smiling brightly. "Oh yes, it has been truly amazing. Please give him our compliments and let him know we will be sending our friends his way."

The waiter beamed. "I will let him know. Please stay as long as you'd like and have a wonderful night."

"Thank you," I said as he walked away.

Mother stood from the other side of the table, and Father joined her. "We will not discuss this further," she commanded as she grabbed her shawl from Father's outstretched hand as he pulled it from his micro bag. "The decision is final." She wrapped it around her shoulder when it was done expanding, and Father gave her his arm. We waited for the valet to escort me out, and entered the cool, late June night of Old Colorado.

"I will never forgive you for this," I promised as I settled back into the car. They didn't respond as we made the drive back to my dorm at Sally Brown.

Chapter 2

"You can't be serious," Sarah hissed.

"Oh, trust me, I am," I countered as I flopped onto my bed. Kathy's slight form bounced as I did.

"Do they realize that those Buckets would rather serve your head on a plate than welcome you to their fold?" Sarah paced in front of me in my small dorm room as she scratched at her PortMed, leaving bright red lines on her pale skin. I watched her, concerned.

"Hey, don't do that," Kathy's gentle voice called as she reached a hand out to stop her.

Sarah pulled away quickly, a glare in her chestnut eyes. They immediately softened as Kathy shrank back. "I'm sorry." Her voice was soft, and she reached out to tuck Kathy's dirty-blonde hair behind her tiny ear. "It's just so itchy. No one tells you that about the MEDs."

"Well, most people don't start them fourteen years too late," I countered with a grin as she stuck her tongue out at me.

Her lush black hair fell in a curtain in front of her and she flipped it aside, her beautiful blue and white bracelets jingling. As she turned, she almost slammed into the desk sitting below my window to the left of my bed. Avoiding it, she continued pacing a hole in my tan carpet.

"It's not my fault my parents didn't want me on this stuff. You know, I'm beginning to believe they were right. What even are the MEDs made of?"

"Oh no, don't you start with that holistic BotJuice," I said as Kathy giggled. "The MEDs are the sole reason our generation is the healthiest and happiest in history."

Sarah huffed, leaving another bright red mark before Kathy swatted her. "You are only going to make it worse," she said. "Loran is right. We are the Pill Perfect generation for a reason. Now get with the program." Her voice was light and teasing, but her eyes were wary. I tried not to wince as Sarah pulled down her blue shirt over her slightly rounded belly, the jagged scar from her severe break last year still zigzagging up her left arm.

"We're getting off-topic," I said. "Today is about *my* problems, remember?"

Sarah sent me a grateful smile.

"Oh yes," Kathy said, turning to me.

Sarah sat down on the beanbag chair across from us. It sagged under her weight, and her long legs bent awkwardly.

"What are we going to do?" Kathy whispered, sounding lost.

I grabbed Kathy's caramel hand as she fidgeted with her gray jacket. Her blue and white pointer finger prosthetic whirled as it grasped me.

"I'm not sure. They're unwavering and have already started the paperwork. I have till the end of this term before I'm out."

Kathy let out a sigh. "Have you told Chris yet? He's sure to think of something."

"Told me what?" We turned to the tall blond boy standing in the doorway to my dorm room.

"Love!" I called, surprised to see him back from basketball practice so soon. He sent me a dazzling smile, opening his arms as I ran to him. I fell into him, grasping onto his blue and white Varsity letter jacket.

"Hey," he whispered into my hair. "I've missed you." Sarah made a gagging sound behind us.

I turned to see Kathy swatting the air at her lightly.

"Please, lover boy, it's only been a day," Sarah said.

"Oh, as if you aren't as bad with Haden," I shot back, settling into Chris's broad shoulder. His familiar scent of honey and leather surrounded me.

He let out a chuckle. "So, what do you need to tell me?" I stiffened in his embrace for only a moment, but it was enough. "Loran." His tone was a warning.

"Come in first, please?" I asked, slipping from his grasp, pulling him in by the hand to my bed. Kathy slid past us and shut my door, locking it. Chris's gaze was wary as he sat down on the bed.

"You're not breaking up with me, are you?" he asked before I could continue.

I snapped my jaw shut, staring at him before I let out a laugh.
His face turned red. "Seriously?"

"I'm sorry," I choked out through my laughter. "It's just after everything...well, that's about as far from the truth as you can get." My mirth was quickly dashed as I remembered my problem. "My parents came by yesterday," I started as I settled down beside him, not glancing his way.

Kathy sat in the desk chair by Sarah and gave me a reassuring smile, her big brown eyes sad.

"Ah, I see," Chris said, rubbing small circles on my back. "Are they getting on to you again for not seeing them more? 'Cause I know you've told them how unusual it is for them to keep coming around. The rest of us haven't seen our parents in at least seven years."

I shook my head. "No, no, that's not it." I took a deep breath, trying to steel my resolve. "They are moving."

"Well, that's good then—"

"And they want me to join them."

The room fell silent. Kathy and Sarah shifted uncomfortably as the temperature dropped.

"You can't be serious." Chris's voice was a deep rumble, and his hand bundled the back of my shirt.

"That's what I said," Sarah added.

"I am," I said before he could continue. "But that's not all. It's where they are moving that has me freaking out."

"Where?" Chris demanded.

"School district *seven*."

Chris was off the bed before I could finish, his hands flying to his spiked hair. His ice-blue eyes were almost manic as he stared down at me. "Do they want you to die!"

"That's what I said," Sarah chimed again, and he spun to her in a fury.

"This is no time for jokes!" he yelled at her.

Instantly she stood, squaring her shoulders, getting in his face. They were almost eye to eye with her ungodly height. "Do not yell at me," she snapped. "I'm not the reason she's heading to her funeral."

"Well, you're not helping now, are you? For once you could get off your lazy Holo-as—"

"Please...quiet down," Kathy demanded, shoving herself between them. "There's only so much noise the dampeners can drown out." Her voice had an edge to it that had Chris and Sarah looking properly chastised. "We don't want the entire school knowing about this. Think about what they would do." Instantly, the two deflated as the atmosphere grew somber.

"Kathy is right. We can't let anyone know." I said, standing and placing a gentle hand on both their shoulders. As they looked down at me, I tried not to cry. "I shouldn't have even told you all. If they find out you knew all along, you could be executed for treason."

Chris brought a hand to my face, catching a tear with his calloused finger. "I'm so sorry. We should be working to find a solution, not arguing," he said. "I just...don't understand why they would choose to do something like this."

I sighed. "They think my grades are slipping because of my schooling." A knowing look passed between the group.

"And you couldn't tell them about The Shadow," Kathy concluded, her voice weak.

I nodded, thinking back to the piece of paper I found in my room three months ago. "Everyone knows he only targets rank two's and a few rank three's. I can't seem to break into the first rank, so..." I admitted as Chris squeezed my shoulder.

"I would never allow him to take you," he said with conviction.

"But that's just it. He almost did. I mean, when was the last time you heard about him leaving a warning? If Haden hadn't come over when he did, I don't want to think of what might have happened." A shiver ran down my spine.

"That's behind us now," Chris said, taking my hand. He led me back to my bed. We fell onto the soft blue covers.

Sarah pulled Kathy over and they did the same on my right. Kathy fell into the crook of my shoulder and Sarah landed on her other side. I stared up at the white ceiling as they both grabbed my hand, awkwardly intertwining our fingers. I grabbed Chris's hand with my other and squeezed. The muffled sound of students passing by outside filtered over us. Everyone except us excited about the start of the term on Tuesday.

"What if we ran away?" Chris's voice was soft.

"And go where?" I asked.

"Into the mountains, of course. There're a ton of abandoned homes left over from the bombings. We could hide out there."

I laughed, giving him a gentle shove. "Yeah, and we would starve in a week."

Chris chuckled. "Come on now, between your years of combat experience and my skills, we could totally hunt for food."

I sighed, squeezing his hand again. "I doubt Muay Thai and basic medical training are going to help me kill a bear. It's certainly a nice thought."

"What if we spoke to the council, asked them to intervene and stop the paperwork," Kathy piped up.

"I don't think that's the best idea," said Sarah hesitantly. "There's no guarantee that they will even listen, and if they even suspect that Loran is leaving of her own free will, then they won't hesitate to make an example of her."

Watching the blue tips of my hair twirl around my finger, I felt my heart fall. "I'll have to change my hair." I pointed out, feeling Chris stiffen next to me. "I won't cut it, just change the dye. But I'll have to time it right. I can't be seen on campus in green and gold, but I can't arrive in blue and white."

"Gold would go best with your hair," Kathy added.

"It's certainly better than puke green," Sarah said, reaching over and grabbing an end to twirl.

"At least you didn't get that tattoo we talked about," Chris teased, and I laughed, drawing his right arm up and turning it to see the blue paw tattoo on his wrist.

"Yeah, that would have been disastrous. Can you imagine trying to explain to Mike why I need him to remove my lion tattoo and replace it with a knight? No thank you. One matching tattoo is enough for me."

Chris laughed. "He would probably take you straight to the doctor to get your head checked." He paused. "We aren't going to tell them, are we?"

I hesitated before answering. "The more people that know, the harder it will be to keep it secret. Let's not add anyone else until we have run out of options."

Sarah nodded. "The JV4 Kent Wood vs Sally Brown football game in two weeks might be a good time to try and gather some intel."

"That's true. We could see how they dress and act. Maybe help you blend in?" said Kathy, her voice growing hopeful.

"We should also set down some ground rules," Chris said, sitting up. He pulled up his PortMed, typing before he stopped. "We can't leave a trail." He swiped away, letting the screen dissolve before he headed to my desk. I sat up, watching as he rummaged through the drawers, pulling out a pen and paper pad. "Alex was telling me recently that they have been working on a way to monitor the PortMeds. We can't be too careful." He returned with the supplies, and we rearranged ourselves around him on the bed. He placed the pad in the middle of our circle.

"First things first," I said. "We will need to find another means of communication. I couldn't bear the thought of not being able to talk with you." Chris wrote, *Find a form of communication*, in elegant script.

"Oh, and you'll probably need some kind of disguise—for cover," added Kathy, and he wrote, *Costume?*

"You will also avoid any form of sports, especially combat," Chris said. I felt my heart tug at the thought, but knew he was right.

"What else?" Sarah asked.

The first week after learning about my transfer was spent throwing around ideas on how to either get out of it or survive long enough to make it to The Picking. If I could get Paired with Chris, I would be able to transfer back without a problem. The standard set of lectures filled my days as I prepared my term project, feeling a sense of loss as I realized I wouldn't be able to bring it with me to Kent

Wood. The following week was packed between the second lecture week, basketball practice, work, and helping Chris prep for the JV4 football game.

Chapter 3

I enjoyed the feeling of the sun on my skin as I made my way home from my last lecture class of the day. Already my mind was running with ideas for my project, thinking of ways I could include all my subjects when working weeks started in four days.

"Hey Loran, wait up!"

I turned to the boy calling me, smiling when I saw his twisted long hair. "Hey Haden, what's up?" I asked, stopping for him. Groups of students filed past us, moving at different speeds as they got on and off the path and grass surrounding us.

"Not much," he said as he twisted to dodge a biker before he settled beside my path, his tall slim build allowing him to pull off the move. "I've been looking for Sarah. Have you seen her?"

I laughed. "Last I saw, she was headed to help Mike and Chris prepare for the game tonight."

"Oh yeah, I forgot she was scheduled for that." He rubbed his hair sheepishly, his green eyes squinting. "Are you planning to get to the game early?"

I nodded, motioning to my bag by my side. "Yep, just going to drop off all my supplies. Then I'm picking up Kathy and heading that way."

"Cool. Mind if I join?" he asked.

"Not at all."

"Bring back the lion!" called a voice, and I turned my head to see a boy with a Megabot standing on the lawn. He was surrounded by posters and flyers covered with the symbol of an African lion.

"The lion never left, you idiot!" yelled a boy passing by and his friends all laughed.

"You know, I never thought people would be so upset when we voted to change our mascot," Haden noted as we turned down another path, heading to the dorms. The large, tan brick buildings of the lecture halls and labs gave way to a wide grassy knoll filled to the brim with students. School spirit was in the air as people emerged, covered in white and blue, from dorm buildings up ahead made of the same boring tan brick as all the others.

"Yeah, I don't really understand what the big deal is," I agreed as I watched someone throw up a Holo-work. It exploded in the air above us, releasing a large mountain lion into the sky that ran away, fading into the clouds above. "I mean, we are still the lions. Now we just have one that represents our home."

Haden opened the dorm door for me, and we squeezed through just in time to avoid a large group of first-year students running out. The two-story lobby was packed, the thunderous noise of excitement filling the air as Haden made a hole for me to follow through.

I waved to Violet, a girl in my art class, as she sat on one of the many occupied lobby tables. She waved back before turning to her conversation. Once we made it to the elevators in the rear, we headed to the second floor, where my dorm was. I quickly unlocked it with my PortMed and threw my stuff inside. Grabbing a baseball cap, I returned to Haden, and we zigzagged our way down to the communal bathrooms.

"There you are!" called Kathy as she spotted me in the crowd, standing on a sink. "Hurry up so I can paint your face in time." Grabbing Haden's hand so we weren't separated in the gaggling group of girls, I made my way to her.

Kathy sat on the sink's edge when I arrived and quickly got to work. The cool face paint made me shiver as it hit my skin. In the mirror above her head, I watched as she covered my tan skin in a royal blue. My freckles disappeared, replaced by twin paw prints. An old white eyeliner bot was put to my eye and instructed to paint two winged lines. It come to life, fluttering its winglike back, gripping slightly onto my skin before it crawled to my eyelids. I closed them as it *beeped* for me to stay still. When it was done, it *beeped* twice more, and I felt Kathy take it off. Next, we pulled my thick wavy hair into a ponytail, my hair band, The Wrap, opening as I placed it. Gathering all the stray strands, it straightened out the bumps and clamped down. I put the baseball cap on, pulling my hair through, and nodded.

"You shouldn't be too easily recognizable now," Kathy whispered as I helped her off the sink.

I gave her a bright smile and turned to Haden, who was patiently waiting for us off to the side. He only looked mildly uncomfortable as another pair of girls left the stall, their undergarments hanging from their hands before they saw him and blushed, hiding them in their shirts.

"You ready?" I asked, and he nodded. Together, we filed our way back out of the dorm and into the bright day. It took us ten minutes to make our way through the line outside and onto the bus that would take us to the stadium. The feeling in the air was electric.

"We are set for the semifinals, right? If we win today, I mean," Kathy asked.

I nodded, pulling up the game's stats. "Yep. Trident is already out due to their two losses in a row last week, and the Florida Falcons never had a chance. It's going to probably come down to Sandy Village, Michel Thomas, Water High, and then us, 'cause there is no way we are losing today." I scrolled through the list of players from Kent Wood.

"Wait, is that Kyle Patson?" Haden asked, halting my hand.

"Oh yeah," I paused, seeing one of only two images on the roster. "What is *the* varsity basketball captain doing on the JV4 football team?" Tapping on the image, I watched it expand. Bright coffee-brown eyes stared back at me, a smug smirk on his lips.

Kathy let out a laugh, inspecting the boy. "People could ask the same question of Chris," she pointed out.

"Yeah, yeah," I said with a dismissive wave, taking in the long scar under Kyle's left eye, pale against his light brown skin. The image moved. He lifted one large hand and ran it through his short, spiked brown locks, the look remarkably similar to Chris's. His toned muscles strained with the movement, his smirk growing.

"Looks like he's at it again," Haden commented as he watched over my shoulder. I turned to him in question. Haden raised a dark hand to circle Kyle's hair. "Copying Chris? Last time I saw him, he had waist-length hair that he tied back. He joined football, only one season behind Chris. I guess stealing Chris's basketball title wasn't enough."

I sighed, knowing that when Chris heard the news, things were going to go south fast. "Is it too much to hope that he'll be benched the whole time?"

"For you? Yes. You have the world's worst luck right before your boyfriend," Kathy stated matter-of-factly.

Haden chuckled as I groaned. "Hey, don't worry about it. It will all be fine."

The bus pulled up at the stadium five minutes later. I piled out with my friends, talking animatedly as we pushed toward the entrance. The building was styled in the same manner as the Roman Colosseum. Its decorative designs and large arches made it come alive as the roaring sound of the crowd filtered out. We filed through, giving a DNA sample at the gate to ensure we were noted on the mandatory attendance list. The VIP section was mostly empty. *Being the girlfriend of a player has its perks,* I thought with a smirk. We took the front row seats, the smell of freshly cut grass filling the air.

Across the stadium, the seats were filled in green and gold. An enormous wall cut the stands in half, blocking us from our rivals. It didn't, however, stop their annoying chanting from coming my way. Thirty minutes later, the stadium was full. Alex, Sarah, and some of our friends forced their way through the masses to us.

"Thank goodness we have VIP seats, or we would have been forced into overfill," Alex said as he settled down two seats to my right, his long legs tangled as he tried to get comfortable.

"Why are you all so late?" Haden asked as Sarah pushed past me to him. She bent down, giving him a peck on the cheek before she sat beside him.

"Chris heard the news about Kyle," she said with a mischievous wink at me.

I groaned. "This isn't going to be good." My head fell into my hands.

She reached over and patted my back. "No, it's not," she stated, just as the announcer took center stage.

"Hello and welcome to the Den!" he said, his voice booming around me. "Let's rise for our national anthem." The crowd rose and turned to the giant flag in the middle of the stadium. I watched the silver and gold striped banner wave back and forth above us. The eagle, our nation's symbol since the founding of the United States of North America, stood in the middle, its beak holding the Document of Change for the People. As one, we sang. The many voices in the stadium rang in a strangely haunting melody.

As it ended, the announcer smiled at the crowd. "You know them, you love them, their roar can make you run in fear. The Sally Brown Lions!" My side of the stadium erupted into cheers as the team flooded the field. Deep base music filled the air, and I watched for number 85. Chris was ramped up, he swung his arms in the air, his helmet in hand, and his mouth opened in a roar. I cheered for him as they settled on the sidelines.

"And now for the visiting team. Please welcome the Kent Wood Knights!"

I booed loudly as they filed onto the field, the deafening roar of our competitors winning out. The game began. I enjoyed watching as we trampled the Buckets into dust. My blood ran cold as the second half started, and number 36, Kyle James Patson, stepped on the field.

"Here we go," Alex said as Kyle took his position opposite Chris. I could feel their anger from the stands.

The ball snapped, and the two collided. It was only the beginning. Every bone-shattering hit, every head-snapping tackle, every foul play had me on the edge. Then it all came to a head. A bad pass by their quarterback allowed Chris to intercept. Kyle was hot on his heels and when he went for the tackle, my world slowed. I watched as Chris's body caved inward, an audible snap ringing through the stadium from mics attached to the uniform of each member. He was down.

The teams rushed the field as Mike, Chris's best friend, threw a hit at Kyle, trying to get him off Chris. Fights broke out as he lay defenseless on the ground. In a flash, I was scrambling forward, down the stadium wall, rushing onto the field before I could think. Right as I almost made it into the fray and got myself maimed; the assistant coach caught my arm.

"Not here!" he whispered, pulling me to him right as cameras turned my way. He buried my face in his chest as the chaos continued.

I cried. I could hear others rushing the field, the guards and refs stationed along the sides taking action. The assistant coach didn't let me out of his chest till the fight was overheavy and a hand was on my shoulder. I turned to look up at Mike, his face bruised and bloody, but otherwise unscathed.

"He's been taken to the infirmary," he explained, and I took his offered hand. In one swift move, he placed his helmet on my head, the light material sitting awkwardly above my baseball hat. "He said he didn't want them to see your face."

I nodded, the helmet shifting back and forth with my movement, and followed him down the sidelines. I didn't care that the game was still going on, nor that we were winning. The only thing on my mind was Chris and his safety.

Chapter 4

I waited in the infirmary for Chris to get out. The sterile walls and floors made me slightly uncomfortable, but I ignored the feeling. When the door before me opened, I looked up. Chris staggered from the room, a crutch bot floating under his right armpit, the only thing keeping him upright. I eyed him as the doctor followed him through.

"You're the girlfriend, I assume?" he asked with a smile.

I nodded.

"He will need plenty of rest. His scratches should be healed by tonight, but he has some internal bruising that will take three or so days to heal, and we were forced to use stitches for the wound on his chest. It might scar. Also, he has a broken rib. That alone should keep him out for a week."

I nodded as Chris let out a groan. "Don't worry, doc, I'll make sure he does as instructed."

"Holo-sticks!" Chris exclaimed as I finished unwrapping his bandages from his torso.

"Take it easy," I said as I inspected the small scar across his chest. Four days after the game, it was mostly healed, and with time would almost fade, joining the plethora of other scars across his skin. His internal injuries were a different matter. "You need to be careful. You heard the doctor. The MEDs won't be done patching your ribs for another two days, at least."

"It would have been sooner if that stupid Bucket hadn't come back from more," he grumbled as I made him lie back on his bed.

"Is he complaining again?" Mike asked from the doorway.

I turned and gave him a grin. "Yeah, but what's new?"

He chuckled as Chris let out a string of grumbled obscenities. Mike shoved himself off the doorframe, making his way inside. He was careful to not distribute too much of his weight onto the bed as he sat, his long legs straining from the angle. "Hey, look at the bright side," he said, patting Chris on the leg with a sharp slap of his brown hand.

Chris let out a small yelp and Mike chuckled. "You'll be all healed by the time basketball starts in the September term."

I smacked Mike on the back of the head, his shaggy mahogany brown hair flying as I did so.

"Hey, now, sis, what was that for?" he asked, rubbing his sore spot.

"For messing with my patient. He needs peace and calm during his recovery—not your annoying teasing." His dark chocolate eyes gleamed as he pouted and I crossed my arms.

"I think I know what the patient needs," he said with an eyebrow wiggle.

I felt my face flame. "You." *Smack.* "Are." *Smack.* "The worst." *Smack.*

"Hey now, this is elder abuse," he cried, raising his hands to defend himself.

"If you kill the buffoon, he'll just come back to haunt you."

Mike looked at his savior with pitiful eyes as I spotted Sarah over his shoulder.

"He deserves it," I grumbled, but concluded my assault.

"Great. The more the merrier," Chris groaned from his bed. Sarah rolled her eyes, stepping in, Haden following behind as he slipped in from the hall.

"Hey, we just wanted to make sure you were okay, bro," he said, slinging an arm around Sarah and smiling.

A group of boisterous boys passed outside the hall. I sighed as they yelled good wishes into the room.

Haden turned and closed the door, sealing us in relative silence.

"Thank you," I said, rubbing my temples. "It's been nonstop for days. Everyone is so worried we'll lose the basketball season and won't leave us alone."

"Trust me, we get it," Mike said, dragging his hand along his face, his scruff pulling as he did so. The tattoo that went from his neck to collar bone seemed to stand out against the strain. The three jagged rips inked across his skin were a dark gray, three long blue claws protruding from the bottom and two smaller tips poking out on either side, looking like a paw ripping him apart.

"You haven't been sleeping again, have you?" I asked, and he avoided my gaze.

"There isn't time for sleep. The finals are in three days and we need to prepare, or the sharks will crush us. Then I have to help the basketball team get ready for the season, so we aren't behind when Chris is healed. Also, The Cubs are making plans for the next raid on Trident and the freshman are helpless—"

I stopped him before he could continue down the rabbit hole. "Is Alex not helping?"

Mike sighed. "He is, but it's still a lot to spread between just two people. Normally, the three of us can tackle one commitment each."

"You realize I'm still right here," Chris said, groaning as he forced himself to sit up. He batted my hand away as I reached out to help. "I'm not an invalid," he dismissed, looking to Mike.

Sarah took a step toward me, laying a comforting hand on my shoulder before I could process my bruised emotions.

"Have Alex take over the basketball team; he should be the go-to, anyway as my second. You will take over the football stuff, and I can balance The Cubs," Chris commanded.

Haden exchanged a weary look with me. I gave him a slight nod, and he stepped forward, drawing Chris's attention. "If you're going to do all that, at least let me or Loran help." He held up his hand to stop the impending argument. "Nope, there is no negotiating here. You haven't been this injured since we were kids, and I don't think either you or Loran have it in you to go through that again."

My hand flew to my left shoulder, my skin tingling at the reminder of the day I lost my best friend and almost lost Chris. My raven tattoo, its beautiful wings spread in flight, its head craning toward the sky, was momentum to her.

Chris sighed and sat back down. "Fine, but I'm going to complain the whole time." He grinned, reaching his hand out to me. "I'm sorry. I shouldn't have pushed you away." As he pulled me forward, I shrieked tumbling onto him. "I can understand why you were so stubborn after the accident now."

Sarah laughed as heat flooded my cheeks, Chris's fingers tracing the base of my spine where a rough jagged scar lay. I ran my hand along his chest to his left shoulder, tracing the peaking beak of his complementary tattoo. Unlike mine, his raven was mid-flight, her wings pulled inward as she shot upward.

"Stubborn is certainly a word for it," Mike teased, and I kicked out at him, not breaking eye contact with Chris.

He caught my foot, patting it away.

"Well, next time you get struck by lightning and are forced to stay in bed for a month, let me know." I heard a deep sigh behind me.

"Please tell me we aren't arguing about this again," Kathy's soft voice filtered into the room.

I flipped over, landing beside Chris, facing her. "How in the—"

She smirked, twirling a small black rod on a ring on her finger.

"Oh," I said. I recognized her custom-made destabilizer. A device she created to help her hack the school systems. The gold streak of wire along the side was new, and I had to guess it was a feature that allowed her to hack the security locks on the dorm.

"Don't worry, I'm not planning on mass producing this one," she said before Sarah could speak up in protest. "Even I know it's not safe for this tech to be available to everyone."

My shoulders relaxed as she sent me a gentle smile.

"How long did it take?" Chris asked, leaning on his elbows.

Kathy blushed, looking down to the side. "Since I know you and can guess your go-to wiring preference, it's faster. So only two minutes."

"Nice. That has to be a new record."

Kathy nodded at Mike. "Yep. But I'm not here to show it off. I came for Loran." The ice in her eyes made me go rigid. "I think I found a solution to the problem you're having with your project." Chris stiffened under me, and Sarah coughed as she drew Haden down into a kiss to distract him.

"I didn't know you were struggling with your integration?" Mike sounded offended. "You know, I would have been more than willing to help out."

"I know," I sputtered out. "But Kathy was just there, and it involves a lot of high-level computer tech. I promise I wasn't ignoring you."

Mike grinned and I relaxed. "I'm just teasing you." He swatted at my foot.

I got up, turning to kiss Chris on the lips before I walked over to Kathy.

As I spoke, I didn't look away from her. "I'll let you all know how it goes, okay?" I worked to control my voice from trembling.

"Sounds good." Chris's voice was strained, following me as I left with Kathy.

Chapter 5

"Her name is Lovota Miller."

I stared at the moving image of a ten-year-old playing in a lake with her friends as Kathy explained her plan.

"She goes to Willow Creek and is top rank three. She even runs cross-country and plays basketball. Almost all your interests are the same."

I traced the tanned cheeks, looking at a set of freckles not so different from my own.

"The eyes and hair are a bit off. You can just claim it's the style and a trick of the light if anyone manages to find her pictures."

"Won't people be suspicious if there are two of her in the same place?" I asked.

"That's the beauty of it. She's just a small, no-name, alternate schoolgirl with a slightly above-average ranking. No one will think to look. As long as you stick to the shadows and play the part, you should be fine."

As Working Weeks started, the two weeks following Kathy's discovery were packed. Between project presentations, midterms, practice, work, and clubs, I barely had time to fit in preparing for the move. To help give me a cover, Kathy started a new club for me to disappear to. We spent the hours there running over cover stories and learning all I needed to to pass myself off as Lovota.

"No, again!" Kathy commanded lightly.

I let out a frustrated shout, pushing up from the chair I was sitting in. It tumbled to the ground with a *clang* as I began pacing back and forth in the small gray room.

"BotJuice. I have been over this five times in the last thirty minutes alone and it's Monday! I swear if I don't get my last off-day this week, then I'm going to scream. What did I get wrong this time?" I asked.

Kathy sighed, watching me from her chair across the cold metal table.

"You can't seem to get the location right. When you mention public school kids, you don't talk with enough disdain." She raised an eyebrow at me as I spun to her. "Also, you can't use the term BotJuice. That is a Sally Brown curse. Holo-sticks is best from now on as it's neutral."

My hands flew to my hair, tugging in frustration. "And how exactly am I supposed to sound? Because I'm feeling plenty of disdain at the moment." I ignored her first point. *So, what if Willow Creek was in Vail, not Aspen? Would any Kent Wood student know that? I certainly don't.*

"You need to find a balance. You wouldn't hold the same hate you do to Kent Wood, but you wouldn't be indifferent to them like you would be with Trident." The Holo-screen before her flickered.

"How would you know that?" I demanded.

"Because I spent the last football game schmoozing our alternate school guests. Unlike some people." She gave me a pointed stare, which I ignored.

"You know, I was busy trying to help Chris keep the team running."

Kathy let out another sigh, her eyes growing sad. "Listen, you can't just go to your default mode of pretending everything is normal and ignoring your problems. I get it. This is hard on all of us. Whether we like it or not, you are leaving, and we only have so much time to prepare." I snorted.

She leaned forward, placing her palms on the metal surface, making her small five-foot-three frame feel twice as intimidating. Her voice grew louder as she spoke. "The football team doesn't matter anymore. Your clubs don't matter anymore." She stood, shoving her own chair to the ground as her volume increased. I was taken aback by her frustration and anger.

"This school doesn't matter! You no longer belong to Sally Brown. In three weeks, you will be a slightly above-average girl coming from a small alternative school, hoping to find a better life for yourself through the amazing studies available at Kent Wood."

She spat the name, the entire sentence making her face crunch in disgust. "And if you aren't, then they will figure you out. You will be turned into the council for treason. You will be paraded before the schools as an example of what happens when you try to leave the system after freshman year." Each point felt like a stab to the heart, my anger depleting. "They will make it look like an accident. They will kill you. Then this amazing precious life you have dreamed up of a picket fence and perfect Pairing to Chris will all be mute because you won't be around to see it. Do I make myself clear?"

Tears rolled down my cheeks. "Yes," I croaked, looking down at my intertwined hands. I felt more than saw Kathy's fury turn to a dull simmer. With a sigh, she made her way to me, her boot-clad feet echoing in the tiny room. She placed a gentle hand on my shoulder. I looked down, seeing the fear, heartbreak, and sorrow I felt in her gaze.

"I don't want you to go," she breathed.

I raised my hand to hers, pulling it from my shoulder and drawing her into a hug. Her small form trembled against mine as she also began to cry.

"I don't want to leave either," I said, smoothing down her hair. "I know you're right, as always. I'm just so scared. What if I mess up and get caught because I couldn't keep everything straight? What if I'm not angry enough, not sad enough? What if...I can't keep her down?"

Kathy pulled away as I heard the faraway sound of a scream. "Those dreams. Are you having them again?" she asked in concern as she inspected me.

I shook my head. "No…I just…The last time I was in a stressful situation like this, I just snapped. I can't go back to that, Kathy. I can't be *her* again." My hands trembled as I pulled the memories back, shoving them into a box in my mind.

"I think you have more control now than you did back then," Kathy reminded me gently. "You were seven."

I scoffed. "It took four years for me to come back from that. Two more for me to find myself again. If it hadn't been for Chris—" I stopped. I didn't want to think of those dark years when all I cared about was others suffering, wanting to get my revenge for an accident I should have prevented.

"What happened wasn't your fault. Hannah was at the wrong place at the wrong time." Kathy shook me, drawing my eyes to her, giving me a gentle smile. "You don't need to worry. You have your Gold pills, right?"

"Yeah. I made sure to ask Father for extra, just in case."

"And you remember the signs, right?"

I wanted to sigh but instead, I answered. "Yes, unknown screaming, my world starts tilting or shifting around me, breathing becomes hard, pink tints my vision, I feel like I'm falling, the world doubles and mirrors itself, I see strange images, then red settles in and it's over. Oh, and of course, my nightmares increase."

"Good." Kathy nodded as she inspected me. "Remember one or more of these and you need to take the golden pills. No exceptions."

"I know, I know, trust me I don't want another incident, I'll do my best to take the pills when needed." I tried to sound sincere instead of panicky as I pushed back memories of my past.

Seeing my distress, she smiled gently. "Then there you go. If you are struggling, they will bring you back. As long as you have them, you will be okay." She rubbed my arm in comfort as her voice took on a melodic tone.

"How did a little junior get to be so wise?" I asked.

"Because she was lucky enough to have you in her life," Chris said. My head snapped up to the single metal door in the room opposite me. He shut it quickly behind himself. The various locks twirled into place, the dampening system taking effect and cutting off the subtle sound of students in the distance. "It looks like today's been a rough session." He walked over to us, pulling us both into a hug before leaning over Kathy to give me a gentle kiss.

"Yeah, that's my fault," I admitted as we pulled away. "I kept messing up and kind of lost it on her."

Chris gave me an understanding smile, stepping away to pull up both the stray chairs.

I watched him, my arm around Kathy till he was done.

He turned to me. "Come sit and let's try this again," he said. I nodded, breaking away and taking his hand as he led me to my chair, sitting me down in it. He stepped back, placing two powerful hands on my shoulders as he stood behind me. "Have you decided on a Focus yet?"

"Yeah, I think I'll pursue marine biology," I said as Kathy took her seat across from me, pulling up her Holo-screen from the small tablet she had on the table. "If I'm going to be forced to pick my major before college, I might as well try it out. I've always wanted to study the life cycles of white dolphins." The map of our country filled the space before me. I looked it over.

The seven school districts of North America were clearly highlighted, ending slightly above the old border between The United States and Canada. Seven golden blobs were scattered about within them, showing the borders of the schools themselves. I longingly traced the long, scar-like image that Sally Brown left in the middle of the country.

"I think that's a good idea," Chris said with a squeeze.

"Now, which is Willow Creek?" Kathy asked as eight gray blobs appeared across the districts.

I scanned our district, struggling to remember which was Aspen and which was Vail.

"That one," I said, pointing to the upper blob in the Rocky Mountains.

Kathy sighed. "Well, at least this time you were closer and didn't point to Honesty Prep in Montana."

I gave her a hard look. "That wasn't my fault," I snipped. "The first map you gave me was hard to read and I couldn't tell which part of the districts I was looking at."

"The good news is you have time to learn." Chris intercepted Kathy as she opened her mouth to counter.

She closed it with an audible *click* and sighed. "Fine, let's move on." She pulled the map down, turning the screen to privacy mode so I couldn't see the answers past the blurred surroundings. "Now, what is their school mascot?"

I sighed, but answered.

As we continued through the questions, Chris's presence kept me grounded. Kathy's words rang in my head, and I reminded myself that this was important. I needed to live and breathe it until I knew it by heart. The other outcome wasn't an option:

life without Chris. Well, it wasn't a life at all. Though I knew The Picking would put me with my literal perfect partner, I just couldn't see how they could choose anyone but him.

Ever since the day I met Chris on a snowy hill near the dojo my parents sent me to as a kid, I'd been star-struck. He was everything I wasn't at the time. Smart, smooth, cool, and overall kind. As we grew, those qualities did as well. When we were seven, Chris saved my life, the memory of that day tattooed on my shoulder blade. When we were eleven, he won his first basketball game and became the most popular boy in our grade. At thirteen, he hit rank one, solidifying himself in the school hierarchy and on our school site. By the time we were fifteen, I had finally caught up to him. I had secured myself a place at the top of the cross-country team. I was rising in basketball and hit the lower Varsity leagues. I had made friends with everyone in my class and got voted prom queen. From everything I knew about The Picking, the only thing keeping us apart was our rankings.

"That was better. Good," Kathy encouraged as I finished talking about the last time I saw a public-school football game. Mentioning how I thought it was so annoying that it broke into another fight. Of course, I liked Trident vs. Sally games better as they usually ended in less violence. "That's just the right amount of disdain, annoyance, and exasperation. Just remember that from now on. Now let's go again."

I groaned, flopping back in my chair.

Chris chuckled, placing a kiss on my forehead. "Just one more time. I promise if you do, I'll make it worth your while," he said with a wiggle of his eyebrows.

I let out a barking laugh, sitting up. "All right, but only one more and then I get a break for today," I said. "Besides, I can only disappear so long before the others start to ask questions."

Kathy nodded. "All right." She adjusted in her chair, putting on a forced smile as she held out her hand. "Hi, my name is Kathy. It's so nice to have you here."

Forcing a softer smile to my face, I grabbed her hand, careful to add a small amount of hesitation to my motions, as if scared she would hurt me.

"Hi, I'm glad to be here. My name is Lovota Miller. I just transferred from Willow Creek."

Chapter 6

The smell of fall was in the air, the summer heat slowly letting go, a gentle warmth taking its place. Final Projects were due in five days and with it, the pit in my stomach grew.

I sighed as I walked home from drama club. My hands were covered in paint from working on props, and I quickly typed a reminder to have IT come fix the décor bot. Luckily, my clothes were still relatively paint free, unlike my partners'.

The flashing date on my home screen made my heart skip a beat.

5:23 p.m. Thursday, August 14th, 2121

Only seventeen days before I left my home forever. My PortMed squeezed, the MEDs slowly calming my racing heart. I'd noticed I was relying on them a lot more to keep down my growing anxiety. Reaching into my pocket, I fiddled with the small package of red pills Father had Drone Dropped to me. According to him, they should help for moments when I was especially anxious. Though, like the golden ones, they were for emergencies only. The expansion packs weren't mainstream yet as most people didn't need them, the MEDs being more than enough to keep them healthy.

Those who did could access them with doctor prescriptions soon as they hit the market in five months.

Having a father who had served on the board of the Medical Evaluation and Disease Society had its perks.

"Did you hear? The Falcons apparently attacked the common arts building," I heard a girl say to her friend as they passed me on the path.

"Yeah, but I heard it wasn't too bad, just some stink bombs. *Though* I heard they modified them again. The agent we developed last time isn't working to nullify the smell," the boy replied.

"Oh gosh, I can't even imagine what that must smell like. I'm so glad I'm not in any common art courses at the moment," the girl continued as their voices faded from hearing distance.

I looked to the west where the common arts buildings sat inside the foothills. The tall tan brick buildings were visible even from my distance, a large circle cut from the largest one's middle. I could barely make out the featured piece of the month within; a grand work of a mountain lion hunting. I slid between a large group of students taking up the path, not wanting to traverse the currently wet grass beside me.

"Dude, you need to stay at least ten feet away!" a voice exclaimed, and I turned to see two boys walking to my right. One was holding his nose closed, waving at the air in front of him.

His friend turned around, stopping as he snapped back, "It's not my fault you keep getting too close."

A group of girls heading their way quickly diverted their path, traversing the wet grass in favor of passing within smelling distance of said boy.

He watched them go, disgruntled. "Seriously, the faster we can get to the labs, the better."

I made a slight detour to my left as I drew close, wanting to stay away from the faint smell of feces floating my way.

"You are so not going to be allowed on the bus like this," his friend shot back, stepping back another few feet. The stinky boy threw his hands in the air, and I held my breath as the movement increased the smell.

"Fine, then I'll walk. Maybe by then, they'll have found a solution to this mess." The disgruntled boy turned from his path, traversing the lawn to cross to the path that would take him to the labs by foot. People scattered away from him.

"Chris will certainly be holding a meeting about that tonight," Alex said as he made a wide approach to me on the lawn, his red hair bright in the afternoon sun.

I laughed, nodding at one of my closest friends. "Weren't you in art class? Why are you stink free?" I asked.

He gave me a big smile, two dimples forming on his red cheeks as we turned to continue to the dorms. "Well, turns out teachers don't really find my pranks funny," he said, and I groaned.

"What did you do this time?"

He had the gall to look offended. "Why, I never!"

I shoved his shoulder with mine and he let out a deep laugh, his rumbling voice surrounding me full of mirth. His blue piercing in his right ear shone. "I was just trying out a mini version of our plans for the Kent Wood attack in a few weeks."

"And?" I raised a single eyebrow, pursing my lips.

"Well, Mr. *Grouch* didn't really like my interpretation of his angry face. Especially not when it was splattered against his wall."

I stopped, making the girl behind me release a string of curses as she worked to dodge me. I ignored her.

"You didn't!" I said in disbelief. Mr. Crouch was one of the strictest teachers in the arts district. He believed the current system of teaching was too lenient.

"Student-based learning only leads to hooligans and riff-rafts," he ranted on an almost daily basis, despite the proof in the fabricated pudding. The average level of education had only been on the rise in North America for the past seventy years. His attitude and his lecture-only based style of teaching meant he was by far the least favorite teacher on campus. I expected him to be out within the next year.

"I did." Alex grinned. "And let me tell you, it was a piece of art unlike any other. Even Superintendent Michela said so."

I forced down a sigh, my lips twitching as I held back my smile. We headed toward Chris's dorm. The doors opened before us as a boy walked out and I caught it, holding it for Alex.

"So, how long do you plan on being out this time?" I asked, heading to the elevators. The lobby was mostly empty, students heading off to work or coming back from working sessions.

"Well, the whole thing will last about three days, but I'll only be gone one, since I can only miss two of his lectures before he tries to knock me down a tier," Alex said as he caught the elevator. I stepped in and he hit the fifth floor. "The others, though, should be gone the whole time, as it will be during a working week. Chris has The Cubs splitting into lots of smaller units this time so we can hit more spots. I think he wants to leave them with a lasting impression since it's his last basketball season and all." We exchanged matching grins. "We also have to find a new hideout as the Buckets found our last one. It will probably have to be farther from their borders." The elevator *dinged*, and we stepped out into the hall. Immediately, the hair on my arms stood. A small cluster of students huddled to my left outside a room.

"What's…"

Sarah turned at the sound of my voice. Even from the distance, I could see her eyes were red. Before I knew what I was doing, I was rushing her way. *Please, not Chris*, I prayed as I neared. I opened my mouth to ask as Chris stepped out into the hall.

From Haden's room.

"No." The word slipped from my lips as I skittered to a stop feet away.

Chris looked up, his eyes troubled. He turned back to the group, acknowledging a boy there. "It's him; send out the notification."

The boy nodded, and his fingers flew along his PortMed in a blur. The room quickly filled with a shrill sound, and I didn't lift my arm to see my PortMed light. The hall was cast in an eerie blue glow as multiple images of a white tree with twisted roots filled the space. Moments later, a picture of Haden flashed around us. I stared at the image, looking at his bright, smiling face as he stood over Sarah, his chin on her head.

"Alert! There has been a Shadownapp!" The room echoed with the alert three times. Instructions were quick to follow, telling people to keep an eye out for Haden. The warning was clear: "Don't approach anyone with him. Call the authorities."

Sarah crumbled to the ground before it could finish. I was on my knees beside her in seconds, pulling her to me as she sobbed.

"Let's get moving," Chris commanded the group. "If we retrace his steps, we might have a chance of finding him." The hall emptied as everyone rushed to see if they could get Haden in time. As Chris passed, he placed a gentle hand on my head. I didn't watch him go, knowing that it was pointless. Other than my incident, we had never successfully stopped a Shadownapp. Still, we always tried. The only other option was to do nothing, and when faced with adversity, Sally Brown never stayed still. Soon Sarah and I were the only ones left in the hall, her cries filling the air.

It took a lot of time for me to coax her off the floor and settle into Haden's room; she refused to return to hers, continually telling me she would rather wait for him in case he returned. I didn't comment as I sat her on the bed and pulled his blankets up around her.

My heart broke.

She looked so small huddled under them, her head peeking out, eyes red and puffy. I heard her take in a deep breath of his scent as I went to his mini fridge and grabbed her some water. She drank greedily, gasping as she finished it in one go. I sat down beside her, grabbing her hand from under the blanket and giving it a gentle squeeze. I could feel as the MEDs got to work, a somber atmosphere replacing her manic one. She lifted her other hand, drawing it across her face to wipe her tears away.

"You know, I always had a feeling this day would come," she whispered. I watched her empty eyes. The brash girl I knew looked lost. "He was always one to draw attention, you know." She paused. "You remember the first day we met him? He was so full of life, of light. Instantly, I knew I wanted him to be mine." Her forlorn smile fell. "I once asked him to either apply himself harder to get to the first rank or drop to at least the bottom of rank three. He laughed, you know." Her eye stared blankly at the wall opposite us. Haden's favorite poster, an image of the rock band, New Metallica, shimmered.

"I had been so offended. Asked if he wanted to be Shadownapped. But he stopped, and after giving me a big kiss, told me the only way someone was taking him from me was if he was dead." I saw her mood drop even lower. "What if *he* killed him?" she whispered.

I grabbed her other hand, forcing her to turn and look at me. "You would know if Haden was dead. You are too close to not be able to sense that." She brightened only slightly, my words and the MEDs helping her mood. "Besides, The Shadow doesn't kill."

"How do you know?"

"Simple, if he did, then why would he bother taking the bodies? No, if he killed, I would imagine it would be like Sandy Village, leaving the evidence somewhere we could find, in a way that would scare us." With a sigh, she leaned against me. I rubbed her back through the blanket.

"Who will I Pair with now?" She sounded so lost.

I had no response.

"We couldn't find him," Chris's voice was broken when he returned the next day. I could tell by the bags under his eyes that he hadn't slept in the last twenty-four hours. "They are going to keep looking, but I got sent home."

Silently, I stood from my desk chair, grabbed his hand, and led him to my bed.

"You have done what you can for now. Sleep. I'll watch for any news and wake you if they need you." I knew he was exhausted when he didn't argue, collapsing onto my bed instead.

He was out in seconds.

I couldn't help but feel empty as I headed home from my final presentation a week later. Sarah had refused to go to any of her work sessions and, though it wasn't required, I could tell the teachers were getting concerned with her absences. I didn't know if she showed up to any of her finals or finished any of her proposals for her project as she wouldn't let me into her room and dodged me when she saw me. My PortMed squeezed as my anxiety spiked. The calm that washed over me was comforting. I had to believe everything was going to be okay, even as I prepared my things to leave.

"Is everything packed?" Chris asked as he watched me pace my room.

"Yeah, Mother grabbed the last of my things yesterday by drone. All I have left is this." I gestured to my small backpack sitting on my bed. Tears sprung to my eyes as I looked at it. "How did Break Week pass by so quickly?"

Chris came up behind me, pulling me into a hug. "I'm so sorry," he said, his breath fanning the back of my ear, sending shivers down my spine. "I wish I could say you could stay."

Chapter 7

I used to think life was predictable.

Each day, I knew the MEDs would keep me fit and healthy, my friends would always be around to support me, and the students at the seven schools would continue to hate each other.

Now, I stared at my reflection in the dingy, under-used train station bathroom, knowing nothing would ever be the same again. My hair dyeing machine was in my hand before I could question my decisions. I quickly scrolled through it, picking out a shade of gold I could live with. My hand trembled as I raised it to my hair. Layer after wavy layer, I pulled the machine through. Watching my blue tips fade to gold hurt more than a knife to the heart. When I was about halfway, I paused, stopping to reflect on the new look.

The golden ends shone against my brown locks and made the green in my eyes pop. I leaned in, inspecting the bags under them, noticing how the freckles on my cheeks seemed more prominent with the purplish tint. My blue chipped nails reflected back at me, and I glanced at the green nail polish on the sink with disgust. With a sigh, I stepped back, pushing a thick layer of hair behind my ear, forcing a smile. My reflection grimaced back, my wide ears poking out, sending a wave of insecurity through me. I flipped it back to cover my ear and continued. Just as I was about three-fourths of the way through, a knock at the door resounded through the room.

"Are you almost done?" Chris called.

"Almost," I responded, quickly working through the rest of my hair.

"Okay, don't take too long. Your train will be here soon, and we'd all like time to say goodbye." Even through the door, I could hear the sadness in his voice.

"I won't, I promise," I said as I finished with my hair. I cleaned and painted my nails, blowing on them to activate the drying chemicals. Within seconds, they were hard and ready. I took a last look at myself. My favorite gray jacket was pulled over a simple green shirt, its tattered ends frayed from years of abuse as I nervously fiddled with it. The two rips in my jeans showed off a little skin, but not too much to be inappropriate. I bent down to grab my bag, slinging it over my shoulder. With a little bounce, I turned and headed out the door.

The station was almost empty save for my friends and a middle-aged man farther down the single track. We chose it specifically for that reason, since there was no way to explain four unsupervised students out in the world of adults. Especially with no paperwork for three of us, and no golden bands to declare us as private school brats, free to do as we liked.

Chris turned at the sound of the door closing, pushing from the wall he was leaning on, and approaching me. He looked me over, his smile bittersweet.

"I hate to admit it, but these colors look good on you," he said bitterly, raising a hand to my hair. He twirled a strand of golden brown in his fingers. "It's almost like you belonged there the whole time." I smacked his hand away with an annoyed grunt, almost missing as he said, "He was right."

"What?" I asked.

Chris blinked as if waking from a daze and sent me a kind smile. "Nothing, Lightning." He kissed my head as I hissed at him.

"Not so loud."

My eyes flew to Kathy and Sarah.

"Don't worry, they can't hear us, and even if they could, they know you're leaving, so it's not a big deal if they know the new code name." Grabbing my hand, he led me back to the bench where they were sitting dejectedly.

"Still, I just..." I paused, feeling warm as I thought of the night he gave me the nickname. "It's a special thing, okay? Only you can call me that."

"Yes, of course, dear," he said as we stopped in front of the girls.

"I hate your parents. Officially," Kathy ground out, glaring at my hair as if it had personally offended her. The whirl of her electronic pointer finger rang in my mind as she tapped it on the bench. Sitting next to her, Sarah fidgeted with her chocolate bar, ignoring everything and everyone. The scent wafted across the bench, making my stomach roll.

At that moment, my PortMed *beeped*, letting me know the train was on its final approach. At the sound, Kathy's big eyes suddenly watered and before I knew it, she was whimpering. She wiped at her face with her rough gray jacket, so like my own, leaving behind angry red streaks on her cheeks.

"I know, trust me, I know," I said, bending down to wipe away a stray tear. "You've given me everything I could ever need to succeed and for that, I'm eternally grateful."

She smiled through her tears.

Sarah let out a noncommittal grunt next to her, and we both turned to watch her with concern. Her comatose state since Haden was taken had only grown worse the closer we got to my departure. It broke my heart.

I searched the station for something to help hold me together. My eyes passed Chris, his large form folded in on itself behind me, and old flickering signs and cracks in the floor, till it landed on the man standing at the other end. He was rugged-looking, glancing at his PortMed as he tapped his foot impatiently on the ground. His suitcase lay next to it, shiny and new. His black necklace, though, was not. Yet, I didn't feel bad for the Unpaired man.

"You know, we could still run," Chris said, drawing my eyes back to him. The pain in his voice broke my heart.

"Chris..." His name stuck in my throat, and I cleared it as Kathy and Sarah glanced up, worry in their expressions, before Sarah returned to her fidgeting. "I can't, just please drop it, okay? It's too late now." The letter from my new superintendent burned a hole in my bag and my mind, holding my tongue before I let him know about the threat it contained.

"It's still not fair," Sarah snapped, glaring at the floor. "First Haden, now you! When is this all going to end?" Her voice grew steadily and Kathy quickly shushed her, glancing nervously over to the man. He shot us an aggravated glare but kept to himself. I grimaced and pushed past her outburst.

"It's almost time for me to leave," I said, offering my hand to the girls. They each took one, and I helped them up.

We walked to the train tracks in somber silence. Precious minutes slipped away, yet I was afraid to speak up, as if one word would shatter the fragile atmosphere. A gust of icy wind whipped my hair into my face as the Hyper Train raced into the station tunnel. My PortMed *beeped* moments before it pulled to a stop, the doors opening with a long *sigh*. The Holographic countdown clock began on my wrist, five minutes till I left my life behind. With a deep breath, I turn back to my friends. It was time.

"Goodb—" I whispered, stopping as Kathy rushed up, hugging me. Her tears stained my shirt, but I didn't mind. Holding her close, I took in everything that was her one last time, her tiny frame in mine and the scent of lilacs. She pulled back, holding me at arm's length.

"We'll miss you." She wiped her tears, which only managed to smear her running mascara across her face and her electronic finger.

I carefully grabbed her hand, cleaning the small prosthetic with my jacket sleeve. Giving her a gentle smile, I patted her head, making her blue and white earrings jiggle. She pouted, but didn't chastise me for treating her like a child.

"Listen..." I paused, staring past her to our dispiriting friend. "I'm worried about her. She's isolating herself and I don't want her to be alone. Can you please keep an eye out?" I asked low enough so Sarah couldn't hear as she hung back a few feet.

"Of course, you know you can count on me," Kathy whispered back before pulling away. The smile she sent my way was the last one I ever got from her.

"I'll plant The Shadow paper the moment we get back," Sarah said, looking anywhere but me.

I winced. It was convenient Haden was taken so close to my leaving. Chris had been able to save the paper left behind from his incident and now it would add validity to my disappearance.

When Sarah didn't move, I stepped forward, pulling her into a hug. She tensed for a moment, then slowly hugged me back. I could feel her fighting off tears as her shoulders shook against my chin.

"Thank you," I said into her hair, reluctantly pulling away. With a deep breath to hold in my suddenly mounting sorrow, I turned to Chris.

"I guess this is it," I choked out. With a heavy sigh, he looked up at me. For the first time that day, my cheeks were wet. I felt so empty when he didn't move to comfort me right away.

"I guess so." He looked at his feet, shuffling them back and forth. His hair was down, his clothes disheveled. It was like his inner heartbreak was reflecting itself in the way he dressed. With a sad smile, I stepped toward him.

"You need to get a cut." I brushed away a few strands of loose hair wistfully as I brought up one of our oldest debates. The golden locks brushed past my fingers like fine silk as he leaned into my hand.

"And you need to grow another inch," he said, finally looking at me. There was mirth in his eyes, yet it drowned in sorrow. I fell into him like one would fall into a dream, anchoring my soul in his arms as the world melted away. "I wish I could pretend this wasn't real," he whispered into my hair.

"Then let's play pretend, princess," I whispered back, memories flooding me of times we played as children. A sad laugh shook his chest as he held me tighter, like he was afraid I'd slip away with the wind.

"As you wish, dear dragon." The words caught in his throat. A small sob escaped me. Instead of confronting my emotions, I stared at the nanobot-powered image of a lion that ran across his jacket. It paused to cock its head, as if to ask why I was crying, before continuing its lap down his arm. I watched it go as Chris's fingers ghosted across my chin. I allowed him to draw my face up.

"You better get going. Make sure to have your phone on you at all times. Okay? I'll check on you to make sure you make it safe."

I sighed, pulling away to draw out the old smartphone from my pocket, the thin little square fitting in my palm.

"I have it. But I don't know when I will arrive, so don't freak out if I don't respond right away, okay? You know how my parents can be."

He nodded, watching me put it in my bag.

"You know I don't want to leave, right?" I stroked his cheek, and a soft smile graced his lips. In the distance, the train bell rang, signaling it was almost time to leave. My PortMed blinked, and I dismissed the notification. I broke from Chris's grasp, grabbed my bag, and turned to the train, ripping everything away like an old-fashioned Band-Aid.

The man from the station sat two cars down, staring at me through the window with impatience as he whispered to a middle-aged lady next to him. I was stepping onto the train when Chris's hand fell onto my shoulder. The pain that simple gesture brought was more than I could bear.

"What—" My voice cracked as I tried to glare at him. The flexing of his hand on my shoulder told me he was barely holding himself together.

"I got this for you." He held out his other hand. The gold necklace with a glass cherry blossom, my favorite flower, hanging in the middle, took my breath away. I smiled at him, looking through blurry eyes.

"You're shameless," I chastised with a grin. He had made sure it was just short enough it couldn't be mistaken for a Mate Necklace.

"Thank you." His smile was forlorn. "Hurry and turn around." I did as he asked, watching his blue paw tattoo flash at me as the necklace fell against my clavicle with a gentle thud. "Don't forget about us," he whispered in my ear. Before I knew what was happening, he shoved me into the train.

I stumbled, catching myself at the last second on a pole. The doors groaned to a close behind me and I whirled back to my friends. They stood on the other side of the smudged glass, huddled together as if weathering a great storm. Their tear-filled eyes haunted me as they disappeared with a blur and the rushing sound of the wind.

Chapter 8

Ads for food and clothes popped up on the glass around me as the lush landscape of Old Colorado flashed by. I passed hours reading them and pretending to be in the past, in a time when my trip could have just been another vacation, where I wouldn't be separated from those I loved forever. A world without rivalries.

The train sped through the western countryside, leaving no time to enjoy the view as mountains, deserts, and forests passed by. It stopped twice before my destination, and three more people joined me. Two of them were young, identical twin girls, and they clung to each other desperately as they sat down on the bench farthest from me. I watched them whisper to each other, their hazel eyes scanning the horizon for danger, and wondered what brought them there. The third passenger, an elderly man, sat in the opposite corner. I was surprised to see him, as most working adults preferred personal transporters or company teleporters. As I watched him stare outside with longing, I realized that for him, this ride was probably more than just a means to a destination.

A small bell *dinged*, startling me, as the train slowed.

"Last stop, Santa Monica. All passengers depart," announced the computerized voice, clicking in and out from years of use. With a deep sigh, I stood, grabbed my bag and swung it over my shoulder. I could hear the soft crying of one twin as she stood next to me. I forced myself to ignore her as I focused ahead.

The train came to a gentle stop with a gasp of air and a *beep* from my PortMed. The doors groaned open, revealing a large and ancient station.

As I stepped out, I was instantly hit with the sticky feeling of humidity clinging to my clothes and skin. A constant roar surrounded me as clusters of people rushed around, heading to and from their destinations. My fellow passengers pushed past me as signs lit above, advertising clothes and products I had never seen or heard of before, each tailored to the individual. I felt better as my PortMed squeezed and released my death grip on my bag strap. With a deep breath, I gathered myself.

"Come on, girl, you got this," I whispered, continuing forward. Looking around, I spotted the exit past two large red trains. I made my way toward the hovering scanners, looking around for my parents.

"Loran!"

On reflex, I smoothed out my outfit and ran my hand through my hair, catching my knots before I looked to Mother. She stood in all her glory on the other side of the security gate, waving at me, a giant smile on her face. Next to her, Father stood with his arm around her, smiling. The wat they held each other in a loving embrace reminded me of the life they were forcing me to leave. My bitterness grew.

The security line was short, the AI detector allowing a steady flow of people each minute. Once I was clear, Mother rushed me, almost tackling me back into it and an old woman trying to get through. She shot us a dirty glance as she passed by, mumbling about spoiled private school children.

"It is so good to see you," she said as she kissed me multiple times upon my brow. Her hair fell around me, obscuring my view as she shook me about. More people filed past us, parting around us like the Red Sea.

With a grunt, I freed myself from her grip. "It's only been two months," I said.

"Here, let Father take that." She grabbed my bag before I could protest.

Father took it from her as he approached and smiled down at me. "Good to see you, bear," he said, rubbing my hair with his large hand, his kind eyes squinting.

I smiled back, a genuine smile. Begrudgingly, I had to admit I was happy to see them. I had missed them, surprisingly. They escorted me through the crowded station, talking about the weather and their new office.

I followed them to Lisa, their new AI Hovercar. The doors opened as we approached, and Father stored my bag in the trunk as I slipped in. I settled into the soft leather seat as the windows tinted; the roof turned black, and screens lit up all around me.

I quickly dismissed the notification on the news and weather in favor of glancing outside.

Father and Mother got in, starting our drive to Kent Wood. The streets were relatively clear, as only a handful of people could afford cars, allowing us to zip by at breathtaking speeds. The SMART system kicked in, allowing Father to release the wheel, and turn his and Mother's chairs around to face me.

"You are going to love this school," Mother said, as she applied a layer of red to her pouting lips, her AI reflection in the hand mirror helping to guide her in a perfect application as it traced a path along its own.

I lifted my hand to my chapped lips in envy.

"I went there yesterday, and it was so nice." She smacked her lips twice before closing the mirror with a snap. Father took it from her, storing it on the side. "Much better than Sally Brown. Though I am not surprised; after all, it was founded by the illustrious Kent Wood, and we all know his money was not a thing to laugh at."

The words stung, and I clenched my hands together to keep from lashing out. She continued to drag on, ignoring me in favor of scrolling through her PortMed.

My hands stung from the bite of my nails as I clenched tighter. "Stop it, Mother!" I snapped, trying, and failing to keep the anger and hurt out of my voice.

She looked up at me, freezing. Her face fell as she turned toward the dash with the flick of a switch. With a sigh, her head drooped, straight hair cascading around her.

Guilt overwhelmed me as I realized I hurt her again.

"Alright," she croaked.

"You didn't tell them I'm coming from Sally Brown, right?" I tried to change the subject, pushing down my feelings. I had to be hard as steel. Any wayward emotions could get me killed.

"Of course not, dear. You have been so good these last few months and we know you didn't want to move. If that is what it takes to make it easier for you, then we were happy to do so." Father said, drawing my attention away from Mother. With a gentle hand, he turned her back around, soothing her with strokes along her wrist.

"I would've preferred not to leave in the first place." I watched as they exchanged a look, but didn't press.

"Teenagers." The car grew silent as I pretended to not hear Mother. Past arguments hung in the air.

I turned away from them to the window, watching the world outside. Tall buildings and bustling paths filtered past, giving me my first view of the world of the adults outside the vacation spots my parents took me to. People blinked in and out of existence as teleporters delivered them to their destinations. Windows shone with barely visible circuits as solar panels soaked up the sun. Drones delivered packages to individuals as they went about their day, and clothes changed designs with a flick to match the newest trends.

"You know you could have at least dressed up," Mother sniffed, pulling my attention to her.

"I have told you a thousand times before, if I go to school in the dresses you buy me, I will stick out, and not in a good way. If you wanted me to dress like you, you should have sent me to a private school like all your friends did with their kids."

Mother glared at me, her cheeks growing red in anger.

"Not now," Father said, placing a hand on hers and giving me a stern look.

Hours later, we turned into a section of thick redwoods. I stared at my royal green nails, pushing down the urge to pick at them, and didn't look up until I saw the enormous shadow of Kent Wood's main high school building looming overhead.

The seven-story building was beautiful, the base level covered in pristine white brick, rising into floors of black glass. The sun bounced off the windows, reflecting deep shades of green and gold.

We passed the imposing school gates as they dissolved before us, continuing into the depths. I turned to watch the shimmering lasers flicker back into their places. When I sat back, I saw tall towers of both brick and shimmering glass dotting the landscape as far as the eye could see, surrounded by beautiful sections of trees. Smaller, intricate buildings nestled between them. Doors opened and closed, filtering the students walking about the grassy nulls.

As the second biggest school in North America, Kent Wood held over two hundred thousand kids, kindergarten through Ph .D. Spanning across the northern part of the west coast of lower North America, no other school came close, except for maybe Sally Brown in acreage and Water High in population. The high school was split into two parts, north and south, both next to the beach near the upper part of California. I'd been assigned to the north side where I'd stay in the Science and Fundamental Foundations dorms with my like-minded peers.

"Like-minded, my Holo-a—"

"What was that, dear?" Mother's sickly-sweet voice cut off my thought as I realized I had voiced it aloud.

"Nothing, Mother," I chimed, sending her an overly sweet smile.

Father gave me another disapproving glare. "Most kids would be grateful for such an opportunity. People move to this district from all over to receive a quality education." Father's tone had an edge, but I couldn't stop my snarky reply.

"You mean for the money it used to get ahead—" There was an intensity in his eyes that stopped my rant before it could start. With a sigh, I turned my head away, allowing my thick hair to block my view of them. As the car pulled to the entrance of the North High Science Sector, I went over the story I prepared in my head, checking it once again for holes. Random facts on Willow Creek filled my every thought, and I chanted my cover name in my head till it stuck. With a deep breath, I pulled my hair back and looked out. An imposing brown structure with horse statues lined in gold loomed before me at each corner. The blatant show of excess made my skin crawl.

Father opened the car door. I stepped out, raising my hand to block the bright sun hitting my eyes as it peaked from a cloud above. Father took my bag from the back of the car and came to stand beside me. Mother trailed after him, almost timidly.

"Hello. Welcome to Kent Wood High. My name is Mrs. Adams, and I am the superintendent of this grand institution," a sweet, cheery voice greeted us. A tall olive-skinned woman strutted toward us at a crisp, abrupt pace, not stumbling or shuffling despite the pin skirt strangling her legs. As she descended the marble stairs, her hand reached to adjust a button on her suit jacket with vicious precision. The smile on her face countered the glare from her hazel eyes looking down over a pinched nose. "You must be Loran. We are so glad to have such an excellent student gracing our halls." She put her hand out almost hesitantly, and I shook it firmly. Her thin lips drew into a grin, letting me know I made a good first impression. "Mr. and Mrs. Black, thank you for coming. I will take it from here." She turned from me dismissively, grabbing the bag from Father's hands before he could protest.

His hand hovered before it dropped, watching it as if it was his last landline to me. Mother nodded to Mrs. Adams and turned to me. Her smile was soft and strained, like she didn't know whether to cry or laugh.

"Be good," she said, hugging me. "We won't be available until October, but we'll call."

"Mother, I'm not a kid anymore," I whined, but accepted the hug, knowing it was the last I might ever have.

"We know, darling, but it's been so long since we spent real time with you," Father said from beside her. His voice was sad. Father was always the logical one; it seemed he knew this was our last moment.

"I will miss you both," I said as I hugged him.

"I know. You are going to do great things," he whispered into my hair. Before I could turn away, Mother grabbed my hand and pulled me into one final hug.

"I'm sorry." She kissed me on the forehead, lingering for a moment. Her lips were soft like cotton, yet they stung like the kiss of death. I pulled away, surprised to feel a few tears fall down my cheeks. I swiped them away. Turning, I followed Mrs. Adams into the building, not looking back.

Chapter 9

"I trust you will behave yourself," Mrs. Adams said, her voice cold. All pretense of kindness disappeared the moment we stepped inside. "We will not tolerate any petty, internal drama here."

I followed her down the empty, back maintenance hall, the lights flickering above us, the paint on the walls chipped. We stopped in front of a small black door.

"I understand," I said, looking down at my bag in her hand. The urge to grab it and bolt was strong, but I held it back.

"It says on your transcript that you transferred from Willow Creek. Do your parents know about that?" She eyed me like a puzzle she couldn't figure out.

"I told them I had to change it to avoid conflict. The excuse worked for them."

Voices floated past from the other side of the door, disappearing as quickly as they came.

"And your name change?" There was an edge in her voice.

I gritted my teeth. "They don't know and don't need to."

"Good!" I watched as Mrs. Adams brightened. "You know the rules. What happens in school stays in school. Everything you need is here. Our students never leave campus." She laughed, the sound shrill and dry like her personality. "If your parents ask you to visit, we will tell them you have plans. From this point on, you will cease all communications. You will also keep your mouth shut about your past. We cannot afford an incident."

I clenched my fists and glared at the floor, holding in my anger and sorrow. Mrs. Adams was efficient and to the point. Like a gardener, she trimmed away each straying branch.

"I understand the rules, and I know the risks. Can I leave now?" I caught the grin that floated on her face. She thought she had tamed me, had put me in my place. I resisted the sudden urge to punch her as she passed me my bag.

"Yes. I'm sure I'll see you around."

I yanked it from her hands as she turned with a triumphant smile. Quickly, I stepped into the small room past the door. The area was devoid of students; a lone elevator stood at my left across from a sign pointing to the main lobby. I could hear voices filtering through the door to my right. Peeking out through the small window in it, I could see a vast area with tall columns. Students were scattered about on tables, couches, and huddled in groups. Two-story grand windows let light in from the afternoon sun on two of the four walls. I could see a set of golden elevators to my left; on the opposite wall, two wooden doors led to the outside.

I ducked back as a group passed by a few feet away, my heart racing. As my PortMed squeezed, I ignored the pain shooting through my hand as I slammed the button for the elevator behind me.

The ride to the fifth floor was quick. The elevator *dinged* open to a wide hall littered with black doors. I quickly walked past the single occupant, a tall thin girl with chestnut-brown hair, avoiding her eyes as I searched for my room. I found it, pressing my hand against the door as I pushed. It unlocked, registering my signature, and I slipped inside.

Carelessly, I threw my bag against the wall in front of me and went about setting up my personalized lock system on the door panel. As the small screen turned green, I let out a sigh of relief, turning and sliding down it to the ground.

Mother was right. My room was nicer than my one at Sally Brown. I had an entire apartment to myself. A small kitchen sat to my right, already stocked, based on the open cabinet full of snacks. The wall separating it from the living room was hollow in the center, two feet of the counter jutting out, creating a place to sit and eat. The living room itself was a decent size, with a small couch on the right wall, a desk, and two comfy-looking chairs on the opposite side. A panel on the wall above was my HTV. On my left was an open door showing off my small bedroom.

With a sigh, I pushed myself off the ground, grabbing my bag and heading farther into its depths. I noticed the bathroom across the short hall as I passed. Stopped in the doorway I took stock of my room. It was a decent size, slightly bigger than my room at Sally Brown, with a mini-queen bed to my left and a desk sitting across from me. My beanbag was already situated beside it.

I headed in and dropped my bag on the desk with a small *thump*. Reaching inside, I pulled out my phone, setting it down. I stared at it and it seemed to stare back, the implications of my new life within its small square screen. Reaching to pick it up, my hand stopped inches away. My heart raced as I tried to force it to calm. Another squeeze and I could breathe.

With a shake of my head, I turned and quickly unloaded the rest of my bag. Spare clothes went into the already-full closet and school supplies into their proper place. I moved furniture with a flip of a hover switch.

As I prepared for bed, I tried not to notice the silence surrounding me or the vast space before me in my private bathroom. The porcelain walls, sink, and toilet felt bright and new in the worst kind of way. I dropped my pajama top as it slipped off the floating hanger, bending down to grab it. I almost hit my head on the hangers above me as an unfamiliar *buzzing* sound filled the room, startling me.

My heart racing, I spun. Pinpointing the noise, I let out a breath as I realized it was my phone. Quickly, I headed back to my desk, pulling my shirt on as I went. I picked it up, unlocking it. The screen came to life with a flicker. Though most of the pixels were dim, I could still make out Chris's name in the small box in the center.

Did you make it safely?

I opened the app.

9:25 p.m. Me: *Yes, thank you for checking. I'm in my room now. I hate to admit it, but those brochures weren't lying. It's really nice here.*

I hit send, my pulse racing. It felt like hours before the phone *buzzed* again.

9:32 p.m. Chris: *Is your nose ok or is it too long for function now?*

I let out a small laugh before replying.

9:34 p.m. Me: *No, I can't believe I'm saying this, but I'm serious. Too bad all this luxury is wasted on brats.*

9:35 p.m. Chris: *Ha, that's true. I'm glad you're safe and not in a ditch somewhere. These last few hours have been torture, not knowing if you were ok. If you were still alive.*

9:39 p.m. Me: *Trust me, I know. I miss you so much already; I don't know how I'm going to get through this.*

My finger hovered over the button before I forced it down.

9:39 p.m. Chris: *I miss you too! You are my world. I'm feeling lost without you.*

The reply came back instantly, and my heart skipped a beat.

9:40 p.m. Chris: *I know you can do this—you are strong. Besides, it shouldn't be too long. We just have to make it to The Picking.*

Chris's words warmed my heart and gave me hope.

9:42 p.m. Me: *You're right, like always.*

9:43 p.m. Chris: *I know. I'm a genius, that's why you love me.*

I barked out another laugh, my fingers flying.

9:43 p.m. Me: *One of many reasons. I'm just so nervous about tomorrow. What if I can't fool anyone?*

9:46 p.m. Chris: *I know it's scary, but you got this. Just remember what we practiced, and don't try to show off. Ok. Your goal is to stay in the shadows and away from The Shadow.*

I suppressed a shiver, thinking of the being that took students without warning or prejudice before replying.

9:49 p.m. Me: *Yes, yes, I know, you've only reminded me a hundred times.*

9:51 p.m. Chris: *Hey now, Lightning, you know I am just looking out for you.*

I felt my lips involuntarily twitch as I reread the nickname.

9:55 p.m. Me: *I know. I love you.*

9:55 p.m. Chris: *I love you too! Sleep well, ok? You have a big day tomorrow.*

9:57 p.m. Me: *I will, goodnight.*

9:57 p.m. Chris: *Goodnight.*

I pressed the side button, watching as the screen flickered to black. With a heavy sigh, I went to put it back down on the desk. Hesitating, I pulled it back, holding it to my chest as I turned and walked to my bed. Pulling the sheets up tight, I got comfy.

"Lights off." As the room dimmed, I turned, pulling the phone back from under the sheets and flipping it back on. I reread the last few messages, smiling for the first time that day.

Chapter 10

Flying from my covers, I looked around, panting. My PortMed squeezed as I took in my room. Flopping back down with a grunt, I closed my eyes, trying to block the world out as reality set in. I laid there for another hour, glad that I still had a day before school started on Tuesday.

A knock sounded out through the dorm.

"One moment," I called, flipping my covers off. I quickly got dressed, pulling on a loose pair of sweats and my jacket. As I approached the door, I tried to straighten the rat nest I called my hair. Giving up, I opened it, coming face to face with my unexpected visitor.

"Hello, my name is Hayley. I'm like the dorm mother," said the cheery girl in front of me. Her voice was slightly high in the peppy way that bordered on annoying. It made my ears ring. A blinding white smile made me begrudgingly smile back as she bounced on the balls of her feet. I tried to process what I was seeing as she stuck out her hand. "You must be Lovota." She waited for me to accept her hand.

My brain caught up with her words as I shook. "Yep, that's me." I inspected the rest of her, watching as she did the same to me.

She was wearing a bright white, green, and gold cheerleading uniform. The top was small, her big bust filling it out. It showed off at least six inches of her flat pink stomach, which displayed a small gold belly button piercing with a tiny green stone. The skirt was green and gold striped, two swords clashing over and over on the left side, drawing my eye to it, and a slit up the opposite side. It ended at the upper part of her thighs. The obscene amount of skin disturbed me, but I tried to push past it as she spoke.

"We're so glad to have you here." She flashed another blinding smile, emerald eyes squinting as her arms crossed over her body at the same time. Sharp nails dug into the skin of her elbows.

"Thanks, I'm glad to be here," I said as cheerfully as I could, trying to imitate the friendly Lasa-fair attitude Kathy had pounded into me.

"So, Lovota, that's an interesting name. Like, how did your parents come up with that?"

"Oh…" I rubbed the back of my head, stalling for time as I tried to think of a response. My fingers caught, pulling out a few strands. I tried not to wince. "You see…it's from my mom's side of the family. They immigrated here back in the 2000s from Greece."

Her eyes lit in interest. "Oh, that explains why you have such beautiful, tanned skin. I wish had skin like that. I'm prone to burning." Hayley flipped her long blonde hair, and I watched it fall back. The light waves bounced as they settled past her waist.

I laughed, giving her a genuine smile. "Yeah, I got that a lot back at Willow Creek. It was hard for most of my classmates to get a tan in the winter months," I said, remembering how pale Willow students seemed to be.

Hayley's shoulders relaxed as I talked. When she smiled again, it felt more real, though her eyes were still guarded. "Oh yes. I noticed that. I, like, always thought it was because you all stayed inside studying too much."

"Oh no, we aren't that bad." I forced an awkward laugh. *Add some disdain.* Kathy's voice rang in my head, and I gave Hayley a tight smile. "Though, unlike some people, we don't have the time to slack off."

She was unaffected, pushing past my insult like it didn't matter. "So, are you a freshman?" Her gaze was calculating.

"Oh, um, no, I'm a senior, actually." Another squeeze and my heart calmed again.

"That's unusual. Why are you transferring so late?"

I hesitated, carefully picking my words. I was uncomfortable with the way the conversation was turning. "My parents recently moved. They offered to help me transfer. I...well, listen, I'm going to be frank. It's a long story, and I'd prefer to be comfy as I tell it." I stopped, stepping back to invite her into my room. She didn't budge, waiting for me to continue with distrustful eyes. I let out an aggravated sigh. "I don't know what your problem is, but I'm tired. It's been a long week and if you don't want to talk, then that's fine with me." I made to close the door and she stopped it with her foot.

"No, no, I'm sorry. I'd love to sit down." Her smile was once again forced. Without a word, I let her into the room, closing the door behind her. We headed over to the couch and I settled in at the far end while she sat at the other, her back facing my door.

"Well, where to begin..." I weaved a story, filled with grains of truth, of a girl from a small school looking for her place in the world. After losing her friend to The Shadow, her grades slipped, and she jumped at the opportunity for a new start.

Hayley listened, nodding along. Her defensive posture lessened as I spoke. By the end, she was relaxed, though her gaze was still guarded. "I'm sorry to hear that," she said, placing a gentle hand on mine as she reached across the couch. "Hopefully, despite your past, you can, like, find your place here." I gave her a softer smile, my heart slowing as I relaxed.

She bought it for now. I thought. A knock sounded through the room, and Hayley turned to my door. With a flick on my PortMed, it opened.

The girl from the hall the day before stood on the other side. She was dressed in a pristine cheerleader uniform that clung to her tall, pale, lethal-looking body. Sharp long nails decorated with diamonds and green flowers sat on narrow hips. As I made eye contact with her, her thin red lips pursed like she ate something sour.

"What is it, Lilith?" Hayley's tone was far from friendly as she addressed the girl. It took me by surprise. A quick flash of pain shot through Lilith's hazel eyes, a sneer on her face covering it as she ground back.

"We have practice soon, *captain*." She spit the last word like it was poison on her tongue. "And we can't start without you."

Hayley's shoulders tensed. "I will be there on time. I always am," she snapped back.

"You should be there early," Lilith grumbled. I leaned back as the atmosphere grew cold.

"What was that?" Hayley's tone was deceptively sweet. As Lilith paled, I knew the look on Hayley's face had to be deadly.

"Nothing. I'm sorry. I just wanted to make sure you were okay." She flicked a glance past Hayley to me, drawing me back into the conflict. As if she had forgotten I was there, Hayley whipped around. Her eyes flashed, her expression shutting down before I could read it. She gave me a once-over.

"No, everything is fine. I appreciate you stopping by." She didn't look back. Lilith fidgeted before shooting me a dark glare.

"I'll see you there, captain," she gritted out. Her ponytail whipped around as she turned and stalked down the hall. I watched her go, avoiding Hayley's gaze.

She stood swiftly as I made to close the door, stopping me. With two sharp swipes at her skirt, she straightened, looking down at me. Her eyes were cold.

"It was nice meeting you," she said with an overly large smile. "I'll be back tomorrow to help you get to class."

My heart dropped. "No, no, that isn't necessary," I sputtered out, and she went rigid. "Not that I don't appreciate it," I quickly amended. "It's just...I would hate to inconvenience you."

She relaxed marginally. "It's no bother. It's like my job as the Dorm Mother to make sure everyone is settled in. Usually, I spend my time showing the freshman around." She turned and headed out the door. "It will be a pleasant change for once to keep an eye on someone—" she paused, turning back, " —my age." She disappeared into the hall before I could reply.

I watched the empty space, my heart beating rapidly despite the squeezing of my PortMed, feeling as though I had passed *and* failed some unspoken test.

Chapter 11

I EXITED THE GOLDEN elevator into the lobby of my dorm building the next day. It was filled with students milling about, getting ready for the first class of term. The excitement was electric, reminding me of the atmosphere Sally Brown had on game days. I could feel all eyes on me as I shadowed the cheer captain, Hayley, to a table on the side, pulling my jacket closer. My fingers fiddled with the ends as she stopped, a small bounce in her movement.

"Morning!" she chimed to the three girls sitting before us. They turned from their conversation.

"Morning," ground out a small brunette in a cheerleading uniform. Gold bangles covered in green stones jingled as she stood. A henna tattoo of an otter bounced along her brown flat stomach.

"Hi," whispered a girl across from her. She quietly stood from her seat, shuffling about as she gave Hayley a tiny smile. She tucked her dirty blonde pixie-cut hair behind her pale ear.

"'Sup, cap'," chimed the girl with flaming red hair pulled into a ponytail sitting beside the tiny girl, as her vivid sea-green eyes, surrounded by freckles, flickered past Hayley to me. Instantly, my hackles raised as flashes of memories surfaced, my hand flying to my stomach where a particularly nasty scar sat. I cursed my luck. Jaz Swift. Though I hadn't seen her in four years, thanks to her reaching the varsity leagues before me, my last memories of her were hard to forget. I noticed her left ear was missing the tip, leaving behind a jagged line, her only reminder of that day. "Who is this?" she asked. The other two watched me with guarded looks.

Hayley spun to me. There was a bright bounce in her step as she replied. "This is Lovota. She, like, just transferred here from Willow Creek." She grabbed my hand, pulling me forward, and I tried not to stumble. "Since she's new, I'm showing her around."

"Oh, it's nice to meet you." The tiny dirty blonde stepped forward, giving me a timid smile. "I can't imagine how scared you must be coming all the way here. Luckily, you're in good hands. My name is Lucy."

I took her offered hand, giving her a kind smile. Her black eyes were soft, and I could already tell I would like her.

"Thank you," I said. "It's definitely been an experience so far. All of this is so much…" I paused, looking around at all the students walking about on white marble tiles. "More than I'm used to." She gave me an understanding look, her pointy nose scrunching as the brunette stepped up beside her.

"Name's Sally. Yes, I know it's an unfortunate name but it's mine," she said bluntly, giving me a once-over. The glare in her brown eyes framed by short, wavy, golden-brown hair sent a shiver down my spine. "You sure dress funny for an alternate school kid."

As I felt a squeeze, I bristled. "I'm sorry?" I asked, not having to fake my disgusted and insulted tone. "How am I supposed to dress, *Pleb*?" I threw the newly familiar insult with all the disdain I could muster.

The group was quiet for a beat before she let out a barking laugh. Her button nose scrunched, and her hair flew about tiny ears as she threw her head back.

"Oh, I'm going to like you."

"You really need to be nicer to the new kids," chastised Jaz as she also stepped forward.

My blood froze as I met her calculating gaze.

"Jaz. It's nice to meet you," she said, extending a hand. Her green and white varsity letter jacket was stained, and the dirt-speckled golden cuffs rubbed my hand as we shook. As she pulled away, she tucked a stray strand of hair behind her undamaged ear. Two piercings stuck out from the top. One a soft gold ball, the other a green jagged spike. Despite her rugged looks, her face and eyes were surprisingly soft. I let out a breath as I realized she didn't seem to recognize me and forced down my anger.

"It's nice to meet you as well," I said.

"Well, now that you all have met, we need to head to class," Hayley chimed, bouncing forward. "We can't let Lovota be late. She will be gathering too much attention as is."

I winced, falling into step behind her and the others.

The air was pleasant as it swept over me the moment I stepped outside. I looked over the green grassy knolls. Like Sally Brown, the paths moved at an accelerated pace, but I noticed they seemed to be personalized per student, people walking at various angles and paces that didn't match the basic flow. Sets of oak and tall sequoia trees sprinkled the land and, in the distance, I could see a large forest. The girls chatted as we turned onto a wide path, filing past a set of slower-moving students.

"What classes are you in?" Jaz asked as she paused a step, allowing her to fall back beside me.

I instantly felt on edge, forcing my body to relax as my PortMed squeezed. "I have calculus, physics, and basic English today. Then I'm taking biology and a four-hour class called the Arts of the Past tomorrow," I said as I pulled up my class list, scrolling through the day. "Not sure exactly what it is, but it sounded interesting." Kathy had picked out my classes, working to find ones that would help me stay in the rankings with Chris without also drawing attention to myself.

Jaz hummed, placing her hands behind her head, and I noted she was only wearing a black sports bra under her jacket. "That's a PE, specializing in the study of combat arts," she explained.

My stomach dropped, and I stumbled.

"Are you okay?" she asked. Yet as she helped me stabilize myself, there was a glint in her eyes that set me on edge.

"Yeah, yeah. I'm just not used to this," I said, gesturing to the path.

"Oh, I never thought of that," she said as the others turned to see if we were coming. "Your campus must be too small to need help getting to class on time, hum?"

I nodded. "Yeah, in comparison, I guess it is. Especially since it's squeezed up in the mountains near Aspen." I tried not to grimace the moment I realized my mistake. Luckily, it didn't seem to faze her or the others who were now walking beside us. No one complained as we took up a good portion of the path. Instead, I noticed that they gratefully stepped aside when need be, some of them almost bowing as they did. It seemed like I was right and Hayley's group were near the top of Kent Wood and highly respected. I ignored the glares I was receiving.

"I can't imagine what that must be like," Lucy piped up.

"It's a lot of hiking for sure," I said.

"Sounds like elementary all over again," Sally said. "How annoying. I'm glad the campuses slowly get less hilly as we age."

We hit a fork in the path, and Hayley stepped across Jaz to me. "I'll take you from here and drop you off at the calculus class." She scooped my hand into hers, surprising me before she pulled me forward. I waved goodbye to the others as I sped up to keep pace without stumbling. We turned toward a set of buildings. Three small towers seemingly made of gold and a single brick one-story building surrounding a tall gold and green-tinted glass tower sat ahead. I noticed a team of students scrubbing away at one of the walls, the face of a lion fading as a bot passed by. I shoved down my pride. We filtered into the tall tower with other students, our way made easy as many of the boys stumbled from Hayley's path. She gave them a kind smile and more than one smiled like a buffoon back.

I could see all the way to the top of the tower. Above us, stairs twisted and turned, leading to the other floors. Various drones and bot tech flew about as we ascended a set of stairs to the left. A few humanoid bots walked the halls we passed, their metal feet *clicking* along with the students', and I glimpsed a research lab across the building.

Math was one of Kent Wood's strongest subjects, and the class filing into the two-story lecture hall we stepped into reflected that. As I followed left, down a set of stairs, I spotted tablets built into each desk already alight, beaming up images of symbols and video games. Space around each allowed students a place to work on projects and utilize VR technology to interact with the lesson. A flash of envy shot through me as I saw the sleek glasses on the desks. Unconsciously I tightened my hold on my backpack, my older model of haptic gloves making me suddenly feel inadequate.

I followed Hayley to a row near the middle. Students greeted her, and she gave each a large smile. Finally, she stopped by an olive-skinned boy with shaggy brown—almost black—hair. He looked up from his desk where thousands of lines of code filled his Holo-screen. Spotting Hayley, he smiled a wide smile. I noticed his lips were just the right shape to pull off that taunting smirk most boys tried to make.

"Hey Shan," Hayley called, and he stood, giving her a hug. "Where have you been? I swear it's been like a lifetime since I last saw you." His skin darkened as he blushed, stepping back.

"It's only been a week," he said, his voice melodic. He rubbed the back of his head in embarrassment. "Besides, it's not my fault. Kyle took up my break, insisting I try to hack the system to find Michel Thomas's basketball plans."

Hayley let out a sigh. "Tell me he didn't..." Her tone was exhausted and bemused. Shan nodded with an amused smile.

"Excuse me." I quickly stepped aside as a small girl made to pass. The movement drew Shan's attention to me. When we made eye contact, my breath caught. Almond-shaped blue-gray eyes swirled like a storm on the sea. I felt like I was drowning in their depths, unable to look away. A cough broke the connection, and we both turned to Hayley. There was an amused glint in her eyes as she watched us.

"Shan, I'd like you to meet Lovota," she said by way of introduction, and I held my hand out to him. Immediately, his blush returned. He shook it, looking down, his hair flopping into his face.

"It's nice to meet you," I said, giving him a gentle smile. He brightened as his hair fell into his eyes. With an annoyed sound, he flipped it back out of his face, glaring up at it as if it had done him a great wrong.

I smiled, finding myself instantly at ease with him.

"It's nic-ce to meet you," he stuttered.

"Lovota just came from Willow Creek and I'm dropping her off. Where is Kyle? I was hoping he would be here." Hayley looked around the room for said boy.

"Should be here any moment," Shan said. "I left him with his fans in the hall. You know how he can be."

Chapter 12

Before Hayley could reply, a boisterous laugh filtered into the room. I turned to the door we came from, watching as the last person I ever wanted to see walked through it.

Kyle James Patson.

A mix of fear and fury filled me. Four gorgeous girls surrounded him, his arms wrapped around the shoulders of two, showing off a tattoo of a gold sword piercing a green shield on his left bicep. As he let out another laugh, they giggled, batting their eyes at him. He shot them a wink.

"Thank you. I appreciate the compliment," he said, stepping away. They actually whined as he did so, and I felt like throwing up. "Now, now. I have to get to class. Gotta maintain my top tier Rank One spot, you know." With frantic nods, they left, heading to their own classes. Kyle watched them go before he turned to us.

"Kyle!" Hayley stepped forward, bouncing.

Seeing her, his eyes instantly lit up. "Hayley," he whispered her name like a prayer, pulling her into a bear hug as he rushed forward. "It feels like it's been years." I heard him whisper into her hair.

I was suddenly uncomfortable, like I was witnessing something private, and looked away.

"That's what I was just telling Shan," Hayley said. "I heard what you've been up to. Like, you can't be serious. You know even Shan's skills can't hack those Hooters."

Kyle laughed, and I looked back in time to see him place a gentle peck on her head as he stepped back. He opened his mouth to reply, his eyes flying up to Shan and spotting me. Instantly, he was on guard, stepping forward slightly in front of Hayley. Another squeeze from my MEDs and I had to remind myself that he shouldn't know me. That every time we met, he should have been focused on Chris instead.

"Who's this?" His voice was cold, almost a growl.

Hayley placed a hand on his shoulder, her golden green nails digging into his skin. "This is *Lovota*." The way she emphasized my name made me wary, but I forced an uncaring look onto my face. Her tone stopped Kyle, and he looked around. I followed his gaze. Everyone was watching us, their postures, and eyes hesitant as they waited to see what would come next. I realized that moment would decide my fate. Pensively, I waited.

"She is from Willow Creek."

Like watching a sunset, the anger and defensiveness fell from Kyle's face. He flashed me a heart-breaking smile. "Well, why didn't you just say so," he said, coming up to me. He held a large hand out, and I took it, acting like I could care less what he thought of me as I prayed he wouldn't be able to tell my palms were sweaty. "It's nice to meet you. I'm sure you heard, but my name is Kyle." I gave him a once over, pretending to put a face to the name.

"Oh, you're that basketball kid," I said with a bright smile. "You won the best player of the year award, right? My friend talks about you all the time."

Kyle puffed up at the acknowledgment, and the room around us relaxed. "Yep, that's me," he said. "I'll get it again this year. Just you wait." I nodded enthusiastically, pulling my hand away and subtly wiping it on my pants, hiding my disgust.

"You totally will," called a boy from behind Kyle, and he turned enthusiastically to greet him. Hayley stepped up to me with a big smile, some of the hardness in her gaze gone.

"It's crazy to think how far his name has spread," she said, watching him with admiration.

"Is he your boyfriend?" I asked. I didn't remember hearing about Kyle dating anyone. He was a notorious playboy.

Hayley let out a gruff laugh. "Gosh, like no," she denied even as her cheeks slightly pinkened. "We've been friends since, like diapers. It would be like dating my brother." Her eyes watched him with longing.

"Right." I drew the word out in disbelief.

"Anyway." She bounced. "I must head out. Will you be okay here?" I looked to Kyle, then back to Shan, who was already at his desk, engrossed in his code. Sensing my eyes, he looked up. The blush was back as he looked back down.

"Yeah, I think I'll be fine," I said.

"Good. I'll see you later, okay?" She bounced away, giving Kyle a small peck on the cheek as she passed. He waved, continuing to talk with the group of boys gathered around him. I turned around, walking up to one of the empty seats next to Shan.

"Mind if I sit here?" he nodded, his hair obscuring his eyes as he did.

"Is there any way to transfer out of Arts of the Past?" I asked a blushing Shan as we walked along the path from biology class the next day.

"Well, of course, but trust me, you don't want to," Kyle butt in on the other side of me. "Professor Grant is one of the best martial artists in the country. You won't want to pass up a chance to learn under him."

"You only say that because you haven't seen me fight," I countered, playing my part and cursing Kathy for not digging deeper into the class descriptions. "Put a basketball in my hand. I'm good. Tell me to run for multiple miles, fine. Fighting, well, how do you feel about a hospital visit?"

Shan let out a chuckle. The sound sent a pleasant shiver down my spine that I ignored.

Kyle's wide smirk wasn't as aggravating when it wasn't derogatory, but I still had to force down my anger.

"You should be okay," Shan said quietly, giving me a blushing smile. "I'm sure you're not that bad if you can do those other things."

I sighed. "Yeah, okay. That was an exaggeration, even so, I don't really like violence. I would prefer to avoid it where I can."

"I heard basketball?" I turned in time to see Jaz jogging up to us from the path she had followed the day before. A tall boy I distantly recognized from the basketball team jogged beside her. His clean crisp varsity jacket bounced with every step, the mascot on his arm galloping across.

"We were talking about our next class," Kyle said in greeting.

"Oh yes! I'm so excited," Jaz said with a vicious glee in her eyes as she looked at me. My heart skipped a beat before she continued. "I've been waiting to knock that smug smirk off your face for years," she told Kyle.

He let out a barking laugh that had the group of girls passing us giggling. "You only wish you could," he teased.

"You better watch yourself. We both know Jaz could kick your butt if she puts her mind to it," taunted the boy next to her with a grin.

Seeing the question in my eyes, Jaz introduced us. "This is my boyfriend, Zack. Zack meet Lovota." Zack held his hand out with a bright smile. Behind the thin layer of his blond hair, I could see two scars zigzagging along his cream skin. They went down his left side, one to his ear and one to his jaw.

"It's nice to meet you," we said at the same time. He laughed, wrapping his arm around Jaz, releasing my hand, and glanced down at her. The look revealed a small tattoo behind his ear of the Kent Wood shield. His green eyes softened as they met Jaz's. My heart ached as I was reminded of Chris, but I pushed the feelings down.

"I'm guessing you guys play sports. Which ones?" I waited a beat before repeating the question.

Jaz's eyes focused back on me, dilating like waking from a dream. "Sorry, what was that?" she asked.

"Ignore them when they get like this," Hayley chimed from the side, and I turned to see her approaching with Sally and a group I hadn't met yet. She quickly introduced us. I took in their names and appearances as we walked.

The boy with a birthmark shaped like a paw on his right cheek was Sam. The tiny, frizzy-haired brunette with hazel eyes, dark skin, and ruby-looking sneakers around her small feet was nicknamed Dorothy. She told me, in a thick southern accent, she had a small dog that looked like Toto from the Wizard of Oz. The girl next to her, her twin, was nicknamed Bee. I could see why, as she constantly buzzed around, hopping and fidgeting even when standing. They had matching tattoos on their right wrist of an intricate green and gold sword, Bee's freckled face their only distinction.

The last two members of the group were two brick walls nicknamed Tweedledum and Tweedledee, or Dum and Dee for short. Dum had a tattoo of a green shield on his pale left ankle while Dee had a gold sword on his. It didn't take long to figure out that the names were far from accurate, coming more from their perpetuality to get in accidents then their intelligence.

We turned toward the athletic sector as Bee, Dorothy, the Tweedle brothers, and Lucy headed off to the arts sector.

"So, Jaz and Zack are close?" I whispered to Hayley.

She nodded. "Inseparable. Like, I wouldn't be surprised if they are Paired."

Sounds like Chris and me. My emotions raged as I fought to keep a calm façade. I could feel my cheeks flush. *I wish I could just forget my old life and move on.* My MEDs activated with a squeeze and I shoved the thought down as my heart slowed and my flush receded.

"So they say, anyway," said Jaz, rubbing the back of her head as she heard us. "It's not personal. I just kind of get lost in him sometimes."

"It's all right. I understand." There was something off in Jaz's smile as I turned my attention to the plaque, stating we were entering the athletic sector. Dorms, stadiums, and training facilities surrounded me, giving me my first view from a home vantage. Though not as grand as Sally Brown, they were still beautiful, each decked out in green and gold with black accents, making the colors stand out. The basketball stadium had always reminded me of an enormous bird's nest with gold and green sticks jutting from the sides.

"Yeah. It's beautiful, isn't it?" Shan asked behind me.

I turned to him, nodding. "Way bigger than I'm used to." I forced a smile. "It's amazing you all have two of these sectors just in high school alone."

"Only the best for the best," Kyle said with pride, and I squeezed my hand into a fist, pulling in my anger and the retort on my tongue. We ended up turning to one of the brick buildings sitting to the side of the stadiums. Kyle and Zack took the lead, pushing open the doors. Instantly, I was hit by the familiar sounds of fighting and conversation and the smell of rubber. Bleachers lined the walls on either side of a large sparring mat, which was occupied by a middle-aged man and a large boy with brown hair. They wrestled, their muscles visibly straining, as the crowd cheered them on.

As I took a seat in the bleachers, the man twisted his body, flipping the boy and effectively pinning him to the mat. The class roared as they counted down, declaring him the winner.

"And that is why I am in charge of this class," the man said as he stood, straightening his Gi, the white robe slightly crinkled from the fight.

"Serves Robert right," Hayley giggled to Jaz as she watched the disgruntled boy get up from the mat and walk off. A group of boys was waiting for Robert on the side and passed him a water bottle with wide smiles.

"Well then, I think it's time we get down to business," said the man. The class was instantly silent, hanging onto his every word. "My name is Professor Grant. I'm warning you now, this class will challenge you physically and mentally. There's no shame if you want to drop out." I vaguely recognized the dark-skinned man with a bent right thumb and bright gray eyes. He was an assistant to Master Nako when I was a child. As he scanned the crowd and spotted me, his lips twitched slightly. My heart skipped a beat, but he didn't draw any attention my way. "No takers? Very well. Welcome. Since this class is a PE, we will be working all weeks of the term. If you skip, you won't be docked unless it gets excessive, but be warned. Missing could equal a painful loss later on. For the first few days, we will practice basic forms of fighting from a variety of styles. In two weeks' time, we will then put them to practical use in one-on-one spars, group fights, and dummy practice. Now then, today, let's talk about wrestling."

I fiddled with my jacket ends as he spoke, worry overtaking me as I tried to think of a way out of the situation. Despite what Kyle said, changing classes was close to impossible since all the ones for the slot were full. When Professor Grant finished and we were called to practice moves, I made sure to stumble about as I imitated the flips and grapples he was showing. I caught Grant's curious gaze a few times, confusion clear on his face before he would go about helping other students.

"Did you do something to piss him off?" Jaz whispered to me as we completed a roll.

"No?"

"He's helping everyone else who is struggling, but won't even approach you."

I cursed in my head as we did another roll. "Oh, I—um—didn't notice." I stuttered out, making sure to miss my landing. Jaz quickly stabilized me, shoving me slightly and apologizing before we went back through the set.

Chapter 13

"Go on without me," I told Shan. "I need to talk to the professor really quick."

He gave me a concerned look, but nodded. "I'll w-wait for you outside," he stuttered as I turned and headed over to Professor Grant.

"Professor," I called, and he turned from his bag, smiling.

"Lor—"

"My name is Lovota," I interrupted. He raised one eyebrow, but nodded for me to continue. "I wanted to speak to you, if you have the time."

He gave me a smile, motioning me closer as he said, "Of course, I always have time for my students."

"I need you to check on me in class from now on," I whispered once I was inches away.

"I can't do that, Ms. Black—"

"Ms. Miller now," I corrected.

"Of course," he whispered back. "Unlike some of your classmates, you do not need help."

"Please," I pleaded. "If you don't, it will look suspicious. My life literally depends on this."

He gave me a long assessing gaze, realization lighting in his eyes. "They sent you to Sally Brown?" I nodded, feeling slightly confused. "Hum, I guess I thought. Never mind. I understand. You don't need to say more. But I also can't give you everything. So, let's make a deal. You agree to improve at a pace rapid enough to not need my attention all the time, and I'll make it look like it's because I'm an excellent teacher. Okay?"

I nodded, my face hurting from the bright smile on it. "Deal. Thank you so much!"

As I left, my fingers made contact with a thin hand with diamond-studded nails on the door handle. My heart thumped as I met eyes with Lilith.

Did she hear us?

She sent me a forced smile, pushing the door open. "Please after you," she said sweetly, but the glint in her eyes didn't fool me.

"Thank you," I said, walking past and feigning nonchalance.

"H-hey, that was quick, did-d you get everything..." Shan trailed off as he spotted Lilith behind me. She looked at him, raised a single thin eyebrow, and walked off. He watched her go with a broken gaze till Kyle smacked him on the back, startling him from his trance.

"You good to go?" he asked me, giving Shan a moment to recover.

I watched the interaction with interest, nodding. "Lead the way."

We headed out of the athletic district and back to the dorms. The group met up on a path along the way, and I listened as they all talked excitedly about a party coming up.

"You can be my date," Kyle said with a wink.

I sputtered, feeling disturbed. "I have a boyfriend."

He smiled wider. "And?"

Before my anger could explode, Sally slapped me on the back, laughing. I glared down that the little cheerleader, watching the annoying otter bounce around. "Oh, you have a lot to learn about Kent Wood," she said, with an evil glint in her eyes.

Waking up the next day, I quickly dressed and rushed out of the room to avoid Hayley. Her friend group was full of the last people I cared to be around. They were the top students of the sector—if not the whole school—and because of them; I had more eyes on me than I wanted or planned. Not to mention, being around most of them made my skin crawl half the time.

I tried to ignore the hurt look in Shan's eyes as I dodged my usual seat to head to the back of class. *He'll get over it. He won't want to be my friend, anyway.* I thought as I tried to hide.

I thought I'd succeeded in avoiding Hayley when she popped up beside me with a sharp smile as I walked from calculus.

"Oh, there you are," she called. Her grip on my arm was unyielding and the look in her eyes made my PortMed squeeze. "We were just looking for you. Come on, it's Saturday, and we always eat at Numan's Best on Saturdays."

I had no choice but to follow as she dragged me along.

"You're not, like, avoiding me, are you?" Hayley asked out of nowhere as I sat under a tree in front of the dorm, enjoying the warm September sun.

I looked up from the presentation I was preparing for class, amazed that a week had already passed, and stopped. The look in her eyes sent my heart into overdrive and I noticed how her hand hovered over her PortMed.

"No, of course not," I quickly denied, waving my hands in front of me as I felt a squeeze. "What would give you that idea?" I tried not to let the tears flow as I realized avoiding her would be impossible.

I pulled up my project map. The weaving class tree swirled around me, my entire academic history on display. The five students in my review and the calculus teacher Mr. Talon sat in front of me, looking it over with wide eyes.

"As you can see, I have a varied background in arts, math, biology, physics, and English," I said, confidently. I was in my element, and there was no way I was going to play my intelligence down, no matter what Chris said. "My plan is to utilize these to create an encompassing project. I've gotten it cleared with my other teachers. If you're okay with it, then I would like to move ahead."

Mr. Talon looked my map over, turning to my proposal. "Based on your ranking, I would say you could get this done by term end and pull it into calculus three next term. *But* I would push you to consider taking a few parts out. It might be a bit strenuous."

I cursed Lovota and her new bottom-tier third-rank status as I smiled tightly. "I understand, sir, but you can see that ranking is new. Due to extenuating circumstances, I was unable to push myself last year. I guarantee that if you let me continue, you won't regret it."

Mr. Talon eyed me thoughtfully, scrolling through my academic record as he did. From behind him, I noticed Shan still staring at my chart with a look of wonder. As we made eye contact, the blush grew on his face, but he didn't look away. It felt like he was viewing me in a new light. I sent him a nervous smile, which he returned with a taunting grin that made my heart skip.

"Alright then," Mr. Talon declared. "I think you're good to go. Now please tell me how you plan to tackle the charting of the migratory patterns of the Carcharodon Carcharias."

My excitement grew as I explained my plan for charting, designing, and building a safer path for the fishing systems to take to avoid the sharks while also still saving the fishing companies' money. As I spoke, I watched Shan's eyes grow wide. By the time I was done, they had gone dark, an unknown emotion, like boiling lava in them. When he noticed me staring, he blushed, looking down quickly. "Well then, Ms. Miller. I am excited to see what you come up with."

I nodded, smiling as Mr. Talon dismissed me. Sending Shan a bright smile as he took his place at the front of the group in the small white room, I made my way into the lobby. The circular area with five doors was relatively quiet, the students selected to present to their groups first standing about or gone. I leaned against a wall near my door, ignoring the stares I received from a group of boys clustered in the corner nearest the hall leading to the other math rooms. Closing my eyes, I allowed myself to think about my friends back home for just a few minutes, fingering my necklace and feeling the weight of the phone in my pocket.

"Hello there, you must be new," a smooth male voice woke me from my daydream. I tried not to groan at the sound of a sniffle as he finished speaking. "My name is Thames, but you can call me Tom." I opened my eyes, surprised to see a beautiful boy standing in front of me, his hand outstretched. Despite his slouch, I had to crank my neck to look him in the eyes as I shook. The nerdiness of his appearance contradicted the smoothness of his motion as he smiled, pushing his glasses, of all things, up his nose. Onyx eyes gleamed from behind the rims.

"I'm Lovota," I said shortly, showing I wasn't in the mood to talk, ignoring the way my heart raced. *Am I scared?* I tried to pull away from his grip but found my hand caught in his. My eyes flew down as he rubbed the back of it with his thumb, his grip unyielding.

As if realizing what he was doing, he let it go, a sheepish smile on his face as he rubbed the back of his pale neck. "Sorry," he apologized, seeming genuinely guilty. "Lovota, you say...that's an interesting name. You don't look much like a Lovota to me." He pushed his glasses back up his nose. I couldn't tell if they were for show, or if he needed them. It was uncommon to see someone with impaired vision that the MEDs or a doctor hadn't fixed. But the reflection told otherwise, and it piqued my interest.

"Why would you say that?" I asked.

Tom's shaggy black hair fell around his face as he glanced down. He ignored it, letting it catch in his eyelashes without blinking. "Well, Lovota means fast wolf, and you just don't strike me as the wolf type," he explained with a chuckle and grin. The sharp edge of his jaw tensed. His eyes searched me, hunger flashing across his face. The look sent a jolt of fear down my body. But as fast as it came, it was gone. *Get a hold of yourself. He isn't dangerous.* The panic in my heart eased, and I found the way his eyes lit with mirth amusing.

Throwing a sassy hair flip, I responded. "Well, I don't know about the wolf part, but I can assure you I'm pretty fast."

"Oh, I bet you are." There was that look again. His glasses reflected as he adjusted them and when I saw his eyes again, they were filled with a kind warmth. *Is the stress getting to me already?*

"Hey, Lovota, is this guy bothering you?" Kyle's voice broke in before I could continue our conversation. He shut a door two sets down loudly behind him and I winced from the noise, shooting him a glare. Crossing his arms, he ignored me as he glared at Tom, who shrank back from me, revealing the top of a black and gray tattoo over his left shoulder. By then, his group of friends had slowly inched their way over, but as Kyle stalked toward us, I watched many of them shrink back and hide in the shadows. Something about the movement was off. The look in their eyes far from fearful.

"Kyle, I'm fine," I snapped, forgetting for a moment to be passive. "I don't need your violent Pleb attitude right now."

"What are you doing here, *Thames*?" Kyle ignored me, invading Tom's space. Despite Tom's cowering posture, he was still taller.

"Nothing, Kyle. I was just trying to get to know the new girl is all." Tom put his hands up in defense, yet an intense hate lingered in his eyes. It made me wonder what Kyle did to make him so angry. Well, other than being a Defect. He began to back away to his friends, his stance reminding me more of a fighting crouch than that of a coward.

Kyle didn't seem to notice it as he glared down at the boys, his chest seeming to swell with pride at their fear. He sent Tom a cocky sneer, stepping beside me, making me dislike him more, if that was possible.

"She doesn't need to know you. Understand?"

Tom backed up again, falling into the crowd of nerds behind him. "Completely," Tom said, shivering. His eyes flashed to mine. For a moment, I swear I saw a grin sneak on his face, sending another shiver down my spine, causing me to step toward Kyle.

"Good." As Kyle was about to continue, the door to my classroom opened.

I turned to see Shan walking out, rubbing his eyes. His entrance broke the tension in the room, but he didn't seem to notice as he looked at Kyle. "That was killer. I don't think I'll ever get used to presenting. Felt like sleeping the whole time," he growled. I was surprised at the anger in it, but it didn't faze Kyle.

With a laugh, he stepped beside Shan and slapped him on the back, causing him to stumble forward a bit. "That's what you get for staying up late last night doing all that hacking. I'm telling you dude, you should make people pay you for that instead of doing it for free."

Shan opened his mouth to reply, snapping it shut as he spotted me, looking like a deer in headlights. I caught the slightest blush on his face as he looked down at his shoes. Kyle grunted, huffing, and smiled at me. "Now that we're all here, let's head out." Kyle took the lead, Shan falling in behind him.

Turning to Tom, I tried to flash him a friendly smile. "Sorry about that." If I didn't have class, I would have tried to talk longer and figure out why he made my brain itch. But I couldn't fall behind, so I continued down the hall with Shan and Kyle.

From what I could tell in the week since I arrived, cliques at Kent Wood were tougher than Sally Brown. Though my old group wouldn't hang out with the likes of Tom, we also wouldn't have been so rude. Though it could have just been Kyle.

Chapter 14

After my last class of the day, the group headed to dinner. Hayley picked a small restaurant in Block D in the science section near the main building. As I packed into a large booth at the back beside Hayley and Sam, I noticed no one bothered picking up a menu. I scanned through the items quickly so as not to hold up the order.

The table was bustling with life, and I watched my new friends with interest. Despite moments of tension and overall awkwardness, I had to admit: so far, Kent Wood wasn't like I thought it would be. All the stereotypes and hateful stories we shared around the lobbies and fires at events weren't ringing true in most cases. I didn't know how to process the information, flipping between anger, confusion, and fear far too often to be healthy.

The server came around to take our orders and Kyle flirted with her shamelessly before she left, glancing my way as he did, sending me a wink.

I rolled my eyes, turning to the conversation Hayley and Jaz were having.

"Yeah, I agree. We will like, so beat them this year," said Hayley.

"Beat who?" I asked.

"Sally Brown, of course. The varsity team plays them in basketball in three weeks," Jaz said.

"What!" My shout caused people to turn and stare. I blushed in embarrassment, hiding behind my hair.

Ignoring the stares, Hayley continued as if nothing happened. "Yeah, I know it's like early in the season. Whatever. Might as well get it over with. Then we'll have more time to improve before the championships." She flipped her hair.

My heart was like a sledgehammer in my chest, my PortMed working overtime. Through all the chaos, all the planning, how could we have forgotten about the games? Attendance was mandatory for all school events ranked JV5 and up. Everyone had to go unless they had extenuating circumstances. Even remote events had to be attended, though some were virtual, with fans projected on the seats at the stadium. There was no way I could avoid it other than getting lucky and falling into the overflow buildings. I took a deep breath before a panic attack could set in. *I'm one in thousands.*

"Lovota...Lovota." I came back to the present, remembering that was now my name. Hayley's hand was on mine; my stomach rolled at the sight.

"Oh, sorry." I pulled away, trying to do it slowly so as not to raise suspicion before hiding my trembling below the table.

"Food's here." She pointed to my plate.

"Thanks." I picked up my burger, taking a bite. I eyed it as the conversation continued to roll. *Maybe if I choked and died, I could escape. No, that would never work.* I was sure Jaz or someone else knew the Heimlich and would save me. I sighed and took another bite.

"So," Hayley continued between bites of her tortilla. "Like, who do you think has the best chances?"

"What do you mean?" I asked, not following.

"With the Kent vs. Sally game," she continued.

Oh Right.

"Who will win? I heard the Browner's aren't as good this year. You were just there, right? How did they look?" Her tone implied there was more to her question. Everyone's eyes were on me.

Of course, they are good. This year is our year.

I wanted to yell, rant, and fight. Instead, I stopped myself by taking a bite and chewing diligently.

"Well, they passed through for a scrimmage against Water High a few months back. They seemed pretty good, but I'm probably not the best judge. If you heard rumors we will win, then I think you're right." I sprinkled in a small grain of truth, hoping by doing so, I wouldn't get caught. I took a bigger bite so Hayley couldn't ask more questions.

Maybe I'll get food poisoning. I snorted to myself. *That would be too lucky for me.*

"I hope so. It's about time someone knocked them off their athletic pedestal." Hayley sighed, looking down at her food. "This year is supposed to be ours." The table grew silent.

Once we finished and headed our separate ways, Jaz stopped me and offered to join me on a walk around campus. "I can tell you're still struggling to get around," she explained. "I know it's been a week, but better now than never, right?"

My rolling emotions calmed as she smiled bashfully. *Maybe she isn't as bad as I remember?* We walked the north high as she explained how the divisions of studies allowed students to navigate to classes faster.

In the arts sector, I commented on the buildings. Even their architecture seemed to express the creativity with twisting spirals, graffiti art, murals, and more. I found myself a little envious of the site, wishing Sally Brown had presented such a creative expression; it was a core of our philosophy after all.

I made a mental note to call Chris as Jaz went on a rant about how Zack never remembered to take her out on game weeks. We ended up skipping the athletic sector since I'd become quite familiar with it. She ignored the admiring looks we gathered when we neared. Once we were out of earshot, she told me the attention was uncomfortable for her, and she didn't venture there outside of practice and classes with Zack. She spoke of the hardships and pressures of being a starter on the basketball team. I realized despite her rampant popularity, she was humble, and a wall fell between us.

By the time we made it home, I felt more connected to the school and her. Kent Wood really was a beautiful campus, I was loathed to admit.

I tried not to cry as I nursed a nasty bruise on my cheek from my spar with Jaz.

"Hey, you're getting better, at least," she said as she held an ice pack up to me. I grabbed it, giving her a forced smile, wincing. Her eyes flashed with joy for just a moment, putting me on edge.

"Yeah, it's like, only been a little over a week. Don't give up now," Hayley encouraged with a sharp smile.

I can't wait for the weekend. Each of my muscles protested as I got out of bed. Looking at my PortMed, the home screen read:

Saturday, September 13th, 7:10 a.m.

I sighed, making my way to the bathroom and looking in the mirror. My cut from the day before was healing, at least.

"Now, if my internal bruises would get with the program, that would be awesome," I mumbled to myself.

As I looked over my equations, I hummed a tune from one of my favorite songs. Shan grabbed one of my floating equations as he sat beside me and began making notes. I tried not to stare as he not only understood my work, but could break down the complexity of my thought process. *He is Kent Wood after all*, I remembered.

"You're close; but I was actually hoping to take in this sub-species here," I corrected him as we worked. The heat of his gaze wasn't uncomfortable as I explained my plans and I had to push down the flutter of my heart.

He is Kent Wood!

The smell of sweat filled the air. I observed the three pairs sparring on the mat with rapid curiosity. A sharp yell rang out, as Jaz delivered a nasty left hook to Lilith's face. She went tumbling out of the circle and someone called the match. The other two pairs continued.

"And that's match," Shan whispered next to me as Zack was taken out by the boy from the first day, Robert. The final match was called moments later, and everyone clapped as the participants headed over to medical to make sure there wasn't any severe damage that would take the MEDs more than a day to heal without help.

"Next up, we have Shan and Trent," Professor Grant read out from his PortMed.

Shan stood, and I eyed the large boy he was going against, feeling a sense of dread for him.

"Hayley and Dean."

Hayley headed to the middle circle along with a wiry boy.

"Lovota and Kyle."

My heart skipped a beat, and Kyle stood next to me.

"Ready?" he asked, holding out a hand and flashing a winning smile. I ignored the sudden skip of my heart as I reluctantly took it. He pulled me up.

Why couldn't it have been next week, I thought as we settled into the ring, *at least then I might have a good excuse to try to win.* I took stalk of the twenty-four-foot circle. The pairs behind Kyle were settling in for their own fights and I watched as he fell into a kickboxing fighting stance. I mimicked him, making sure my feet were slightly off and my bounce wasn't as stable.

"Begin," Professor Grant said.

Kyle immediately sprang into action. I dodged his blow and he began to circle me.

"I'll go easy on you," he said with a kind smirk.

Irritation filled me. "Don't," I snapped. "It would defeat the whole point." I sent a punch his way, and he dodged it as I pulled back slightly. A kick and a dodge, and I got a feel of his fighting style.

"Lovota, I admire your passion, but we both know you aren't good enough to take me at my best. Few are."

I used my anger to fuel my speed as I dodged a hit and landed one next to his crotch. With a grunt, he staggered backward, his eyes widening.

"I'm faster than you realize," I countered.

His demeanor changed as his eyes grew hard. When he came at me again, it was with more force and speed than before. I dodged his hits as best I could without showing off, a few nicking me.

One sent me reeling.

I staggered backward, barely avoiding stepping from the ring as I danced back in. I was sure to never be more than would be expected from two weeks of tutoring, but I used my speed and agility to my advantage. I managed to land a hit on his right cheek, and I watched in satisfaction as it turned red. When he left an obvious opening, I took it, kicking him hard in the side.

Miraculously, I snagged a rib and he staggered backward, holding it with one hand. I took the opportunity for a break as he backed up.

My breaths labored, and my steps began to stagger. I saw recognition in his eyes as he watched me, replacing the primal glint that had been there since my first hit. I decided I wasn't going to go down so easily.

The hit that did me in was a vicious left hook to the ribs. It took me out in seconds and I found myself wheezing on the mat as he stood over me, panting. Seeing my immobility, the student running our mat called the fight.

Kyle straightened from his crouch, with questions in his eyes. As he reached out to help me up, he let out a painful grunt, hand flying to his ribs. He looked down, then back up, and his face fell into disbelief. There was a sudden hunger in his eyes I didn't care for.

I pushed myself up, wincing as I did. "Good fight," I said, rubbing the forming bruise on my side and slowly feeling the MEDs take over. As the pain became a dull throb, I turned and headed over to medical. After an initial scan that showed I hadn't broken a rib, I headed back to the bleachers. I was surprised to see Shan already there, sitting quietly with no visible markings.

"How did you do?" I asked as I took the spot beside him. Jaz and Zack turned from their convo, flipping around on the bench to face us, Sam listening overhead.

Shan blushed heavily but answered. "I-I won." He blushed even harder as I tried not to look surprised. "I g-got lucky." He said in leu of an explanation, and I suddenly wanted to see him fight. He gave me a subtle once over, worry in his eyes. "He went hard on you?"

I ignored the slight anger in his tone as I replied breezily. "I told him to. The only way I'm going to get better is if people take the kid gloves off." Before Shan could respond, Kyle was flopping onto the benches beside me.

"Yeah, well, it's not like that was too easy a fight," he groused. "You're a quick one. Even managed to land a good hit or two." There was a hint of adoration in his voice.

"Well, I told you I played basketball and ran. I might not be a great fighter, but I have stamina and agility." My explanation eased the concern in everyone's eyes, and Jaz brightened.

"Speaking of, you should go out for the team. We are holding last minute tryouts since our small forward is out for the season Sunday."

I gave her a hesitant smile. "No, I don't think I should." There was a look in her eyes that chilled my bones. "I mean, I only ever played in alternate divisions. I have seen you all play. I don't think I'm ready for that." Jaz's eyes softened and Hayley took the seat beside her, a slight bruise forming under her left eye.

"It wouldn't hurt to try, right?" she pushed.

I didn't argue, already learning that when it came to her and Jaz, I wouldn't win. "Okay, I'll think about it."

Conversation died as Professor Grant took the center of the room. "Each of you did a good job today. I know it's only been two weeks, but I'm very impressed by how many of you have grown." He gave the room a brilliant smile. His golden Mate Necklace shone as he turned, the thick chains holding up a dragon pendant. "By the end of the term, I will have made fighters out of all of you." The room brightened at the compliment. "You're dismissed." Chatter surrounded me as I followed my friends out of the room.

Chapter 15

"I'm, like, totally going to need a shower," Hayley whined as she wiped a spot of blood from her hand. Her bot spar hadn't been easy, and the thing had managed to nick her.

I laughed as Jaz took a sweaty hand and rubbed it across Hayley's stomach. She let out a shriek, swatting at her friend as the others egged them on.

"At least, it's the end of the week and the last lecture week. Saturdays are the worst. I hate having to stuff all the classes into one day," Sam chimed in behind me. "I'm ready for the party."

The excited chorus of agreements reminded me I was going to have to go to said party the next day.

"My offer still stands," Kyle whispered in my ear, his breath tickling the back of my neck and sending a shiver down my spine.

I gripped the phone in my jacket. "I have a boyfriend." I hissed.

"Unless you're Paired, it doesn't matter here," Sally whispered as she overheard. "To be exclusive like Jaz and Zack takes years of time and fighting off the competition."

I turned my attention to the two love birds as Zack threw a hand over Jaz's shoulder, pulling her close.

"Well, where I come from, that's not how things roll; it's all in or all out. I would appreciate it if you would stop pushing." I could feel Kyle take a step back, but Hayley stepped up to me.

"It would be wise for you to remember you are no longer in Willow. This is like your home now, and you wouldn't want anyone getting worried about you because you refuse to conform. Right?" She said it lightly, but the look in her eyes had me on edge.

I forced down the lump in my throat as I felt a squeeze. "Right," I said.

Satisfied that I had been cowed into submission, Hayley nodded and turned back to the group. "Now then, what are you all planning to wear?" she asked as the others joined us along our path home to the dorms. Jumping on the topic change, I joined as the girls discussed their outfits, the boys sighing loudly.

"If you've got nothing to wear, you can borrow an outfit from me," Lucy offered me sweetly.

"Oh no, I'm sure I have something," I replied. "I'll probably just grab a nice pair of pants and shirt." I would have thought I killed their pet the way Hayley and Jaz's eyes widened.

"You can't be serious," Hayley said.

I dodged a stray biker. "What did I do this time?" I asked in exasperation.

"That won't do at all. That's like bringing a football play to a basketball game; it's just not done," Jaz said.

"This is like literally the biggest party of the year!" Hayley's voice pulled up an octave as she bounced, and I tried not to wince.

"Well, what else would I wear?" I immediately regretted asking as the two fell into a rant about clothes, boys, and social pariahs.

I watched with wary eyes as we approached the dorms, looking to my other friends for help. They pointedly ignored me.

"Now you've done it," Kyle said with a chuckle behind me as everyone disappeared, leaving me alone with two scheming girls.

I stared wide-eyed up at Coach Sharky.

"I'm sorry, what?" I asked, not believing my ears. All that time I had trained and practiced just to make it on the top varsity spot had all paid off. *For the wrong team.*

"You made the team," she smiled widely. "Congratulations." I knew those words should have made my day, if not my entire high school career, instead, I felt a sense of dread.

"Oh."

"I can't believe you just told coach 'no'," Jaz ranted as we headed back to the dorms.

As I responded, I didn't look at her. "I just couldn't handle the pressure." I ignored the pointed frown Hayley and she shared as my MEDs activated.

"Fine. If that's all it is." Before I could stop Jaz, she had my arms and was pulling them back, restraining me with my jacket. The wicked glee in Hayley's eyes made me shiver. "We are heading to the cross-country tryouts." I sputtered in protest as Jaz dragged me away.

"Don't worry," Hayley said gently, though her eyes were bright in a way I didn't like. "You know the cross-country teams always wear ridiculous costumes for the events. No one will know who you are, so no pressure."

I tried not to slam the door behind me when I got back to my dorm, my heart racing. I quickly grabbed my phone and sent a message to Chris.

5:43 p.m. Me: *We have a problem. I just made the cross-country team.*

My phone was *buzzing* before I could put it down.

"Loran, it's totally time to get ready for the party. Will you let me in?"

I looked up from my phone to the door. "I'll have to call you back," I whispered.

"Okay, be safe. I love you," Chris said on the other line. Quickly, I placed it in the drawer of my desk and headed to my door. I opened it for Hayley and let her in.

"You look horrible," she said as she barged in and took in my room with a critical eye. She was already ready for the night in a gold dress that hung off her form, ending at her mid-thigh, show-ing off her smooth legs.

"It's been a long day," I said, heading back to my closet. As she looked around, I fumbled about, trying to grab clothes. I spotted Chris's jacket, slinging it over my head and pulling the hood up to bury my face in. His scent still lingered in the fabric, and my anxious heart calmed.

"Nice setup," she commented, glancing over my desk. She began to open drawers.

"We! We had better get started," I said, trying to distract her as I pulled out the clothes I was planning to wear. "Don't want to be late to the party."

She stopped and turned, eyeing my outfit before lighting up. "Yeah, you're right, and looking at that, we have a long way to go."

I let out a breath as another knock sounded at my door. Jaz came in. She wore a shimmering green halter-top and a black skirt that showed off her long, toned legs. She looked around, spotting the options on my bed, and let out a groan.

"What!" I demanded.

"Tell me you brought the stuff," she said to Hayley, ignoring me.

"Totally. We are good to go. But first," Hayley replied, passing me, rummaging through my closet. She laid out a pair of short shorts with tattered edges and a hole in the side. On top of those, she laid a dark blue slit-covered short sleeve. It was one of my more risqué shirts and I usually wore something under it. When she stood back looking triumphant, I was reminded again of the differences in what Kent Wood considered appropriate.

"No," I said.

Jaz sighed.

"What?" Hayley asked, clearly confused.

"The shirt will need something under it. I won't look like a Holo-stripper."

She picked it up, seeing what I meant as the large slits revealed themselves under her wandering hand.

"Come on, it's totally not bad. Be a little risky tonight," she protested.

I raised my eyebrows at her. "I'm not comfortable in that," I said, leaving no room for argument.

Jaz sighed louder.

"You Midwest folk and your modesty. Like, you would think you're from Sally Brown with that attitude. Fine!" Hayley picked out a thin silver tank as my blood ran cold. "Happy?"

"Yes." Taking the outfit, I stripped, trying to calm my shaking limbs, hoping her comment was just a passing thought. A squeeze calmed me slightly. "You know it's hard to dress risky like you all do when the weather is cold enough to freeze limbs half the year," I countered, trying to laugh at the end.

She let out a laugh as well, easing my nerves. Jaz sighed even louder, looking in the bag she brought along.

If something as small as clothing choices can lead me to being exposed, I need to start making a change, I thought.

"Yeah, yeah, now get dressed," Hayley commanded. I rolled my eyes at her, pulling on the shorts and stripping off Chris's jacket.

"Is that a tattoo?" Jaz asked as I turned to grab the shirt on my bed. My hand flew to my left shoulder. I couldn't stop the soft smile on my face.

"Yeah. I've had it forever. It's a raven," I said with a small shrug, pulling the shirt on. Hayley pulled up the camera on her PortMed and linked to mine. I twisted, watching my PortMed show off her view of my outfit. The slits around the shoulder were smaller, and only the tip of the lower wing was clear. Satisfied, I headed to the bathroom, the two on my tail. "It's part of a set. My boyfriend got one too, but his is mid-flight."

"That's really sweet," Jaz said with a bright smile as she pulled out her makeup and hair supplies from her bag.

"Now we're totally going to have to fight off the guys tonight," Hayley teased with a devious grin, grabbing a makeup bot from her bag. "Kent Wood boys are suckers for a good tattoo."

I huffed. "I already have someone, and back home, we are loyal to those we are with."

"Let's not start this argument again." Jaz cut Hayley off as her eyes grew hard. They exchanged a look that made my heart race before Hayley relaxed. "Besides, that doesn't mean you can't tease the others," Jaz sang.

I gave up.

We set up around the counter, grabbing the necessary accessories we would need.

"I noticed you seem to like the color blue," Hayley said, spotting my makeup bag. As she started brushing through her hair, she made eye contact with me in the mirror, and I froze.

"I mean, it's my favorite color, not to mention the color of my school," I replied hesitantly, cursing the little details.

"Like, I know, Sally Brown shares the same colors as Willow. You should totally be careful about it though. You don't want people thinking you came from there now, do you?" Her gaze was pointed.

Jaz avoided my eyes as I searched for support. So instead of replying, I sent Hayley a tight smile as I nodded, my palms sweaty.

"Hey, let's turn on some music," Jaz said as she headed to the panel by the door and scrolled through the options. I turned my waves into tight ringlets with the help of my style bot and pulled out my makeup bot to start on my face. The small silver disk sat in my hand as I clicked to my desired pallet, colors flying on the screen, twisting it to activate.

"Speaking of boys, I can't believe the rest of you aren't dating anyone," I said, trying to make small talk as it got to work

"You kind of came at a troubled time for relationships," said Jaz as she set up her makeup bot to apply her mascara. The screen popped up as a Holographic image with multiple categories and options available to her. Settling on a wingtip design, she selected it and sat as still as possible as the small bot began working. I watched in envy at the ease the bot applied her look compared to mine that started and stopped over and over.

"How so?" I asked as I moved it again.

"The Picking is this summer," Hayley explained as she finished crimping her hair. "And like we said, most of us don't take their relationships as serious as Jaz and Zack. Like, so, there are a lot of breakups in senior year." She ran a hand through her perfect hair. "Everyone wants the chance to date around before they are pinned down for good."

"I guess I get that," I said. "Some people are like that back home, but it's always no emotions attached kind of thing."

"See, that totally makes sense," Hayley said. "I just like don't get risking an attachment when you might not end up together." Jaz stopped her bot, giving her a pointed look. "Come on, you knew that. I totally spent three years trying to convince you to give Zack up. At this point, you are so evenly matched it's like almost impossible to not be together."

Jaz rolled her eyes, giving me a conspiratorial smile. "Says the hopeless romantic," she countered. I laughed, finishing my make-up. "Though tonight we are hoping to help Sally get with the boy she has been pining over for months."

"Oh?" I asked.

"Yeah, Garret and she are totally close, but when he decided to switch Major Focus and moved over to the arts district, they've had less time together," Hayley sighed. "Then there was Shan and...Lilith."

My eyes widened as I turned to her. "No," I said in disbelief. *It explains his reaction before.*

"I know," Jaz lamented.

"What about you and Kyle? There is chemistry there. Why aren't you together?"

Hayley sputtered, almost dropping her nail polish. With a faux calm, she set it down, twisted the lid, and looked at me. "...what?" Her voice went up an octave.

"Lovota, Hayley and Kyle are close, but not like that," said Jaz in a tone that told me to stop while I was ahead.

"Yeah, like, I mean sure, I used to have a crush on him when we were younger." Hayley flipped her hand in the air, letting out a strained laugh. "But that's like beside the fact. He plays around and, like, well, my feelings for him have like disappeared. Oh, um shoes. I need those!" Hayley quickly stammered out an excuse, rushing from the room. I watched her go before Jaz pulled my attention back.

"Don't bring that up again, alright," she said while making eye contact through the mirror. "Hayley definitely has feelings, but she won't admit it. He is always benching her for others, and she thinks he can't do serious. I won't believe it either till he does. The only person he has ever put energy and time into is Chris, his rival from Sally Brown. Off the court, well, you've seen him."

"I'm just surprised she would care for him. He...." I hesitated. "He seems to be a bit of a...well you know. He's certainly not my type after how he treated Tom."

Jaz's hand stopped its descent to the counter, her eyes growing cold. "Listen, I know you wouldn't know about this, but you can't judge Kyle too harshly." She paused, glancing at the door before continuing quietly. "A few years back, there was an incident involving Tom and Hayley. She ended up being sent to the hospital. Kyle didn't take it well, and blames Tom for it to this day, despite multiple witnesses saying it wasn't his fault."

I immediately felt guilty for judging Kyle's actions before. "Oh." My voice came out hollow.

"Don't worry about it, it's ancient history. Just try to cut him some slack, okay?" The matter dropped as Hayley returned. I laughed at the jokes told, but on the inside, I was choking down the memories flooding me of Kathy and Sarah. *No. Not tonight. I won't think about the past.*

"You alright?" I nodded, forcing a smile.

"We're going to knock them dead," said Hayley triumphantly.

I followed her out the door and to the crowded lawn.

Chapter 16

THE PATHS WERE PACKED as students spilled from the dorms all around us into the cool night air. Stars shone brightly above, and the almost full moon lit the sky. The energy in the air was contagious, and I found myself growing excited. Like a school of fish, we twisted and turned, flowing down paths I hadn't walked before toward the forest.

Eventually, the buildings dissipated and gave way to mountainous trees. Red bark smelled of pine. Below our feet, a smooth gravel path kicked up dust as the sound of idle chatter filled the air. As we pushed into a clearing, I stopped, causing people to bump into me. Ignoring the grumbling, I couldn't help but gasp at the sight. Hayley turned around when she heard.

"What's wrong?" she said in faux concern, a smirk upon her face. Jaz stood beside her with a wide grin.

"I thought you said we were going to a park," I said, my voice weak.

"Yeah, we are. Welcome to South Park!" Hayley announced.

The building before us and those beside it were the farthest thing from a park. Well over five stories high and made of glass and marble, spanning back as far as I could see, it was the fanciest building I had ever laid eyes on. The words Kent Wood were chiseled in black above the front entrance. Tall white marble columns lined the sides. Gold trim accents highlighted the roof and windows. A beautiful fountain filled the space in front of a shining black door which was a story high, propped open with ropes tied to its giant silver snake handles, showing off a vast interior filled to the brim with students.

"South Park is the biggest mansion in the country. Used to belong to Kent Wood himself," said Jaz, grabbing my hand and dragging me forward. "The South Park party is one of the three parties on campus. Everyone in high school and up is invited. Here, people don't care what you've done or where you come from. We're all one family tonight."

I smiled at the thought. *Could I be free to be me?*

As we drew near the entrance, I noticed artsy kids wearing unique outfits made of all types of materials and colors, shirts with wings that fluttered, pants and skirts that changed color and shape. They mingled with the nearby jocks, dressed in sport shorts and jerseys, each adorned with a moving knight or pair of swords. We headed to the stairs, and I spotted a jock walk over to a fairy dressed girl and flirt with her. She smiled back in a dazed way that showed she wasn't all there, but he didn't seem to mind. In fact, I heard him tell her about his feelings and watched as she blushed. They kissed as I looked away.

The marble staircase was spotless despite the crowd, and I noticed college students mingling, clearly marked by their necklaces from The Picking. The air about them felt more sophisticated as I passed, and I couldn't tell the different majors just by style or attitude. Twisted gold necklaces of varied designs hung to their mid-chests and tattooed rings on their fingers reminded me of what was coming. Seeing them was captivating, and I wasn't the only one staring.

Someone elbowed me in the gut as a rowdy group passed by. I turned to say something, my mouth snapping shut. The Unfortunate, those who hadn't been paired, were marked with a simple black chain around their necks that bounced as they jumped and weaved into the crowd, mingling with the younger students. My heart went out to them, knowing their only hope of finding someone was in our class.

"This doesn't seem like something the adults would be okay with," I said, as a group of boys ran by with a keg of what I was guessing was beer on their shoulders. They shouted and hooted as they passed. Everyone was smiling and laughing, letting them through and slowing our progress up the last few steps.

"It was the school's idea, actually," explained Hayley. "The teacher council totally came up with it, something about unity in college. Even though pairings are mostly based on ranks and interests, they are also judged on personalities and other factors. A jock could end up with a nerd. Really, it's just an excuse for a wild party." She shoved a hole through the crowd, letting us up the last step.

Almost immediately, everyone dispersed into the massive building and only Jaz's hand in mine kept me moving forward. The entrance was just as beautiful as the outside. A shining white marble floor spread out before me. Gold, black, and silver weaved and twisted through it and the walls in intricate bands. A grand black staircase with hand-carved banisters lined with gold towered above, reaching the top floor. At each level, it branched, creating access to long balconies. Over the gold rails, I could see multiple doors, some open, some closed, leading to unknown places. Every detail, every stone, was the perfect mixture of dark and light, chaos and elegance.

Jaz pulled me toward the floating tables covered with food on the ground floor as Hayley spotted Kyle across the room. She waved frantically. I scrambled to keep up, avoiding stray elbows and plates. Kyle waved back, a slanted grin on his face as the others joined us.

"You guys ready to party?" he yelled unnecessarily as we met up. The boys joined him, hooting and laughing as Jaz and Bee cheered in response. Kyle turned to lead the way through the building.

Navigating off to the left side of the large staircase, past Holo-screens and floating projectors with directions, we headed to a hidden door. I passed more pillars and tight alcoves filled with couples, their faces disappearing from view as the door shut behind me.

"We hang out around the classic arcade and dance floor on the west side," Jaz explained to me. "Takes some time to get there, but it's worth it." She was half distracted by Zack's hand in her hair as we entered the next hall.

"Is that alright?" he asked, smiling brilliantly. I nodded, drawing close as we passed a group leaving from a door on the right side.

"Anything's good with me," I said, enjoying the relaxed atmosphere. We forced our way to the back of the mansion as crowds hoping to pile into other clubs filled the hall.

Eventually, we reached an open door at the end, music filling the space as we neared. The flashing neon lights and hot humid air smelling of sweat hit me hard as the door opened. I was amazed by the giant dance floor crowded with students. It lit under people's feet in various colors and designs that spread when their shoes hit. Computerized music beat in the speakers, a DJ in a knight helmet bobbing at the front, commanding the crowd.

We didn't stop, continuing on the edge of the crowd to another door on the right wall. I had to dodge a few hip checks and stray hands as I waited with anticipation for Kyle to open it and let us through. I stepped into another club, this one larger and blaring a more hip-hop music style as the door behind me shut and sealed off the noise behind. Holographic dancers moved in cages to the sides and on the floor as students swayed against each other.

Jaz pulled me close as the group dispersed. "That room over there is the bathroom." She practically yelled in my ear just to be heard as she pointed to a set of doors near a bar to my left. "The door there, the arcade." I followed her finger to the far corner and a door lit with flashing neon lights. "The third door, the hangout room." She gestured across the room; it was slightly cracked letting in a small sliver of light into the darkened place. "If you get tired, you can relax in there. That's where Hayley and Sally like to stay. They don't really dance, so they just gossip or something. Sometimes, people get a game going as well."

I nodded, and she smiled, rushing off with Zack to the dance floor, leaving me alone. I looked around, feeling awkward, and decided to head to the small bar by the bathrooms, twisting as a couple in an intense make-out session almost slammed into me. When I arrived, I leaned on the glass bar top, spotting the bartender. His gold band with a small emerald at the end swayed as he passed out drinks to the crowd around me. As he spotted me, he flashed a wide smile. I threw my hand up, my pinky out in the universal symbol for water.

He filled up a glass and came over. "Will that be all, doll?" he said with a lopsided grin.

"Yes. Thanks." Unlike some guys standing at the bar, he didn't seem to be sizing me up, just being friendly. It gave me the courage to start up a conversation. "Actually, I have a question," I called, grabbing his attention before he could leave. "What's it going to be like tonight?"

He started prepping another drink, giving me a once-over as he did. I could see his eyes light up when he realized who I was.

"You're the new girl, right?"

I nodded, motioning for him to go on, feeling embarrassed he knew me just like that.

"Well, to be honest, a drunken spur full of love confessions and horrible hangovers." I laughed as he made a swooning noise. He smiled and grabbed another glass as he passed off the next order.

"Well, this is going to be fun," I grumbled, grabbing my drink and gulping it down like a shot. He laughed at my antics, taking the glass and refilling it for me.

"Wish me luck," I said with a tip of an imaginary hat.

"Go get them, doll!" He winked back, leaving to attend to other customers. I found an empty stool nearby and sat, nursing my drink.

"Well, well, well, what do we have here?" said a deep voice behind me.

I turned around, coming face to face with a sweaty, red-faced boy. I recognized Robert as he smiled down at me. His basketball shorts and white tee shirt clung close to his body, showing off well-sculpted abs and arms. The end of a tattoo peeked out from his shorts, looking something like the roots of a tree.

"Want to take a stroll with me, Princess?"

Behind him, his friends laughed, elbowing each other, varsity jackets flapping as they did. A cough drew my eyes back to Robert, a small tongue sneaking out to wet chapped lips as he watched me with a fire in his eyes that made me squirm. The gold and green ring on his pinky finger glistened in the light as he reached toward me.

I flipped my hair and dodged as I turned back to the bar, watching in my peripheral vision as he staggered when his hand hit only air. For a moment he looked confused, his drunk mind taking a second to catch up.

"Looks like we have a wild one here," he said, trying to save face. The group laughed, eyeing me.

I brushed them off, taking my glass and making my way to a small table on the side of the dance floor.

They followed, Robert taking a seat across the table, leaning on his elbows. "Princess, what's wrong?" His handsome eyes were filled with concern as he flashed what I assume he thought was a flirty smile. He shifted in another attempt at trying to be sexy, flexing one of his arms. The movement brought him closer.

"My name is Lovota, not Princess, and I'd appreciate it if you would leave me alone," I spat.

There was a flash of concern. Then he grinned again, excitement in his eyes.

I clenched my fists under the table, resisting the urge to punch him. *I'm trying to keep a low profile, or at least as much as I can at this point.* I reminded myself.

"Lovota." He dragged my new name out as if testing it.

My heartbeat accelerated as he leaned back, giving me a small semblance of space. A familiar squeeze calmed me.

His eyes searched mine, an unknown expression in them. "I recognize that name... You're the girl that tried out for the basketball team, right?"

I didn't respond. *How did he know, it's only been five hours?* I took a sip of my water wearily. *I guess I shouldn't be too surprised.*

"So what?" I asked, setting down my glass.

"So? You turned down a starting position on varsity! I must say. I'm impressed. And curious. No one says 'no' to joining the ranks of The Elite."

I recognized the name Kent Wood gave its top athletes and tried not to scoff. *Elite, BotJuice. Everyone knows Sally Brown has the best athletes, not counting combat sports.* I eyed his group warily as they encircled us.

"Though I heard they dragged you to the cross-country team instead. You made that as well and just after arriving from a small alternate school. Interesting..."

"It really wasn't a big deal." I got up to walk away, his hand catching mine as I passed, stopping my momentum, and my glass *shattered* on the ground. He didn't budge as I tugged. "Let go of me!" I demanded, my reaction making him grin.

I swear I heard him whisper. "Not this time." His eyes glinted with a different type of hunger. Fear broke through my armor of anger. Without letting go of my hand, he stood, pulling me to him. "I don't think I will." His breath fanned over my face, the stench of alcohol making me gag.

"Let go or I'll—"

"You'll what? Smack me? Please. No, you're going to be my girl, you understand?" To anyone looking, the way he held me close could have been mistaken for a lover's embrace. "I promise to take care of you." His fingers danced along my back, sending fearful shivers down my spine. I shoved at him, trying to push back, but he was too strong. My eyes darted around, searching for help in the crowd, but no one was looking our way, no one cared. The feel of his fingers flowing down my left shoulder blade over my shirt seemed like he was tracing my raven tattoo, but I knew it wasn't visible.

"Let me go." Again, I pushed, to no avail. He grabbed my chin, forcing me to look at him. My cheeks hurt in his grasp as he brought his face inches from my mouth. *You can't expose yourself.* Chris's voice whispered in my ear as I prepared to punch him.

"Make me." Robert's breath fanned along my lips, a challenge in his eyes.

Screw my cover. I'm ending this now.

"She said let go," a deep melodic voice startled me.

Robert let go, turning to the boy furiously and blocking my view of my savior as he pushed me behind him. Glass skittered under my feet. "Stay out of this, man," he growled.

"No. Let her go." The grip on my wrists tightened. I heard his friends behind me and before I knew what was happening, I stumbled back, falling to the ground, catching my hands on the shards below. I cried out in pain, his friends grabbing my wrists as I made a run for it. My head snapped into one of them. He let out a string of curses. A firm grip on my neck kept my head bent as I watched two shadows face each other through my hair. A crowd gathered.

"Make me," snarled Robert.

"I won't have to. You know if he saw you treating her like that, he would have your head," the boy said.

"He's not the boss of me," Robert growled.

"I'd beg to differ." The boy taunted, riling up Robert. With a shout, he charged. The boy spun on his heel, dodging, and positioning himself behind Robert. Grabbing his upper arm, he used the momentum to swing Robert around and threw him toward the table. He hit it on the way down, knocking himself out.

"Anyone else?" The boy's voice was soft, but there was an edge to it. The group quickly let me go, scampering away into the diminishing crowd, dragging Robert with them. I looked up at my savior.

"Thank you," I said, my voice failing as I met stormy blue eyes.

"You're welcome," Shan said with a bashful smile.

"Shan?" The surprise in my voice had him rubbing the back of his head and looking away, the familiar gesture taking away any unease creeping in.

"H-hey." His familiar blush flooded his face. "Sorry about that. Sometimes people can be real gear grinders." He winced in pain as he put his arm down.

"You're hurt," I said, reaching out to see what was wrong. He waved me off with a smile.

"It's n-nothing," he stuttered. "Been through worse. Plus, the MEDs will kick in soon." He rolled his shoulders to prove his point. "Hayley sent me to find you. They want to play a game with their new friends." He awkwardly gestured to the door behind him, asking if I wanted to join.

"Alright." I agreed. As he grasped my hand to lead me away, I felt the sting of my open wounds. Hissing, I retracted, cradling it to my chest. Shan's face turned dark as he grabbed my hand back, palm facing up. I could see the slices from the glass, some cuts deep, some clotting already.

"Did he do this?" There was that edge again that I was unfamiliar with.

"Kind of. When he pushed me back, I stumbled and fell on the glass."

The darkness on Shan's face disappeared, his eyes softening. "I'm sorry." He realized he was still holding my hand and quickly dropped it, his blush returning. "S-stay here, please. This is too deep for the MEDs to heal tonight." Grabbing a few napkins at the bar, he returned with a glass of water, dipping them in. Gently, he took my hands, his blush at full force as he dabbed them, pulling up the remains of blood and glass. Once they were clean, he took a cloth from his pocket and ripped it, wrapping it around and tying a small knot on the back of my hands when he was done.

"Do you always walk around with medical cloth in your pocket?" I asked, trying to break the awkward tension as he dropped my hands.

"Oh, y-yeah actually. I used to get nosebleeds when I was younger. I never stopped carrying them, don't know when someone might need it." Standing tall, he offered his hand, refusing to meet my eyes.

I took it, allowing him to lead me through the crowded dance floor. A few guys bumped into me, eyeing me. I ignored them as Shan gently pulled me closer and weaved me in front of him, his hands resting on my hips as he helped me navigate, his body protecting me from the crowd. I could feel the definition of his abs and the subtle muscles in his arms, a blush rising on my cheeks. As we neared the door, he stepped back, leaving a cold spot where his hands were. I ignored the sense of loss and the absence of my phone.

Chapter 17

THE ROOM WAS FILLED with bodies that occupied five large couches and three reclining chairs. Doors lined the walls, leading to who knows what, and groups huddled around tables, laughing and talking. Kyle and Hayley sat on the floor next to one of the couches, talking to a set of people I didn't recognize.

She turned to me, a mischievous look in her eyes as we approached, making me regret coming immediately.

I sat down next to her, Shan's leg brushing mine as he did the same.

"Now that everyone is here, let's start the game. Lovota, this is Jace, Tyler, and their friends. Tyler, Jace, this is Lovota."

I waved to the group, fidgeting uncomfortably under their gazes.

"So, this is the famous Lovota who turned down Coach Sharky?" said Jace. There was happy mirth in his brown eyes.

I smiled at him and nodded.

"It's nice to see you again," said a girl next to him. She was Bella, center starter for the team.

"You too," I said, giving her a smile. "So, what are we playing?"

Hayley's face lit up like a cat catching the canary as she announced the game: "*Seven Minutes in Heaven.*"

"Really, that old game? Do I have to play?" I whined, earning a few chuckles from the group.

"Yes, miss grumpy, it's like totally a Kent Wood classic, and we need you or there won't be enough girls. Now the rules. Guys, pick an object on your person or on the table over there—" Hayley pointed to a table full of objects on the far wall. "Then put it in the hat. Girls will pick an object from the hat and close their eyes. The boy she picks will go into a closet and wait for her." Hayley pointed to the set of doors to our right. "In case you didn't know, you must kiss at least once."

I felt like a middle schooler again as I watched people shuffle in anticipation and anxiety.

"'Kay, girls, come over here, and guys pick out your objects." Hayley popped off the ground and headed to a refreshment table on the opposite side of the room from the hat table.

Feeling exasperated, I got up and joined her. "I can't believe you're making me do this. This is such a lame game," I complained as I picked up a piece of chocolate from the table.

"Relax, you don't have to, like, kiss the guy if you don't want to," said Hayley.

I exchanged looks with Lucy and she rolled her eyes playfully with a shrug, as if to say, what can you do? I giggled, agreeing with her. We snacked as the guys finished, then made our way back to the couches, other people in the room joining us as they saw what we were doing. I sat back down next to Shan.

"Alright, Sally, you go first." Hayley passed her the hat with a conspiratorial wink.

Are we playing this game just so that Sally can get with Garret?

She grabbed something from the hat that looked like a key ring and closed her eyes. Sure enough, a boy who Shan whispered in my ear as Garret got up from the couch.

I took a moment to observe him. He was tall with dark skin and short, darker hair. His right arm was covered in ink, inter-crossing chainmail, and plates of armor, looking like they had always been there, his light brown eyes lighting up when he spotted Sally. He had to angle his body as he stumbled into the closet, broad shoulders almost hitting the frame. A single gold earring in his right ear glinted with the movement. Once he was inside, Hayley tapped Sally, and she opened her eyes, joining him. More couples went to the other closets as the rest of the group dispersed to wait. A group of boys started a game of beer pong at the back table, and I went over to watch.

"Time's up," announced Hayley, and I turned to see her head toward the closet. She opened the first one to reveal Sally and Garret making out intensely. They pulled away quickly when they realized they had an audience, Sally blushing a deep red as some of the boys' hooted at them. Garret helped her up and they left the closet together, heading to a couch.

Their escapade was soon forgotten as more couples were found in compromising positions. Others sat in the opposite corners of the closet awkwardly. My turn came as I was about to start a round of beer pong. My stomach did a backflip as Hayley approached with the hat, all eyes on me.

She waved it in my face, that mischievous glint back in her eyes. "Lovota, you're up."

"Really?" She glared at me, and I sighed, giving up. "I won't be kissing any boys," I mumbled as I reached into the hat, searching around. I pulled out a Z keychain. As I closed my eyes, I could already tell who I didn't get by the looks I caught. It didn't take long before I heard the closet door open and close. Hayley dragged me to it before I could see who was missing. She shoved me inside and I stumbled, hitting someone on the way as my hands braced the opposite wall. The lock slipped into place as I gathered myself and tried to maneuver my way down to the floor. The darkness was all-consuming. The smell of sweat was overpowering. The sound of the other occupant's breathing filled the air.

I managed to sit down without bumping my partner and settled in.

"Whoever is in here, if you try to kiss me, I will hit you so hard you won't wake up," I said breaking the silence with fake bravado.

"Wow, that's harsh."

My heart stopped. *No, anyone but him!* "Kyle?"

I heard a chuckle in response. "Nice guessing their fish, girl."

"Stop calling me that. I told you dolphins are mammals, not fish," I snapped, pulling my legs close to avoid being anywhere near him. My eyes were adjusting to the dark and I could see my boyfriend's rival sitting legs crossed and hands thrown behind his head, planning who knows what as he watched me. Anger simmered just below the surface; I was overwhelmed. I shoved down the scream filling my ears, clamping my hands to them. *I don't need a pill I am fine.* I chanted in my head over the noise.

"Loran?" I lifted my head.

"What?" I asked on reflex before I realized my mistake. "What are you talking about?" As he shifted in front of me, I couldn't tell if my recovery worked.

"I was asking why you seem to hate me, Lovota?" I blinked a few times, wondering if I really had misheard him *and* missed his whole question.

"I don't hate you," I said, shifting my numb leg.

"I'd disagree. I've been nothing but nice to you since you arrived, and you repay each effort with anger." As I realized he was right, I cursed myself.

"I don't hate you…. You just annoy me." I tried to find a way to explain myself.

"Why's that?" He pushed, leaning forward, his eyes searching in the dark.

"Because…I don't like guys like you." The excuse sounded lame even to me, but I was going to stick to it.

"Guys like me?" he drawled, testing the words. I could tell he didn't quite understand. *Play the alternate girl.* I chanted in my head.

"Yea, the player, always flirting with every girl, treating us like we're a trophy to be won. Others like they're trash. The typical pleb jock." Silence followed. I shifted uncomfortably under its weight, hoping I didn't misstep.

"I don't think you're a trophy," Kyle replied after a moment, his voice soft.

"What?"

"You're not a trophy to me. I know we haven't known each other very long, but I'm drawn to you. I want to get to know you more." There was something more to his tone, something I didn't trust.

"Listen, I don't mind being friends, but it will take time."

"We are very compatible. You have a fire in you. I saw it in our fight." Kyle's hand reached out to me. I dodged it, letting it hit air and land back on his lap.

"I don't think we are compatible," I hissed.

"It's really not hard to get your record, you know."

My heart stopped beating for a moment. "What?" I squeaked out.

"Hayley is a talker," he replied. "She told me you used to run everything back at your old school. Captain of teams, leader of clubs and committees. I'm the same way. Don't you see? We'd be perfect together."

"Kyle, stop! Please don't look into my record. That's such an invasion of privacy." It didn't take much for me to sound upset as I felt a squeeze. "I don't do players. They're never loyal, and besides, I have someone back home. Someone I love!"

"Come on, forget him. He's far away and I'm here right now." Kyle leaned closer and, with nowhere to go as he took up the space around me, his hand fell on my knee. The smile on his face was gentle, but the shadowed look in his eyes screamed danger. "We could be together, you know. They will Pair us if we work at it. In fact, I have some connections I'm sure I could pull. Being with me would open doors for you." His words seemed like a love confession, but it was off.

"Please just stop." My voice wavered. "Leave me alone. I just want to get through this year in peace." I didn't realize how close he had gotten till I felt his breath on my face. It smelled of candy and alcohol.

"You're so far away from home." He sounded sincerely sad for me. "All I'm asking is for a chance. A chance to get to know you, your thoughts, dreams, secrets. Besides, there's almost no chance for you to end up with him now."

Immediately, anger boiled up in me. I swung out, trying to hit him. I hit air as he dodged.

"How dare you!" Tears threatened to spill down my face. I furiously wiped them away. "You have no idea what could happen."

"I'm sorry," he said after a beat, his gentle tone back. I couldn't tell where he was through my bleary vision, but I couldn't feel his body heat. I took a breath, collecting myself.

"It's fine. Just never say that again." I looked up in the direction where I thought he was. "I underst—" The feeling of his lips against mine stopped me. It was a quick kiss, lasting only seconds, but it froze my heart.

"Just think about it." His voice tickled my ear and just like that, he was gone. Before I could think of a response, the door opened, a bright light filling the room. I blinked away the pain but didn't move.

Kyle got up from across the closet and walked out, not turning back to look at me. I felt sick as I thought about what Chris would think.

Disapproving boos followed Kyle, but he didn't say or do anything. Hayley helped me up, a worried frown on her face. I took her hand, grateful for the gentle gesture. Heading to the couch in a daze, I flopped next to Shan and Jaz.

Chris will be so mad.

I tried to hold in the tears as Jaz talked. The group partied the night away around me, Hayley finally taking me home early the next morning, the girls joining us.

"So?" said Hayley, breaking the silence as we walked down the moonlit path home. "I totally have to ask. What happened to you and Kyle?"

"Hayley!" scolded Jaz.

"What! We're all thinking it. I mean, like really, don't tell us nothing. Because the look on both your faces said otherwise." Hayley's smile was strained.

"Nothing happened," I whispered, looking away and leaning toward Jaz.

"Yeah, right. Kyle's look certainly said different," Sally offhandedly replied, inspecting her nails and glancing over at me.

"What do you mean?"

"Well, Kyle always gets this look whenever he throws a touchdown or shoots a three-pointer. It's this cocky grin and a sparkle in his eyes." Lucy did a small impression. I held back my laughter. "It's his 'I conquered the impossible' look and was amplified by ten tonight. Plus, you had this utter look of shock. So, tell us what happened."

"I told him I had a boyfriend," I said hesitantly, thinking over the conversation and feeling a sense of dread.

"And?" Bee said, nudging me.

"Then he kissed me," I whispered under my breath.

"No way!" exclaimed Jaz.

I nodded as my face heated, avoiding Hayley's eyes.

"Man, I knew he was bold. But tryin' to kiss a taken girl, especially ya. I would have thought that ya would've punched him out," said Dorothy in her thick southern accent, imitating a punch.

"Told you Kent Wood boys are ruthless," said Sally, her eyes shining in amusement.

"It took me by surprise—I didn't have time to react, or I'd have decked him." I sighed as I thought about it, the guilt coming back tenfold.

"So...was it good?"

"Sally!" chastised Jaz.

"What?" Sally pouted back.

"*Really?*"

"Come on, just tell me. I've always wondered if he was a good kisser. I mean, he has to be with all the girls falling for him." Despite Jaz's efforts, the group was watching me, intrigued.

"Yeah, I guess so," I admitted, ignoring the disgusting butterflies. "It was too fast to tell and to be honest, I'm trying to forget it." *And all the possible slip-ups I had.*

"Wow, I can't believe it," sighed Bee.

"Speaking of boys," Hayley turned to her next victim. Sally lit up like a Christmas tree.

Chapter 18

"I-I know you're lying."

Shan's soft declaration caused me to stumble along the path we were walking on my way back from my Saturday work shift at the lab. Steadying myself, I turned to him, ignoring the cool fall breeze that blew over me.

"I'm sorry what?" I asked, glancing around to make sure no one was in earshot as I tried to feign nonchalance.

He did the same, shuffling awkwardly. Very few students were out in the late night, most home asleep or preparing presentations. I caught the eyes of a group some distance away.

"Follow me, please." With a sudden determination, he grabbed my hand, pulling me down a path, heading for a stucco building. We passed a couple chatting below a floating streetlight before Shan pulled open a small door several feet away from the main entrance. We entered a hall, the cracked and stained old fabric tiles and flickering lights making me uneasy.

The echoing of our feet on the scuffed tiles thundered, accompanied by the beating of my heart. The smell of chemicals and the sound of whirling fans cooling computers filled the air as we turned down another path. Through a glass panel, I saw a small computer room, thousands of tiny machines stacked on top of each other, glowing blue. The sign on the door we passed read *AS Servers*. Next to it was another door reading *Maintenance.* Shan pushed it open, pulling me in with him.

I took a moment to catch my breath as I watched him flutter about the small room. A simple table sat in the far corner, wrappers and empty energy cans laying upon it, surrounding a Holo-screen. I stepped forward to see what was on it as Shan passed me to the door. The lock sliding into place chilled me to my bones as I read the words before me.

Lovota Miller.

Below were paragraphs of information, the same information Kathy found for me. However, a giant gold mark was stamped across the page: *Taken by The Shadow, September 13, 2121.*

I didn't move as I sensed Shan come up behind me.

"I've been looking into you, Lovota," he said softly, my cover name sticking to his tongue.

I refused to respond as he gently put a hand on my shoulder and pushed me aside. He guided me to a chair and I sank into it, unfeeling.

With an awkward cough, he patted me. Pulling his swivel chair up to sit across from me, his screen to his right, he leaned over, resting his elbows on his lap, and intertwined his fingers. As he rested his head on them, I saw his familiar blush, yet his face was determined.

"I think we both know it doesn't take a lot to find a person's information if you have the skills. A click here and there, a little bot grease, and there you go," he said without stuttering or flopping, in his element when it came to computers.

"Have you told anyone?" I asked, my voice hoarse.

He gave me an assessing look before leaning back. "Not yet. I wanted to talk with you first. From what I can tell, there are two possibilities. I've been watching you..." He blushed as he realized the implications of his words. "You're not good at this kind of work," he said with a gesture to the computer. "So, either someone found the info for you to steal, or you're actually Lovota and somehow you are here despite the fact you've been taken by The Shadow." Shan paused, allowing his words to sink in.

I glanced back down at my hands in my lap, fiddling with the chipping paint on my nails. As silence filled the room, I opened my mouth to run with the first story that popped in my head before snapping it closed. After a beat, I sighed and looked up at him.

He hadn't moved, his face soft, but his eyes guarded. Letting out an awkward cough, he diverted his gaze, turning to what I assumed was his desk. He fiddled with some papers, moving them about. "It's time to be honest."

"You're right, I have been lying," I said at the same time, stopping.

There was another beat of silence before he spoke again, his voice measured as he looked at the screen. "Go on."

"The truth is, I'm Lovota, but I'm not here because of my parents. I promise, though, I'm not here to hurt anyone." The words rushed out, my mind going a thousand miles a minute. I knew I had to find a way to sprinkle enough truth into my story to be believable. "About a year ago, I was invited to see a public-school game between Trident and Sally Brown. It was like nothing I'd ever seen, the violence, the crowds, and the cheering—it was over-whelming. I ended up running out in a panic attack, hiding in the first room I could find." I paused as he turned to me. His eyes were kind, and he motioned for me to continue.

"It was the locker room for one of the teams. Mid-panic attack, one of the players found me. He helped me calm down. Once I was okay, he took care of me until one of my friends found me. We kept in contact, and over time, fell in love. About a month ago, one of my friends got word that a player at the rival school had heard about our relationship. Since I was a no-name girl from such a small school, he thought he could kidnap me and use me against my boyfriend to help him win a game."

Shan's eyes lit with understanding, and I could see him filling in the missing pieces for me as I continued.

"My boyfriend offered to have me transfer to his school, but when we asked permission from the student council, they denied us." I allowed my voice to catch as I spoke, watching Shan as his guard fell more. Ignoring the twinge of guilt as I took advantage of his caring nature, I pushed forward.

"My friend proposed I transfer to another school instead. He knew if we went about it through the official channels, then we wouldn't have to ask the council for permission. He was the one who got my paperwork filed, and in a few short weeks, I was ready. My boyfriend worried that if news got out about my transfer, the player that was after me would just follow me to my new school and get me there. After some thought, we produced The Shadow Plan." I gestured to the computer behind Shan, shakily.

"It was simple. A week after my transfer, my friend would lay the trail of a Shadownap, hoping that by doing so we would divert any chance of me being followed." I held my breath as I finished, waiting to see if he would believe me.

He closed his eyes, taking measured breaths before he opened them to look at me. They shone in the dim screen light.

"I'm sorry you had to go through all of that," he said, moving to place a hand on my leg. He paused right before he did, awkwardly hovering before he pulled back.

"Thank you," I croaked out as relief filled me. A new type of determination filled Shan's eyes. A sense of peace washed over me as he stood up and reached out to me. When I took his hand, I felt more protected than I ever had in my life.

"N-no, thank you," Shan said, his signature blush in place as he opened the door for me to leave. "It means a lot that you were willing to trust me with your story. I promise to do what I can to keep you safe." As we left the dingy halls and walked back into the cool night air, I pushed aside the guilt gnawing at me.

You should have told the truth. I ignored the voice.

"I'm just glad you believe me," I whispered to the night air.

Shan and Kyle whispered to each other ahead of me on the path. They seemed to be arguing, Kyle throwing his hands in the air repeatedly and Shan running his hands through his hair.

This has been going on for days. I sighed.

"What is it this time?" Jaz asked as she stepped beside me as we headed from calculus.

"Your guess is good as mine," I said. "They won't tell me." I ignored her pointed gaze.

"So, I think I'll have time to sneak away and see you," Chris said on the other line.

My heart soared as a smile split my face.

"You mean it?" I tried not to sound as desperate as I felt.

"Yep, meet me at the visitor's building Thursday after class, and don't get caught."

"Wow, someone's happy today," Hayley called as she saw me walking toward her. There was a slight bounce in my step, and I knew I was wearing a giddy smile.

"Excited for tomorrow's game, that's all," I said, not caring about the strange look she sent my way. We met everyone and walked to class. Kyle came up behind me, bumping me lightly on the shoulder as he passed. I looked up at him and he sent me a flirty wink. Shan joined as we headed to lunch, and I smiled at him. He gave me a shy smile, blush in place and joined Kyle.

I could barely pay attention during class. When the last bell rang, I rushed out of physics, leaving Jaz, Hayley, Kyle, and Shan in the dust. It was a short two-mile walk to the athletic sector, but I ran the whole way. As soon as I reached the plaque, I realized I should've gone home to change. My tattered jeans, green shirt, and jacket stuck out among basketball shorts and varsity jackets.

Ignoring curious gazes, I made my way to the middle of the sector where the visiting teams stayed. The area was one I was familiar with, and now I knew it was half as nice as the rest of campus. I reached my destination and didn't see Chris. Shooting him a quick message on my location, I leaned against a tall tree. Autumn leaves fell around me in the gentle breeze and the cloudy day told of an impending storm.

Chapter 19

"Well, well, well, look who's here."

Robert's voice stopped my heart. Chills raced down my spine. My head snapped to a group of boys heading my way down the main path. I hated to admit they were an attractive bunch; even some girls at Sally Brown confessed to fantasizing about them behind closed doors.

"Did you come all this way to see me, *Lovota*?" Robert approached, his posy laughing nervously, looking around for Shan. When they didn't see him, they relaxed, regaining their cocky attitudes.

"Leave me alone," I demanded, but he swaggered forward, a kind look on his face, his eyes surprisingly soft. His breath ghosted against the top of my head as he bent over me, hand resting on the tree behind me.

"I'm sorry, I didn't mean to scare you the other night. I can get a little wild when I'm drunk."

I saw his hand descending to my cheek. In an instant, I dodged it, kneeing him in the crotch as I did. He fell to the ground with a grunt of pain as I smirked down at him.

"That should teach you not to touch a girl without her permission," I snapped as I spun to leave—right into a chest.

The boy grabbed me as I staggered back, keeping me from falling and running away. I struggled against him, kicking his shins, but he didn't let go, his meaty hands encompassing my arms, pinning them to my side as he turned me around. Robert finally got up, pain still in his eyes as he stalked toward me with a sneer.

"That wasn't very nice. You're on my turf now, and I'm going to make sure you understand what that means."

I was shaking as his hand came up to cup my chin.

"Hey! What are you doing?" The sound of Chris's voice was surreal, my heart fluttering as I drank it in. He stepped from behind the tree. The sight of him made my heart swoon, but the anger in his eyes sent a shiver down my spine.

Robert turned to him in a fury. *Clearly, he isn't used to being interrupted when he harasses girls.*

"What do you want, *Browner*," he spat.

Chris crossed his arms over his chest. He glossed over the group, not even looking at me as he sized them up, the move predatory. The guy holding me shifted uncomfortably under his gaze.

"Nothing much," Chris said with a shrug, feigning nonchalance. "I just wanted to make sure that girl is okay. It doesn't look like she wants to be here."

"That's none of your business," Robert growled.

"Oh, but it is." Chris's eyes were hard. "I don't enjoy seeing Defects like you harassing innocent girls." His eyes finally met mine, and they softened slightly before he continued. "Even if they're Bucket slags." I tried to ignore the sting from his jibe, remembering it was all an act.

Robert laughed. He stepped back and grabbed me from the boy, pulling me close in a death grip before I could react. I could feel his toned body against mine, making my stomach roll. I was about to fight him off, but the look Chris sent me reminded me to stay calm.

"Innocent. Really, I don't know if I'd call her that after the other night," Robert taunted.

Immediately, I saw the hurt in Chris's eyes. Then they hardened.

"Back away," he said with an intimidating step forward.

I looked around, trying to see if there was anyone nearby to help, but the walkways were empty, no one wanting to come near the visitor buildings.

"She's in my territory." Some of Robert's friends stalked toward Chris as he got in a fighting stance.

"She is mine till *they* say otherwise." Before I could ask what he meant, a voice snapped through the tension.

"What is going on here, gentlemen?"

As if shocked, Robert let go of me, backing away a step.

"N-nothing," he stammered, and I spun to see a glaring Mrs. Adams. Her aura was frightening, beady eyes pointed down, a well-manicured hand on her hip. I tried to duck behind my captors to hide from it.

"Is that so? What I see here definitely looks like something." Her tone was clipped.

"No, it's nothing, just a little tussle." Robert's voice quivered as he waved his hands about.

Mrs. Adams' eyes glared him down. "Have your little tussle on the court, Robert, not on my school grounds."

"Y-y-yes ma'am," Robert backed away from me.

"Now get going and I better not see you messing with the other team before the game," Mrs. Adams commanded.

Robert gulped. "Of course, war-Mrs. Adams." He turned back to me, shooting me a glare. "Next time we meet, you better pray that your luck holds." He whispered as he passed, his posse scampering after him, leaving me alone with Mrs. Adams and Chris.

"Ms. Black, what are you doing here?"

"I'm just passing through." I stood my ground, meeting her eyes, forcing a smile, hiding my fear. She gave me and Chris a look that said she didn't approve, but then turned and left without a word. I was surprised but grateful. Once I was sure we were in the clear, I rushed to Chris, hugging him.

"Not here," he said, pushing me back. I felt his words like a slap as he turned away. He led me behind the visitor building into the shadows of a large tree. Finally, he looked at me. His arms encircled me as I leaped into him.

"I missed you so much," I whispered into his shirt. He combed my hair down.

"I missed you too." His tone was wary. I pulled away, searching his face, surprised to see a sad smile.

"What's wrong?" I asked, as he let me down slowly.

"What did Robert mean back there about you not being innocent?" I couldn't help as a laugh escaped. When I saw he wasn't joking, I stopped.

"You took that seriously?" He nodded, and I sighed. "I met him at the party last week. He tried to make a move on me. Luckily, one of my friends stepped in and stopped him. They had a fight, and it looks like he blames me for it." The hurt left Chris's eyes as he realized I was telling the truth.

"Sorry for doubting you," he said, taking me back into his arms. This time, he didn't hold back, pulling me close and placing gentle kisses atop my head. "I have been so worried. Everyone knows how Buckets act before The Picking. They have no respect. I hate to admit, I didn't trust you enough to believe you would fight them off." His words stung, but I could see his shame and forgave him.

A subtle breeze blew past, making my hair dance around us as I pulled back. I led him to a bench swing below the nearby tree. We sat down and I leaned against his chest.

"Don't feel bad. I'd have probably felt the same if you left. This hasn't been easy."

He placed a soft kiss on the top of my head. "You're so forgiving. It's one of the things I love about you," he said. The smile on my face hurt. "I know we talk every day, but it feels like it's been months. I've missed holding you."

"I've missed you too. Things are going well, or as well as can be expected here. Jaz has been surprisingly understanding, and I think I might be able to win Hayley over. It's hard to tell, though, especially after this last week." I paused. I hadn't told him about Shan or Kyle. Seeing my reluctance, Chris turned me around to face him and placed a gentle hand under my chin.

"Lightning, what's wrong?" His eyes were soft, exploring mine. Taking a deep breath, I steeled myself and told him. He listened patiently as I explained every detail, his gaze growing cold by the end.

"You're sure he called you Loran?"

I nodded, watching him, waiting for more as he gnawed his lip.

"That could be a problem." When he didn't say more, I placed my hand on his.

"You're not upset about the kiss?" I asked, searching him.

"Oh no, don't get me wrong, I'm livid. I mean, how could you put yourself in that kind of situation, Lightning?" His words were like a knife to the gut, his tone sharp, but he stopped and breathed. "I also think there is more going on. My first priority is your safety. Especially since your cover's been compromised by The Shadow."

"I know. Chris, I'm so sorry." I apologized, seeking his forgiveness.

He didn't meet my eyes as he played with my hand in his. "Things aren't the same back home. We always knew you played a big role, but well. People are upset. It's getting harder and harder to keep the truth a secret, to keep you safe. Everyone wants to know where you went. No one believes The Shadow could have taken you." His voice cracked, and I pulled him to me, allowing his head to fall onto my shoulder. "There is pressure for me to mourn. I.... The pressure. I just.... it's hard. I had to see you. And you're doing well, adjusting...Too well. I mean, glitching. I thought we discussed how you wouldn't join a sport, and here you are on cross-country. Plus, a combat class!" Chris was on a rant, hands gripping my back, keeping himself together.

Indignation filled me as he brought up our newest argument. "Hey! I had to avoid suspicion, and the class is Kathy's fault," I snapped.

"I know, but it's still too much. Now not only are you friends—" He pulled away, his gaze hard.

"Acquaintances," I interrupted.

"...With my biggest enemy." He continued ignoring me. "But he also stole a kiss. He already took my title—was that not enough?" Chris ran his hands through his hair, looking disheveled.

I put my hand to his heart. Feeling the erratic beat as I took a deep breath, attempting to be calm for the both of us. I maintained eye contact.

"I'm sorry. I know how this must feel, but it will be okay. I'm doing my best, but I'm all alone here, figuring it out as I go, and I'd appreciate a little sympathy. People will forget about me, eventually. The world will go on."

He took in a deep breath.

I could tell my words were working, so I continued, "Remember when you first asked me out? The fear and panic. I could have died that night, but I didn't. If we can survive a literal lightning strike, then we can do this. Together."

Chris sighed deeply and all the tension left his body. "You're right, I'm sorry." His hands roamed my arms gently. They came around my biceps and swiftly he pulled me so I tumbled over as he laid down and ended on top of him. The bench swung and the grass below us danced in another breeze. "I can be a bit of an idiot, can't I?" he said, pulling me into a kiss.

I laughed into it, pulling away to the loving smile on his face that I missed dearly. "I love you," I whispered against his lips.

Our kiss started gently before we lost ourselves. Life had been harder than we wanted to acknowledge, but the feel of his hands roaming my body reminded me I was home. His soft kisses danced along my neck and chest. I returned the favor and smiled as our eyes met.

Much too soon, Chris pulled away, panting. "Holo-sticks, I missed you," he said as he leaned his head so our foreheads touched.

"Me too."

Sighing, he pushed me up, settling beside me. As we moved to continue, a raindrop hit my cheek. I turned to the gray sky above.

"Get going before the storm gets bad. The boys will be back soon too." Chris helped me up.

We walked to the edge of the building and kissed goodbye in the shadows, the rain already starting to soak my shoulders.

"I'll see you at the game tomorrow."

I shivered in delight as his breath tickled my ear. "I'll be cheering for you in my heart," I replied.

He smiled, turning and walking away to the other side of the building. He hated goodbyes as much as I did, and I could tell it was getting harder for him.

I made my way back to my dorm right as the rain picked up. Winds blew the pelting water at the glass panes of the entrance. A thunderous rumble shook the building as I watched the storm roll on the horizon.

Chapter 20

Hayley was banging at my door, demanding I get up and help her.

If I ignore her, she should go away, I thought as I put on a baggy pair of sweats and Chris's hoodie. Pulling my hair into a ponytail, I didn't put any further effort into my looks, trying to be unrecognizable.

Luckily, I didn't run into Robert as I made my way through the athletic sector to meet Hayley at the stadium like we had originally planned. Old metal doors creaked as I pushed them aside, filing in through the maintenance entrance. I followed the long hall till it widened, opening to the court. Students were milling around, some in uniforms, others setting up for the game. I spotted Hayley as she rushed to me, wearing sweats and a crop top.

"What, like, took you like so long?" she demanded, looking me over. I could tell she was nervous by the way she bit her upper lip, her bounce slightly off.

"Had a rough night, just moving slowly. What's the plan?" I shoved away her concern and followed her back to the group of cheerleaders stretching in the corner. I spotted the back of Kyle's head near the team's entrance as he jockeyed with Zack, the team filing out of the gym.

"We need you to critique our routine. It needs to be, like, perfect for tonight." Hayley explained as she pulled me over to the benches to join some other girls who had been dragged along. We all mumbled greetings to each other, not quite awake as we watched the team's routine. Sally waved at me from the end of the line before they started, and I smiled back. Lilith was surprisingly absent.

I finished helping make banners two hours before the game and headed back to my dorm to get ready. Hayley tried to coax me into wearing my outfit from the party, but I refused.

"Come on, show those Browner's what they're missing," she insisted again, practically shoving the clothes in my face.

"No means no," I said, shoving her away.

"Fine, then," she said with a huff as she chucked them away. "Will you at least, like, help *me* get ready?"

I agreed and helped her find her best cheer outfit in the mess she called a closet. I did her hair in a French braid as she chatted idly about the latest gossip.

"Loran." My head snapped up as she called my name.

"Yes?" I said before I could stop myself. My heart went still as she made eye contact with me in the mirror, her eyes calculating. "I'm sorry. What was that?" I tried to play off my response, but the wariness in her gaze didn't change.

"I was saying I think we'll have a distinct advantage tonight in the game," she drawled. "Rumor is, their star player Chris just lost his girlfriend, Loran, to The Shadow. Apparently, they totally have been keeping the whole thing hush hush, but he's quite devastated."

I prayed she couldn't feel the shaking of my hands as I continued to weave her hair.

"Oh, that's crazy news." I barely kept the hysteria from my voice. "I hope she's okay."

Hayley watched me, inspecting my face as she drew her hand up, brushing past her PortMed. "Yeah, well, if The Shadow really did get her, then I doubt it."

As I activated her hair tie, I sent her a strained smile. "I know but still..." My words hung in the air as I watched it tighten around her ends, clamping her hair together, not a golden strand out of place. "I'm finished. We better get going or we will be late." I stood, brushing invisible dirt off my jeans as I worked to calm my breathing and ignore the screams in my head.

You need a pill. Kathy's voice whispered in my ear but I ignored it.

"Oh, you're right, we totally need to hurry," Hayley said, the cheer back in her voice as she grabbed my hand and dragged me out.

We met Jaz outside the dorm; Sally was already at the gym getting the team ready for Hayley, the rest of our friends saving us seats. By the time we reached the stadium, a large crowd was forming. Students filled the area from all angles, walking along the grass and forcing their way onto the path that would let them inside.

I was jostled by a boy in green body paint as he called out for his friend to wait. A small girl in a sports bra and gold paint turned and waited for him to catch up. Everyone pushed, wanting to be at the front so they could ensure they made it inside the stadium.

"Hey, make way!" called a girl nearby as she spotted us. "Head cheerleader heading up!"

With a murmur, the crowd parted, making way for Hayley and us. I felt eyes on me, ignoring them in favor of watching her strut forward. She took the attention with the grace of nobility as she smiled and waved to those around her. Jaz meanwhile looked grateful to not have any eyes on her. At the entrance to the stadium, we were redirected to a VIP booth. I gave my name and identification—a prick of blood—for entrance, like always.

Hayley left us at the tunnel and Jaz grabbed my hand, leading me forward. We walked through the tunnel, the echoes of the crowd muted until we reached the entrance to the gym floor. The noise hit me as we stepped out, overpowering.

We were right on the court. The only thing separating us from the players was a short glass wall. Jaz moved to our front row seats, and I noticed they were in the war zone. I pulled Chris's hood up over me, ensuring my hair was tucked inside before I followed. Greeting the rest of our group, I made my way to one of two empty seats near Shan. He smiled as I sat down, his body blocking me from the blue and white crowd a few feet away, separated only by a tall chain-linked fence.

As Jaz passed out the banners we made to our section, some-one else passed clappers and noisemakers to the other. I chose a sign that flashed Garret's name, avoiding Kyle's altogether. With a knowing look, Jaz passed it along. In return, she was given everything to do with Zack. It was amusing to see her holding a giant version of his face, which winked occasionally, while waving a flag with his name. I winked back at it, turning my attention to the court, avoiding looking to my left as the chain links *rattled*.

"Bucket head!" Someone yelled and the crowd booed. I pulled my hood up around me as Shan turned to them.

"Takes one to know one," he called back as a guard stepped forward.

"Stop that!" he commanded to the Sally Brown student, shaking the fence, his electric baton buzzing dangerously as he raised it. The boy backed off and turned to his seat.

A deathly silence washed over the crowd as the announcer entered the court. "Hello and welcome to Barracks Stadium, home of the Knights," he said. Cheers erupted from my side of the stadium. I tried to join them, not feeling the enthusiasm. "Now, for the starting lineup! From the visiting team number two, Mike Hall." Mike ran out of the visiting entrance. Boos filled my side as he waved widely. I smiled inwardly as I hid my face, longing to go give him a hug. "Number six, Alex Montaven..." The announcer went on and on, mentioning names of friends and surprising me with some of the new players.

"Finally, the team captain voted one of the top players of the year. Number one, Chris Manteno." The other side of the stadium erupted in cheers. The large screen filled with his smiling face as he entered with a calm stride. Chris raised his right hand to the crowd, his paw tattoo highlighted as he waved. It took all my will to not scream for him as our eyes connected and his smile grew.

"That Browner needs to keep his eyes on the court," snarled Bee two seats over, surprising me.

"Yeah, seriously, doesn't he know we aren't interested?" agreed a girl I didn't know.

"Turns out he's not as broken up about his girl as we thought," chimed in Jaz from my right. "Shouldn't be surprised. Could've been a nice leg up though."

"The home team! Number seven, Robert Duncan," the announcer continued. Robert ran out, waving his hands wildly in the air as people cheered. "Number four, Garret Manro." I cheered and waved my sign as Garret ran out. Kent Wood players filed onto the court, fists and chests bumping. Jaz swooned as Zack entered, and I laughed at her, earning a playful glare. "The team captain and nominated best player of the year, number one, Kyle Patson." As Kyle appeared, it was our turn to overpower the other teams booing. He walked up to Chris, and they shook hands, the wide screen featuring their exchange. Both held a forced smile, their knuckles white, before they split apart and headed back to their own benches. Everyone broke into cheers as the cheerleaders entered. Hayley waved at us, causing a yell to erupt from the crowd as I watched Sally falling in at the rear.

The referee blew the whistle, signaling the beginning of the game. The teams made their way back onto the court, settling into their positions, Chris and Robert facing off for the tip-off.

I could feel their hatred from my seat, their glares plastered above on the giant Holo-screen.

The crowd quieted, all noise a whisper as the suspense grew. Feet shuffled, filling the stadium with the sound of squeaking. The ref threw the ball up and the silence was broken with a roar as Robert won.

By the time the first quarter was up, three members of each team had fouled out, including Garret and Zack. The second quarter began with the score tied 20-20.

I felt torn as I outwardly cheered for Kent Wood, but inwardly cheered for Sally Brown.

By the third quarter, everyone was on their feet. 92-88, Sally Brown. Each play had me biting my nails. Kyle scored two more three-pointers and Chris got two shots in as the clock counted down. At the two-minute mark, Kyle got the ball and made his way to the basket, Chris right on his flank as the crowd roared.

The two battled for the ball, the refs ignoring the shoving and hits of the team members, keeping their opponents at bay. As Kyle went for the shot, Chris jumped, swiping it from his hands and hitting his arm. The ball flew out of bounds. As they landed, Chris shoved Kyle, almost passing it off as ancient as a whistle blew. The two ignored the ref, the crowd quieting.

"Hey Browner, what was that for?" Kyle yelled as he stood. His voice boomed through the stadium mics as the court acoustics amplified it. The screens focused in. I was frozen as I watched Chris stagger from the force of Kyle's shove.

"That's for trying to take what's mine!" Chris was pissed and he practically spat at Kyle.

"I won the title fair and square. It's not my fault you weren't good enough to beat me even when I was out half the season," Kyle taunted.

With a roar, Chris swung. Kyle dodged it, aiming, hitting him right in the eye. In seconds, both teams were at their sides, holding them back. The gym erupted with cheers and hollers as the fight got out of hand. I gasped as I saw Chris stagger back, Kyle getting free and sucker-punching him. Involuntarily, I stepped forward.

"Not now," Shan hissed as he grabbed my wrist. I turned to look at him. His face was stone, staring straight ahead, not acknowledging me, but a subtle blush was growing. "If you get involved, you will get hurt." I turned back in time to see Mike rush forward, striking at Kyle and the situation dissolved. Sadly, Chris had made enemies of him and Robert. The two were on him like no tomorrow. Zack helped Garret try to hold back other team members, but it was pointless.

The refs fought to gain control of the situation as guards poured onto the floor, and it took almost ten minutes for them to stop the fight. My heart broke as I saw Chris limp back to his bench, but Shan's grip around my wrist reminded me to stay still. An illegal play was called on both sides, the game paused. There was a painstaking thirty-minute break before it started again. Shan didn't let me go until it ended. In the end, Sally Brown won 100-98. Both Kyle and Chris were sent to the infirmary. The crowd dispersed and guards escorted the students to the door, making sure that we wouldn't bump into Sally Brown. Hayley found us outside and we followed her to the back of the stadium. She flashed her badge at a guard, and they let us through begrudgingly.

Chapter 21

"Kyle is in room 501. All the other infirmaries are full, so we are being forced to share," Hayley said quickly as we almost sprinted down the hall.

I pulled my hood up farther as she opened the door, stepping to hide myself behind Jaz. I suppressed a gasp when I saw the two tables before me, Kyle and Chris, beaten, bloody, sitting on them. Two guards blocked the meager distance between them as they glared at each other, the doctors patching them up. Through a glass door, I spotted Robert sitting in an ice bath. Luckily, he hadn't spotted me.

"Kyle!" Hayley rushed to him. She gave him a hug and he winced. "Sorry," she apologized, backing up.

"It's okay," he said as a doctor pushed her back, muttering about annoying cheerleaders and damn teenagers.

I'd think with what they pay the school's private doctors they would like kids a bit more, I mused, a smirk tugging at my lips.

"How are you feeling?" asked Jaz, earning a painful-looking smirk from Kyle.

"I'm fine. He doesn't hit that hard," he said with a glare at Chris.

Chris returned it, his rebuttal dying as a guard powered up his stick. He snuck a quick glance at me as the group shifted. I gave him the best sympathetic look I could muster, wishing I could join him as I fell back against the wall. He nodded. It was painful to watch the doctor fill a cut with skin glue and see it slowly mend together without being able to hold his hand. We waited for twenty minutes in silence, Hayley and the others glaring at him, the tension growing.

Sarah, Kathy, Mike, Alex, and boys from both teams joined us sometime later. Once again, the doctor complained under his breath forcing himself through the crowded room. A guard made it clear there would be no fighting as everyone split off into two groups, facing each other down. I caught Kathy's eyes across the way. She gave me a sad smile but didn't move to acknowledge me. I was grateful for her control, but it still hurt. Seeming to mistake my hunched form for fear, Jaz pulled Zack to her, using their bodies as a shield. With them, none of the others could spot me and I was grateful for my new friend, even when I caught the glare Sarah sent them.

Once Kyle was patched up, Hayley helped him off the bench, and a guard followed us out, blocking my friends from touching him. I was the last one out and stole one last look at Chris before I fell into line with the others.

"You need to quit the team now." Chris's voice was cold on the other line.

"I told you I can't." I ran a hand through my hair. *It's been three days of this. When will he stop?* "Hayley already watches my every move. None of the excuses I've tried so far are working, and if I keep pushing, I will expose myself."

"You realize that by pining over a guy you'll probably never end up with, you are just setting yourself up for heartbreak, right?" Kyle pushed as I stepped out of the work session for calculus.

We were mostly alone in the math hall as a large portion of the school was skipping work day or joining The Sword on a prank run on Michel Thomas.

"You need to let him go."

An unexpected rage filled me as I heard a scream, and I spun, hitting the wall behind him. As soon as I saw the fear in his eyes turn into hard determination, I regretted it.

I returned to my room, slamming the panel behind my mirror. It flew open and I grabbed one of two bags inside. Taking the first red pill as my grip on reality felt like it was shifting, I flipped open the small panel in my PortMed, sliding it in. I slammed it shut and the screams faded.

"And you have your mask ready for the game?"

I sighed, staring at the phone on my bed in annoyance. I grabbed the black mask and waved it around, though Chris couldn't see. "Yes," I said.

"Good, and your nickname?"

"I've got it covered, Mother," I ground out, and Chris *humped*.

"I'm just looking out for you. You only have two more days before you'll be back at Sally Brown and in danger of being exposed."

I felt properly chastised, and my annoyance vanished. "I'm..." I paused. "Going by Lightning." There was a beat of silence.

"To honor me?" He sounded genuinely surprised.

"Yeah, I hope that's okay?"

Chris's chuckle on the other line had me smiling for the first time since he left the week before.

"I think it's perfect. I love you."

My heart skipped a beat in all the wrong ways. "I love you too." The words were hard to get out, and I ignored the pit in my stomach.

Classes flew by and before I knew it, the calculus pre-presentation was upon me. I walked into Mr. Talon's office, pulling out my gloves as he pulled on a VR headset. I showed him the basic migration patterns I had mapped. He took down notes, nodding, then finally asked me the dreaded question.

"How do you think you did?"

With a sigh, I told him honestly that I didn't feel it was my best work.

He nodded, jotting down a few more thoughts before giving me a gentle smile. "I'd be more confident in your abilities, my dear. For now, keep working on this. I'm excited to see the completed project."

I left, my heart hammering. My future with Chris rode on my ability to improve my work in the next few weeks before finals.

"Ready?" Hayley asked.

I nodded, following her to the bus in the athletic sector, yawing, not used to waking up early on Sundays. The gang was waiting for us along with a small cluster of people saying goodbye. Bee was giving her last hug to Dorothy as the sun began to rise, before she loaded the bus.

"Got everything?" asked Jaz.

I nodded again and shot her a slight glare. *No talking from me today, traitor.*

Jaz rolled her eyes, reading my thoughts easily. "You know you're happy I forced you to join."

"We'll meet you there," said Sally, stepping aside to let one of my teammates through to the bus.

"Totally. Run hard, okay?" directed Hayley. For once, she wasn't wearing her cheerleading outfit to a game and she tugged at her long sleeve shirt as she fidgeted with the ends.

"Will do," I said as I waved goodbye and headed to board the bus. Before I could take my first step, a hand grabbed my wrist. I turned to see Kyle smiling at me with one of his signature smirks. I couldn't help it when my heart skipped a beat. *Stupid hormones!* I sent him a glare, but he ignored it, turning up the charm.

"Hey fish girl, I forgot to give you this." He handed me a small keychain.

I stared at the Z in confusion. *Why's he giving me this?*

Kyle's smile grew. "Run hard." The doors closed before I could reply.

I headed to a bench at the back. Part of me wanted to push down the window and toss the chain out, but the other part wanted to keep it. *I don't want to be rude,* I told myself as I tucked it into my bag. *Am I still in love with Chris?* I squashed the thought as quickly as it appeared. The drive to Sally Brown's cross-country terrain was several hours long by hover bus. My seatmate left twenty minutes in when she realized I wasn't up for chatting, joining the team as they mingled, excited for the meet. I wrestled with my feelings as the familiar mountains of Sally Brown filled my view four hours in, spotted with yellow and gold from the changing leaves. I pulled out my uniform. After I laced my shoes, I grabbed my new mask, slipping it on. The hard plastic settled on my face, leaving the bottom half exposed. Grabbing my black cap, I twisted my hair to tuck under it.

"Hey Lovota, what's with the mask? No costume?" asked Ken as he walked up the aisle to me. He was a nice guy. Short, with unruly black hair and a laugh that sounded like a hyena. He was by far my favorite teammate besides Bee.

"It's my good luck charm. I wear it at every meet," I explained with a smile.

"And the hat? Don't you get hot in that?" he asked as he sat beside me.

"Not really. It has cooling and warming bots, so I can make it comfortable. I really prefer it to the costumes."

Ken gave me a bright smile. "Oh, cool."

"Has everyone checked the roster?" Coach called from the front of the bus. I replied to her in confirmation with Ken. I used to think Kent Wood was trying to one up everyone else, but now I loved the fact that they used nicknames over real names.

Speaking of one-upping, I glanced over at Ken, who went by Terminator during races. I had never been able to inspect the fake gun strapped on his back, or the sunglasses on his head up close. He resembled the few pictures I'd seen from the old movie, with red contacts to complete the look. It brought back memories of when I used to run against him. I was lucky my costume before had been an intricate headpiece with heavy makeup to make me look like a lioness. Bee joined us in the back, sitting on the bench opposite mine with a makeup pack in hand.

"Let's do this," she said with a stern expression. I laughed at her. She painted a beautiful lightning bolt on my upper right arm, then turned to Ken to have him paint her face with black and yellow stripes. Not surprisingly, she used her nickname as her roster name. I smiled as I watched her flirt with him. Each time he shushed her, trying not to smudge her lines.

Just like Chris.

I reached behind my neck, unclasping his necklace. Gently, I wrapped it around my wrist and secured it with some athletic tape. *Now I can see it as I run.*

We arrived at Sally Brown not long after everyone was ready, a giant crowd already waiting for us. People patted us on the back as we made our way to the lockers. Kent Wood was hungry for a win. The crowd ended at the double doors in the building's side that housed the bleachers and locker rooms. When we reached them, we took a quick reprieve to pack our stuff in the lockers, then gathered in the center.

"Alright, you know the drill. Run hard and focus on yourself. Don't let the crowd or other team get in your head," Coach said and we all nodded to her, the laughing faces from the bus replaced by determined looks. It was our meet. Even I wanted us to win, it didn't matter who I had to beat. Coach put her hand to her ear and looked at us. "It's time."

I fell into line, taking my spot at the second-place position behind Ken. The cheering of the crowd filled the air, as we filed out of the building, the beating of feet echoing in the walls behind us as people stomped on the bleachers above. I knew our faces were on the big screen, so I stared straight ahead at the starting line. The Sally Brown team was waiting. I nodded to them as I took my spot, noting the new members and admiring their intricate costumes.

The run was a 5k, one of the hardest terrains in the nation, filled with booby traps and mud pits. Luckily, I was familiar with each one. As the ref took to the line, I closed my eyes.

One Mississippi. I counted.

The crowd grew quiet.

Two Mississippi.

The sound of my heartbeat filled my ears.

Three Mississippi.

The *bang* of the gun sounded as I launched forward.

After I passed the first bend into the woods, I slowed down, pacing myself. Some of the more experienced kids joined me and we worked together, keeping each other's pace, and avoiding obstacles. Ken flashed me a grin around the 2K mark as he sped ahead. I laughed at his challenge and bided my time, watching as he gained ground.

When others grew tired, I took the opportunity to pull ahead. I passed Ken, flashing him my own grin. A faint laugh accompanied me as I turned a corner down the track, dodging a trip wire.

As I passed the 3K mark, I could hear the announcers' comments. Speakers were set up along the track to mess up the visiting teams. I welcomed their intrusion as I raced by.

"And there goes number 7. It says here her name is Lightning. That's very fitting, it seems, since she's leading the group."

"Yes, but what's with the mask, Joe?"

"Costumes are one thing, but we have never seen an actual mask before. They are often too constricting for the runner. Brad, it looks like she's going for the ninja vibe."

The announcer's voices faded as I passed the last speaker. I passed the 3.5K mark without any competitors in sight. The 4K marker was gone in a flash before I slowed down, knowing the last kilometer was the hardest. Uphill most of the way, there were four mud puddles and a small stream with a hidden trip wire you had to run through to finish.

I hit the stream before I heard feet behind me. One of the Sally Brown kids was sprinting toward me. I didn't recognize him, but

I had to admit I was impressed, he was good. Another pair of feet joined him, and I glimpsed Ken's red eyes. Passing the 4.5 k marker, I decided it was time. After taking two long strides, I sprinted.

The boys were on my heels as I ran the last hill. I felt a strange squeeze as adrenaline filled me. A burst of energy spurred me on.

Euphoria filled me as I threw my hands in the air, hitting the laser. I ran a few more feet, then slowed down, bending over as I caught my breath before throwing my hands on the back of my head to stand straight.

The cheers of the crowd hit my ears as my blood stopped rushing. I turned around as the Sally Brown kid arrived. When he caught his breath, I headed over to him and we shook hands. He forced a smile, his vampire fangs peeking out. We walked over to the end of the strip to wait for those that made it.

Ken was third, and he arrived with guns literally blazing, the faux fire from them heating the area. I shot him a glare at the uncomfortable addition to my overheated state, and he laughed.

Slowly but surely, people appeared over the hill after him. Four people followed in a small pack of their own, Bee among them. The last person to cross was Monaca from Kent Wood. When it was clear no one else had made it, we turned to the crowd; the official coming over, lining us up in order of rank.

"I think we can all agree that this was a great meet," said an announcer, the speaker booming as our faces filled the flat screen.

"Our winner today is Lightning from Kent Wood," the ref declared. I stepped forward. Ken came from behind me, throwing my arm in the air, and the crowd went wild. The boy who finished second stepped up, waving. The crowd settled down and the official handed us our trophies.

"We did it," exclaimed Ken, throwing himself at me for a hug. I embraced him, feeling euphoric. Bee bounced about, drawing looks from our competitors as they huddled. Laughing, we pulled her into the hug. Students filed from the stands, the air still abuzz with excitement as I said my last goodbyes to our rivals and we walked back to the locker room with renewed vigor.

Chapter 22

"I'll meet you guys at the bus," I said as we headed out of the locker room, noticing Chris's necklace was no longer on my wrist. "I forgot something."

Ken and Bee exchanged worried glances. "I can go with you," Bee offered, but I shook my head.

"No. I'll be quick. I just need to find something." I tried to keep the panic out of my voice as I forced a smile.

"Okay, if you say so. Just be careful. You never know when a Browner will strike," said Ken, taking Bee's hand and leading her away.

I watched them go before turning back to the locker rooms in a sprint, searching frantically, then returning to the hall.

I know I had the necklace when I finished the race; it has to be nearby.

"Hey, good running out there," called a familiar voice behind me.

I spun to face Mike, my heart jumping into my throat.

He leaned on the far wall of the hall, my golden necklace swinging in his grasp. I eyed it, then him, cautiously as I approached, nodding my head in thanks, worried that if I spoke, he would recognize my voice. His eyes followed my every move with a dangerous gleam. I pointed to the necklace in his hands, and he glanced down at it, a wicked smile on his lips as he looked back at me. "Oh, is this yours?" he asked, his tone taunting. The necklace unfurled from his grasp as he held up his hand, the chain swinging from his finger.

I reached for it, but he snatched it back. "If you want it, you're going to have to ask nicely."

I ground my teeth, holding in my anger as I held out my hand expectantly.

Mike stared at it distastefully. "What's wrong, Bucket? Am I not worthy enough to hear the sound of your voice? All I'm asking for is a simple 'please'. Or is that something you only reserve for your secret boyfriends?" His words took me off guard, the snarl on his face scaring me.

"What in the world are you talking about?" I snapped before I could stop myself. My hands flew to my mouth, my eyes widening as his face changed.

The anger was still there but confusion was rising. "Loran?"

Quickly, before he could get closer, I punched him, sending him reeling as I bolted for the exit.

"Loran!" Mike's voice echoed in the hall, but I didn't stop, flinging the doors open to the outside. I hit the crowd right as he caught up with me. Twisting out of the reach of his hand, I disappeared into it. As I made my way through, people recognized me. They patted me on the back, some even standing aside.

I broke through the other side as Ken called my name. He waved at me, motioning for me to join him on the bus. I rushed to him, grabbing his hand and dragging him in with me. The doors closed with a *whoosh*, and the bus lurched forward, making us stumble. I turned around to see if Mike had followed and felt my heart stop. At the edge of the crowd, he stood holding his bruised chin, his eyes blazing. The look on his face told me he knew the truth. I couldn't break eye contact even as Ken shook me, asking what was wrong.

Voices echoed around me but I couldn't hear a word. He and Bee led me down the aisle to an empty seat. After a few failed attempts at trying to break me from my panic attack, they let me be.

My world came crashing down as we headed back to Kent Wood. The bus was full of chatter, but I sat alone in the back, filled with despair. *What will Mike do now that he knows?* My bare neck felt cold as I dragged my hand along it, questions ringing in my ears.

10/13/2121 8:01 p.m. Chris: *Loran, are you there? You need to respond to me now! What happened?*

Ten missed calls. I couldn't make myself answer a single one.

"You okay, Lovota?" Jaz asked as we walked to class.

"Yeah, I've just been stressed with term end coming up is all."

Hayley gave me a look. "Are you sure it isn't something to do with the Browner chasing you after the meet?" she asked potently. Before I could reply, Shan was by my side, awkwardly diverting her attention to the topics of her project. They walked ahead. I tried to stay aware of my surroundings, but it was so hard to be present when worry overwhelmed me and I could feel the MEDs working overtime. After the conversation died, he stepped back, joining me.

"Was it *the* boy?" he asked, and I knew who he was talking about.

I felt guilty as I lied. "Yes."

With a nod of understanding, he placed an awkward hand on my shoulder. "You're safe here."

I fiddled with the red pill in my pocket as I nodded.

10/14/2121 4:22 p.m. Chris: *Listen, Mike is saying crazy things. He's got some absurd story in his head of cheating and a kidnapping conspiracy. I need to know what you said to him so I can play damage control before something bad happens.*

17 missed calls.

I shoved the phone into my desk drawer as it *buzzed* again. "Get a hold of yourself," I chastised myself. "You need to respond to him." As I reached for the drawer, the sound of screaming filled my ears. Quickly, I slammed it shut and went to find a red pill. "Everything is fine."

"I have to tell you something," I said.

Jaz looked me up and down as I shuffled nervously in the doorway of her room. "Alright, come on in." Relief flooded me as I stepped in. "What's going on?

"I think my boyfriend is going to break up with me!" The words flew from my mouth before I could stop them.

Her eyebrows shot up. "This calls for cocoa. Go sit down and tell me everything." *You can't trust her.* Ignoring the sudden pit in my stomach at Chris's voice, I sat, pulling my phone from my pocket. Jaz walked to the couch, stopping as she saw it.

"What is tha—"

I interrupted her. "I fell in love with a boy from Trident."

There was a flash in her eyes before she took a deep breath and sat down. "I think it would be best if you start from the beginning."

Telling Jaz my polished story I gave to Shan made me feel sick. *Maybe I should just tell her the truth?* I thought.

She will kill you if she knows.

The voice sounded suspiciously like Sarah.

"Can you believe fall break is, like, almost here," said Hayley, excitedly bouncing on the path next to me. "I'm going to cry just waiting for it."

I stared up at the falling leaves, ignoring her and the others. My phone was heavy in my pocket, my fingers flicking over the cold metal as I stuck my hand in. My last message weighed heavily on me.

10/17/2121 5:02 a.m. Me: *Chris, I didn't say anything; I can't say anything. I've been in a panic attack for days. What did he say is going to happen?*

It had been three days since he left it on Read.

"I'm more excited for the Halloween homecoming dance." Jaz brushed her hand against my arm on the right, drawing me into the conversation. "So, what's the plan for the break?" she asked, and I turned to Hayley.

"We might go to south KW for a beach party. But like, I'm not sure yet," she said as she checked her shopping list. "Seems like we are out of makeup cartridges as well," she mumbled.

"I would die to be a regular teenager for once," said Sally distastefully. Although I hadn't seen my parents for almost two months, they had tried to stay in touch. Sally's parents, on the other hand, were there every other week. Mrs. Adams was fighting them off, but it was slow going.

"Yeah, I agree. Let's go," I said, surprising myself as well as the others. Jaz gave me an assessing gaze and my hand a squeeze.

"Well, if Lovota's up for it, then I'm game," Bee cheered happily. They continued to chat, scarves pulled tight around each of our necks, the cool air of the oncoming winter blowing around us.

It hit me how much my life had changed in such a brief time. Despite everything, I found myself beginning to care for my new friends. It caught me off guard at times. I followed them down new paths and past smaller clusters of buildings as we headed for the mall that sat between the two high school campuses.

"Alright, we need a game plan to tackle the crowds," Jaz said with a serious face.

"Not everything is competition," Sally countered.

"We can just play by ear, right?" Lucy asked nervously.

Jaz groaned as we pushed open the doors.

"Look over there!" Hayley exclaimed the moment we stepped into the warm building. She rushed past a group of girls to see the dress in the display window.

I followed her, fighting the crowd. Later light shone through the mosaic skylight above as we went to find a dressing room. Hayley chose a strapless, bright pink sequin dress with pink high tops. Each step she took released colored MicroBots from the heel, making it look like she was splashing through a puddle.

Jaz teased her about the choice. "Wow, who are you trying to impress?"

"Like, do you think Matt will like it?" she asked nervously.

"Of course! He likes you for you and not what you wear, but this will definitely knock him away," I encouraged her.

Her eyes lit with surprise, but her smile softened. "Thank you, Lovota." Her voice was gentle, and I felt as though I had just taken a huge step forward with her.

"The boy has only known you for two weeks. He'd probably like you in a sack." Sally pointed out as she dragged her dress off, tossing it into a pile.

Jaz chose a black and white strapless, skintight dress that ended mid-thigh and showed off her long legs and athletic build.

Sally took a gray dress. It was tight on top and puffed out at the waist, with one strap on the left shoulder.

I ended up choosing a midnight black dress that was tight on the top and flowed loosely down to my knees. On the right bottom was a silvery sequence of flowers that moved when I did.

Listening as Hayley told us more about Matt's newest feat of romance, we headed out of the store to meet the others.

"Did you know midnight black is totally Kyle's favorite color?" she teased, causing my heart to seize up.

"Why didn't you tell me before I bought it? I thought all you Kent Wood kids hated blue!" Jaz smiled wickedly behind her.

"It looked too good on you. We knew you wouldn't take it if we told you, and besides midnight black isn't blue," said Sally. I didn't believe her for a second.

I glared at Jaz. After hearing the state of my relationship, she'd made it her mission to "get me a guy" and pulled the others into it. They were trying to ease me away from Chris, but I wasn't ready. *I don't think I will ever be ready.*

"I can't believe finals are tomorrow," Jaz groaned as we met up with the rest of the group in the food court.

"Don't even talk about it," Bee said from the table, a half-eaten burger by her side. "I barely slept last night thinking about it. I'm just not sure any of my projects are ready."

The sound of rushing water filled the room from the fountain nearby. I spotted a young girl throwing a penny into it.

"I agree," said Dorothy.

"I think you will all do great," I said, placing my order on the panel in the table. "After all, you come from Kent Wood, one of the smartest plebs around."

"Speaking of, how are you feeling?" asked Lucy. "Has the workload been too much?"

I hesitated before I answered. "No, it's been more than I am used to, but the teachers are excellent. The only class I'm worried about is Arts of the Past."

Jaz laughed. "Yeah, I bet. I mean, sure you have improved, but you still manage to fall on your face every other class."

I pushed down my aggravation as I forced a laugh. "True, true. Now tell me more about this dance."

The last week of the term flew by, and I found myself regretting pulling an all-nighter to finish my presentation as my head pounded. I threw my hair into a messy bun, locking it into place with an anti-gravity hair clip before leaving. The sun was too bright as Jaz and Zack met me outside, heads bent over each other. They shot me a cautious look as I approached.

"What's wrong?" I asked.

They hesitated, and the guarded look in their eyes made my blood pressure spike.

"There was an attack...by Sally Brown," Jaz said after a moment. "No one was hurt, but they hit the cross-country building pretty bad."

"BotJuice," I swore. "What happened?"

"It was just a stink bomb," Zack added. "But it took hours to clean." He gave a big yawn, and I noticed how tired they looked.

"Were you cleaning all night?"

They nodded.

"Why?"

Another hesitant look.

"Our group is in charge of running interference and cleaning for this sector," Zack admitted.

They don't trust me. The realization hurt more than it should have. *I thought I'd made some progress.*

As if reading my thoughts, Jaz gave me a bright smile, placing a hand on my shoulder in comfort. "Hey, we didn't say anything because we didn't want to worry you." I pretended to believe her as I nodded. "You're not used to these things. We wouldn't want you failing because you were anxious."

We headed to our finals in silence, and I went straight to calculus. Kyle and Shan saved me a seat, waving to me as I entered the lecture hall. I flashed them a thankful smile as I sat down.

One by one we were called into rooms to present our work to Mr. Talon and his assistances. I left my evaluation in bright spirits, my mind already running with new ideas on how to implement my skills in the next classes.

Shan finished before me, so I met him outside, Kyle coming out right behind me. The boy from the beginning of the year, Tom, gave me a look as I left. I couldn't tell if he was mad at me or the presentations by the scowl on his face. His eyes flashed behind his glasses, glinting as they moved in the light, sending a chill crawling down my spine. Luckily, Kyle grabbed my arm and led me away. I was never so grateful for his forceful nature before then, ignoring Tom's gaze burning my back.

Chapter 23

I finished my biology presentation and headed to the coffee shop, Brain Beans, to wait. The bell on the door *dinged* as I entered the small shack like structure, wood panels creaking below my feet as I crossed the entrance to find a spot at one of the many mismatched couches or tables.

Most of them were filled with students prepping for presentations, but I spotted an empty couch nearby. Laying down, I closed my eyes. Someone kicked my leg as they passed and I grunted, moving it, not feeling like opening my eyes to see my would-be attacker.

"Hey girl, how bad was it?"

I opened my eyes to Hayley standing above me, realizing that I must have fallen asleep. "Fine, I guess." I groaned, sitting up, allowing her to sit next to me. "Feeling a little fried."

"Yeah, I totally felt that way with Advanced Bio," she said, rubbing her forehead. "At least it's over. Hey, looks like you got a paper stuck in your boot. You know we can't take notes into the presentations. You weren't, like, cheating, were you?"

I looked down, laughing at her joke, stopping when I saw she was telling the truth. "How did that get there?" I grabbed the paper, unfolding it slowly. My heart skipped a beat as I read it, and I coughed uncomfortably to cover up the gasp that escaped. Hayley looked at me, her eyebrows raised. I forced a smile.

Crumbling the paper, I put it in my pocket. She was about to press when the door opened, Jaz, Zack, Kyle, and Sally walking in. They joined us on the couch and Jaz toppled onto me, laughing.

"It's over!" she proclaimed, throwing her hands in my face. I shoved them aside lightly and tried to wiggle my way out from below her. "Next stop, homecoming and fall break."

Zack sighed with a smile and helped me push her off. He settled down next to me and she sat on him, wrapping her arms around his neck for support. The rest of the group arrived shortly after, and I used the opportunity to excuse myself to the bathroom. As soon as the door closed behind me, I pulled the paper from my pocket and read it again. The words were still there, written in blood-red ink. I hadn't imagined them.

"Beware the twisted root," I read aloud, confirming they were real. *Not again?* I felt a familiar squeeze as a panic set in. "The Shadow can't get me here," I whispered as screams filled my ears. "I'm safe." My fingers fidgeted with my PortMed longing for a red pill.

Homecoming arrived on Sunday with a bang, the campus exploding with Halloween decorations and themed food for the whole week.

Unlike the party at South Park, the dance was split by Major Focus and each sector had gotten to work on their own themes. Chris was still silent, and each day not hearing from him made my heart hurt.

I put down my hairbrush, heading to my door as I heard a knock, pushing aside my unease. Smiling, I opened it to see the girls waiting outside, piles of clothes and makeup in their arms. Since my place had the biggest mirror, Sally measured, we planned to do makeup there and would use her room across the hall to change.

I listened to her talk animatedly about Garret, praying for my hair to turn out fine as she worked on it. Each pull and distracted twirl as she talked with her hands had me holding my breath. When she was done, I was surprised by the results.

"You should be a hairdresser," I said, awestruck. My hair sat in a beautiful looping bun, the gold ends spiking out at the back and on the sides. Two of the longer pieces curled, falling from the bun at the middle.

Sally smiled proudly at me in the mirror. "Naw, I like science too much. My mom was a hairdresser before she mated dad in her second round though," she said, her eyes gleaming. "She teaches me when we have time." I was about to ask her about her mother, seeing the look of sadness in her eyes, when Hayley came in and gasped.

"OMH! I totally love the hair. You're totally going to knock them dead!" she squealed dramatically.

My lips quirked. It was nice to be interacting with her on a more positive level. "Thanks, your turn," I said, going across the hall to get my dress. Pulling it on, I took a moment to look at the lovely fabric in the mirror, trying not to speculate about the color.

"So, who are you trying to impress?"

I glared at Jaz's reflection.

She ignored it, stepping up to help me with my zipper.

"Why do you keep pushing?" I asked, exhausted.

Putting a hand on my shoulder and giving me a gentle smile through the mirror, she said, "Sometimes the hardest part of life is letting go. In the worst way and the best way, a rebound could help. You never know. You might fall in love on the way." She stared into my eyes, trying to communicate something that I didn't want to hear.

I escaped her grasp, ripping her hand from me and any comfort it might have brought, mumbling something about getting shoes as I walked away. As I pulled on my heels, the rest of the group joined us. Bee, Lucy, and Dorothy took their clothes to the other room when it got too crowded to change in one place. The row of corsages on the counter they passed reminded me that every girl had a date but me.

I sighed. *I miss Chris...but also the feeling of a guy standing by my side, waiting for me.* I shook my head, reminding myself that it was a romantic idea, but not one worth staking my relationship on.

Once everyone was ready, we headed to meet the boys. When I spotted them amongst the crowd in the lobby, I couldn't help but smirk. They cleaned up nicely. The girls went to find their dates. Corsages were exchanged with whispered sweet nothings in each other's ear.

I joined Shan and Kyle, who surprisingly was also going alone, and flashed them a smile. Shan replied with a blush like normal and Kyle gave me a deep bow. With a giggle and sigh, I took their offered arms, and we headed to Café de Fiesta.

The sun was setting, casting a beautiful glow across the lawns and decorations. Filing past the buildings holding lecture halls to a small two-story white brick building nestled between two towers, we arrived and pushed through people dressed to the nines to get to the hostess. She sat us quickly thanks to Kyle's smooth talking. He was the perfect gentleman as he pulled out my chair from the long table set with gold-trimmed silverware and handed me the menu. The chair was soft and I relaxed into it. I hadn't realize I'd been so stressed.

Kyle engaged me in a lovely debate about the best form of combat we learned in class. Shan sat by, interjecting into our conversations occasionally, but mainly keeping to himself. He fiddled with his spoon as I tried to get him to relax, but it was no use.

The conversation at the table was upbeat and lively. I could see the weight of school lifting off everyone's shoulders. When dessert finally arrived, I ate about half before I felt like I was going to burst.

"Please, someone take this before I have another bite," I said, shoving it away.

Kyle took it from me, looking amused. "What, can't handle it?" I glared at him playfully as he laughed. "Okay, okay, I'll finish it." He scarfed the cake down in seconds.

"You're like a bottomless pit!" I exclaimed. He smiled up at me, his eyes squinting, and my heart skipped a beat. I couldn't help but notice how cute his hair looked when he decided to let it hang loosely, hitting partially down his forehead.

"It comes with the job," he said through a full mouth. Immediately, the illusion shattered. "I didn't become the captain of the basketball and football team by doing nothing." I looked away in disgust, catching Hayley's eyes. She smiled at me devilishly, and I knew what she was thinking. Scowling, I turned to stare at the far wall. I couldn't lie to myself. *Yes, Kyle is attractive, but I know our personalities would clash.* Shan laughed as Kyle made a joke and I absently admired it. It had a certain ring, like thunder. It was cute.

BotJuice, you have a boyfriend, I chastised myself.

Dinner finished around eight and we headed to the dance. The moon was full, rising in the sky, illuminating crowds of students walking past gools and pumpkins. By the time we arrived on the second floor of the calculus building, the dance was in full swing. The large room was decorated head to toe in silver streamers and floating fish that swam the sky to match the underwater theme. Tables lined the sides and multiple sets of double doors led to four different balconies.

Jaz dragged me onto the dance floor as soon as we arrived. Bee bumped into us, trying to start what she called a mosh pit. She succeeded. It ended quickly though, when she fell to the ground, taking Dorothy and Sally with her. Lucy filmed the whole thing on her PortMed, and we laughed as she replayed the scene over and over. I jumped up and down to the songs playing over the speakers, enjoying the feel of the bass in the air, loving the smell of sea salt filtered in through the vents. The boys joined us as we made a circle, one of many, for a dancer to take the floor. I watched people show off and after Jaz pushed me to the center, did so as well. When I finished, I headed to the refreshments table for a drink.

"That was outstanding," said Kyle behind me, and I turned to him, smiling.

"Thanks," I said, taking a sip. I was proud of my performance and glad I didn't make a fool of myself. Kyle smiled back at me, stepping closer. I shifted uncomfortably, trying to look anywhere but him, ignoring the heat of his body.

"Lovota, you're amazing," he whispered. I shuddered as his breath ghosted against my ear. "I know you're taken, and I'm working to understand and respect what that means for you. It's hard to keep my distance though." His hand fluttered across my cheek. I had an excuse to dodge him as a girl came up to grab a drink from the punch bowl. He followed me as I walked down the refreshment table.

"Please not again," I begged. I felt Kyle sigh, the distance between us diminishing the effects, but I still had to suppress the fluttering of my stomach. I turned to him. "Why are you so persistent? Can't we just be friends?"

"You're right." He stopped advancing. "But my offer still stands." A dark emotion flashed across his face as he walked away.

Was that suspicion in his eyes? I threw the thought from my head with a furious whip of my hair. Needing air, I headed out to the nearest balcony. Pushing open the doors, I looked around. It was empty. Tables were scattered about, surrounded by chairs.

Lace flowing down the sides, accompanied by silver centerpieces, created a calming glow in the moonlight. I passed them to get to the railing, leaning against it, staring up at the stars, and sighed at the moon.

"When did my life get so complicated?" I asked it.

Chapter 24

"What's wrong?"

Shan's voice made me jump, my hand flying to my heart.

When did he arrive?

I watched him slowly approach me, as if afraid I'd sprint away. His hair glistened from sweat and his stormy eyes were dark.

"You scared me," I whispered, taking my away. He looked me over, concern clear on his face.

Stopping at the table closest to me, but not too close to make me uncomfortable, he smiled. I appreciated the gesture. "S-sorry...I should have made my presence known," he said blushing.

I couldn't help but grin back at him. He could always pull a smile from me.

His face brightened and he closed the distance, taking the space at my side. He smelled of sweat and earth as he leaned against the railing, looking up at the stars. Closing his eyes, his face was serene.

I watched him, feeling comforted by his presence.

"So, do you want to tell me?"

I sighed, turning to the sky. "I guess I could. I mean, you're a guy, right? So maybe you'll understand."

He chuckled. "Thanks for noticing."

I shoved him lightly on the shoulder as he looked down at me with a gleam in his eyes. "You know what I mean. Still, maybe you could shed some light on my problem."

"Okay, shoot," he said. He seemed so relaxed, so sure of himself, and I enjoyed for a moment the confident boy standing beside me.

"My question is, why is it..." I searched for the words, "—that when guys like girls, they either never admit it, or they push too hard? Why can't they just come out and say it without being so—I don't know—annoying or aggressive? Why do guys—" My voice caught in my throat and I coughed as it cracked, suppressing the tears welling up in my eyes and turning my face away. "Why...is it that when you think things are going well, they stop talking to you? He doesn't call or send messages. I'm left wondering...what I did wrong...what made him ignore me?" A tear streamed down my face, Shan's hand on my cheek, catching it.

"Please don't cry, Lovota," he whispered, his fingers lingering as he pulled away. His gentleness caught me off guard. It had been a long time since a boy had shown me such gentle concern. Even Chris was forceful in the way he comforted me.

I took a step away quickly, turning to stare at the campus below, suddenly feeling vulnerable.

"Sorry," I said, wiping at my eyes with a sniff. I heard Shan step away, pacing. "Please don't let me ruin your evening. I know I can be so stupid sometimes. It's just hard, and a new school isn't helping. I-I'm sorry..."

A crashing sound had me spinning. Shan stood in front of a fallen chair nearby as if he had tripped over it, his hands braced on the table.

"Shan?"

He glanced up at me and then back down, staring at it in surprise, like he didn't know it was there.

I raised my hand toward him.

"Don't apologize, Lovota," he choked, taking me aback. My hand dropped in shock as I stared at him wide-eyed. "Please never apologize." His voice softened as he looked up at me.

My breath caught at the raw emotions in his eyes. "Shan?"

"Don't you understand there is nothing you need to be sorry for? It's those boys that should be sorry. We—they—should be able to face you head-on. To tell you how I...they, feel..." He shook slightly, though whether from anger or sadness, I couldn't tell. With a calming breath, he straightened, and when he looked at me, his eyes were guarded. "Any guy lucky enough to have you should never ignore you." He stopped, struggling for words. He ran his hands through his already messy hair, ignoring it as it flopped into his face. I barely caught the next few words as he mumbled to himself. "If only...weren't there. I'd try...Couldn't fight him...wasn't enough...already taken...a Defect." He sighed, then looked at me, his voice barely a whisper. "If only." His fists clenched and unclenched as he looked down.

"Shan?" I said, moving to him and putting a hand on his shoulder. His head snapped to me, his eyes dilating. A blush spread up his cheeks as he gave me a forlorn smile.

"Don't worry about it." Slowly, he put his hand under my chin, wiping away another tear I didn't know was there.

Reaching up, I cupped his face and watched as he leaned into my hand. The air was tense, our eyes locked on each other, each breath matching the next. I was drowning again, but I didn't want to escape.

"Lovota," Shan whispered my name so quietly, so softly, I almost missed it. I longed for a different name to be on his lips. My eyes fluttered as he slowly inched closer, gravity pulling us in.

"How *cute*." Just like that, the moment was shattered.

I jumped away from Shan as he dropped his hand from my cheek quickly. Shame flooded me as I realized what I had almost done.

Shan turned to Robert, a growl stuck in his throat. "What are you doing here? Your kind isn't allowed!" His voice was dark, racking shivers down my spine.

Robert leaned against the far wall. His arms crossed over his chest, showing off his large muscles, and his eyes glinted in the moonlight. "I'm here with a friend," he said, pushing himself from the wall as he walked casually to us. "He wanted me to meet someone. She's inside with him now." Stopping a few feet away, he gave me a slow look and I felt my skin crawl. His grin spread as Shan stepped in front of me protectively. I hid behind him, grateful. In return, Robert looked at him, amused. "But to be honest, I'm more interested in what's out here."

Shan growled.

"Watcha gonna do, nerd? Slap me? We all know those little muscles of yours are just for show." Obviously, he didn't remember the night at South Park.

"Don't make me tell Kyle you're messing with her again," Shan threatened.

Robert's face fell into a scowl. *What's he talking about? What did Kyle have to do with this?* "Leave that punk out of this."

"Why? Are you scared? We both know the rules, so stay away."

Robert's scowl grew deeper, hate radiating from him. Shan's protective stance gave me courage, and I grinned at Robert, trying to hide my fear behind false bravado. I even stuck out my tongue like a child.

He snarled when he saw. "I will find you alone. Then we will see what that tongue can do."

My grin dropped.

Shan stepped forward, seeming to tower over Robert even though he had inches on him.

Robert ignored his advances, continuing to watch me. "You will return to me." With that, Robert turned, pushing open the doors and disappearing back into the dance.

I shivered, trying not to let him get to me.

Shan turned to me once he was gone and smiled, but it was forced. "Ignore that Defect. I'll make sure Kyle puts him in his place," Shan said, putting a comforting hand on my shoulder.

"Thanks," I replied, putting a hand on his.

It caused him to stammer. "I-it's getting cold out. Let's g-go inside and see if we can find Hayley." He pulled away and I followed him inside, sticking close just in case.

When we couldn't find her, I dragged Shan to the dance floor, needing a distraction. I let everything go, enjoying being with him. He wasn't a terrible dancer, and his presence soothed me. The song ended and a slow song took its place. Couples found each other, others filtering off the floor.

"Want to dance?" I asked, putting my hand out. He looked around nervously, as if he would get in trouble. I watched, waiting. Finally, his eyes hardened. Nodding, he put his hands on my waist and I wrapped my arms around his neck.

We swayed to the song as I leaned my head against his shoulder, getting lost in the moment. His steady heartbeat thumped in my ear; his hands were warm where they rested. I should have felt bad it wasn't Chris by my side, but I couldn't bring myself to care. When the song ended, we pulled apart reluctantly.

The DJ announced it was time to leave, and the room whined for one more song, chanting. I laughed as she refused. Shan took my hand and led me around the dance floor. Amidst the chaos, we somehow found our friends, Hayley greeting us with a smile, eyeing our hands with a conspiratorial look. She looked like she had a good night as she hung on her date, Matt.

Shan dropped my hand as we joined Kyle in the back of the group. "Where did you two disappear to?" Kyle asked, an edge to his voice.

"I was helping Lovota with a problem," said Shan, his tone making Kyle inspect him questioningly.

They exchanged a look and Kyle's face darkened. "I see." As we broke into the cool October air, I decided to enjoy the night sky, ignoring the tense atmosphere. I walked ahead as they hung back, whispering, but I caught a few concerning words as they floated on the breeze.

"You need to be careful, dude. I understand you like her and all, but she's dangerous. You don't know where her loyalties lie." Kyle's voice was cold.

When we got to the dorm, everyone headed to Sally's to change and get their stuff. It was two in the morning when I rushed into bed to cry below the covers.

Chapter 25

Hayley invited the girls to her place for a sleepover, and I jumped on the opportunity to grow my bonds with them, tired of feeling alone.

One step into her room, though, and we ended up turning around and heading to mine. I was still reeling from the smell of the forgotten food on the counter.

"Well, it looks like they are done, at least for now," she called from my living room as she flopped onto my couch, the cushions groaning under the force. "This was their longest attack yet. I mean seriously, like two weeks. How did they even maintain that with finals week going on?"

"I'm just glad most of it was concentrated in the south," said Jaz, fixing a pot of tea next to me in the kitchen. Hayley shot me a side glance. I ignored her and the sting of knowing Chris had been close but made no effort to see me. "Don't get me wrong, I feel for them, but I can't afford the distraction with the season picking up."

"They might not be done, you know," Sally said as she flipped through the movie selection on my HTV. "We still have four days before the next term and lecture weeks start."

"Speaking of attacks, have any of you been getting mysterious messages about The Shadow?" The room grew cold as Lucy mentioned the note that had been haunting my nightmares.

I carefully put down the mug I was pulling from the cabinet, my hands shaking, settling on the cool granite.

"Now that you mention it, yeah. I didn't want to say anything cause...you know...but I've been receiving them since last Monday." Jaz's voice wavered a bit, her hands trembling on the counter next to mine.

"Us as well," admitted Bee as she gestured between her and Dorothy.

"Yeah, same. The timing is too strange." The edge in Hayley's tone made me look away from her accusatory gaze.

"I got one right after my bio final," I admitted, studying the speckles in my countertop.

"If we are all getting them, that can't mean it's genuine, right?" asked Sally in a quiet voice.

"Yeah no, you're right!" Jaz pulled the teapot from the stove, pouring the tea into our cups with renewed vigor. She passed me one, then continued into the living room, the drinks trailing behind her. "There's no way they can be real, especially if Hayley and I are getting them." She passed the drinks around.

"You're right! The Shadow almost never takes rank one," said Bee, brightening before her face turned contemplative. "Why do you think that is?"

"I heard The Shadow is a group of top students and they're slowly takin' out the competition." Dorothy's tone was conspiratorial. As she leaned in, an unspoken signal drew the rest of us to the room to sit in a circle. I settled into a chair as I took a sip of my tea.

"That makes, like, no sense. The Shadow only targets Rank three and mid-tier rank two, not one. If it was taking out its competition, shouldn't it target tier one of rank two at least?" countered Hayley.

"No, that would be too obvious. So, they take out the upstarts," Bee said, offended her sister's theory could even be questioned.

"What about the fact that this has been going on for almost twenty-five years?" countered Jaz.

"Well, that's because they don't live in our time," Sally piped in.

Lucy let out a groan. "Not this again."

"What? It's true!" Sally defended, her face scrunching.

"What's true?" I asked, regretting it the moment Jaz whispered. "Now you've done it."

"The Shadow lives in the in-between place." I gave Sally a questioning look and her eyes grew wide. "You know, the space between the teleporters?"

I barked out a laugh. "There's no such place."

"How can you say that? We tear a literal wormhole in space just to get places easier and you don't think there's not a consequence for that? A space or other dimension where The Shadow lies?" Her voice was hard and disbelieving.

"Yeah, no." Before she could protest, I continued. "I heard The Shadow is actually a deformed student from the start of the MEDs." The curious gazes of the girls had me quickly explaining. "Back when the MEDs began, they were super unstable. A young boy named Teddy was one of the first trial subjects. One stormy night, he was called in for his treatment. Right as the doctors were administering it, a large bolt of lightning struck the building, causing electricity to shoot from the equipment, striking him right here." I pointed to my heart, my voice growing deeper.

I watched as each of them leaned in, entranced. "Of course, Teddy ended up passing out. But when he came to, he started to convulse and whither. As he did, his arms began to pop and reform, his back twisting and curling. With a scream, the nurse ran from the room, calling for the doctor. But when they returned, it was empty except for a giant claw mark on the wall and the open window leading to the woods beyond."

Lucy let out a whimper.

"Now he roams the schools, seeking revenge against any he thinks have done him wrong. They say on stormy nights just like that night when the winds howl and lightning streaks the sky, you can hear his painful scream echoing—after—each—strike." I made an explosion sound, my hands bursting forward.

Lucy jumped from the floor and Sally let out a shriek. I laughed, almost rolling from my chair at the force of it. The tension on Hayley's face softened.

Jaz shoved me from my chair. "You're absolutely the worst," she said with a smile.

"But really, does anyone know who The Shadow truly is?" I countered as I slipped back into my chair.

"I do." Lucy's voice was soft, her face twisted in pain. "I've heard rumors it's actually a hidden branch of the government, stealing away children to experiment on for their nefarious purposes."

There was a beat of silence as we all stared at her. Then we burst out laughing.

"No, I'm serious!" Lucy called over the laughter, her face growing red. My sides hurt, but I couldn't stop.

"It's a good theory, Luc, but like, really, you have to admit it's totally ridiculous." Hayley placed a gentle hand on Lucy's shoulder, sending her a kind smile.

"It's true," she grumbled.

Hayley rolled her eyes. "So...anyway, I think that's, like, enough scary stories for one night," she redirected, turning to the group.

Everyone was quick to agree, and we opted to put on a movie. When it was over, I fell onto my bed, sleep taking me quickly.

"We're coming for you," Kathy said, stepping up to me and placing a small hand on my shoulder. "Just hold on."

"What are you talking about?" I asked, but before she could reply, an explosion sounded behind her. She spun as I watched students fly out of the falling wall across the way.

From the rubble, a deformed hand appeared. It curled around the wall, pulling a monstrous body forward.

I screamed and the blood-red eyes snapped toward me. The monster straightened, drawing into a human-like shape. It's back was bent and crooked, and a wing sprouted where a left arm should have been. It let out a grotesque roar and charged toward me.

I grabbed Kathy's hand and ran for it, my heart pumping as we flew through halls, a mixture of Sally Brown and Kent Wood. As we passed by a collapsed door, I spotted a small girl laying underneath.

"Help me!" she called, and I turned to head her way.

Kathy tugged on my arm, stopping me. "What are you doing?" she demanded, frantically looking back toward where the monster was heading our way.

"I can't just leave her there," I said, pulling against her. The little girl lifted her head and I looked into the shining golden eyes of my best friend, Hannah.

"You can't trust her. She's a traitor, Loran. Leave her to die," Kathy yelled.

"I don't care. I have to save her, she's my friend." My hand slipped from Kathy, and I turned to see the hurt on her face.

"You would leave me for her?" she asked as the monster appeared from the shadow, its claws slinking around her neck.

"No, no, don't touch her," I cried, grabbing at it, trying to pry them off.

"Loran," Hannah called behind me.

I turned my head to her to see another claw snaked around her neck.

"Stop, please stop!" I cried, clawing at the monster's face as it surrounded me.

"You will have to choose," its deep voice hissed.

"No," I begged, falling apart.

"Choose."

I looked between the two, turning from Hannah with a heavy heart.

"I'm sorry," I whispered as I grabbed Kathy's hand and ran.

The nightmare followed me into the morning. As the group prepared for the next day at the beach, I slipped a red pill.

Chapter 26

"Fall break!" Jaz shouted as she ran onto the beach, her arms in the air.

Zack chased after her, muttering about troublesome women, the scorching sun beating down on him. I laughed as she tripped, falling to the sand. He caught her just before she hit face first. With a gentle smile, he looked down as she turned in his arms and flashed him an exaggerated grin. He helped her to her feet and they waited for me to catch up.

Hayley waved at us from across the beach where she had already reserved a spot. Trudging across the warm sand, we joined her. The beach was mostly empty, but I knew from when they aired the Falcon and Kent Woods' fall breaks to recruit more kids, it would be packed in less than an hour. Getting a spot early was essential for later in the day when we just wanted to relax.

When I reached Hayley, I put my stuff on the pile with the others and she went about organizing it. Quickly and efficiently, a towel-covered area appeared with a large umbrella for shade and two coolers of food.

I pulled off my coverup, running into the water. It was freezing as I splashed into it, causing me to let out a scream. I jumped up and down, rubbing my hands on my arms, waiting for the heat bots to warm my suit as my teeth chattered. My friends laughed as Jaz ran to join me.

"Leave it to the foreigner to be the first in," she said through chattering teeth. "You know we wait till it warms up to swim, right?"

I laughed, flashing a grin. "Then why are you here?" I countered.

"Couldn't let you show me up." She grinned.

As the sun rose farther on the horizon and the water and bots warmed, we played. Kyle, Zack, and Shan joined us, gathering in a huddle a few feet away, whispering. They turned to us as one, each wearing a devious grin. I ran too late as Shan sprinted to me through the shallow water. I was underwater, feet away seconds later.

Swimming up, I gasped for air, shivering from the light breeze that passed by. Glaring playfully at Shan as he laughed, I swam over and grabbed his head, pushing it under.

Kyle cut my laugh short, dunking me from behind. The crisp saltwater surrounded me, filling my mouth. I came up sputtering and coughing, splashing him in the face as I spit out salt water. He chuckled, flashing a crooked smirk.

Jaz managed to escape for a moment, but Zack eventually caught her. He lifted her up and tossed her in the air. She went flying, her arms flailing, and landed a few feet away.

I laughed as she came up, splashing and glaring at Zack. Lucy was busy fighting Sam a few feet away. I spotted Dorothy on the beach with Bee and Dee. They were burying Dum up to his neck in sand.

The dunking battle continued. Allegiances were forgotten. Chaos reigned supreme. The number of people on the beach multiplied as the sun rose higher in the sky. Others swam around us, and a group of college boys invaded our group. As the afternoon drew on, I got out and pulled on my coverup, sitting down with Dorothy for lunch.

"You are one crazy gal," she said with a grin that I returned tenfold.

Kyle split a sandwich with me, and we passed around the sodas.

"You know, Dorothy, I've been meaning to ask, why do you have an accent and not your sister?"

"Well, ya see. When we were young, our Moms thought it would be best to send us to the Florida Falcons. Pops wanted us to go here. We were split up until middle school when Moms passed away. Pops brought me up here," she explained with a sad smile. That explained a lot, as the Falcons were known for their thick southern accents. "It was hard to lose my Moms the way we did, but I have to say 'm grateful. My sister is my world. I know 'm only four minutes older, but sometimes it feels like years."

I could see the depth of emotion Dorothy held for Bee as she watched her play across the beach. It felt bittersweet.

"I have to admit I'm jealous. I always wanted a sibling. But my parents were too busy to try again," I confessed with a sad smile.

Dorothy flashed me an understanding look. "I can't speak for the others. But Bee and I, well, we consider ya to be a sister. In the brief time ya have known us, ya've been kind to both of us, something that hasn't happened often in our lives, especially after my transfer. Like those times ya just stop and talk to Bee." She paused as Hayley walked by to grab a soda, starting again when we were alone. "Yar support in cross-country, including her in warm-ups. Well, it meant a lot to her, still does. It means a lot to me too. All this to say that ya're a good friend and a kind person. Bee and I would love to be yar honorary sisters till ya don't want us." Dorothy's speech caught me off guard and before I realized it, tears were falling down my face.

Quickly, I wiped them away and gave her an enormous smile. "I'm honored." I hoped she could hear the sincerity in my voice. When she sent me a wide smile, my heart filled. We talked about the struggles of transferring as we soaked in the sun. As I watched my friends play, I enjoyed the brief moments of peace that the break provided.

I stood and caught a stray beach ball before it could hit Dorothy, tossing it back to its owners as a group of boys passed by, playfully shoving each other, and laughing.

I watched them, surprised, as I spotted Tom inside their ranks. He was smiling broadly, his pale skin shining in the sun. I was shocked by the defined muscles of his arms and stomach. From up the beach, someone shouted, a small girl ran down the sand, chasing her hat flying away in the breeze.

I moved to grab it, but before I could stop it, it flew into Tom's group. The girl followed, stumbling into him, making them both fall to the ground. Shouts rang out. Kyle beat me to the girl. He quickly had her up and on her feet, dusting her off and checking her over. His movements were soft and kind, concern in his gaze.

"Are you all right?" he asked gently.

"Y-yes." She sniffled. "My hat."

Kyle shooshed her gently, wiping a tear from her cheek.

"We'll find it." I quickly went to the edge of the water where her hat had fallen and grabbed it, turning to see Tom stand, dusting himself off.

"You need to watch where you're going," he said. His face was kind, but there was an undercurrent to his tone that made me shiver.

"*You* need to leave," Kyle snapped, shoving Tom away.

He staggered backward, clumsily.

As Kyle made to advance, the girl placed a hand on him, stopping him. "Please, don't fight, big brother," she begged.

He inspected her as I approached them, his eyes softening. "I'm sorry. Are you sure you're okay?"

She nodded quickly.

Tom slunk away before Kyle could turn back to him, his friends following.

I watched them go, worried. "Here," I said, handing the little girl her hat. She gave me a wide smile as she put it on.

"You're a little young to be on this beach, aren't you?" Kyle asked.

"Violet!" a voice called. A tall girl similar in build to the one beside us was running our way. "Oh, there you are." She pulled the little girl into her arms. "Don't ever run off like that again. I was so scared."

The little girl wiggled in her grip. "I'm fine," she whined. "Big brother was here to watch out for me."

The older girl stopped smothering her sister, looking up to see Kyle and me. Her face turned red. "Oh." She stood, gripping the little girl's hand. "Um, thank you."

Instead of flashing her a cocky smirk or wink like I expected, Kyle smiled softly. "It's really no big deal," he dismissed.

The girl's blush deepened. "W-we better get going." She turned, dragging her sister along.

"Thank you, Lightning," the little girl chimed, waving as she was pulled away. I watched her go with an open mouth.

Kyle chuckled beside me. "Let me guess. You're not used to people just knowing you by sight?" he asked.

I looked at him, shaking my head as I tried to take comfort from the squeezing of my PortMed. *Not since my days as Blades,* I thought. Instead, I said, "Not really, no." I played bashful as my heart calmed.

Kyle gave me a gentle smile and I was surprised by the kindness in his eyes. "You'll get used to it." He stopped, shrugging. "That, or you'll hate every moment and play it off like it's no big deal."

I inspected him, seeing an unexpected vulnerability in his eyes. "Is that what you do?" I was surprised to see a blush on his dark cheeks.

"Naw," he said dismissively as the arrogant boy I was familiar with took the place of the one I wanted to be friends with. "I've always been this awesome. It's only right that I embrace it."

"Uh-huh," I said noncommittally. "Well then, great one, I think it's time for dinner. You coming?"

Most of the beach was settling down to relax until the Holo-work show. The atmosphere was calm as the sunset.

As I lay down on my bag, I felt it vibrate. Shocked, I open it, pulling out my phone.

Chris.

The caller ID read loud and clear. My heart skipped a beat, and I looked around. Everyone was preoccupied, no one noticed my sudden change in attitude. I made excuses to leave and skittered off. Once I was out of earshot, hidden behind a nearby cabana, I answered the phone.

"Hello," I whispered, just in case. "Where the Glitch have you been?"

"Loran, is that you?" Chris's hushed voice replied. He sounded winded and spoke as if he was in a hurry. "We need to talk."

"AI's above, we do. Where have you been?" I demanded.

"I need to tell you something. I need to tell you that...well...Listen, we can't be together anymore."

With those simple words, my world shattered. My knees locked up and my hands trembled. "Chris? What are you saying?"

"It's time we faced the facts. There will never be an us, can never be an us. Pretending otherwise is childish."

My pain was replaced with anger at his indifferent tone. "What are you talking about? We discussed this! We agreed it didn't matter. What happened? Why are you pulling the plug and after ignoring me for weeks!"

"Nothing happened..." He trailed off.

"Liar! What's going on Chris? I know you're lying!"

He sighed, the sound brittle across the speakers. "I'm telling the truth, we can't be together..." He paused. "But it's not because of The Picking. Things are happening, Loran, bad things. Everything's going to change. People think it will be another war." He sounded tired and my anger depleted slightly.

"What are you talking about?" A familiar squeeze did nothing to help my shot nerves.

"It's complicated, and you're in the middle of it. Listen, I'm trying to protect you." His voice was hard again. Yet it was lacking the anger from before.

"Whatever it is, I'm willing to face it with you. Just tell me," I begged.

"I'm sorry, but no. I'm going to figure this out on my end, and you don't need to be involved. I'm making this decision for you. We are done."

"Chris—"

The phone *clicked*. The *beeping* of the dial tone blasted in my ears. My legs gave out. I hit the sand hard. The phone slipped from my hand, landing somewhere below. Around me, the world lost all color and sound. My heart beat violently against my chest, daring to break through.

Did that just happen?

My body ached in ways I didn't know it could. I had never thought about the end. Never imagined there would be an end, even after the last few weeks.

Now it's over.

We will be together forever. I promise. I won't let anything get in our way, he had promised.

Why did he go back on his promise?

I put my head onto my knees, grabbing at my hair as I heard screams fill the air around me. I didn't feel the pain as I lost a few strands. All our memories flooded me, hurting more with each passing second.

What was Chris talking about? What change? Was the world tilting?

I vaguely heard footsteps behind me, but I was too busy trying to keep myself together to care, forcing back the pink in my vision that warned me I was starting to lose control. *Not here, not now.*

"It's going to be okay," said Hayley, kneeling next to me. I didn't know how she found me, but I was grateful she had. She put her arm around me, and I cried even harder.

How did it come to this?

My world had transformed in a few months, then shattered in a matter of seconds. Hayley continued to comfort me until my tears ran dry.

"It's getting late. We should probably meet up with the others."

I nodded and rubbed my eyes raw. As I sat on the towels, I tried to hide my face, but it was useless. Jaz exchanged a look with Hayley. She nodded, giving my knee a squeeze. Knowing she tried to prepare me somehow made the ache even worse. Lucy offered a small gesture of understanding as she passed me a piece of chocolate.

We sat silently, the surrounding chatter dying as the sky lit with Holo-works. Each bang and shatter of color accompanied the shattering of my heart.

Chapter 27

The world seemed to lack color. The vibrant Monday sun shining through my window felt harsh instead of comforting. I could hear Dorothy in my kitchen, fiddling with the mugs.

"I hope ya like coco," she called out.

I sniffled, grabbing another tissue before I replied. "Yeah." My voice broke.

Minutes later, she was at my bedroom door, a steaming cup in her hands. Looking me over, her eyes were full of concern. "Here, take this." She handed me the mug and sat down on the bed beside me.

I took a sip, my tears falling into the drink.

"Do ya want to talk about it?"

I shook my head, and she nodded.

"Alright." She stayed with me until I cried myself to sleep.

I woke up early for the first day of the new term and pulled on my best outfit. Looking in the mirror, I tried to smile. *I am my own person. No boy defines me,* I thought over and over, trying to convince myself not to cry. My eyes were puffy and red from two days of crying, and no amount of makeup or MEDs could hide it.

Haley was waiting for me outside my door, and I forced a smile. She smiled sadly back and put her arm around me protectively. Neither she nor Jaz had pushed me into talking, and I appreciated the gesture.

Jaz met us on the first floor as we walked out together to meet the group, the mood somber and awkward. Hayley and Kyle had history class with me, so I followed silently behind them as we headed to the building. We picked seats in the back of the small room as people filed in around us, chatting as they caught up after the brief break.

"Hello class, my name is Mr. Connor, and this is History Three," said a middle-aged man as he walked in. "In this class we will learn, we will discuss, and we will have fun, as long as you don't disrupt others and respect each other. Understand?" His eyes roamed the room.

"Understood," said the class in response, and I nodded.

He sat down and leaned back in his chair, grabbing a ball from his desk. Mr. Connor took a spin and tossed the ball to a boy in the front row. He caught it with ease and tossed it to his friend.

As it made its way through the room, Mr. Connor continued, "Good. We are going to jump right into the lesson. We will talk about your term projects next week." The ball passed overhead. "Today's topic, The Picking. Now you all know what it is. The seniors will take part this year, beginning your new life with that special someone. Therefore, I think it's important to discuss its history and how it works. First question, how did The Picking start?"

A hand shot up. Mr. Connor acknowledged it and a boy in the front row stood.

"They instituted The Picking because of the divorce rate in the old America in the early 2000s," he said proudly.

Mr. Connor gave him a gentle smile. "That's right. In 2035, the divorce rate in America was at ninety percent. People's view of love and relationships were almost nonexistent. Casual flings and hookups were prominent. You might think it wouldn't be a problem, but it sent America trillions of dollars into debt." Mr. Connor clicked a button and a Holo-screen popped from the floor. Images and articles from that time swirled in its light, filling the room.

"People grew violent, lashing out at their lovers. The crime rate shot up. To protect its people, the government enforced a new law: The Act of Separation, which made divorce illegal. Of course, this did not settle well. What if you got stuck with a dangerous partner? What if they paired you with someone you weren't attracted to? The list went on and on."

A kid in the back coughed, covering what sounded like the word *idiots*, making the class laugh.

Mr. Connor smiled before he continued. "Despite the protests, the law stayed in place. As time passed, they worked out the kinks, but it wasn't perfect. Now that people were stuck with each other, marriage rates dropped or ended in disaster. After a mass murder in 2045, when an abusive husband burned down his lover's building, the government stepped in. From then on, they decided whom people married. This way, everyone would have a perfect match." Mr. Connor stood from his chair, grabbing the ball thrown at him midair, passing through the hologram.

Some boys cheered at his skill, and he did a slight bow. I cracked a smile at his antics.

A headline filled the room. "As you all know, this didn't work out at first. The Prank of Holland Road is a good example. So many people were paired wrong the system had to be shut down. The Picking was put on the back burner during The America's War in 2053, when we united with the nation once known as Canada against countries in South America allied with the Chinese and Russian forces. Our population declined after the bombings of 2056, leaving the country in shambles."

Images of said bombings flashed before us, sending shivers down my spine.

"Then a man named Kent Wood at *A Better Future for Tomorrow* came up with a solution. Two years after the war, he discovered by compiling data about a person, from their social life to their grades and dreams, he could match people perfectly. It was quickly and widely accepted and is still implemented today. So, how does The Picking work?" he paused, smiling. "Well, I'll show you." Mr. Connor pulled up *The Board for A Better Tomorrow* site and turned to us.

Excited buzzing filled the air as a pit formed in my stomach.

"Now I need two volunteers." He scoured the room and his eyes fell on me. "You and you." He pointed to a boy two rows in front of me. "Names please."

I felt my blood run cold, watching a small boy in the second row stand up.

"Raphael Montez 5559," he said.

"Lovota Miller 168," I replied, praying I had gotten the numbers right.

Mr. Connor plugged in the names, and I watched as our data was pulled up.

"Now this is just an example, the pool for Pairings coming only from the students at this school. Don't take the results too seriously."

Slowly charts, paragraphs, and images popped up on our screen. I let out a breath as I saw no mention of The Shadow. I watched as Lovota's life played before my eyes in pictures of sports events and paragraphs. Like most students, her familiar freckled face disappeared from record once she hit middle school.

"Now the government starts by taking certain things into consideration. First, they look at the subject's rankings. They often pair people in the same ranking together."

Lovota's number three ranking popped on the screen. Raphael's was five, a more common rank, but low for Kent Wood. I received unwanted looks from my classmates.

"After that, they eliminate."

A list appeared, so long I could barely read it.

"Next, they look at the person's personal life, what they like to do, what clubs they're in, so on."

A list of about half of Lovota's clubs popped up and small boxes next to each name on the list appeared. Words scrolled quickly. The list shrunk.

"Each one of you has a device in your head called The Monitor. Invented in 2060 by *MegaPlex Technologies*, it's located right above your frontal lobe. It receives signals about your heart rate, health, even memories. As you know, it also helps doctors know when to distribute the MEDs, and uses the PortMed to notify you if disaster strikes internally. The government takes these readings into account, looking at the situations that make your pulse quicken, your mind wander. They assess these situations carefully, considering what type of people make you nervous or scared. Then they eliminate again."

The screen flashed, showing numbers across the room, names passing too fast to see, the list shrinking. I could make out the twenty or so names and began reading. My heart raced as I recognized three.

"Finally, they interview your friends, family, teachers, and you. They learn about how others see you to complete the picture they have. They compile all this info together and gather a list of the top ten people for you."

I saw Kyle's head jerk, along with some others in the room; a small girl in the corner was especially eager. My heart pounded as the list continued to shrink, the three names not going away.

"After the interviews, they bring it down to two people. They look at other lists to see who else was paired with your chosen two, then compare your matching with theirs to see who's more compatible."

If it was possible anymore to die from shock, I would have. Tom and Kyle's names remained as I watched Shan blink from view.

"After all that work, they choose your other half. Then comes Picking Day."

The names faded as a video played and Holo-graphic boys walked the room all around us, approaching doors and resting their hands on them. I could relate to the worry and anxiety I saw as my world continued to crumble around me. Then they turned the handles.

"After all this, it takes only a few seconds to meet your Mate."

Doors opened and girls seated in comfy chairs appeared around us, some immediately rushing out of them to hug their new Mate, others stayed seated, nervous, or surprised.

The video died, and the room was left in darkness.

It's just an example. I'm not Lovota, I chanted in my head, trying to take comfort in the words, ignoring the fact that despite her rank, Lovota and I were eerily similar. *I won't end up with either of them. I can't.*

"For some, marked with a black necklace, a Mate is not found, and they are forced to wait another year. Others are given the option of sitting out, allowing their chosen to go with a person who will be more compatible. These people are sorted into the next years Picking, marked by a blood-red necklace in the meantime. Those who abstain from the program permanently are respected and marked in silver. However, they are expected to hold jobs that the rest of society can't or doesn't want to perform because of familial duties."

The lights flashed on, making me feel like I was waking from a bad dream as I blinked, looking around.

I met Mr. Connor's eyes and he watched me with a calculating gaze. "The Picking makes pairings that are completely accurate. There hasn't been a false pairing in over forty years. For many, even some of you in this room, it can be difficult as you are currently with another partner. Some couples get matched others don't, but let me assure you, it will make you happy. Questions?"

Hands shot up. We spent the rest of the time discussing aspects of The Picking. The bell rang as he finished, the class filing out. Everyone was chatting about the results, speculating on who would be with who. All I wanted to do was find a bathroom to throw up in.

"So, you're a number three rank," said a boy from our class as he walked up beside me. I nodded, continuing to look straight ahead, ignoring my anxiety spike as Kyle glared at him.

"Why do you want to know?" said Hayley. As word of my breakup spread, boys had come out of the woodwork, desperate to be a shoulder to cry on.

The boy looked at her with too wide of a smile. "Hey cheer captain, what's up?" he asked, trying to divert her wrath.

"I said, why do you want to know?" Hayley stalked toward him.

"Never mind." The boy walked away, defeated and shaken.

"You would think by now they would know," whispered Kyle to Hayley as they walked in front of me, assuming I couldn't hear them. "I've tried to make it clear."

"You know they won't listen. That would totally require an ounce of self-preservation."

I blocked out their conversation and retreated into myself, alone, and lost. Thoughts of Tom, Kyle, and Chris filled my head. *Why do all my matches leave me feeling sick?*

I was snapped from my musings by a sharp pain in my shoulder. Tumbling to the ground from the force of the hit, I tried to catch myself before I smacked the concrete. Gravel and sand dug into my palms as I landed.

Chapter 28

Faintly, I heard Hayley snapping at someone as I blinked back stars. With a grunt, I pushed myself up, spinning to face my attacker and tuning into the shouting match Hayley was having with them.

"You're either stupid or naïve! Knowing you, though, I'd say it's the latter," snapped Lilith. Her sharp long nails sat on her narrow hips. As I made eye contact with her, thin eyebrows pinched downward over angry eyes. "What are you looking at, Browner?"

Instantly, my heart jumped into my throat. "What?" I choked out through the lump, feeling a squeeze through the fog. Fear threatened to overwhelm me, sending me into a panic attack.

She sneered, her eyes turning darker. "You heard me. I'm not sure how you're getting away with it or what lies you told everyone else, but you're obviously a Browner."

"Shut up, Lilith. You're just jealous 'cause Hayley doesn't have time for your clingy Holo-ass anymore," Kyle said, stepping next to me. This diverted Lilith's attention for a moment before she stopped and looked around. I followed her eyes, noticing the crowd that had gathered in the hall. People whispered to each other with wary looks.

When her eyes snapped to mine with a vicious glee, I knew it wasn't going to be good. "You always were one to go for anything on two legs, Kyle, but I never thought you would stoop so low. You all must realize how suspicious she is, right?" She turned her attention to the crowd, calling for support. "She came here in the middle of the year, claiming to be from some small school that's in the same district as our major rival. She immediately makes friends with the most popular students in our sector. Not only that, but the same ones in charge of dealing with attacks. She pulls you in further by claiming an imaginary boyfriend has broken up with her, begging for sympathy. I bet you've told her our secrets. I bet she's taking them back home and destroying us from the inside out."

Every point Lilith made was like a stab to the heart. It would be hard to deny the truth.

I looked around the crowd, seeing many heads nodding along, and it hit me. I'd been naïve. Despite lying through my teeth, I thought I could make friends and live a new life without consequences. The moments of guarded suspicion from my friends flashed before my eyes. *Have they ever truly trusted me?* A glance to my right confirmed my thought as Hayley watched my reactions with calculation, as if she had been waiting for that moment.

How many people have been watching me, waiting for me to mess up? Waiting for an excuse to attack. I have to try to stop this now!

"I'm not sure where you got all this info unless you've been watching me, but I think you have been misinformed. Though all the points you made are true, you put quite an evil twist on it," I said, stepping forward, my chin held high.

"Oh, really?" Lilith's voice was sharp as she approached me.

Kyle tried to step between us, but I put a hand on his shoulder, stopping him. I couldn't let him protect me; it would only put fuel on the fire.

"All the things you just accused me of are suicidal at best. At worst, they are the most pathetic attempt at spying I've ever seen," I said.

Kyle stepped back as I stepped forward.

"How do you explain it then?" she asked, our faces almost touching as I snapped back.

"Simple. You saw me the day I arrived. Even then I could see Kyle's right. Hayley didn't want you there and you reacted like a child would, throwing a tantrum. You know, as dorm mother, her job is to greet everyone and help them feel at home. From there, I was lucky enough that she befriended me and help me adjust." I pushed forward, causing her to stumble back. "Unlike you, she and the others have been willing to give me a chan—"

"Please. You really believe that? You're more stupid than I thought," Lilith interrupted, making me pause in my advance. "Unlike you, I've known Hayley for years. Before you came around, *we* were best friends. She does nothing without a reason. She only befriended you to monitor you" She poked my chest with a sharp nail. "But obviously on the way, she and the others have been tricked. It's about time someone spoke up. We all know who you are, so stop trying to pretend."

I shrunk back as if slapped. "You don't know what you're talking about..." When neither of my friends spoke up, my heart fell. I tried to keep the tears from spilling out. I wasn't the only one who noticed the lack of defense, and the whispers in the crowd turned to a subtle roar.

Lilith leaned down to whisper in my ear. "Your lies can't save you now, Browner. You can bet I won't let this go. I will make sure everyone sees you as the liar you are. You know the punishment for traitors. I look forward to watching you burn." Her words made my blood run cold as tears fell down my face. "*Loran.*"

"How?" I choked out.

"You should really make sure a room is empty before you go talking to teachers about sensitive information." Her smile was sharp as she pulled back. "You never know who might be listening." There was a commotion in the crowd before I could ask why she didn't just tell everyone my name.

Over her shoulder, I saw Shan shove his way through along with Sally and Zack. One look at my face and Shan's confusion morphed into a deep anger. "What are you doing here, Lilith?" His voice boomed around us louder than I'd ever heard.

Immediately, Lilith's face changed. With a twist, she turned to him, stepping beside me. It was hard to miss the adoration in her eyes as she looked at him.

"Shan," she said, her voice octaves higher than before. She almost skipped to him, clinging onto his arm. The lack of her presence caused me to stumble and fall to the ground. The longing in Shan's eyes as he watched her had me breaking all over again.

I didn't care how bad I looked as worry overtook me and screams filled my ears. The PortMed worked overtime as I forced them out of my head, wishing I had my pills.

"I was just putting this little sneak in her place." Lilith shot a glare at me.

Even through my tears, I could tell Shan wasn't thrilled. With a shake, he had her off his arm, stumbling away. The shock on her face reflected how I felt as the tender look in his eyes morphed to disgust. "You haven't changed one bit," he spat at her.

The hurt on Lilith's face was replaced with fury. "So, she's got her little claws in you too. I thought you, of all people, would know better, but it seems you're still the same sad little boy I dumped months ago."

Shan flinched at her jab, but his glare remained. The crowd was eating it up. "I don't know what you've been saying, but we both know it's all lies. After all, that's all you do. I bet you've been waiting for an opportunity to attack and accuse her in front of everyone. I bet you twisted the story in the worst way, making yourself look like the good guy while she burns." Shan shoved past a seething Lilith to me. With gentle eyes, he squatted down, giving me a forlorn smile. "H-hey there." He brushed the tears from my face.

"Hi," I choked out through a sob. He grabbed my hands, stopping as I hissed in pain.

Shan paused, turning them over, seeing the gravel-filled scrapes. The fury returned to his eyes, but he gently helped me up, ignoring Lilith's ranting as he did. Once I was on my feet and stabilized, he turned on her.

"I think you've done enough. You have one minute to turn around and leave. If you stay here, I won't be responsible for what happens."

Fear filled Lilith's eyes. With one last glare, she pushed her way through the crowd. The moment she disappeared, Shan spun around, his ire directed at Kyle and Hayley who were still standing behind me. "And you two. I can't talk to you right now. How could you just leave Lovota to deal with Lilith alone? You both know how she can be."

"Hey dude, you don't know what happened. So don't jump down my throat!" Kyle snapped back, finally finding his voice.

"From what I can see, you were letting her take the brunt of Lilith's anger." Shan advanced.

Kyle took a step forward. "I told you not to—"

"Both of you stop. This is not something to discuss in public." Sally's sharp voice cut off the impending argument.

Both Kyle and Shan took a step back, looking around. People in the crowd looked guilty and quickly dispersed.

I knew the incident would be all over school by the end of the day. All I could do was pray people didn't take what Lilith said to heart and dig deeper.

Kyle and Shan exchanged glares before Shan turned to me and gently pulled me to him. "L-let's get you home." His voice was soft, his breath a little ragged as he realized how close he was holding me, and a steady blush rose up his face.

Sally walked on my other side as Shan cradled me under his arm. I was left at my dorm, the others making excuses to leave. I watched them walk away and headed to my room to grab a red booster pill.

"Good morning." I forced a smile as I met my friends for class the next day.

An awkward silence followed for a moment before Jaz piped up. "Good morning. Sleep well?"

I grimaced. "Not reall—"

"Let's get to class." Hayley's tone was hard as she turned and headed out before I could finish.

I watched her go, feeling defeated and sad. All the progress we'd made was gone and I didn't know how to get it back.

Days passed in a blur. I felt aimless and alone, even with my friends nearby. Kyle was a silent observer, and Shan, the only one to come to my defense, was a constant shadow. Jaz still supported me, but made it clear she wasn't going to take sides between her best friends. The others agreed with her, still warm but refusing to get in the middle. Lecture classes flew by in a blur and before I knew it, we were nearing the ninth of November, Unity Day.

"You guys look great. Like always," said Kyle as I walked outside with the others. I watched his eyes roam Hayley before they landed on me with a glint. Shan caught my eyes before he looked away, blushing.

"Thanks," the girls all said together, the tension breaking as Jaz shouted jinks and we laughed.

Zack took her hand, and Garret swept Sally off her feet. I cooed as Dorothy's date gazed at her, struggling to speak, receiving a light shove from Bee for it.

We headed to South Park, joining a giant group filing through the woods. As we neared the mansion, I noticed it was notably less crowded than before. A single large door was propped open, keeping out most of the crisp winter air. We stopped in a line waiting in front of a small booth at the entrance.

"Name please," asked a boy behind the booth. Several students dressed in suits stood beside him.

"Kyle, party of sixteen," Kyle answered.

"Follow me," said a girl with menus next to him.

I did, passing multiple tables of people along the way. Instead of heading behind the stairs we went to the left and down a wide gold painted hall.

She opened a door to a room decorated with pumpkins and streamers. Five large circular tables sat within, two of them already occupied. I inhaled deeply, smiling contently at the smell of sweet potatoes and turkey.

"My lady," Kyle said, pulling out my chair as I sat cautiously, wondering why he was being so sweet.

"Thank you," I said. Shan sat down on my right, Kyle on my left.

The table was full of lively conversation and my somber mood began to brighten. I ate so much turkey I felt like exploding, but not even that could get my spirits down. Everything about the atmosphere was light and playful, something that had been missing for a while.

"Wow, you're like a bottomless pit," teased Kyle with a laugh, and I punched him on the arm.

"You need to work on your moves," Shan laughed next to me, making my heart flutter. It was so good to be with my friends like before, feeling somewhat normal.

Chapter 29

"No way, it's her!" someone exclaimed.

I turned to see a young girl pointing at me. With a shriek, she ran over. "I can't believe it's you. Can I have your autograph?" She pulled out her PortMed and flipped a paper toward me.

It hovered in my face as I processed her words. I was still adjusting to the fame my third win in cross-country had earned me.

"Hey, we're eating here," snapped Kyle, putting his arm around me.

"No, it's fine," I said. I waved my hand over it, a Holo-pen appearing. Grabbing it, I signed.

"Thank you so much! You know you're my hero," she gushed. "I want to be just like you."

I nodded awkwardly. One of her friends grabbed her hand, dragging her away while muttering apologies.

"You okay?" asked Shan.

I nodded again with pinched lips. "Yeah, I'm just not used to this type of attention."

"You are handling it remarkably well," Kyle complimented. I smiled at him gratefully.

"So," said Zack, pushing back his chair and holding his hand out to Jaz. "I think it's time for us to go. We have a Unity Day after party to attend."

I filed out of the room, the boys leading us to the back of South Park. Passing by more groups eating on the dance floors, I ignored the murmurs that followed.

"Okay, close your eyes," said Kyle once we reached the oh-so-familiar game room, and I obeyed. Someone grabbed my hand and led me through the door.

When we stopped, I heard Shan speak. "Open."

I did, gasping at the sight. The room was covered in Unity Day decorations, making it look like someone puked up orange and black, yet I found it beautiful. There were various games lying around and multiple couches to relax on.

"Hey, are we late?"

I turned around to see a group of kids Garret hung out with from his Spanish class in the doorway.

"No, you're right on time," said Garret as they walked in.

"Let's party!" called Bee.

Within minutes, the party was in full swing. I made a turkey with a caramel apple, feathers, and a stick. With a grin at Shan, I put it in a flowerpot next to a combat helmet; he smiled back before blushing and walking away.

A girl from Garret's group laughed at me saying, something in Spanish, the immersive class requiring they speak the language whenever they were together. Since my main study language had been Chinese, I could only catch a few words, nodding and chuckling awkwardly to her. She smiled at my embarrassment and walked away.

As I finished my second apple, this one to eat, Hayley grabbed my arm and dragged me over to the couches. I spotted Shan across the room, talking to a girl I didn't know. He was blushing, his hand rubbing the back of his neck as she let out a giggle.

I ignored the feeling twisting in my gut as my PortMed squeezed and the MEDs got to work.

"I think it's totally time to play a little truth or dare," Hayley announced as she pulled me forward, settling me on one of the couches.

"I am not—" I started.

"I'll tell the group all about that time you lost your pants at the zoo." She stopped me with a whisper in my ear. The smirk on her face was devious as she pulled away.

I glanced nervously around at the group watching us, regretting sharing that story. "Don't you dare," I hissed low enough only she could hear.

Hayley looked around. "Kyle—" I pasted my hand to her mouth, stopping her before she could start.

Kyle looked at us from his spot on the other couch, his eyebrows raised in question. I shook my head, telling him it was nothing.

When he turned away, I whipped my head back to glare at Hayley and pulled my hand away. "Fine, but only if you agree to never speak of that again."

She split into a grin and stuck out her hand. "Deal. Since you're so against it, you totally go first. Truth or dare." I made eye contact with Shan across the room. He gave me a small smile, turning back to the girl and my heart fell.

"Dare," I said. Hayley smiled and turned to the girls in our group. They whispered among themselves, then turned to me.

"Alright," said Hayley. "I dare you to go into the closet and wait until we let you out."

I sighed again and stood, making my way to it. "Remind me to never let you drag me to a party again," I muttered as she locked me in. *At least it's not as dark as last time.* A faint light shone through the base of the door. I sat in the corner and closed my eyes.

Minutes ticked by. I wondered if I'd ever be let out when the door opened. Standing, I dusted off my pants and prepared to leave, but it closed before I could look up. With a sigh, I slid back down, my head in my hands.

"Great," I groaned to myself, and heard a laugh.

"Thanks, glad to know I'm enjoyable company." My heart fluttered at the sound of Kyle's voice and my head shot up. It felt like a lifetime since we had been in that closet together.

I watched him sit in the corner opposite mine. "Do you remember the last time we were here?" he asked, mirroring my thoughts as he crossed his legs.

"Yeah, I was just thinking about that," I said cautiously, remembering all that had gone wrong that night.

"You know what I said that night still stands. I'm into you Lovota, and I would like to get to know you on a more intimate level. We are a perfect Pairing after all."

"Stop right there." I put my hand up as he tried to advance. "Not too long ago, you were letting me fall to the ground as Lilith tore into me. I'm not stupid, Kyle, I can see how you treat me. I don't know what you're playing at with this lover boy act, but I would appreciate it if you could stop."

Kyle sat back, his eyes calculating. "You know, the day you landed that first punch on me, it was in that moment I realized I was doomed." The subject change had me reeling. "Very few people can hold their own against me, let alone land a hit. The last time someone nicked me outside of a game was Shan. We had just met, and he took my toy. It was a silly thing really, but I pushed him and in return, he punched me right in the jaw." He let out a laugh and I caught a peek of the boy on the beach, the one that made my heart soften. "It worked out then, but ever since I have made it my mission to hold everyone at a distance, just in case."

His cockiness returned. "Then you came in, blazing. The truth is, I don't think I can trust you. I can tell you're dangerous, yet like a moth, I can't resist getting close enough to be burned." The cocky boy fell away. "You're being blunt, so let's be blunt."

I felt a familiar squeeze as he looked me over, hatred and desire in his eyes.

"You are nothing like the girls I grew up with. Strong but timid, smart but naïve." He hesitated. "It feels like an act. Since your breakup, things have been off. There have been more attacks than ever from Sally Brown, yet they are mild compared to their normal MO."

I tried to hide my shock at the news. By the way the girls talked at the sleepover, I'd thought they were done.

"I'm sorry to hear that, but I don't know how that's my fault," I countered. "It's not like anyone has told me this before."

He eyed me up and down. "You would think so, wouldn't you? But I just can't shake the feeling there is more to the story, more to you."

"I'm nothing special," I argued. "Just some girl from an alternate school that is too far below your high and mighty gaze to be noticed."

He winced at my tone, his gaze growing soft. "I really hope that's true."

Before we could continue, the door opened, light flooding in. I blinked rapidly as Hayley looked down at us.

She turned to at Kyle, communicating silently before her eyes fell to me. "Let's go," she said with a forced smile, and I took her offered hand without question.

"Do you ever wonder what life was like back then?" Shan's voice was quiet, and I looked up, my humming stopping as I put away my calculus project. The lecture hall was emptying, most people rushing from it to enjoy the sunny Tuesday.

"What do you mean?" I asked.

He looked up at me, a blush rising on his cheeks. "Before The Picking. You know. Dating someone and knowing that it could end in more. That they would choose to be with you without outside influences."

I searched his eyes, feeling warm as they stormed. I reached out to him hesitantly, grabbing his hand. His blush intensified, but he didn't pull away.

"I think it's a nice thought," I said.

The brush of his lips was soft against mine, barely a passing taste before they were gone. My face flamed, and I looked away with a cough, not letting go of his hand as my heart filled with warmth.

"The great school war of 2070," began Mr. Connor as I sat down for class on Friday. "Who can tell me about it?"

A girl at the front raised her hand.

When he called on her, she stood. "It started with Sandy Village and Florida Falcons," she said. "Two students, a boy and a girl from rival schools, fell in love. It was forbidden, and they had to sneak away to meet in secret. Luckily for them, this was before the schools had strict traveling policies. When their friends found out, they ripped them apart and declared war, claiming that they had sent the other as a spy. The war lasted two years, ending when the girl was shot down trying to save the life of her enemy. After that, the boy killed himself. The two schools stepped in, held a funeral for them, and declared peace in their honor."

Mr. Connor nodded in approval. "That's about it in a nutshell. We are going to look at it a little closer." He clicked a button, and the room dimmed, the Hologram in the floor activating. I caught his eyes past the image and was surprised by his hard gaze. I was instantly on edge.

"Now let's start at the beginning. In 2028, the universal school system was founded. Education in America was dropping further and further in the rankings. So, to solve this problem, the original board of education was demolished. They decided having many small schools with too many students per teacher wasn't working. To fix this, they split the US into seven equal parts based on population."

A map of the United States popped up and the pit in my stomach grew.

"In these School Districts, or SD's, one to two schools were established along with one or more private or alternative schools."

The map zoomed in, highlighting the areas he talked about.

"SD1 comprises of one school near Alabama, Florida, and Georgia, The Florida Falcons. After some time, a private school joined the district, Bankings."

The world around me swam with swamps and beaches before dropping us in the middle of The Falcon campus. Stucco buildings connected by glass canopies towered over me.

"SD2 is small, with one school in Michigan and Indiana, Trident."

The map zoomed out and flew to the next one. The small half-underground buildings and school boats of Trident surrounded me.

"SD3 covered most of the old states. They created two schools, Mesa Verde in New Jersey, Delaware, and Maryland, and Liberty in New York and Massachusetts, abolishing them after The America's war. With casualties reaching the millions, the population wasn't large enough to support two schools. They moved the students and school to Virginia and Kentucky, an area now called Water High."

A campus filled with glass buildings comprised of the most beautiful shade of gray-blue filled the space, the architecture making me feel like I was back on a campus from the 1800s.

"SD4 has one school, even though a voucher was sent in for two. A compromise allowed a small private and alternate school to be located nearby the main school, Gelfied Prep and The Honeybees. The public school in Nebraska and Iowa holds Michel Thomas."

Brick buildings and lawns featuring the newest in technology swirled around us.

"SD5 comprises of one school and two alternative schools, Plainfield High and Tenfold. Most of the public school is in Arizona and New Mexico with the graduate school in west Texas, Sandy Village."

Sandy-looking domes and tall stucco buildings with great balconies were intimidating in their reach.

"SD6 was one of the few allowed to house two private and alternate schools. One private school in Aspen, Colorado, Honesty Prep, the other in Agency Montana, Crystal Lakes. The first alternative school in Vail, Willow Creek, and another in Pueblo, New Dawn. Sally Brown is the most spread-out school. Each grade crosses at least one of the original state boundaries. The elementary through middle schools in and near Idaho and Montana, and the high school through Ph.D. in Utah, Wyoming, and Colorado."

The familiar campuses of Sally Brown sped around us, filling me with longing and dread. Mr. Connor gave me a pointed look as a scream filled my ears. *Shut up.* I tried to drown them out.

"Here in SD7, we have one school, located in the upper part of California and most of Oregon. All the surrounding states were integrated into this section. Now we reach into the High Canadian region."

Mr. Connor pulled up a map showing us the dividing lines of the old states. The room grew cold as he looked me up and down with a calculating gaze.

"As time went on, the population changed, and schools grew or shrank. To accommodate the students, they adopted a boarding school structure in 2045. Before the war of 2070, parents often visited on the weekends and students left to see families in the summer. But for security reasons, those privileges were restricted for the sake of the children." The tilting world didn't righten as my PortMed squeezed. *I need a golden pill now.*

Chapter 30

"Yes, that's a good point, Klara," Mr. Connor said, finally looking away from me.

It didn't make me feel better.

"Though the schools were supposed to be equal, they didn't stay that way. Some parents sent their athletic children to certain districts, while others kept their academic children in the highest-ranking ones. The founding of the *Medical Evaluation of Diseases Society*, or MEDS in 2047, was the beginning of the end for the rivalries."

A boy in the back row cheered when he saw the blue speckled medical symbol, the image of MEDS, making everyone but me snicker. For a moment, breathing was hard as my hands twitched for a pill I didn't have.

"With the release of a pill that solved both obesity and mental illnesses, the world changed," Mr. Connor continued. "MEDs increased people's health, overall physical appearance, and ability. The newly enhanced children changed at a rapid pace, their behavior volatile at best, deadly at worst, escalating the tension."

I avoided looking at the images of the failed tests as pink flooded my vision. *Why am I panicking? I need to get a grip now before it's too late.*

Mr. Connor watched me intensely. "Then in 2070, when most of your parents or grandparents would've been in school, the sophomore class of Sandy Village visited the Florida Falcons. It was there that Jessica Holmes and Aaron Mathews met. Aaron was a trial subject of the MEDs and had excelled faster than most."

A security video played of their first meeting and I watched it with trepidation.

"They got to know each other and soon fell in love. When Josh Sholtis, Jessica's ex, found out, he gathered his friends together and attacked the Florida Falcons' main building, and the school sided with him. They believed Aaron to be a danger because of his MEDs. Acting out of this fear, they declared war. The attacks grew from small pranks to kidnappings and more."

Tension rose in the room, people shifting uncomfortably. Mr. Connor didn't break eye contact, and the MEDs weren't helping me from feeling like I was falling.

"On the evening of September 13, 2072, the Florida Falcons attacked the main building of the high school at Sandy Village, killing thirteen people and injuring seven more. Sandy Village struck back, killing fourteen, injuring ten. Jessica couldn't take it anymore; in desperation, she threw herself in front of a young Falcon freshman. She was shot in the chest and died immediately. The fighting stopped when Aaron saw her. He took his gun to his head, the first suicide in 22 years. After this incident, the school stepped in. Regulations were tripled, everything monitored. Guns across the country were banned and production ceased."

The image of an old gun flashed on the screen before it was tossed into a burning fire. The explosion that followed brought another scream to my mind. I shook my head, willing the noise to stop.

"MEDS soon perfected their drug, distributing it around the world." Mr. Connor shut off the image, turning to the class.

I felt some tension ease and the desire to grab a pill faded.

"As you all know, the rivalries and pranks haven't stopped. Still, we administrators hope that one day you will all be able to live together in peace."

The bell rang and Mr. Connor nodded to the class. "See you next week."

We got up and grabbed our bags. Everyone shuffled from the room in a buzz of conversation. I ignored Mr. Connor's eyes on me as I plotted how to get to my dorm as quickly as possible to grab a red pill.

"Don't you think it's totally strange how history seems to be repeating itself, even over fifty years later?" said Hayley absently as we walked down the hall. "I mean, sure, we aren't, like, in a war right now, and we're missing a forbidden romance, but there's no denying tensions are totally close to snapping."

"Hayley!" Kyle chastised. "Don't you think that is a bit pessimistic?"

She shrugged. "I just call it like I see it."

"I hope that's not the case," I said, fiddling with the end of my jacket as I tried to shake the feeling of danger from my mind. "I can't imagine what a war would look like now." Hayley and I shuttered at the thought, but Kyle's eyes were hard.

"I can tell you, if it comes to that, I won't hesitate to join. There is nothing more important than keeping those close to me safe." I could tell he meant it, and silently I prayed that there would never be a reason for him to follow through.

A *bumping* noise woke me from my nightmare. Groaning, I rubbed my eyes and walked to the door, but when I opened it, no one was there. I looked around the hall, confused. Not a person in sight. The *bumping* continued as I turned back to my room, realizing it was coming from my window.

Cautiously, I walked to it and pulled it open, peeking out, trying to see in the dim twilight. As my eyes adjusted, I spotted shadows moving around the building below. One threw something against the wall with another *bump*.

"Hey, what are you doing?" I shouted down at the group, and they looked up. My heart stopped as I gazed into the lion-masked faces.

"Run!" one of them yelled. The voice was faintly familiar past the thumping in my ears. The group dropped their things and ran for it, laughing. The last person to leave turned back to me and lifted his mask. I couldn't stop the small gasp that escaped.

"We will be back," yelled Mike, turning to leave with a dash into the trees.

My heart thumping wildly against my chest, I crumbled to the ground. *What's Mike doing here?*

As the shock faded, I quickly grabbed my jacket to cover up my skimpy sleepwear and headed to Hayley's. I banged on her door until she opened it, annoyed.

Her hair was a mess, and she looked like she wanted to kill me. "You like better have a reason to be waking me up early on a Saturday morning."

"Get dressed and call Kyle. Something's up." Every fiber in my body screamed to go back and hide. Yet I knew in my bones I had to face what was to come head on.

Hayley's expression changed to a mixture of curiosity and fear as she disappeared. She returned with her hair brushed and a pair of sweats on.

She fiddled with her shirt as she came out. "Kyle and Shan are on their way. What's up?"

"I don't know, but someone was throwing things at the building. They were from Sally Brown," I explained, feeling a squeeze.

"Show me." Her voice was ice.

I nodded and led the way outside. We made our way to the other side of the building cautiously, a LightBot leading the way as it flew from my PortMed.

"It was right—" I stopped as I saw the damage.

The wall was covered with paint, gruesome and terrifying in the bot light, the picture no less crude than the sloppy style it was in. A mountain lion stood on the left side, his paw outstretched, longing and anger on his face. On the other side was the knight of Kent Wood, in its arms a small lion cub. It was unconscious, blood seeping from its paw, a bright silver lightning bolt on its rear left leg. Under the image were the words: *Give us back what's ours*. My blood ran cold. There were missing pieces around the edges, but the picture was still clear as day.

"Back what's theirs?" Hayley said to the empty alcove.

I heard footsteps behind us, turning as Kyle and Shan appeared on either side of me, panting. There was a pause as they read the message.

"What do they mean 'theirs?'" Kyle asked, glaring at the wall as if it had committed a great offense.

Fear overtook me and I forced myself not to take a step away from him. *Would he kill me?*

Shan stepped forward, eyes scanning the image. "Do we have something of theirs..." A noise escaped his mouth as he trailed off, barely loud enough for the others to hear. He turned slowly toward me, the betrayal in his eyes as he stared down, hurt. As if disgusted by the sight of me, he turned away.

My heart broke. I longed to reach out to him. He knew I had lied, kept lying to him, and there was nothing I could do to take it back.

"Shan," I begged him to understand. I didn't mean to hurt him. I couldn't tell them I was from Sally Brown. Couldn't he understand that?

He pulled away from my outstretched hand. "Why?" His voice was hoarse.

Please stop. I pleaded, staring at him. *Don't tell.*

"Why what, Shan?" asked Hayley.

I looked to her and Kyle, then back at Shan. I waited for him to explain, but he just stood there watching me, waiting for me to voice his suspicions aloud. *He won't tell.* No, he wanted me to, and that was so much worse.

Hayley sensed something was up and turned to me, the suspicion back in her eyes. "Lovota?"

Better tell them now. Shan wasn't the only one who would understand the image right away. I'd need friends on my side when the news got out. *If they still want to be my friends.* I pushed back my fear as I faced them. "There is something that I have to tell you." I prayed fervently and silently that they would understand and wouldn't turn me over the moment I confessed. "I'm...I haven't been completely honest with you guys...when I told you about my old school."

"What are you saying?" Kyle asked, his hand hovering over his PortMed. Hayley was glancing between him and Shan, shoulders tense, waiting for clarity.

I took a deep breath and looked at her. "I'm not from Willow Creek."

Hayley stepped back from me, her eyes glossy. Her fear felt like a slap to the face. I heard a scream that sounded too much like my dead friend as her eyes darted about.

"Jamie? Or Loran?" Her voice cracked, and I looked down at the ground in shame. "You were right?" The question wasn't directed at me.

My head snapped up to Kyle, his eyes blazing with anger. "I didn't want to be. I was hoping it was Trident." I remembered Jamie then, the girlfriend of one of the basketball players at Trident. We were similar enough I could see the confusion. She had disappeared a week before me, lost to The Shadow.

"I-I wanted to tell you," I stammered out stumbling forward. They all took a step back and I pulled my arms inward. "I knew I'd be your enemy. I was worried about what you would do. You know how they treat transfers like traitors. I didn't want to lie. Well, I did, but I didn't want anyone to be hurt. I was just so scared. When you guys accepted me, I saw no need to ruin things."

"Loran?" Shan said, the name sounding foreign on his tongue, and I tried not to cry.

I have no right to cry. I'm not the one who's been betrayed. Why was I so stupid to think I could keep this secret?

"I'm so sorry. I should've told. I thought that we'd only have a year…Then Chris broke up with me. I was going to tell you, but when you didn't step up with Lilith, I feared what would happen." The words flew from me.

"And she was right!" Kyle roared.

Shan put a hand on his chest, stopping his approach.

"No! No, you need to believe me. I really came here because of my parents. I promise I'm not a spy." I cried then. "Please, you need to believe me—"

"We don't need to do anything but report you to the council. We let it slide before since we weren't sure, but no more!" snapped Hayley, opening her PortMed.

"No!" Shan and I called out at the same time.

My head snapped to him, my eyes wide in wonder.

He didn't turn to look at me. "Listen, I'm as upset about this as you all but let's hear her out. There has to be a good explanation. There has to be." His tone was pleading, and Kyle and Hayley backed down. All three turned to me, expectant.

"It started when I got a note from The Shadow at the beginning of the year." Before I knew what I was doing, I confessed everything. Their faces didn't soften, and more than once I watch Hayley's hand hover over her PortMed. Things that weren't relevant tumbled from my mouth like vomit as I collapsed to the ground, the grass cold and damp under my legs and hands. Tears streamed down my cheeks, and I could barely breathe through my stuffed nose and panic. When I finished, there was a long pause.

"You could have said something." Shan's voice was soft, hurt. "You could have trusted me."

"I'm so sorry."

Shan nodded awkwardly, stepping back when I tried to reach up to him.

I hung my head, wrapping my arms around myself. "I really didn't want to come here. My parents really did force me. I promise I'm not a spy." I repeated through tears, turning my head to see Hayley and Kyle.

They exchanged a heated look before Hayley bent down. "I'm so sorry, Loran," she said. Her voice was soft, but my shirt balled in her hands momentarily before she quickly realized and let go. "You shouldn't have to be afraid. I'm glad you told us, even if it was, like, kinda late." She rubbed my back.

Kyle stood beside Shan, keeping his distance, and didn't look at me. There was a chill in the air. The last bit of cold before the dawn. But I didn't break away from Hayley, didn't turn to face the day.

My tears dried as the sun peaked over the horizon. *When the school sees this, my loyalty will be under scrutiny. People like Lilith will come out of the woodwork, calling for my head. I have to be ready.*

"Let's get you back to your room," Shan said. "We will wait for you outside and when you're ready, come join us. Please."

They waited outside as I dressed quickly. I tried to wash the redness from my eyes, but I couldn't stop crying.

I could be dead in just a matter of hours if I'm lucky. Days if I'm not.

I had to believe Sally Brown thought I'd been taken against my will and weren't trying to put me in harm's way.

Still, why didn't Chris correct them or attempted a more subtle form of rescue?

I quickly grabbed a red pill from the drawer under my sink. I felt no relief, the world around me turning pink as it tilted on its axis. Quickly, before I could fall victim to the fog filling my head, I slammed the mirror door open and fetched the golden pills there. I couldn't avoid them anymore. The moment after they released into my system, the world rightened and cleared.

With a breath, I walked to the door, my heart thudding with each step. My hand rested on the knob, and I watched it shake. It took a few minutes to gather the willpower to turn it.

Hayley, Shan, and Kyle were still waiting for me. They stopped talking the moment I walked out. Shan couldn't even stand to look at me. Hayley took my hand and helped me out of the building, walking beside me as if in support, but it felt more like she was making sure I couldn't run.

Chapter 31

A crowd was waiting when I returned to the site, people whispering and pointing, speculating on the meaning of the image. My friends' PortMeds had already beeped to alert them of the incident during our short walk. As the crowd saw us, they parted way. No one seemed suspicious of me yet, but I knew that wouldn't last.

I took a deep breath. Letting go of Hayley's hand, I shoved my way through to the front. I heard Shan yell after me, but I didn't stop.

I can't have rumors going around that aren't at least half-true.

People stepped aside as they recognized me. When I reached the wall to a clearing a few feet wide, I turned to face the crowd. Many of the underclassmen quieted down first, seeing I wished to speak. The rest followed suit, resulting in an uneasy silence.

All eyes were on me as I took a breath. "Hello," I said, my voice squeaking a little. My hands shook and twitched, longing for something to play with. But I wouldn't show weakness.

"Hey," replied a boy at the front, causing others to chime in.

I cracked him a thankful smile. The crowd was slowly growing as people woke up and headed to class, stopping at the terrifying sight. Curious whispers fluttered across the yard.

"So, I bet you're wondering what's going on," I said, gathering my courage. I tried to speak up, but my voice did not travel far when it trembled. "Obviously, we've had a visit from our old friends Sally Brown." The crowd murmured as they passed my words back down the rows. "It's abnormal for an attack to have a message with it. What does it mean?" I turned to the picture. "Give back what is ours," I whispered, more to myself than anyone else.

I turned back to the crowd and attempted to stand straight. "What is theirs? We can assume they believe we have taken a cub—or rather, a student." A subtle roar began. "If that's the case, why not bring it to the council? Get justice for this student that we've stolen? We all know the proper procedures. Why sneak around?"

I caught Hayley's eyes as I scanned the restless crowd. She was making her way to the front with Shan and Kyle. She gave me a sad smile, nodding her encouragement. I could already tell who had figured out the end of my explanation. They were the ones who looked at me with hate.

I took a breath and said the words that I felt would change my life forever. "Why paint a lightning bolt on the cub?"

The bubble *popped*. My reputation as Lightning of the West made the symbol well known.

"No, it can't be."

"Really?"

"How could she?"

"I knew it."

"Lilith was right."

"She shouldn't be allowed to wander about. Someone, grab her."

"Shut it, do you really think she could run now?"

I wish I'd stayed in the shadows, I lamented to myself.

Older students spit at the ground near my feet.

"I see many of you already know or suspect what I'm getting at." I continued, and the crowd quieted slightly. "Those who know me know I arrived this year.... Now that I think about it, everyone knows that." I tried to chuckle, but it was stuck in my throat. "My name is Loran Black and I'm from Sally Brown—"

The crowd erupted in boos and rude remarks. I flinched.

I hadn't finished what I was going to say, but it was too late. The relative peace was gone. There was only chaos. I heard a few demands for my life, but I didn't falter even as people moved for me. I caught Sally's eye in the crowd, and she looked at me like I just killed her best friend. The looks from my other friends as I scanned weren't better. Jaz watched me with a resigned acceptance that I didn't have time to process as a boy from my physics class, Dan, stormed up to me. We had become friends during a project and often spoke about The Picking. He was sweet for some girl from his art class; I helped him get the courage to ask her out. Now, as he glared at me with hate, it was like none of that mattered. The worst part was I knew that's how he saw it. Whatever I was to anyone before was moot I was a traitor and nothing more.

"So, then, whose side are you on? Are you their Lightning or ours?" he demanded as he pointed to the wall behind me. The question took me aback.

"Yeah!" Shouted the crowd.

I gulped down the sour taste in my throat. I never expected them to make me choose. *Why do they want me to choose?* I was confused. *If I say I belong here, then things could hopefully settle down. But if I say I'm Sally Brown's, I won't last two seconds.* It was a harder decision than it should've been, my self-preservation at war with my heart.

"Settle down," Kyle said, stepping up beside me before I could respond. "Why should we make her choose?"

I was shocked by his support but as he turned a cold shoulder to me, I realized that wasn't what it was. He said he would fight if it came to war, and now his moment had come. The crowd settled down, but the tension didn't fade.

"Kyle, you know better than the rest of us. Loyalty is every-thing," yelled a boy farther back. I recognized him from the JV4 football team.

I looked at Kyle, wondering what he meant. He looked around with hard eyes, many shrinking away from his gaze.

He stepped in front of me. With one movement, the atmosphere changed, a wary calm settling in. I never realized the effect he had on the population until then. "Yes, I know. But we can use this to get—"

I stopped him, putting my hand on his shoulder. He looked back at me, shocked, and I shook my head. "Please," I asked, look-ing for an opportunity to stop the impending chaos before it went further.

He nodded and reluctantly moved aside.

I took a step forward and held my head high. I knew what I had to do to see the next day. Sally Brown had abandoned me to the wolves. "If it is loyalty you want, it is loyalty you will get. My last connection with Sally Brown has already been severed. Though I know many of you will still doubt me, I can tell you now. I am loyal to Kent Wood!" I stated, my voice strong. I amplified all the feelings that I had developed in my short time there and forced them out. Kyle tensed and then relax beside me. The crowd was silent for a long time, my words sinking in. I knew I could have just sealed my fate.

"We will stand by you," said Dan, but he glared. "If you turn on us, there will be no mercy."

I nodded to him to show I understood. He grabbed my hand firmly and shook it. It felt like I had just made a deal with the devil.

Kyle came up beside me, a victorious smile across his face, and grabbed the other. With a nod, they turned to the crowd, and I was shocked as they threw my hands into the air.

"This is our Lightning. We will strike down anyone who tries to challenge us," Kyle yelled. The crowd cheered, making me feel dazed. He put his hands up to quiet them. They fell silent immediately, the air electric. He took center stage as I backed away to join Hayley and Shan, who had made their way behind us, the others not far away.

Shan's presence was cold, mirroring Zack's angry glare. The crowd had grown to the point I could spot people in the trees nearby. They hung from branches, trying to get an unobstructed view.

The walls surrounding us allowed for Kyle's powerful voice to ring to the edges of the crowd. "Sally Brown has declared something today. They think they can just barge in here and take what's ours."

My heart fell as I realize what I had just done.

"To ignore procedure," he continued, "and do as they want. We've let them walk on us for too long. For too long, they have installed fear in our hearts. Those Glitchers!"

I flinched as he cursed.

"It's time we fight back. This land is ours. These people, ours. They want what's ours? I say come get it! We will give nothing—and no one—up. This means war!"

The crowd went crazy as he finished. I was overwhelmed by the noise. Looking out into the angry, determined faces, I felt like crying.

This isn't what I wanted.

I realized then the violence wouldn't stop with pretty words. The hate ran too deep, the tension like a rubber band waiting to snap. All it needed was a push and somehow, some way, I became that push.

"Shan, please." I couldn't corner him in classes that day as I was exiled to the back of every single one, so I waited till he was off work the next day to jump him and ask for forgiveness.

It hadn't worked.

As my hand lay on his, he spun, pulling from me.

"Don't touch me," his voice was cold, but his eyes were hurt.

"Please, listen—"

"No!" His gaze broke and he whispered. "You should go before I say something I will regret."

I felt my heart break as he left me alone in the room where he discovered my secret all those weeks ago.

Chapter 32

"We can't allow this to continue!" Blake, a chemist major and college freshman, called out. His golden Newly Mated Necklace bounced against his chest as he moved with passion behind his podium on the stage.

"We must take action," the crowd yelled in reply.

"I say we try to solve this diplomatically if we can. Stop this war before it starts. Lives and valuable time will be saved," argued Abby from her podium. She was an art major and a friend of Lucy.

Sally Brown had attacked, trashing the sports sector with images of the lightning cub right after I spoke with Shan, but some were reluctant to go to war. Like Abby, they wanted to resolve things peacefully.

I looked around the golden and green rows of the largest theater on campus. Being a Monday, it was packed to the brim, everyone on edge.

"We all know it won't work. Browner's are bloodthirsty. Diplomacy won't last. We must act," countered Blake.

The plastic chair under me *squeaked* as I shifted uncomfortably.

"I don't think that's true. We have proof that diplomacy can work. Loran is an example of this. Let her speak." Abby turned to me.

I tried to hide my horror as everyone looked past the podiums toward me. I thought I was done speaking for the day, having already declared my loyalty for the school to see. Jaz's hand squeezed mine, giving me the strength to stand and walk to Abby's podium as I ignored Kyle's frigid attitude coming at me from the other chair.

"Don't you agree that diplomacy could solve this?"

"Um, well, to be honest, I don't know." I looked down at the floor, refusing to make eye contact with the crowd as my PortMed squeezed.

"What do you mean you don't know? You lived there and obviously you were popular. Could we not—could *you* not—reason with them?" she pushed.

"Well, it's hard to tell." I paused. "I wish I could say diplomacy would work. I really do, but I can't guarantee it. I know, like here, there will be people fighting for peace. But there will also be people wanting war. It's no secret that our two schools hate each othe—"

"See, she admits war's the answer," interrupted Blake.

"I'm not finished." I glared at him. "I believe we all have misconceptions about each other. Trust me when I say we aren't that different. If we put aside our feelings, we could end this conflict now."

"We are as different as night and day," Blake snapped. "Do you want us to lose this war? By letting our guard down, we could very well open ourselves up to attack." His eyes were hard.

"No, we're not," I cried out. "I've seen both sides. When it comes down to it, we are the same."

"I knew it! I told you she was on their side."

A sour taste filled my mouth as I turned to see Lilith standing up in the middle of the crowd. Her voice echoed in the room through the speakers in the ceiling.

"Stay out of this," said Jaz, walking next to me.

"Why should I listen to anything yo—"

"Both of you shut up." I stopped the argument. "I've already shown my allegiance, but that doesn't mean I don't still have feelings for those I left behind. I don't want to see people on either side hurt." I ignored the way Hayley stiffened in the front row.

"I don't know if that's possible," said Blake. His voice gentle, taking me by surprise. "I see where you're coming from, but if these attacks don't stop, then we will have no choice but to engage."

"I say we send a party. See if they will talk," said Abby, taking the podium back. She turned to Blake, looking him straight in the eyes. They nodded and turned to the crowd.

I shrunk back into the background with Jaz as they spoke. Kyle's glare hurt as I sat back down in the farthest of the three chairs.

The debate ended, and we took a vote. I voted with Abby, even if I didn't believe it would last for long. Jaz didn't vote, but I saw her hand twitch when Blake asked for war. Meanwhile, Kyle stood proudly with the call. In the end, diplomacy won out, and Kyle looked livid.

"It's decided. We will send a party as soon as possible," said Abby.

The meeting ended, and Kyle stormed backstage, meeting Shan, Zack, and Hayley. I trailed behind him, Jaz at my back. As soon as the curtains closed and we were obscured from view, he spun on me.

"You just had to go and defend them, didn't you?" he demanded, advancing. Only Shan's steady hand on his shoulder stopped him from getting in my face.

"I don't want anyone to fight!" I snapped back. "Why are you so keen on running headfirst into a confrontation?"

"Why can't you just keep your mouth shut?" he growled.

I tried not to wince. "Because I truly believe we could solve this peacefully. I've been on both sides. I've seen both people. Sure, we have our differences—who doesn't—but they aren't so big we couldn't work past them."

The area grew silent, the sound of the backstage hands pretending to work as they watched us the only noise.

"You disgust me."

I stepped back, watching the anger in Kyle's eyes grow.

"You need to realize you are lucky to be alive. You live only because we say you can. Your purpose in life now is to help Kent Wood and no more," he said, and Hayley gasped.

I didn't let the tears fall. "That's not what you were saying a few days ago," I countered.

Kyle and Shan went rigid. "Don't you dare," Kyle began.

"What? Can't handle knowing you fell for a Browner?" I didn't know who I was addressing the question at.

They both flinched as if slapped.

"I think that's enough." Shan's calm voice intervened before I could say something stupid. I looked to him. He avoided my eyes, and I could see his pain. "At this point, it's all moot, isn't it?" He looked up, making eye contact with me and I felt like drowning, and not in a good way. "You lied."

I winced that time.

"To us," he gestured to the room. "And to me." A tear fell as I felt his pain. "Everything we know about you is built on that lie."

"No, it isn't," I begged. "Sure, I didn't tell you which school I was from, but everything else was the truth. Where I came from doesn't change who I am."

"You can actually fight." He countered and I stopped, dread filling me. "I looked up your records. Your real ones."

An unhelpful squeeze and I winced again.

"You were once one of the top combat specialists in the nation, more commonly known as Blades."

Hayley's eyes widened and she took an unconscious step back.

BotJuice, I thought. *Why did he have to find those records?* They were buried deep, the luchador mask burned, multiple better fighters including my rival, Hunter, taking the spotlight; there shouldn't have been a reason that name was still connected with mine.

"That's not who I am anymore." I pushed back images of bloody fists and gleeful laughter.

"You were truthful about your basketball and running records, at least. But we both know that boyfriend of yours wasn't some new l-love." His voice cracked with a stutter. "Did you two laugh together that day?" He took a step forward, awkwardly but forcefully, his eyes shining with unshed tears. "When you realized you had tricked me, did it make you happy?"

"No," I breathed, guilt overwhelming me. "No, I wanted to turn right back around and tell you everything." Tears flowed freely down my face and the rest of my former friends shifted uncomfortably.

Shan looked at me, truly looked at me, and when he looked away, no blush on his face, I felt like I'd been found lacking.

"I think it would be best if you kept your distance for now," he whispered. "I need some time to think."

Kyle stepped up to him, putting a comforting hand on his shoulder as he glared at me. "Loyalty means everything, Loran. Where does yours lie?" he asked.

It felt like I had been stabbed.

Together, they turned and left the room. Zack watched them go, conflicted.

"Go on, I don't mind," Jaz whispered to him as she stepped around me. He placed a gentle kiss on her head before running off. The backstage crew was no longer pretending to work as they watched us curiously.

"I'm, like, not sure what to think of all this," Hayley spoke up, watching her hands instead of me. "I suspected you were lying all along but—" She stopped, looking at me, tears falling down her face. "I totally wish it had been Trident." She turned and left. Jaz watched her go, then turned to me. She didn't say a word, just raised an eyebrow.

"What do I need to do to gain their forgiveness?" I asked as she made to leave.

She paused, her back to me. "Prove them wrong."

Then I was alone.

Chapter 33

Masked faces surrounded me, people in the stands screaming for my blood. My heart thundered in my chest as I was shoved to the ground. Out of the shadows, Robert, came to me, a knife in hand. He spun it casually as he sneered down.

"Beg princess, beg," he said, and I did, falling to the ground and weeping.

He laughed at me. "Pathetic," he spat, kneeling next to me. Grabbing my chin, he forced me to look at him. I saw danger and death in his eyes. My tears rolled down his hands as he smiled hungrily at me. "I told you, you would return to me. I can save you, but you must give in to me. You did it once before, you can do it again." He leaned in to kiss me and I bit his lips at contact. Growling, he pulled away, licking the blood.

"I didn't choose you then, and I won't choose you now," I cried.

"Have it your way." He grabbed my hair, pulling it upward, causing me to cry out. Holding the knife up to the crowd, he flashed a smile. "It's time for her to choose. Us or them." He turned to a group of boys nearby. "Bring out the prisoner!" he shouted.

They complied, disappearing, and coming back out with a body. I watched Chris being dragged from the darkness, his body bloody and battered, his right eye swollen shut. His beautiful blond hair crusted with blood.

I tried to fight Robert off and rush to him, but he held me back.

"Choose, darling," he cooed, shoving the knife into my hand, pushing me to Chris. I stumbled forward. In the corner I spotted Lilith, her vicious smile cutting as she clung to Shan. He held her close like a lover, his eyes empty when they looked at me. The hollow feeling of those eyes strengthened my resolve. I couldn't back down. I walked to Chris slowly, his smile weak.

"It's okay," he said.

I raised the knife, my hands trembling. Then spun and dug it into Hayley's gut. Shocked, I let go, staggering back as I watched her bleed out. Her hands gripped the knife, and she looked up at me with wide eyes.

"No, no!" I cried, rushing to her.

Sarah's hand stopped me. "I knew you would choose us," she said.

"No!"

"How does it feel, Browner?" Lilith spat as I passed her on the path to my calculus class Thursday morning. Her spittle hit me on the cheek, waking me from the memory of my nightmares.

I tried not to cry as I wiped it away. *It's been three days; when will she leave me alone?* The surrounding path was empty as people made a wide berth, as if I had the plague. *I'm alone.*

As if reading my thoughts, Shan turned from up ahead, looking me up and down before he turned back to Kyle and continued walking.

Lilith watched them go with glee. "I knew all along you were nothing but trash, and now it seems like your friends have finally realized it as well. How many days has it been now since your lies came to light? Five, I believe, and they still can't stand you."

People passed, watching with vindictive glee.

I ignored Lilith as I continued to the doors of the calculus building.

She skipped to me, matching my pace. "Oh, is the little Browner deaf now? Or are you just too high and mighty to speak to me?"

I dodged a foot in my path, almost falling into Lilith.

With disgust, she pushed me off her as the boy laughed. "Don't touch me, filth."

"Just leave me alone," I implored.

She dusted off her skirt like I had left a mark. "No, I don't think I will," she sang, following me into the building. "See, I haven't had this much fun in months. Do you know the last time I was right over Shan? It's been years, and it was over the color of a beetle, of all things." There was fondness under the disgust in her voice. "Then you came along." She barked out a laugh as I attempted to lose her in the crowded stairs.

I was unsuccessful.

"You precious gift, you." She pinched my cheek painfully and I let out a shout, swatting her.

"Do that again and I will deck you," I threatened. I wouldn't though. I was too scared of the possibility it'd be pinned on me, and the council would decide I wasn't worth the effort to keep alive.

Lilith knew this too, so she pinched me again, just for fun. "You are just too cute, sweetie. Let me ask, was it fun playing pretend these last few months?"

I hoped she would leave me alone as I entered the lecture hall, but she didn't, following me to the back of class. Shan and Kyle watched us go with guarded looks and I tried to pretend I didn't feel my heart break. I fingered the extra red pill in my pocket, wondering when I could slip it into my PortMed without anyone noticing.

Lilith looked down at the two still watching us as I settled into my new desk, none of my seatmates saying "hi".

"I thought I tore out that boy's heart when we broke up, but you somehow managed to do even worse, and you didn't actually know each other," she whispered from behind me, her hair tickling my cheek. "You'll just have to tell me how you did it some time."

"I don't know what you're talking about," I said, searching the room for Mr. Talon, knowing Lilith would have to leave when he arrived.

"You don't, do you?" She sounded amused. "Oh, I think I'm going to like this new arrangement. What say you?"

I didn't reply.

"You're practically friendless, you know. Sure, the girls stick around, but it's more from paranoia and pity than actual friendship. Couldn't you use a buddy?"

Mr. Talon saved me from having to reply and Lilith disappeared as if she was never there.

When class concluded, Kyle and Shan walked ahead, dashing any effort I could have made to catch up. Like a wraith, Lilith appeared with a wide smile. Before she could continue our talk, Tom stepped forward from the crowd. Both of us looked at him questioningly.

"Hey Loran, I was wondering if you had a few minutes to spare," he said awkwardly, surprising me. "I need to ask you a question about your project."

His eyes were kind, and I jumped at the opportunity. "Oh yes, of course."

Tom smiled widely as people turned to watch us. "Sorry, Lilith, but I'll have to steal your friend for a bit." Something flashed between them as they made eye contact, but I couldn't read it.

Lilith gave Tom a tight smile. "Of course." She turned to me, pulling me into a hug. I struggled as she squeezed hard enough to bruise. "Have fun, okay?" She gave me a smirk as the hall erupted in chatter and skipped away.

I caught the boys' eyes at the top of the stairs as she passed. Kyle watched me and Tom with guarded suspicion as Shan looked on, worried.

I suddenly felt a wave of anger and offered my hand to Tom with a wide smile. "Shall we?" I asked.

He looked at it as if such a gesture was foreign to him before taking it. He led me down the stairs, past my so-called friends and outside.

"Browner," someone hissed as we walked by. "It wasn't enough for you to ensnare the basketball captain. Now you want to sink your claws into our valedictorian."

"Now, Harold, that's not a very nice thing to say." Tom's tone was light, but it set me on edge. "Please apologize to the lady." There was an awkwardness to Tom's movements so like Shan, yet so different.

Harold flushed in embarrassment as he was chastised. "I'm sorry," he grumbled, not looking at me.

"No worries," I said amazed. Tom continued down the path, dragging me with him. "Thank you for that," I told him after a beat.

"I understand what it's like to be on the outside. Kids can be very cruel." Tom's face was sad. "Though I shouldn't be the one doing this for you. What is going on with your friends?"

I swallowed the lump in my throat. We turned on another path and he led me toward the English building.

"They don't want to have anything to do with me." I tried not to cry. "I betrayed them."

Tom stopped, looking me over. His glasses glinted, blocking his gaze. "I'm sorry to hear that," he said. "I do think they will come around, eventually."

"That's a sweet thought, but I doubt it," I said.

"I have known them longer. You can take my word for it," he contended.

I let out a sharp laugh, catching Hayley's angry eyes as she met up with Kyle on a path to my right. "And Kyle still hates you for something you did as a kid."

Tom followed my gaze to see Kyle glaring daggers. His face darkened. "Yes," he said, his voice deeper for just a moment. "But that was a unique and unfortunate accident. This is something minor in the face of what is to come."

Dread filled me. "You don't really think it will lead to war?" I asked.

"You were called in for the meeting tomorrow, no?" he pushed, and I nodded. "Then yes, I do. They will use you, you know. You are the beacon of this fight." His posture softened as I winced. "I don't mean to upset you. I'm only telling the truth. Just be prepared, and you should be fine."

"Well, I'm sorry we got so off-topic," I redirected, not wanting to acknowledge what he was saying. "What was it you were going to ask me about my project?"

Tom grinned. "Oh, I didn't have one. I could tell you were uncomfortable with Lilith and wanted to give you a different partner to walk to class with." He stopped and I blinked, realizing we were standing in front of the door to my creative writing class.

"Well, well, well, looks like Lightning has graced us with her presence." Robert's voice made me feel like vomiting. He approached from around the corner, cocky as always. He opened his mouth to taunt me more, snapping it shut as his eyes widened. "No," he breathed.

I was confused as the color drained from his face.

"Good afternoon, Robert," Tom said from behind me. He placed a firm hand on my shoulder, and I didn't bother shoving it off. Robert watched the movement, growing paler, if that was possible. "I hope your weekend was enjoyable."

He gulped. "Yes, it was quite pleasant. If you'll excuse me." Like a kicked puppy, he skittered past, filing into the class. I watched him go, confused and concerned.

Tom cleared his throat, drawing my attention. He gave me a bashful look. "I'll leave you here then. I hope the rest of your day is better."

I nodded dumbly as the awkward boy walked away. What just happened?

I watched my friends laughing across the lobby on the bright Sunday morning, feeling like my heart was breaking. A group of tormentors blocked my path to the elevator, I lowered my head and pushed forward. I felt their words like jabs and their jabs like knives to the heart. The screams in my ears hurt and I couldn't tell if they were all in my head or around me. Reaching my room, I pushed open my door and locked it quickly behind me, blocking the people in the hall.

"That door won't stop us, Browner. You will pay one way or another!" a voice called as I threw open my drawers, grabbing a gold and red pill.

Chapter 34

"Diplomacy has failed us!" Blake yelled to the crowd. "It's time to take up arms, my friends. War has begun!"

The crowd cried around me, pumping their fists in the air.

"No, stop, please. There could still be peace!" Abby begged. But she was drowned out before she could say more.

"There will be no peace! Sally Brown has sent us a message." Blake held up a picture for the world to see on the big screen.

The three representatives were tied up, their faces painted yellow with black whiskers resembling a lion's face. Each of them had multiple bruises and cuts on their body, obvious even with the paint. It broke my heart. Only one of our representatives returned from their mission on Sunday. The rest were being held captive until Sally Brown's demands were met, one of them being my return. Of course, it was ignored.

"They have proven by taking what is ours that war is the only option. The Board refuses to help, so we will fight back! We will rescue them!"

The crowd yelled louder. I winced in my seat.

"Things have totally escalated a lot faster than I thought they would," whispered Hayley next to me.

I nodded.

"It was bound to happen sooner or later," Jaz added beside her.

Sally stiffened to my right, and I could hear Bee's nervous bouncing behind me next to Dorothy.

"I was hoping to avoid this," I said to no one, met by silence.

"So, boys, men, what do you say? Will we go to war?" Blake called to the crowd.

The boys cheered. I wasn't surprised. When Kyle heard the news, he was pissed, ranting and raving in the lobby for anyone to hear, though I was shocked to see Shan join him. I had always thought he was the peaceful one. It seemed even he had his limits.

"Girls, women, are you with us?" Blake yelled, and a chorus of cheers was his reply around me. I sat in silence. "We have selected students for our first Alpha and Beta squads. They will rescue the prisoners, and when that's done, we will attack. Let the war of 2121 begin!"

The room shook as people stomped and jumped.

"Won't Mrs. Adams stop them? Why isn't the Board worried?" I asked.

Jaz shook her head. "Word is the Warden's encouraging this, says it's good for school spirit. I think it's because she's too lazy to step in," she said.

"Or she totally wants us to go to war," added Hayley.

"I'm guessing you all are part of the alpha squads?" I asked, eyeing them with worry.

"Yes. I don't care what people might say. They have no right to threaten innocent lives," said Jaz with conviction.

"We will stand for what is ours even when others don't," Kyle hissed behind me. I ignored the pain of his words as my PortMed squeezed.

Blake dismissed the meeting, and everyone spilled from the building. Hayley and Jaz allowed me to walk beside them as we went, and fewer people called for my blood as I passed.

"It isn't right," Dorothy whispered to someone behind me as we made our way from class the next day.

"She made her bed. Now she must lie in it."

I was surprised to hear Shan whisper back. The tear falling down my cheek was wiped away before any of them could see.

I hid in the corner of the lobby, hoping to say goodbye as my friends left early that Thursday morning. I cared for their safety even when they didn't seem to care for mine.

Prove them wrong. Jaz's words rang in my head daily and I was trying to figure out how to do it.

Another student passed my lone table with murder in their eyes.

What would they do if I just ran away? I could go back home to Sally Brown, make it all go away...

Some nights when I lay in bed, I debated the option. *Would I be accepted?* Despite the claims they were attacking to save me, I doubted it. It wouldn't have taken much for them to find me and save me from this hell. Yet they hadn't.

The elevator dinged and I watched as the girls came out, decked in black. The ski mask Bee wore had two swords crossing on the right temple.

In perfect timing, the front doors to the building opened, and the boys piled in with a large number of others in the same outfit.

I stood, walking to the edge of the crowd to say goodbye.

"What are you doing here?" I was thrown to the center as a girl violently shoved me.

Tumbling forward, I tripped on a foot in my way, and fell on my hands in front of my friends.

The room was silent.

"You have no right to say goodbye. A Browner like you should be dead."

Multiple people in the crowd jeered.

"I'm so sorry," I cried.

"Stop this," Kyle demanded. My head snapped up. He refused to meet my eyes, but Shan watched me with concern next to him.

I felt a sudden jolt of anger at the look.

"You're right, she is just a Browner." The word hurt more than it should have. "But she is our Browner now and we protect our own." He looked at me then, but I couldn't read the emotions in his eyes. "Even when they don't deserve it."

"She shouldn't even be here," the girl who shoved me proclaimed. "Why doesn't the council take care of her?"

"Because she's worth more to us alive than dead."

I looked behind me, watching as Robert pushed from the crowd.

"What are you saying?" the girl demanded, mirroring my thoughts.

Robert looked down at me with a hunger in his eyes as he continued to defend me. "For some reason, the Browner's have decided she is worth all this effort," he gestured widely with his arm, "even though she left them. Don't you wonder why?" The room was silent. "She serves a greater purpose alive than dead, and she is our first and only inside resource."

My blood ran cold as understanding dawned on me. I felt all eyes on me as I searched the faces of my friends. They wouldn't meet my gaze. Murmurs filled the room.

"I think that's enough for now." A hand was suddenly in front of my face as I looked up at Tom awkwardly standing above me. I took his hand and he helped me up. "Our brave friends here are about to leave on a dangerous mission. We should give them the chance to say goodbye before they go."

Surprisingly, the crowd listened, and people began approaching the team, saying goodbye.

"Thank you," I whispered as I watched my friends receive well wishes. "I seem to say that to you a lot lately."

Tom sent me a huge smile. "It's really no big deal." He rubbed his hands on his pants, an award-winning blush on his face.

The team filed out of the room.

I caught the Tweedle brothers' eyes and sent them a kind smile. They returned it with crooked smiles of their own.

"Please stay safe."

I was surprised when Dorothy and Bee approached me.

"We really don't want to lose a sister," Bee said. Dorothy nodded, glancing back at the group to make sure they weren't watching.

"Shouldn't I be saying that to you?"

Dorothy gave me a pointed look. "He's been waiting for an opportunity to get to ya. Don't give it to him."

I followed her gaze to Robert. He was surrounded by dozens of people wishing him goodbye. Though he addressed each one, his eyes never left me.

"Stay in yar room if ya can."

"It's not like I have anyone to hang out with anyway," I said begrudgingly.

She gave me a sad smile and the two of them merged back into the team.

"I told you they would forgive you." Tom's amused voice made me smile slightly.

"Yes, well, those two have always been understanding." I caught Kyle's eyes through the glass of the lobby windows. They were molten. "I don't think I'll get so lucky with the others."

Chapter 35

The masks around me taunted me. Voices screamed and jeered. I looked around, frantic.

No, I couldn't be back here, not again. The floor was clean, no sign of Hayley's blood.

"Pathetic," Robert spat, kneeling next to me, grabbing my chin. He forced me to look at him. I saw danger and death in his eyes. Tears rolled down his hands as he smiled hungrily at me. "You always were such a weak thing. Full of emotions. Let me ask. How does it feel now? Was all of it worth it?"

I yelled, butting him in the head. He staggered back, his face morphing for a moment. The red glint in his sunken eye disappeared as he straightened.

"I won't choose, not again."

"You don't have a choice. You never did." He grabbed my hair, pulling it upward, causing me to cry out.

Chris was dragged back out from the darkness, his body bloody and battered like last time.

I tried to fight Robert off, tried to wake up from the nightmare.

"Choose, darling," he cooed, shoving the knife into my hand, push-ing me toward Chris. I stumbled forward. The knife felt wrong in my grasp. I looked down to see it already covered in blood.

"It's okay," Chris said, his voice hoarse. "It's better this way." He closed his eyes, a smile on his lips.

I thrust the knife down—digging it into the wooden floor below me.

"No!" My legs crumbled beneath me as I gave in to my great exhaustion.

I heard Robert behind me, his voice a husky growl. "So be it."

My head was yanked back, and I felt the cold metal of the knife slide across my neck.

I shot forward from my bed, feeling my neck and stifling a scream as an insistent *pounding* filled my room. Pulling on Chris's jacket, I popped in an extra pill into my PortMed, ignoring my growing dependency on them to stay sane. I opened my door, coming face to face with a red-faced Kyle.

"After everything you've done, now you befriend him?" he shouted before I could ask what he was doing. He was still dressed in his clothes from four days ago, dirt and grime littering the black.

"What are you—?"

He barged past me into my room, a whirlwind of fury and hands. "You know, the first time I could forgive you. After all, I thought you didn't know better," he continued as I shut my door, locking out the curious faces passing in the hall. "But no! I learned you knew the whole time, and you still choose to associate with that Defect. You have stooped to a new low, Loran."

"If I knew what the BotJuice you were talking about, I could probably say sorry," I snapped as I turned to him.

"You know exactly what I'm talking about," he hissed.

"No, I don't." I ran a hand through the tangles that were my hair. "Why don't you enlighten me?" The sarcasm in my voice was heavy.

"I'm talking about your relationship with *Thames*." He spat the name.

It took me a moment to remember that was Tom's full name. When I did, I couldn't help but laugh.

"What's so funny?" he demanded.

"You really think that's what's going on?" I asked. The anger in his eyes was my answer. "There is nothing going on between me and Tom." I shuttered a little at the thought. "First off, he is not even my type. And second, what gives you the right to be angry about it? We haven't spoken civilly in weeks, and I haven't seen you for four days, but here you are giving me a lecture about who I can and can't see."

"Don't try to fool me. I know your type. The Picking chose him as one of your perfect matches," he argued.

I felt my anger depleting, replaced by exhausted amusement. I resisted rolling my eyes, knowing it would only make the situation worse. "That was just a simulation," I countered. "And if you remember correctly, it also told me you were the other choice." A flush ran up his cheeks. "Plus, it wasn't even my paring. All of that was based off Lovota's personality, not mine."

Some of the anger left Kyle's eyes. "You are so frustrating, woman." He gripped his hair.

I couldn't help but watch his strange, conflicting emotions with amusement. "Says the boy who continually flips his feelings on a dime."

He sighed. "Yeah, well, a lot has been going on." He flopped onto my couch.

A hint of anger flared up. "Oh, really? I didn't notice." My voice dripped with sarcasm. "It's not like my world hasn't been turned upside-down." I threw my hands in the air as he watched me guardedly. "See, this is what I'm talking about. You think your last three weeks have been hard? How 'bout you try to live in fear for months with the very people you have grown up being told to hate?" Kyle cast his gaze away. "Wondering how you will trick them long enough to make it to The Picking, and then hope you end up with the boy you have loved since the first moment you met, despite a ten thousand to one chance. How would you feel if all your friends, new and old, just up and abandon you because of some stupid school rivalry that isn't even your fault? Hm?"

Kyle's anger returned tenfold. "Don't you play innocent here. I know who you are, Blades," he spat, standing. "The most ruthless fighter in the ring. Willing to do anything to win, even if it almost killed her opponents."

I shoved down the screams in my head, the world seeming to tumble to the side as a fog with a pink tint filled my vision. *I don't need another pill, I'm becoming to reliant.* I tried to tell myself even as my fingers twitched.

"I'm not that girl anymore," I said, my anger depleting as my body turned cold.

"You were once, though." Kyle pushed, almost gently. "How can I know you won't be again?"

How indeed.

"There is nothing I can say that will make you believe me," I said, my breathing difficult as my heart filled with sorrow. "Why don't you just leave?"

Kyle shot me a glare, storming past. "Fine, then." He grabbed the handle, yanking my door open. "Stay away from Tom." The door slammed shut behind him, reverberating in the room.

I felt like I was falling through the floor as I fumbled into my bathroom. Grabbing a gold pill, I slammed the pack into my PortMed. Panting, I watched my crazed eyes soften as the shadows slowly faded, the voices leaving, and I sighed. A *knock* sounded in my room again.

"I swear, Kyle, if you don't leave me alone," I snapped, pulling the door open. I stopped as I saw Jaz standing before me. She hadn't changed since the attack, either. A clotted red scratch adorned her right cheek. She was smiling at me and in her hand was a small box of chocolate.

"What the..."

Chapter 36

"So, are you going to let me in?" Jaz asked, her smile growing at my confusion.

I snapped my mouth shut. Nodding cautiously, I stepped aside.

She walked into my room, looking around at the few changes I had made. I saw her eyes darken as she noted the extra lock I had installed on my door.

"What are you doing here?" I asked.

She gave me a soft smile. "We just got back from the mission," she said in lieu of an explanation.

"Yeah, I know, Kyle already stopped by and gave me an earful. If you're here to do the same, please leave." I gestured to the door, but she didn't move.

"You know, I never considered what all of this must've been like for you," she said, ignoring me and moving to the couch to sit. I watched her cautiously as she settled in, opening the box of chocolates she brought and placing it on her lap. "I bet it was hard to leave your family behind just because your parents said you had to."

"It was," I admitted cautiously, not moving as she gestured for me to join her.

She sighed, turning to grab a piece of chocolate and popping it in her mouth. "You know, the moment I saw you, I knew exactly who you were."

My heart skipped a beat. "But you…"

She gave me a pointed look. "Did you really think I wouldn't? We have history, and it's not the sort one forgets so easily." She traced the jagged line of her missing ear tip. "I still have nightmares about that day," she confessed, focusing on the next piece of chocolate in her hand. "I was so excited for that game. It was my first one as the starting point guard. I'd worked so hard for it. Spent every waking moment training just so I could beat you." She smiled forlornly. "You weren't even a starring player, yet even then I knew exactly who you were. Loran, the most ruthless player in Sally Brown middle school, JV. Should have been a Sandy Village kid with that blood thirst. Everyone was so scared of you then. You weren't afraid to play dirty and knew how to make it look like an accident. Coach had searched far and wide for someone who wasn't afraid to go toe-to-toe with you."

Those years after I lost Hannah, filled my head. I felt aimless in the world, as if I had lost my purpose and took my anger out on those around me.

"When they put you in, I was ready. I was going to prove my metal and earn my place in varsity next year."

My hand traced the long scar on my stomach, feeling the gentle rise of a wound long healed. "I spent years trying to figure out how you slipped that knife past security," I whispered.

She sent me a sad grin. "Oh, that was the easy part. One of the high school team members flashed the guard as we passed through. Poor guy didn't know what to do. The hard part was hiding it in my underwear until the right time and not stabbing myself in the process."

I remembered the moment I spotted the blade, only my years of combat training keeping it from sinking into my gut.

"Despite what you think, I never wanted to kill you. Just maim you in a way that would prevent you from stepping on the court ever again."

I winced.

"I never expected you to be able to turn it back on me." Jaz pulled her hair from her signature ponytail. Red strands fell around her face, and she carefully pulled a section up near her ear.

I inspected the large gash on her scalp, the line matching the point where her ear used to be.

"I guess I should have known then there was more to you than meets the eye, *Blades*." She let out a mirthless laugh. "The doctors told me that if you had been even an inch closer, you would have dug into my skull and hit my brain." She visibly shuttered, and a pit formed in my stomach.

"I didn't know that," I whispered. When we'd both been sent to the hospital that day, I thought I had the worst of it. After all, she returned to the court a week later despite her supposed suspension, while I was benched the rest of the year in recovery.

"Oh, I'm not surprised." Jaz gave me a cocky grin. "I made sure they kept the whole thing hush-hush; even returned to practice two days later. It was my perseverance through the incident that landed me my first varsity spot on team five." She motioned to the couch again.

I hesitantly walked over, perching on the edge farthest from her.

"I should really thank you. It's because of you I made it in and kept climbing. I kept an eye on you, you see, and every time it seemed like you were catching up, I pushed myself harder."

"Why didn't you say anything?" I asked.

Her eyes glinted in a predatory manner. "Simple; I wanted my revenge. I knew that if the others knew about you, they would send you straight to the council and I would lose my chance." I shuttered, moving back, but she stopped me. "I'm not here for that." The kindness in her eyes was the only thing keeping me put. "It took some time, but I began to see you weren't the girl I knew in middle school. You've changed, and begrudgingly I had to admit I liked the new you. I meant it when I called you 'friend'."

"That day changed me, too." I paused, searching for the words. "I was so tired, you know. When I lost Hannah, my world just kind of fell apart. I couldn't face the pain, so I pushed it outward, never stopping." I lifted my shirt, showing her the scar. "The day I woke in the hospital with four cans of skin glue in me and a nicked rib, Chris was crying. I'd never seen him cry before, and he'd witnessed me being struck by lightning. I realized then what my actions were doing to my friends." I gave her a surly smile. "If it wasn't for you, I would probably still be down that path."

We fell into a comfortable silence.

I took a deep breath. "Why did you wait till now to say all this?"

Jaz's face went stony. "Oh, don't get me wrong, I've been pissed about this whole thing. Still am a bit, if I'm honest. I guess in my fantasy world, we would have gotten close enough that you would have divulged everything to me, I would have been able to tell you I knew all along, and we would have become the best of friends." She let out a chuckle.

"We still could be?" I said.

"I think I'd like that..." She gave me a small smile. "We were able to find the representatives," she revealed, grabbing another piece of chocolate. "They were in worse shape than we expected. We had to be careful with the extraction. I got caught in the crossfire on the way out, met one of your friends." My heart sped up as she gave me a pitying look. "Sarah says 'hi' by the way." I almost choked on my breath. "Things...happened and well, it hit me. I was acting no better than the people you once called friends by expecting you to just...move on and choose me." She reached out and grabbed my hand, sincerity in her eyes as she said, "I want to try again if you will let me?"

I watched her, inspecting the cuts and bruises on her. Knowing they came from Sarah left me feeling a strange sense of anger toward one of my oldest friends. Though Jaz refused to say, I could guess what Sarah said wasn't something that would inspire loyalty toward her. I sighed. "I don't know."

"I understand you are hurt. So are the others. Our friend group hasn't been the same since all this started and well, I don't think it will be until you are part of our family again. If you're willing to give me the chance, I'd like to help you rebuild."

I looked at the box of chocolates, then back at her. I knew if I accepted her offer, it would be the start of something I didn't know if I was ready for.

"I want that too," I admitted. "But I don't think I can give you all what you want. I'm not ready to choose."

Jaz placed a gentle hand on mine. "I won't ask you to," she said. "Though I can't speak for the others. All I'm asking right now is that you try to see this from their perspective and do what you can, where you can, to help. Can you do that?"

I looked at her hand. *Could I?* I didn't know, but I did know I was tired of feeling so alone. "I can certainly try."

Chapter 37

I stood in a small lab the next day. The room was chilly, matching the eyes of the occupants as they watched me warily. I shifted nervously, standing slightly behind Jaz as she acted like nothing was wrong.

The walls surrounding us were covered in monitors, images of Sally Brown filling each one. A small table sat in the center, occupied by Blake, Abby, and my friends. Other students helping form the new combat teams waited in clusters around the room.

Kyle was the first to speak up. "What is she doing here?" he demanded of Jaz.

She cocked her head as if she didn't understand the question. "I invited her," she said.

Kyle opened his mouth to argue.

"Did I ever tell you I knew the whole time?" Jaz continued.

His mouth shut with an audible *click*.

"And you never reported it?" asked Abby, sitting up straighter, her eyes calculating.

I was suddenly worried for Jaz's safety. "She didn—" I started, stepping forward to defend her when she cut me off. The atmosphere in the room shifted as they noticed my actions.

"I had no reason to at the time." Jaz sent Abby the fakest smile I had ever seen.

Shan eyed me, a question in his gaze, and I tried not to shrink back from it.

"And what would lead you to believe that you would have no reason to alert the council of an imminent threat?" Blake's voice was cold.

Jaz didn't budge. "That is personal and not really relevant anymore now, is it? Sure, you could take action against me, try me in front of the school and let me die, or we could focus on the issue at hand and work to end this war before the Browner's get ahead." I could hear a pin drop in the silence as they stared each other down.

"Do you wish to help?" Blake stared straight into my soul as all eyes turned to me.

I nodded, pushing down my panic as I spoke. "As much as I can. I..." I stopped choosing my next words carefully. Jaz gave my hand a small squeeze that had Hayley's eyebrows shooting up. "I don't want to do anything that could lead to others being hurt or killed, but I also can't just sit by. If I can help in any way that doesn't involve combat, then I'm willing to try."

Zack hid a smug smile in his hand as Abby grinned next to him.

Blake searched me and I stood taller. "Alright. you can stay."

I let out a breath and Jaz relaxed beside me.

"But."

I stopped my movement forward to the table.

"It's on a trial basis only. I won't be the first to tell you I simply don't trust you. If you are willing to listen when I say you have to leave and you don't argue against any decisions made in here, then I will allow it."

I gnawed at my lip, thinking. "I can do that," I agreed.

He nodded, and the occupants of the room returned to their business. Jaz happily pulled me along to the table. Zack welcomed me with a gentle smile as I sat on the other side of Jaz, next to Kyle. I met Sam's eyes across the way, seeing a gentle acceptance in them that made his paw shaped birthmark crinkle.

"Welcome to the team," Kyle whispered beside me, his face bright. I tried to ignore the fact that Shan refused to look my way.

"Okay then, let's get down to business. We have a lot to cover today," Blake said from the head of the table. "First off, we have been reassured that the Board of Education won't interfere in our business. As to why, we don't know yet, but that means we should have some more freedoms to use the school cars and such to get back and forth from now on." Excited whispers filled the room. "We have also managed to secure actual weapons off the black market." The whispers grew to a subtle roar. "You should be aware, most of this won't be high-tech. Swords, knives, bows and arrows, etcetera. We *have* secured a few laser guns. These will be distributed on a first need basis and used sparingly. It costs a lot of money to recharge the systems."

Zack opened his mouth, and Blake held up a hand. "Before you ask, we can't secure any of the older tech there. According to our resource, it's almost impossible to get info on how they made the classic guns and the rumors on the process imply that it's more trouble than it's worth."

Zack sat back, satisfied by the answer.

"The good news is it sounds like the Browner's haven't got their hands on any, so we should have a distinct advantage. Now onto front-line shifts and border patrols."

The next hour was filled with talks about plans for the future, from forming teams to setting down rules of combat. The room was insistent that we send word to Sally Brown, letting them know we would not be involving any students under high school and that they should do the same. There was also talk of finding a place the school could use to house the new headquarters. It wasn't going to be possible to hold everything we would need for the future in the small lab we currently occupied.

As the conversation took a turn toward plans for future attacks, all eyes turned to me.

"I think it's time for you to leave." Blake said.

I gave a stiff nod, stood, and left the room. As the door closed behind me, I suddenly felt as alone as I had when this all started. *You will have to choose.* I shook dream Robert's voice from my head.

"No, I can remain neutral," I whispered to myself.

"You can what?" a deep voice asked.

I looked up, seeing a large boy walking my way down the narrow hall. I watched him warily. A varsity letter jacket hung from his broad right shoulder, and he seemed to be made of muscles. I could see two tattoos on his arms. One on his left bicep and one on his right forearm, bright against his dark skin. The right was a small image of two crossing gold swords. The other, I'd never seen an image like it before. At first, it looked like a small tree, its base normal, with roots sticking out. But as I followed it up, it looked more like a dandelion. Small seeds flew from the top into the air. As they got farther from the tree, they gradually transformed into five small birds flying away. It was an intriguing symbol, and I found myself more fixated on it than the boy.

"You okay there?"

I snapped my eyes up, meeting his hazel ones. Recognition flashed across them.

"Loran?" My name sounded both like a question and a whispered longing on his tongue.

"Yes?" I asked.

He didn't reply, eyeing me like a chess player eyes his board. "What are you..."

The door slammed open, and Kyle stepped out. "You're welcome to come back. Oh, hey, Devein, you're early." Kyle brightened when he spotted the boy, his chest puffing out.

"Hey man." Devein smiled. "I got out of practice early so I decided to swing by. Are you all done already?"

Kyle nodded. "Yeah, mostly, I was just coming to get Loran so she can help us out a bit." Both boys turned calculating stares to me.

"Okay then.... What did I miss?" Devein asked.

"I'll tell you later." Kyle gave me an assessing stare. "Are you ready?"

Shakily, I nodded and followed him back into the room. A rough sketch of the Sally Brown campus floated above the table. I gulped.

"Welcome back," Blake said with a smile. His eyes gleamed in the Holo-light.

I took the seat available beside Shan, Kyle sitting on my other side. Shan stiffened as my hand brushed him.

"As you can see, we have been able to plot a rough map of Sally Brown over the years. However, we are still missing critical data."

My breath quickened as I felt a squeeze. The room watched me.

"Call this your first test."

I took a measured breath, meeting Sally's doubtful gaze across the table before I looked to Jaz. She gave me an encouraging nod. *Prove them wrong.*

"Alright, what do you need?" My answer seemed to surprise almost everyone.

Blake watched me, calculating. "Please give us as much detail as you can on this building here." He zoomed in on a spot of the map I was intimately familiar with, the basketball training facilities.

I steeled myself, praying for forgiveness as I pulled up a Holo-pen and began mapping the building. Everyone in the room hung on my every word as I talked while I worked. I wiped a stray tear from my eye, passing it off as a scratch as I finished.

I'm so sorry.

Blake pulled my rough sketch of each floor, mapping it to the one they had. As he did, I watched as sections turned red. The further he progressed, the more my stomach sank.

They already have a map.

By the time he was done, my superimposed image was littered with small red marks where I misdrew a wall or misplaced a door. It was nothing that should raise alarm as they were simple mistakes, but I still held my breath as Blake analyzed it and me.

"Well then," he said, a slow smile spreading across his lips. "It seems like Jaz was right to trust you. Welcome to Alpha Force One."

The room filled with excited chatter. I watched the faces of my friends begin to soften, a timid kindness returning. It almost made the pit in my stomach worth it.

"I should have never doubted you," Kyle said, softly. I looked at him, seeing a bright grin on his face. "I'm sorry for the things I've said. It was wrong of me."

I expected his apology with a hesitant smile. "Thank you."

"I knew she wasn't a bad person," Dorothy said to my left, and it warmed my heart.

"I'm just happy to have a friend back," Lucy added in her soft voice, pain still in her eyes.

"I'm sorry for lying," I said to the room. "I hope in time you can forgive me, and we can work to win this war together."

"I think that might just be a possibility," Blake agreed with a bright smile. "I look forward to working with you in the future."

A sense of uneasiness settled in my bones as I tried to return his enthusiasm. That feeling followed me into my dreams the following night.

"Beg, princess, beg," Robert said.

I looked around, helplessly. "I already made my choice," I said.

"Have you?" he spat. "If you didn't want to be part of this, you should have run away while you still had the chance."

"I couldn't." I fell to the ground.

He sneered down at me, the knife glinting in his hand. "You could have. There were plenty of chances. But you didn't, and do you know why?" He kneeled down, grabbing my chin to look him in the eyes. "It's because you enjoy this." He ran the knife along my cheek. "You were born for this. For the blood; for the pain."

"No!" I cried, tears falling down his hand. "I gave up that life. I killed the monster." He let out a wicked laugh, sounding like death itself.

"The only thing you killed that day was your best friend." I fought against him, but his claws pierced my cheeks. "Now you're just finishing the job. Bring out the prisoner!"

I couldn't watch Chris be dragged my way, couldn't bear the sight of his broken body.

"Choose, darling."

I crawled to Chris, my hands sliding against the red ground.

"It's okay," he said. "I forgave you a long time ago."

I lifted the knife above his head.

He closed his eyes, a smile on his lips.

I thrust it down.

Chapter 38

I JOLTED FROM MY bed, sweat dripping from me despite the chill in my room. Tears flowed down my face and I scrubbed at them, making my cheeks raw. An extra red pill was accompanied by a golden one as the color tint in my world lightened to white. When I made it to the lobby to meet my friends, I was surprised to see Kyle waiting with them.

"Good morning?" I asked.

They smiled somewhat warily, and Kyle took a step forward. "I thought we could walk to calculus together today?" he said, his words sounding more like a question.

I glanced around for Shan, not seeing him.

"Shan will meet us there." Kyle read my thoughts. "He had...something to do."

My heart fell and I knew immediately that he was still avoiding me.

"Sure, that would be great." I forced a smile onto my face. Kyle started walking, and I followed, stopping to look back at the others.

"Don't worry about us. You two have fun," Jaz said with a wink. The others shuffled awkwardly, and Hayley gave me a forlorn smile. I flushed, confused as I turned and caught up with Kyle, who was holding the door for me.

The cool early December air brought a flush to his cheeks as we headed to class. Less people stared at me with open hostilities, forgiveness coming slowly as word of the things I'd done to help the war spread.

I ignored the twisting of my gut.

"You don't look too well," Kyle stated.

I looked up at him, surprised to see concern in his eyes. "That's not really something you're supposed to say to a girl, is it?" I asked.

He laughed. "No, I guess not. But you could say I've grown rusty." He rubbed the back of his neck, a motion so like Shan that I found myself pining.

"I doubt that the player extraordinaire has lost his skills," I teased.

Kyle avoided my gaze. "You haven't noticed?"

"Noticed what?" I asked right as we passed a group of giggling girls.

"Hi, Kyle!" one called.

Instead of throwing them the wink I expected, he simply nodded. "Good morning," he said, turning from them back to me.

I watched as they glared and one mouthed *Browner*. "Are you feeling alright?" I asked, placing my hand on his forehead. "Have you been sleeping? Is the war already getting to you?"

Kyle's cheeks darkened in a blush, and he swiped my hand away softly. "I'm fine," he dismissed.

"No, you're not. That was prime meat right there and you just passed it up."

Kyle winced. "Is that how you see me?" He sounded so small, and I really took a moment to look at him. The term of fighting had hardened his muscles and the weeks of war talks had already aged his face, but the biggest change I noted was his eyes. They were soft, full of longing when they looked at me.

"No," I whispered. "No, you hate me."

He sighed. "I thought I did too." He looked so lost as he watched the campus around us. My stomach twisted and a different type of anxiety filled me. "But I guess somewhere along the way you wormed your way into my heart as well."

I shook my head.

"Would-you-please-go-out-on-a-date-with-me?" He rushed the words out so fast they seemed to be one.

My breath left my lungs as panic set in. *A date? He wants to go on a date with me?* I couldn't fathom why the thought made my heart race as my stomach fell. I was saved from answering him as we filed into the math building. A group of boys called out to him as we entered, joining us on the stairs. Awkwardness hung in the air.

I thought about Shan and then Chris, two boys I was sure I'd fallen for. Nowhere on that list had Kyle truly existed for me. *But maybe he should? He's seemed to have grown after all.*

What about Shan? A voice in my head whispered. Speaking of the devil, we walked into the large lecture hall, and I saw him. My heart skipped a beat.

Shan was busy at his desk just like the first day we met, engrossed in his project. Pulling my eyes away, I made to turn and hike up to my seat when Kyle grabbed my hand.

"You can sit with us you know."

The pleading in his eyes and the exhaustion of exile made me give in. "Alright."

He led me to the row. I watched as a boy from the basketball team gave me a once over, anger and acceptance warring on his face. Then he stood. Like a well-oiled machine, the room shifted, seats being rearranged just for me. I felt uncomfortable from the glares as Kyle led me to the seat next to him, two down from Shan.

"Morning dude," Kyle said, with a small pat on Shan's back.

"Good morning," Shan said, looking up with a smile. The moment he saw me, it froze. As if waking from a dream, he blinked, looking around the room.

I followed his gaze, catching curious eyes. He returned to his screen without acknowledging me. My PortMed squeezed.

I sat through the short surprise lecture, feeling all sorts of messed up and could barely focus on my new calculations as we split to do individual work. The ending bell felt like years away, and when it finally sounded, Shan stood from his desk and left the room in a hurry. Quickly, I threw my things into my bag, chasing after him.

I weaved through the crowd, catching up to him in the hall. "Wait," I called, grabbing his arm. He stiffened under my grip, but he didn't pull away. "Listen, I know I hurt you, and I understand why you don't want to talk to me. I don't blame you. But I have to tell you something. I know I have no right to, but I I—"

"Oh, there you are, sweety." Lilith came bouncing down the hall, a bright smile on her face.

I winced, prepared for another one of her attacks but it never came. Instead of looking to me, she stopped at Shan, reaching up and pecking him on the cheek. "You ready to go?" she asked.

I felt like I was falling into a darkness I couldn't escape.

Shan gave her a soft smile. "Yeah, just a moment." He looked back at me, his eyes guarded. "You were saying?"

I gulped down the lump in my throat and forced a smile. "I just wanted to apologize. I understand if you don't want to be my friend anymore, but I couldn't live with the thought of you hating me."

Shan looked deep into my eyes as if he was searching for more. "Oh." He sounded disappointed. "I-I've already forgiven you, Loran. Life is too short to hold a grudge, especially with us being at war and all."

I should have felt relief at his words, but as he looked away, I didn't believe him. "Oh, that's good then." I coughed. "Thank you."

"There you are," Kyle said as he slipped in beside me. "Are you okay? I was worried when you rushed out like that. Do you need to see the nurse?" He placed a gentle hand on my shoulder, his eyes full of concern. A small sliver of light pierced through the darkness. Shan eyed the familiar gesture, his gaze growing dark.

"Are you sick?" Lilith asked. "I hope it's not contagious." She gave me a fake smile, vicious glee in her eyes.

"You should really see the nurse," Shan added, his tone caring. "You don't want to get worse."

I felt anger rising. "Oh no, I'm fine," I said, grabbing Kyle's hand from my shoulder and turning slightly toward him. He cradled my hand. "It really was sweet of you to come looking for me," I told him with a soft smile.

He beamed at me and in that moment, I suddenly felt so cared for. "It's really no big deal." He squeezed my hand. "I'd always come searching for you."

"Oh my!" Lilith cooed. "Are you two dating?"

I looked to see Shan's eyes flash, a hint of anger in them.

"Oh, um, no—"

"Actually," I stopped Kyle. "We are just getting to know each other. In fact, Kyle just asked me on a date. I got cut off before I could tell him yes."

Shan's eyes were black as a storm cloud.

I ignored them, enjoying the way Kyle's eyes lit with joy when I looked at him.

"You were?" he sounded amazed.

I smiled up at him. "Yes. I would really like to get to know the real you." I found I meant the words, thinking of the boy I saw on the beach. His smile was worth throwing my feelings to the wind.

"Oh, that is just too cute. Well, we'll leave you to it. Come on, sweety." Lilith tugged on Shan's hand.

He pulled his eyes from us like it was a great effort, following her down the hall.

"I'm worried about him," Kyle said, intertwining our fingers. "She already hurt him once. I don't believe she won't do it again." The kindness in his eyes as he watched his best friend solidified my decision.

This was a boy who seemed to actually care for me and was capable of more than I gave him credit for. My heart fluttered a bit as I thought about the possibilities of a relationship with him.

"He has you to look out for him," I said, giving Kyle's hand a gentle squeeze. "I think he'll be fine."

Chapter 39

I FOLLOWED MY FRIENDS from the fourth day of meetings since that first Thursday, my eyes hurting and my stomach rolling.

"We totally need to celebrate, just us girls. It's, like, almost end of term, and Loran has joined the fight," said Hayley. She eyed me up and down, and when she smiled, it was a little less guarded.

I blushed and shoved her gently, feeling all types of messed up inside. "Come on, it really isn't a big deal," I dismissed, trying to believe the words.

"Yeah right, girl, that was the worst few weeks of my life. To be honest, it was lonely without your constant talking and singing," said Jaz with a grin.

I followed them outside, leaving the boys behind. "I don't sing," I countered.

"Yeah, you do. When you're testing or thinking really hard, you usually hum or sing quietly to yourself," said Sally with a gleeful grin.

My cheeks heated. "Well, that's embarrassing. Why haven't I heard about this before?" I wondered how many people had sat close enough to hear me over the years. My stomach dropped. *Why didn't my old friends mention it? Is this a recent development?*

"I thought you knew?" Bee said.

Dorothy nodded beside her, dodging a stray hoverboard.

I watched its rider chase after it, calling out for someone to stop it for him. When I caught the eyes of a student nearby, she gave me a timid smile.

"No, I didn't! I mean, seriously, I don't sing. I'm tone deaf." I buried my head in my hands.

Lucy laughed at me. "Yeah, it can be a little bad. Still, Shan thinks it's cute," she said with a snort.

"Shan?" Lucy stopped. She and Hayley exchanged looks. Their caution caused my stomach to flop. The others continued walking like nothing was up.

I glanced back, seeing the boys talking by the building we just left. As if sensing my eyes, Shan looked up. I broke eye contact quickly, unable to see the pain still in his.

"Does he—"

"Don't worry, it's, like, no biggie. So, what do we want to do?" Hayley dismissed, cutting me off.

"Let's go to Brain Beans," said Sally, jumping on the topic change. "It's been so long since we've been. Who knows, there might be a performance tonight?"

"I don't know..." said Jaz.

I felt her hesitance, agreeing. I didn't know how I would be received.

"Come on, please?" No one could resist Sally's big eyes begging us to go.

I followed the group to the café, pulling my jacket close to fight the chilling breeze and unwelcome eyes. The bare trees around us were slowly being decorated with Christmas lights and, despite everything, joy was in the air.

When we arrived, we squeezed our way into the shack-sized building past crowds of people milling about. I only had to avoid a handful of feet and hands heading my way. The spit that hit my sleeve was ignored. I enjoyed the smell of hickory and coffee permeating the air as Hayley pushed our way to the front and ordered a round of chai lattes for the group. I grabbed mine with tapioca boba, watching as they made it to ensure they didn't spit in it.

Once we had the drinks, we forced our way to the back of the café. A huge door led to a small meadow covered in tables and couches, strategically stacked on each other and platforms, filling the space and facing the stage. Lights hung above everyone, woven in the trees and along the fence that ran the perimeter. The strumming of a lone guitarist at the stage lent to a relaxing atmosphere. With some persuasion from Hayley, we got a group of freshmen boys to give us their two couches. I laughed into my hand as they walked away, feeling bad.

"To Loran," said Jaz, throwing her cup in the air after settling down on the couch beside Hayley and Lucy.

Sitting opposite them with Bee, Dorothy, and Sally, I responded. "To Kent Wood."

The people around us sat a little less stiffly after that. We clinked cups and took a drink. The night air felt good on my skin and the lights above were bright and welcoming. The café was alive, and I watched the surrounding people with joy. The top of my cup read,

Enjoy every moment. For each is fleeting. I took it to heart as I sat back, happy to be with my friends again. Things were starting to go back to normal. Nothing could ruin the night.

"Well, well, well. If it isn't the famous Brown Lightning."

I spoke too soon.

I didn't turn to Robert, opting instead to watch my friend's faces grow cold.

"Leave us," said Jaz, glaring daggers at him. Sally made a move to cover me.

Though my heart warmed in surprise, I stopped her. The eyes of the students around us told me I would be in a deeper hole if I allowed her to stand up for me. Standing, I turned to him.

"It's nice to see you too, sweet thing," Robert said, smiling viciously at Jaz and Hayley. His little gang was standing behind him, laughing like always. "I heard you and the fabulous alphas made up Princess. Tell me, who did you have to send down the river to achieve that?"

My stomach flopped as he walked around the couch to stand in front of me. He licked his lips and I shivered. "That's none of your business," I hissed.

"Come on, now. I thought we decided to be civil with each other," he cooed, trying to touch my cheek.

As his friends cracked up, I flipped it and him off. "I would never agree to such a thing."

"You don't remember? I do...you were beneath me calling out my name and—" He stopped with a smirk as I let out a shout. Hayley had to grab my arm to keep me from punching him in the face. I struggled against her, Jaz and Lucy cursing him as the air grew cold.

"Keep away from him, Browner," someone hissed so low I barely caught it.

This seemed to amuse Robert. He chuckled, stepping forward. I noticed it was deathly quiet, all eyes and ears on us. The fight left me as I saw the fear in some of them.

"You know, Shan and Kyle were thinking about coming to join us later," said Sally nonchalantly beside me, cutting him off in his next attempt to harass me as she took a sip of her drink.

This stopped most of Robert's lackeys. The surrounding people murmured at the news. I knew that most couldn't believe I had been forgiven by my friends already, let alone started dating Kyle.

"Would you like to keep us company until they get here?" She raised one delicate eyebrow. Robert turned his ire on her. If looks could kill, Sally would be dead. She simply looked down at her nails as if they were more interesting than him. I could feel the hate crashing from Robert like waves. The tension was so thick I could cut it with a knife.

"No, thanks. Me and the boys have stuff to do," he spit through clenched teeth. I saw the way he balled his hands in restraint.

"Aw, too bad." Sally pouted, a smirk in her eyes.

"Have a pleasant night." He flashed me one last strained smile, then disappeared back into the crowd.

The last boy in his group gave me a wicked grin. "Watch your back," he whispered, just loud enough for me to hear.

I felt my breath catch and watched with wide eyes as he disappeared. Bee's hand rested upon my shoulder, grounding me, helping me to calm. With the last of the group gone, people went back to their drinks, the latest gossip already spreading as fingers flew on Holo-screens. I gathered my nerves and slunk down on my chair with a sigh.

"All those guys are complete creepers," said Lucy, visibly shuttering.

"How has he not been arrested for assault?" asked Dorothy.

"He's too good of a player to get kicked out," replied Bee, taking a sip of her drink.

"And no one wants to risk our standing for someone like him," pointed out Sally.

"Besides, he's, like, always known when to stop before crossing the line," Hayley added. She looked me over, her face growing contemplative, her gaze surprisingly worried. "Though he isn't the same with you. There is totally something different in how he pushes you, how he looks at you."

The group let out a collective shiver.

"I've noticed," I said.

"You don't need to worry anymore, okay? The council has put you under their protection, no one will try to hurt you now." Jaz reassured me with a gentle squeeze to my hand.

"At least he won't be at the front with us tomorrow." Lucy smiled.

My mood died at the reminder.

"I'm, like, surprised they agreed to let you come," Hayley said to me.

I felt a squeeze.

"We are in desperate need of more medics on the field. It won't be long till someone dies out there." I really didn't need Sally's pessimism at the moment.

Dorothy gave my shoulder a squeeze. "Learning to heal will be good for ya."

"Yeah," I agreed halfheartedly. We let the subject drop, choosing to talk about more pleasant things. As the evening grew late, I shoved Robert and my mission to the back of my mind. *What can they really do?*

Chapter 40

"Beg, princess, beg."

"Why can't I escape?" I asked, giving in to my exhaustion as I fell onto the slick ground below. "I've made my choice!"

"Pathetic," Robert spat, kneeling next to me. "You have done no such thing. To think otherwise is just you lying to yourself. But you're pretty good at that, aren't you?"

"I don't know what you're talking about."

His claws closed around my face, the red in his eyes seeming to drip down his cheek. "You do. You just won't listen to the voice inside."

Screams filled my ears. I looked about frantically.

All around me, my friends from both schools burned.

"No, no, stop!" I cried, trying to get free to save them.

"I can't. I'm not the one who did this."

There was a match in my hand.

"It's okay," Jaz said, as she suffered, her skin popping, making me want to vomit. "We don't matter anyway."

"No!"

I stifled the scream rising in my throat as I jolted awake. The wind outside blew against the tent, making a popping roaring noise as I looked around. My sleeping bag reminded me of where I was. The other bags were empty, my friends heading out to their mission in the middle of the night.

With a sigh, I got up, rolling my bag as I set about getting the others ready. After two days on the front, our shift was over, and I had never been so grateful to return to Kent Wood.

"How you doing in there, Lightning?" a deep voice called from the other side of the tent flap. It *rustled* and a lean boy entered. Long shaggy blond hair fell in front of his black eyes as he straightened. A charming smile was sent my way, his Mate Necklace and Tattoo, thick with green studs, glinted in the sun before the flap closed.

"Hey, Gang," I said, stuffing Hayley's roll in her bag. "I'm all right just making sure the others will be ready to go. I know they will be exhausted when they return."

"That's very kind of you." Gang's eyes softened slightly, but I noticed he didn't relax. "You ready for training today?"

I nodded. "Yeah, it's been a nice refresher and I'm learning so much." I stood, finished. "You ready to—" I was cut off as sirens wailed around me.

"Injured incoming," called a voice over the PortMeds.

I followed Gang as we slipped out of the tent. The Mobile Army Surgical Hospital style camp bustled as students ran about, various weapons from swords to bows to the few rare L-guns strapped to each of them.

My head snapped to the left as the sound of a hover car filled the air. The familiar set of green and gold vehicles headed our way. My MEDs activated as I ignored the screams in my head, longing for a weapon of my own, but stilled my hands as Gang tightened his grip on his crossbow.

He watched the skyline for pursuing vehicles. I'd learned it was an unspoken rule that the students wouldn't attack medical camps—surely no one was that heartless—but no one trusted the other side to follow the rules, either.

Pushing past Gang, I sprinted toward the med tent as I spotted Jaz's flaming hair.

She stepped from the first vehicle, calling out to the crowd. "We have one red, one yellow, and two green."

The head nurse that arrived by her side nodded. "Grab the red first," she commanded to her colleagues, and they rushed to the boy staggering from the third car, parts of his leg missing.

The world tilted to the right. I slipped in a pill, felt a squeeze, and I was rightening, in control again. "I'll grab the yellow."

The head nurse turned to me. "You will take care of the greens. Even with two, that shouldn't be too hard, right?" There was an edge to her question, but I nodded.

"No ma'am," I said, rushing to the car Jaz pointed to. As I approached, Shan and Kyle staggered out. "Shan." I hurried to him as I noticed the cuts and bruises on his arms and, most likely, the rest of his body. "What happened?"

"You should see the other dude," said Kyle from the other side of the car. I pushed down the urge to hug him, jolting forward as he limped my way. "It's good to see you too." He stroked my cheek as he neared.

"Come on in. I'll take care of those wounds." I dragged them to the med tent. When we arrived, I headed to the part of the floor marked in green. A small bot sat waiting, and as I activated it, it scanned the two boys. They stood still, waiting for the results.

When it *beeped* three times, I let out a breath. "Alright, let's get you patched up."

They nodded, heading to two floating cots and sitting down. I turned to start prepping as the bot went about gathering my supplies based on their injuries. As I looked over my shoulder, I swallowed my concern. I couldn't help but notice the tension between them. Their eyes flickered with an unknown message as they stared each other down, and they looked away with anger.

What happened out there?

As I knelt in front of Shan, I realized his injuries were worse than I first thought. His face was swollen, and I could see a black eye forming. His lip was split, and his neck had a long scratch on the left side that was slowly bleeding. His arms were littered with cuts and bruises, and I didn't want to know what else was wrong internally. Luckily, the bot had cleared them, and the MEDs should oversee that part.

I looked at Kyle. He was in just as bad shape if not worse.

"Please tell me the mission was a success, at least," I said as I wrung out a wet towel soaked in MEDs, placing it on the scratch on Shan's neck. He hissed in pain and closed his eyes as I cleaned him.

"Yeah, it was," said Kyle, taking the ice pack I handed him and putting it on his eye. "The problem occurred later on."

"How so?" I bandaged Shan's arm after spraying it with skin glue.

"The war has expanded," Shan gritted out through the pain, stopping me midway.

"What?" I croaked.

"Sandy Village has joined the party," Kyle explained, moving the ice pack to his other eye as his MEDs got to work. "And they are siding with Sally Brown."

I was growing increasingly unsettled by the way I lost control and my vision flooded with color before the MEDs kicked in.

"They attacked Bravo Two as they were heading home, so we diverted to stop them." I finished Shan's arm and moved onto Kyle, cleaning his cuts. He hissed his last words. "They are a lot more skilled than Sally Brown in hand-to-hand combat."

Hayley and Garret were heading our way from the door. "This is what I was afraid of." I caught Shan's pitying look in the corner of my eye, ignoring him as I focused on Kyle's wounds. I tried not to think about how bad things were going to get.

Hayley and Garret took the empty cots in the green area with us, laying down, clearly exhausted. I had the boys remove their shirts so I could get to the wounds littering their backs and stomachs, wincing as Shan pulled some of the fabric out of a wound in his gut. I washed and cleaned each one.

Staring at their abs, I held back a sudden snort. *So many girls on campus would die to be in my shoes.*

As I washed Shan's back, I saw the tattoo there for the first time. It seemed to be almost identical to Kyle's, except on the hilt. There was a symbol there in a language that I didn't recognize. I moved onto Kyle after a moment, trying not to make it obvious I was staring.

"They made their choice and now we all will pay for it," said Garret with a sigh. I looked up at his tired face. The war hadn't lasted more than a month, and it was already wearing on people. I had seen the lost looks in my friend's eyes. They seemed older and I knew they had seen things and done things that weren't exactly legal or moral.

I'm worried about them.

Giving Garret a kind smile, I finished wrapping Kyle's arm and placed my hand on it. He looked at me and I gave him the best smile I could muster. He grinned back and I saw the effort it took for him to do so.

"I'm done now," I said quietly and stood. Looking down at Shan and Kyle, I held out my hands. They exchanged a glance and stood as well, not taking them.

I tried not to feel hurt by the gesture. A hand was on my shoulder and I turned my head to see Jaz smiling down at me.

"We've been given the go to head home. We have two days before they will expect us back." She told the group as a whole. "The others will join us when they can."

I nodded, giving each of them an assessing gaze. They looked dead on their feet. "I've already packed for you all," I said. "I knew you would be tired and didn't want you all to have to wait. We can grab your bags and head out. I'll drive."

The surprise in their eyes gave way to gentle smiles. A cautious look was passed between Hayley and Garret, but I ignored it, trying not to feel hurt.

"That would be nice, actually," Kyle said, stepping up and placing a gentle kiss on my head. "Thank you for offering."

I nodded and together we headed out, going back home for class the next day. As we neared the parking lot hours later I was starting to stress out about the details of my project and how I was going to get them done in time, the worries of war already forgotten.

Chapter 41

Two days later the war room was filled with static. My eyes glued to the screens around me, waiting with bated breath for them to come to life.

"Rodger, we have visual; signal coming through now," said a girl sitting under one of the smaller monitors nearby.

The static came to life as Kyle's voice filtered through the speakers. "Testing. Can you hear us?"

"Ten-four. We read you loud and clear," the girl replied.

The screen filled with the images of my friends from Kyle's perspective. As he turned his head, I scanned over each of them, glad to see they were okay and had arrived at Sally Brown safely. The other monitors in the room flickered with the cameras from the other members of the alpha team.

"Alpha Leader, how's the situation looking?" Blake called, addressing Kyle.

A laugh reverberated through the room.

"We really need to fix these code names. Alpha Leader just doesn't inspire a lot of fear, does it?" Kyle asked.

I cracked a smile.

The camera shook as he yelped, and Hayley scolded, "We are working, this is, like, no time for jokes."

"Alright, alright, sorry," he called.

"We have visual on the target." Shan's voice cut in, stone cold. He was in full mission mode, as I'd come to call it. "He's exactly where Lightning said he would be."

I ignored the warmth in his voice. All eyes were on me as Abby gave me a kind smile. I returned it wearily, fingering the pills in my pocket.

"Good to know, Alpha Two," a boy said to my right.

"Get ready to move," Kyle commanded.

The camera turned, the snowy woods of the forest around Sally Brown filling the screen. Feet away, two figures crouched. One had a set of binoculars to his eyes, while the other fiddled with a crossbow.

"Remember, team, we want him alive," Blake reminded.

The room was tense as Kyle slowly moved into position. I could hear the crunch of the snow under his feet. As he cleared a pine, a long dirt road curving down from the hill came into view. The sound of laughter filled the air, and two figures appeared at the top.

"Defect," Jaz and I said at the same time. "He's not alone."

I looked at her monitor, seeing a group of five walking before they disappeared from her limited view.

"What do we do, HQ?" Zack asked.

Everyone turned to the far corner where a lone speaker sat. "Proceed with the mission," a deep voice boomed from it. "Incapacitate the others and get out of there."

"You heard Ghost. Move," Blake said.

"Ghost. Now that's a code name," Kyle whispered as someone said, "Go! Go! Go!"

The world was a blur as Kyle began his sprint to the unsuspecting group, the sound of four weapons firing hitting my ears.

I tried not to vomit as the screams from the injured rang out. Mike's familiar face filled the screen as Kyle made his move. I didn't know whose bones cracked as their hits impacted at the same time.

"Kyle," I cried out. He grunted in return, continuing his onslaught. I had to look away, the motion and the sounds around me making the pink shadows grow in my mind. I quickly slipped a red pill into my PortMed, hiding the movement with my hair.

When I looked up, I could see the monitor holding Shan's video. He was sprinting toward Kyle and Mike's fight. He passed the others working to subdue the people who had been with Mike. I didn't recognize any of their faces and felt a small sense of relief.

Mike delivered a hard blow to Kyle that had him reeling backward. Before he could continue his onslaught, Shan was on him. I had to turn back to the main monitor as the screen blurred.

Watching Shan fight was like watching an artist. All his movements were perfectly planned, each step, each blow hitting its mark. I wondered where he learned to fight like that. Even after all my years, I had never perfected such a skill, my fighting style much more like a rabid animal.

Mike didn't stand a chance. He was down as Kyle stood and three people had him pinned. A syringe was pushed into his neck, and in seconds, he was still.

"Alright, we have two hours before the MEDs nullify the serum. Get moving," Blake commanded.

Lucy attached a small button to Mike. Two flicks and the bots inside released. They spread across his skin like a swarm of bugs, encompassing him in a single system. The hovering tech activated as it closed, his body floating into the sky a few feet above the ground.

"We are heading out," Sally said. I watched with bated breath as the team made it to the school cars and piled in, stuffing Mike in the back of one. Lucy and Sam filed into a small ATV at the front and the others jumped into their own vehicles.

The drive toward home felt like a lifetime as familiar landmarks flew by. I fiddled with my PortMed as hours passed, anxious and bored at the same time. The room was mostly calm as people went about preparing for other missions and work. With a sense of déjà vu, the mountains disappeared and a vast desert took their place. Two more hours passed before I heard anything.

"We are an hour out from the first border." Sam's voice was bright as they navigated around a large outcropping of rocks. "We should be home free soo—"

He never finished. The sound of an explosion filled the room. The screens burst with brilliant light, blinding me. Then there was nothing but static.

"Alpha team!" the girl to my right cried, scampering back to her monitor. The room broke into chaos, voices screaming into mics around me as techs worked to get the signal back.

"Respond Alpha One!"

My hands shook and shrieks filled my ears. *No, not today!*

"Get the coms back online now!"

The world was turning. I fumbled for another pill as the pink returned. *Why aren't they working as effectively as before?*

"Someone get eyes on them now."

Beg, princess, beg.

The small bag of five gold pills spilled out.

"There's an old traffic cam a mile out. Hacking in now."

You know what you have to do. I didn't know that voice.

I chased after the pills, grabbing each before they could get away.

"I need those coms!"

I slammed my PortMed so hard that I could feel the needles underneath shift in my skin.

"What do you see?"

My vision returned to normal, but the voices didn't fade. I looked up from the ground, as the main monitor fluttered to life. Hope shattered at the sight of the enormous cloud of smoke billowing in the distance. Cars were overturned this way and that. I couldn't see any movement.

"Alpha Leader, can you hear me?" Blake asked. Static. "Alpha Leader." The sound of a bang. "Glitching! Kyle, are you there?"

A groan filled the room. "What hit me?" Kyle coughed.

Relief flooded me as I began to cry. The room calmed only slightly as all heads turned to the speaker above the monitor.

"Kyle, what happened? Are you okay?" Abby asked.

More coughing filled the air as the other speakers came to life.

"Did we just explode?" Bee asked, amusement in her tone despite the situation.

"I think I broke something." Dum let out a grunt.

"Alpha Team, sound off," Shan commanded. Each person did as they were instructed, and I counted the numbers.

When all twenty-five voices finished, dread filled me.

"Alpha Five, Alpha Twelve, sound off," Kyle called.

No response came. I turned my head to the monitor on my right, static still filling the screen.

"I repeat: Alpha Five, Alpha Twelve, are you there?"

The traffic cam zoomed in and out as the operator tried to get a better visual. My heart plummeted as the smoldering remains of the ATV filled the screen.

"No!" A sobbing howl filled the room as Jaz spotted the wreckage. Her limping form appeared from behind a smoke cloud. "No, no, no." She fell to her knees in front of me as my world tilted despite the pills.

"Jaz, what is it?" Zack called, panic clear in his voice. She didn't answer, continuing to cry into my ears.

"Someone get visual on her now," called Dee.

"Oh no. Sam." Garret's voice was hollow.

"What?" demanded Kyle.

More forms crawled and limped from the wreckage.

"Luc?"

I had never heard Dorothy sound so broken. Tears fell down my eyes as the wailing in the room increased. My body gave out and my knees hit hard on the metal floor. All around me, people were collapsing in on themselves. The world was a diluted red, dripping around me.

"Lucy and Sam are down. I repeat Lucy and Sam are down," Sally called, sounding so broken.

Am I falling?

"What is going on? Do we need to send medical?" Blake stared hopelessly up at the monitors as he searched for a way to help. For a moment, the world seemed to mirror itself, lights reflecting from places it didn't exist and images doubling.

I knew the response before Hayley spoke.

"No. They're dead."

Chapter 42

I should have stopped this.

It was all I could think about as I stood on the main lawn of campus on the cloudy, chilly Sunday. A sea of black surrounded me as we listened to people talk on a small wooden stage before me with two familiar faces projected on it.

"I was five when Sam and I first met," shared an individual beside the pictures as he tried to hold in tears.

"Lucy was a sweetheart. If you ever had the pleasure of knowing her, you would've immediately fallen in love with her gentle demeanor," a small girl spoke up. She couldn't finish her speech, breaking out in tears. A crying friend escorted her offstage.

"No one ever expected Sam to be a jokester, but let me tell you..."

"Once when we were in elementary school, Lucy drew a horse...well she said it was a horse...to this day she still claims it was...still claimed..."

One by one, stories were told. That was how we remembered our dead. If their stories never faded, then they never truly left us, but stories when mourning were hard to share.

I tried not to collapse under the sorrow and pain I felt. I didn't think we would lose someone so soon.

There wasn't anything left to bring home.

My face was sticky with tears and snot as I cried into Kyle's bandaged shoulder. I didn't know Sam well, but Lucy was a friend. Like many of those telling stories mentioned, all you had to do was meet her to fall in love. In all my nightmares, I never expected I'd lose them.

The crowd shifted as Zack took the stage, his voice low and bitter. "They will pay for this. We will not give up until we have won. Sam and Lucy Smith will not be forgotten." The soft-spoken and heartfelt speech that he gave ignited a fire in everyone, including me. The large bandage on his cheek was soaked with tears.

"Few people knew that Sam and Lucy were cousins born days apart. They grew up together," Hayley choked out, leaning on her crutch bots. "The only blessing this brings is knowing neither will miss the other. They left this world as they entered it, together."

When the speeches wrapped up, no dry eye was left. A lovely girl from the art district stood on the stage. She opened her mouth and sang. The melody was sweet and haunting, coloring the scene, moving within my soul. Clouds swirled above as we watched with heavy hearts as the caskets containing mementos to the two, slowly sunk down deep into the dark earth.

Never again would I hear Lucy's soft voice. Her gentle presence or quiet understanding and support wouldn't surround me. I couldn't imagine how hard it must have been for those that were close to her and Sam: Shan who met him at an early age; Zack, who loved her like a sister. These thoughts caused me to cry harder.

"I promise you they will pay," Kyle's voice whispered softly behind me to a person unknown. He held me close, oblivious to the way my body racked harder as I cried for my old friends.

Why did you do this, Chris? Are you pleased?

Kyle placed a gentle kiss on my head that calmed my mind. He pulled back slightly, turning to speak to someone in private. I watched him go.

A hand was on my shoulder, and I turned to see a tearful Shan beside me.

He dropped his hand. "Listen," he paused, looking around as if lost. "I'm sorry. I...." He watched Kyle behind me, his eyes sad. "I forgive you. I really do. I understand why you did what you did, and I shouldn't have held it against you. I know what it's like to carry a heavy secret and well...." He reached to me, awkwardly stopping in midair, his bandaged hand trembling.

I stepped forward into his waiting grasp.

His eyes widened.

"Thank you," I said softly, wiping away a tear on my cheek. "You don't have to say anything more. I'm just glad we are talking again." I softly placed a hand on his where it rested on my shoulder, pulling it off and holding it. "I've missed you."

He looked more broken than he had when he approached. "I've missed you too." He watched me with an emotion I couldn't describe filling his eyes.

"How are you handling the aftermath of the mission?" I asked.

"Are you doing okay?" Kyle asked, stepping up, placing a hand on my waist before Shan could reply.

I gave him a mild smile. "As well as can be," I replied, as he eyed me. "Don't worry, I haven't needed one today, surprisingly."

I didn't speak of the pills aloud, since only a select few were privy to their existence.

He nodded. "Alright. I have to go help with the processions." He looked at Shan, his eyes falling to our connected hands. "I'm glad to see you all made up." His hand squeezed my hip. Before I could reply, he was pecking me on the lips and walking away.

"I'm too late." Shan's quiet voice drew my eyes to him. His gaze was storming in all the wrong ways.

"Don't blame yourself." I gave his hand a tender squeeze. "It isn't your fault. No one could have predicted the explosives." His eyes flashed and a pained smile filtered on his face.

His hand on my cheek stopped the tear there. "Yeah, of course. You're right."

Chapter 43

The woods were eerie, the half-moon above casting an uncomfortable glow around me. Sticks breaking as the group headed up the hill sounded like gun shots to my frayed nerves. I looked over my friends, their faces determined as we followed Blake.

"It's been four days and we still haven't been able to get him to talk," he said, his breath puffing in the air around him. "We are hoping a familiar face will make him open up."

My stomach did a flip as we cleared the hill into a clearing. A small shack sat in the middle, guarded by seven people, a fire in front keeping them warm.

Hearing our approach, they each snapped to attention.

"At ease, men." Blake flashed a kind smile as they relaxed.

"What can we do for you?" asked a guard, eyeing me with suspicion.

"We are here to talk with the prisoner. Please bring him out." They nodded and two of them opened the shack's door. One disappeared, dragging Mike out.

I couldn't stop my gasp at the sight of his bloody face and torn garments of what used to be his clothing. His wrists were bound with a ragged rope in front of him, and he had a limp. A guard forced him to kneel, and he landed on his knees with a grunt.

"How did he—" I asked, unable to finish my thought as worry filled me.

At the sound of my voice, Mike's head flew up.

"He tried to attack a guard when he arrived, almost ended up stabbing them with a hidden knife," a guard explained.

And you have punished him since, I concluded by the fresh cut on his lip, unable to break away from Mike's captivating gaze. Worry, confusion, and anger swirled in them.

"Loran, if you'd please?"

I snapped my attention to Blake, watching as he motioned for me to come up. I didn't move, feeling off. What did one say to the boy, the friend, partly responsible for the death of two other friends?

Treat him with kindness. Abby's instructions rang in my head. *He needs to feel that you are on his side.*

"Mike." I rushed to him, falling to my knees beside him even as my stomach rolled. He gave me a weary smile, then looked at my friends over my shoulder, glaring. I ignored him as I inspected his wounds. Pulling him close to see the damage, I missed Kyle walking up, placing a hand on my shoulder.

Before I could brush him off, Mike pulled away from me with venom. "So, these are your new friends?" he spat. His hate hurt. I avoided it by turning to Kyle.

It was more than an act as I pleaded, "Please try to understand. They are good people. Mike, this war, it's pointless. Our different schools don't change who we are. These petty rivalries need to stop. Already there are too many casualties. Please, just cooperate and we can end this here." Shoving Kyle's hand off me, I reached out to him.

"What have they done to you?" Mike said to me, keeping his gaze on Kyle and the group behind us. There was a darkness in his eyes that didn't exist the last time we spoke.

"Mike?" I asked warily.

"The Loran I knew would never say something like that. Not after what they have done. What they did to Hannah. What they did to you."

Subconsciously, my hand went to my stomach.

"They deserve everything that has happened. The real Loran would know that." Mike reached out to me, his bindings shifting around his wrists, then turned to glare at Kyle. "Is he the reason?"

"It's not what you think."

"You're in denial," Mike said, looking at me with a mixture of hate and pity.

"No, you're the one in denial, thinking this war will end in anything but pain and misery. Two people are dead because of this senseless violence." Indignation filled me. I could hear the group behind me shift.

"You're different," he stated, his voice cold. I resisted shrinking away. "You've changed."

"Well, I had to. I was left all alone here after all. Now I'm trying to prevent a war." I reached out and stroked his bruises, forcing down the mixture of anger and sorrow threatening to take over. *Please listen*, I begged internally to get through his thick skull. *Don't you see the pain this is causing? All that will come if we continue.* "I need you to help Kent Wood end the war."

He pulled away from me as if burned. The movement had feet shuffling behind me, and I heard a crossbow cock.

"What if we want this war? Did you ever consider that? What if we want to fight?"

"Why would you want war? More people are going to get hurt, going to die."

Mike was manic, going from hot to cold, his eyes pleading now. "We started this war for you. Loran, don't you understand? We want to free you and all the others like you. For too long, they have taken our loved ones from us. It needs to stop. Sarah, Kathy, Alex, and Chris—everyone misses you. You have no idea how big a hole you left behind."

"Chris lied to you, Mike. I'm here by my own will. You need to tell me what he's going to do." I was trying to pull us back on topic.

"I don't believe you!" yelled Mike. He grabbed my arm, his binding making the gesture awkward but no less painful.

The guards shifted forward.

"Let her go," Shan commanded behind me.

"Mike, you're hurting me. Please, let go." I pleaded.

"No, I'm taking you with me." In one swift move, he stood, dragging me with him. His ropes fell to the ground, and he brought his hand up to my throat, a piece of broken glass resting against it.

I barely had time to blink before I felt the sting of my skin splitting in two. The world around me seemed to fall to its side, filling with screams; my PortMed squeezed.

You will be mine.

Tears filled my eyes. *Whose voice was that?*

"Loran!" Kyle took a step toward me, his arms outstretched. The pink was coming too quickly, making me panic, breathing was hard.

"Don't get any closer," Mike demanded, pushing the glass hard against my neck.

I gasped in surprise and pain. *I can't be falling, not with Mike holding me this way.*

Kyle took a step back, watching me with wide eyes.

"Put down the glass. You're outnumbered," Shan said, and one of the guards stepped forward.

He held his L-gun high, aiming it at us. The five red lines on the side showed it was cocked and loaded.

I saw no pity in his eyes and I doubted he would mind if he shot me. Fear rushed through my body, increasing at the sight of the barrel staring down at me as the world mirrored itself. I tried to shake away the double images. The pink darkened as it began to shift, flowing like liquid around me. *No not now. I can't lose myself now.*

"Be careful. You wouldn't want to shoot her now, would you?" Mike said, pushing me in the way.

"Shan," Kyle barked.

Shan moved to the right of me, his crossbow drawn, trying to get a vantage point. For just a moment, I was somewhere else, but before I could tell where, I was back.

Mike shifted and the glass dug deeper.

I could feel my blood dripping down my neck and chest. It was surreal, that situation. The Mike I knew would never harm me. *He's different*, I realized. *They all are.* The war was doing exactly what I prayed it wouldn't, changing people for the worst.

"No funny business. I'm taking the girl and we're leaving. Don't follow, or she'll get hurt." Mike's voice shook slightly, but his grip didn't waver.

"You won't hurt her. She told me about you. You're a good friend of hers." Kyle's smile was wide, showing off his cocky side, and he took a step forward.

I felt Mike's resolve waver for a moment as his hands loosened around me.

"Want to bet?" The glass disappeared from my neck, and a sharp pain flared in my upper left arm.

I bit my lip, preventing a scream that settled in my throat. Blood poured down, dripping from my fingertips and the world began to tint red.

Give in!

I shut out the voice that sounded like I was speaking underwater. A deep gash that I could tell had severed at least part of a muscle threatened to make me pass out. A sudden strange sense of calm took over me as I felt a squeeze.

Since when have my MEDs been enough?

The glass was back on my throat in seconds, and I tried to wriggle from Mike's grasp to avoid the pain that it brought, my vision and mind clear.

"I'm sorry, but I had no choice," he whispered in my ear.

I heard the pain in his voice. Though I wanted to be, I found I couldn't bring myself to be mad. He was fighting for what he believed was right. It was something I was unable to do, unsure of where my loyalties lay.

"Stand down," Blake ordered, and everyone lowered their weapons.

Mike backed away, dragging me along with him through the woods behind us. No one moved to pursue.

I watched Shan and Kyle's angry faces disappear as we sunk into the underbrush.

Mike let go of me not long after. Pushing me in front of him, he grunted a command to move.

My blood loss was getting to me as the world spun.

Give in. The voice was back as my world tilted again and made me stumble.

"Come on, let's go," Mike said, running ahead once we hit a clearing.

Without his support, I tripped, stabilizing myself against a tree. When I didn't follow, he turned around, confused.

"I'm not leaving, Mike. I have friends here and my family is somewhere. I can't go," I said, blood dripping far too quickly to be safe.

"I don't understand." The sound of footsteps filled the air, and Mike looked behind me. His very presence seeming torn.

"They're coming. Mike, run. Run and don't come back. Not for me nor for anything else. Tell Chris to stop this stupid war. End this while we still have a chance at peace." I heard Kyle calling my name. "Go!"

Mike took one last look at me, then disappeared into the forest.

I fumbled with two pills as I felt myself falling. I turned to the sound of footsteps directly behind me. "Oh, thank goodness. I was wor—" My words died as I saw Robert's face grinning down at me. His eyes shone with glee in the moonlight.

"Hey there, Lightning."

I ran, all my instincts screaming at me, the pain forgotten. Tree branches hit me as I flew through the woods. Cuts and scrapes littered my cheeks and caught on my jacket and pants. The sound of heavy footsteps behind me kept me going and the world was bright white.

"Kyle!" I cried into the night. Desperation filled me as I spotted a figure in the woods to my right. His blue cap had my heart racing.

He isn't one of ours.

I turned, veering away from the unknown, jumping over a fallen log as I did so. Tears ran down my cheeks. Breathing the cold air began to hurt, and the dizziness in my vision caused me to stumble. I hit an outcropped rock hard and went down with a yell.

"Shan," I cried as the footsteps slowed.

Robert's face filled my view above as the world spun. "I've got you now." The feeling of his hands on my skin made me vomit before I blacked out.

Chapter 44

Everything hurt.

It isn't supposed to hurt. Why does it hurt?

The cool air on my left wrist had me jolting awake, the bed under me squeaking.

My PortMed was gone.

In a panic, I looked about. The room was dimly lit, curtains drawn. A Holo-screen lay on the grand desk before me, casting an eerie glowing map.

Robert was leaning over it, decked out in black combat pants and a tight gray shirt, a small lamp illuminating my PortMed beside him.

Hearing me, he looked up. There was no mistaking the primal glint in his eyes; it sent shivers down my spine.

I made to run, clambering off the bed I was on to the floor, not getting farther than a few feet as the chain around my neck snapped me back. I hit the frame with a grunt. Tears sprung in my eyes at the shooting pain.

I heard a sigh. Clicking a few buttons to change the screen, Robert shut down the map and stalked his way around the desk, coming to rest against it at the front. The surrounding shadows seemed to stick to him like a second skin. Flashes of my nightmares had me wheezing.

"Well, well, well. Sleeping beauty finally woke up." For a brief second, a shadow fell around his eyes, making a claw-like image that descended upon his cheek. It sent my heart into overdrive as the room almost looked like it was tumbling around me.

"Shh," he purred as he approached me, a soft look in his eyes that set me on edge.

I scampered backward onto the mattress, the chain clanking with my movements.

He stopped his approach and tilted his head. "Don't do that, you'll pull your stitches."

I looked down to see the spot on my arm where Mike had cut me; a set of jagged poorly executed stitches barely held my skin closed.

"What have you done?" I asked through my panting, trying to calm my heart with no success.

"I know it's not my best work, but I couldn't have you bleeding out th—"

"Not that!" I screamed.

"No need to yell." He chastised me like I was a small child. "You're going to have to be a little more specific, dear." His voice was surprisingly soft, almost gentle.

It made me cry harder. "Why did you take my PortMed?" I stared longingly at the silver band.

He glanced back at the desk. "Oh, that." When he turned back, his face was full of pity. "It was hurting you." He took another step my way and I pulled my knees in.

He was deceivingly beautiful, I realized as I stared into the depths of his eyes. Like a fallen angel.

With a confused look, he sat on the edge of the bed and I scooted farther from him. "Why do you still cower from me?"

What the actual...

"You have done nothing but threaten me since I arrived," I stated, my heart calming as indignation filled me.

"That was Lightning, not you," he said. "I have always treated you with kindness, my Princess." The confusion on his face matched how I felt as he reached a hand toward me.

I slapped it away as wails filled my ears. "You're crazy!"

His eyes grew hard. "I see." He grabbed the chain next to him, tugging.

I cried out as it snagged my neck and pulled me forward. "Please stop." I clawed at the ring around my neck as he kept pulling. Cold metal bit into my skin and made me bleed.

"No, I won't stop. Not now. Not until you return to me!" he shouted, pulling me up to his face. Spit hit my cheek as I began punching him. He took the blows with ease, leaving me to feel as though I was just a bug.

"I don't know what you're talking about!" I screamed and threw a knee. It landed in his gut, and he dropped me, stumbling off. I fell onto the bed, quickly scrambling across it and to the floor on the other side, as far away from him as possible.

When he looked up, there was no kindness left. "You," he hissed, advancing on me. I grabbed the chain between my hands, stretching it out in front of me.

"Get any closer and I won't hesitate to kill you." I ignored the way the world was flipping around as I glared him down.

He stopped, looking at the chain.

"Pathetic." He flipped open his PortMed and began typing before he finished the word.

A sudden yank pulled the chain from my grip, burning my hands as it curled back to the bed and into a small box on its leg. I couldn't stop it as it reached my neck and tugged me as well.

I had always wondered what whiplash felt like. As the pulling stopped, I landed hard on my hands and knees. Pink covered everything like a second skin taking away the comforting white glow my world usually held.

"No," I whispered to myself as my grip on reality began to slip. My body ached in a new way.

"Ah, it's kicking in, isn't it?" Robert's feet were in front of my face, and I looked up. His eyes glinted red, but his voice was soft again.

Run.

"Yes, I remember how disorienting it was. I would have probably failed if it weren't for you." He looked into the distance as if seeing something I could not. "Your eyes were so kind then."

I glared at him as he squatted down and reached for me.

His face fell. "You will look at me that way again!"

I didn't see the hit coming for me until it connected with my cheek. The air left my lungs as I slammed onto my back, hard. Breathing was difficult.

"I said, I don't know what you're talking about," I wheezed out.

He circled me, a manic look in his eyes. "Yes, they made sure of that, didn't they? Don't worry, you will." His foot pinned me to the floor as he ground it into my stomach.

I flailed under it, hitting and kicking him.

Leaning over, he grabbed my wrists, pinning them down as he straddled my waist. "I don't know what he did to you, but I promise you, princess, I will bring you back. I will banish this *Lightning* from you."

The set of cuffs he pulled from his waist had me flailing.

"Shh," He purred again as he brought my struggling wrists together and clamped them to the ground, securing them so I couldn't move. "There is no reason to be afraid. Everything I have ever done has been for you. I won't hurt you, Princess."

I stared with dread at the strange stick he pulled from his pouch. With a flick, he activated it. A small buzzing sound filled the air as a bright light about three inches long appeared above the hilt. I watched it with wide eyes as the world seemed to mirror itself. It was like watching him and a reflection of something long past at the same time.

"Like it?" he asked, twirling it in front of his face casting sinister light on him. "It's a plasma knife. It's roughly based on a weapon from an old sci-fi movie. This one specifically is just hot enough to cut through your skin, but not too much that you won't bleed. Very similar to the first laser bullets in that way." He looked at me with a serious face. "You know you have to bleed, remember? If you don't, this just won't work."

"Stop, please. I don't know what you're talking about. Don't hurt me!" I cried out, bucking at him.

Give in! The voice in my head was so soft. My world calmed.

Why was I fighting it again?

"Shut up," he said, but he wasn't looking at me. He whipped his head back and forth. "No, she needs to come back, she needs to." Tears streaked down his face.

I saw an opportunity. "Robert, let me go. Please, I promise if you do, I won't tell anyone what you've done."

His head snapped to me, his eyes dilating. "Alright, then."

I felt a moment of relief.

It was dashed as he brought the plasma knife down to my cheek. I could feel the heat of it as it danced a breath away from my skin. The world bled around me. I gasped as the knife settled at the crook of my lip.

"Don't worry, it won't hurt," he said. "I'm just going to free you now, okay? Then you can be mine."

The next thing I knew, Robert's lips crashed down on mine. They were hungry and rough as he bit and licked.

I clenched my lips closed, not giving him the slightest leeway.

He growled and broke away. Frustrated hands gripped me as he bit my neck next, and I gasped. He took the opportunity to stick his tongue in my mouth. I gagged on it.

Tears streamed down my face as I fought him, biting down hard.

With a shout, Robert pulled back, slapping me in the face, hitting hard enough to make my world go black. He grinned down through spots in my vision. Ignoring my tears, he trailed kisses down my neck, licking and biting as he did. I turned back and forth, trying to wiggle out of his way. Angry with my resistance, he shoved my neck down with his free hand, choking me, the knife far too close to my arteries for comfort.

Again, for just a moment, I was somewhere else. The freedom it brought was short-lived.

"No. You're not her." His hand squeezed, then suddenly let go. He drew back from me, a devious smile playing at his lips, a moment of clarity in his eyes. "I'm going to enjoy this," he said to himself.

The pounding of my heart filled my ears. I felt the hot tip of the knife against my neck and screamed as he sliced down my collarbone. It hit me again, this time on my cheek, below my right eye. Again and again on my arms, face, and neck. Each cut blended with the next. It was like fire and ice were mingling in my blood. He shredded my clothes and my skin as he brought it down the side of my shirt and I wanted to protest, but my throat was raw.

I tried to headbutt him and he growled, choking me. With one hand on my neck and the other holding the knife, he pulled back, looking down, admiring me like a piece of art. I cried as the voice in my head screamed to be let out.

Give in!

"I see you," he whispered, leaning forward. "You are right there, my Princess. Come back to me. This time, you will be mine."

I felt the tip of the knife against my stomach and a gurgled cry escaped my throat. The sound of my heart pounding grew louder.

Robert's hand gripped my neck, and I saw stars as he carved into me. The banging in my head crashed, the pain all-consuming. Something inside me gave away.

Give in.

A shadow stood in front of the light in the distance. I reached out to it as it reached back. An icy hand wrapped around mine and the smile that pierced the shadow's face wasn't as chilling as the knife digging into my flesh. A soft voice, sharp as the blade's edge called out around me.

Welcome back.

Chapter 45

I regained consciousness, feeling cold and in more pain then before. I glanced blearily around the red-tinted room, blinking back stars. The movement caused tears to threaten to spill from my eyes as my body lit up in agony. There were still open cuts littering me and the dirt and grime around me dug into them, setting my nerves on fire. As a tear slipped down my cheek it felt like lava as it passed over the open cut there.

Where am I?

The ground under me was rough. As I tried to move, the sounds of chains *clinging* filled the air, my free hand flew to grasp my stomach. Like a slap to the face, memories came flooding back.

"No." I shook my head as hours of torture filled my vision. "No, no." Tears streaked down my face, and they made my wounds scream.

Panicking, I looked around the room. It was empty. I felt a small sense of relief. The map from earlier was visible, and I watched dozens of red dots scamper across it.

Get up.

I did as the voice asked, swallowing a scream as every cut, bruise, and broken bone protested. The chain around my neck *rattled* as I dragged myself to the desk, the rough ground scraping me. It yanked me, stopping short by just a few feet. I could see my PortMed above me, gleaming in the light.

Get it.

I glanced around, looking for something to help.

A broom sat in the room's corner, dusty from years of unuse.

The effort it took to retrieve it and return to the desk made me feel like passing back out, but I pulled through. With a strangled cry, I batted at the desk. The broom flopped about. I heard a *clank* as I hit something and watched as my PortMed tumbled down. Tears of relief filled my eyes as I directed it to me clumsily with the broom.

"Got you," I said as I reached out and snatched it. The familiar pinch of the thousands of tiny needles pushing into my wrist was welcoming. I locked it in place.

Instantly, the MEDs began working. I let out a sigh as some of the pain dulled. My mind cleared, and so did the strange red fog in my vision.

Looking around, I began to plan. I pulled up the messages on my PortMed and typed out my location to my friends. When I hit *send*, it blinked three times, telling me it didn't go through.

How is he blocking my signal? I need to get out of here.

I spotted the box attached to the bed. Standing on wobbly legs, I made my way over to it. I tried to work as quickly as possible, knowing Robert could return at any moment. Gripping the box, pulling and turning it, I tried to free it from the bedpost.

A snap filled the room. I stumbled back as the box gave way, landing with a thump on my butt. The pain was almost instantly soothed.

I gathered the chain around me, wrapping it around my right wrist and tucking the box under my arm. As my body began to mend, my shallower cuts slowly closing, I made my way to the desk. I typed on the screen.

Locked.

I let out a string of curses as I searched for a way out. A small crack of light across the room led me to a barely visible door. I felt around, looking for some sort of lever or handle.

Nothing.

Cursing again, I began to pace. There was only one way out. I would have to wait for Robert to return and attack. If I could make it past him, then I was sure I could find my way back home.

I sat, waiting beside the door, feeling like the minutes were dragging on. When I heard the whirl of locks, my head snapped up and I scrambled to my feet. The box was in my hands and crashing down toward Robert as he stepped into the room. A *crack* resounded around me as he went down. I watched him fall with vicious glee.

"Well, well, well, now that wasn't very nice of you."

My blood ran cold. I looked up slowly, coming face to face with my tormentor.

He smiled a wide smile. I glanced back down, seeing that the body on the ground wasn't his, it wasn't even male.

I screamed as I ran. He caught me before I could pass, hitting me hard in the gut. I stumbled back, dropping the box as I went. It yanked on my wrist as I dodged his next hit. My body protested as

I landed a punch to his face, the fracture in my middle finger gave way. We both let out a shout. I cradled my hand to my chest, on edge as I watched him righten.

He wiped red from his lip and looked up at me. "You aren't her. Your eyes, they are all wrong…" His own eyes shone with clarity. "You want to fight? Well, all right then."

He seemed to move at inhuman speeds, and I didn't see his fist coming. It hit me hard in the cheek, sending me flying across the room. My ears rang on impact and my world turned fuzzy. I pushed myself up, tears stinging my eyes.

Quickly, I turned to block the next hit. His leg swept under me and I fell hard, darkness filling my vision as my head banged.

"This is pathetic. You were tough. You could put up a fight. Now it's all talk," Robert, taunted me as he circled overhead.

I blinked back stars, realizing he was talking mid-rant. Anger flooded me like lava, filling my veins. I liked the feeling. I got up and sprang at him, aiming for his crotch.

He stepped out of the way, but I managed to kick his leg. I received a small grunt in return. Smiling crookedly, I punched him in the face. Continuing my attack, not giving up the advantage, I danced.

The box hanging from my wrist was both a hindrance and an advantage as I moved. Its weight and length was the perfect weapon but keeping it in place, out of Robert's reach was difficult while also blocking his attacks.

He blocked most of my hits and I felt his fist slam into me a few times, but I connected with his stomach and face on more than one occasion, my small form more agile than his, despite my still healing wounds. I could feel them protesting as I twirled out of his reach, but a sudden burst of adrenaline silenced them.

Robert was good, better than I expected.

"You call that a hit?" he taunted as I landed another punch, the box smacking his side as I did.

I felt my moves slipping as pain filled me. The sound of our PortMed's going into overdrive to fix our wounds filled the room with shrill beeps.

I went in for another hit when his hand caught mine. His fist connected with my stomach, making my body bend in. I saw stars as I coughed up blood, collapsing as he let go of my wrist.

Robert was panting, standing above me. "That's better," he said, kicking me down as I tried to get up.

I heard the distinct *crack* of a rib as he did so.

He spoke over me. "I'm going to make you pay, pay for taking her away. When I'm done with you—"

I howled and threw the box at him. It flew out, the chain unraveling, and hit him square in the jaw.

He staggered backward and for the first time since he took me, I saw fear in his eyes.

"You would dare attack me?" He walked forward as I scrambled to my knees, pulling the chain back. He stepped on it before I could finish, yanking it and me forward. "Your better!"

My hands hurt as they hit the ground.

Using the chain to keep me pinned, he kicked me with his other foot. I was flying backward and being pulled forward at the same time, my body feeling like it was being snapped in half.

Another hit. I was kneeling on the ground, crying. He was above me. "You serve only one purpose now," he taunted. "You are my ticket to the future. To success."

I thrashed, pulling on the chain around my neck as he chuckled.

"After all, you're the perfect bait."

My blood ran cold, my eyes widening.

He gave me a twisted smile as he knelt, grabbing the chain and pulling me to him, his hand coming up to possessively stroke my cheek.

I let go of the chain and punched him.

He grunted but was unmoving. "He just can't resist coming for you. Chris was always weak like that. I never understood why you chose him."

"You're crazy!" I wailed.

He let out a mirthless chuckle. "Oh, dear, you haven't seen anything yet." I saw him grab the knife with his free hand and fear took over me.

As the world tinted red, an unexpected strength filled me. I struck him hard. He went reeling. The chain flew in the air between us. I pulled my feet under me. The world was so tilted I couldn't see straight, but I was still able to dodge his attack as I sprang up on the balls of my feet.

"I have done everything in my power to free you from your weakness."

We landed a hit at the same time.

I staggered back.

"I made sure you were safe here," he panted. His eyes flashed with fear, anger, desire, and a longing that made me sick. "I'm the one that kept the doubters at bay, that made sure your secret was safe until it couldn't be any longer."

I flew at him.

He dodged me, grabbing the chain and pulling it.

I hit the desk hard. My side screamed at me despite the MEDs.

"When those friends of yours abandoned you—" He grabbed the back of my neck as I pushed off the desk. I struggled as he dragged me across the room. "—I was the one who made sure the council didn't kill you." He dropped me and I scrambled away. "They wanted you dead." He stepped on the chain again and I choked.

"You're lying," I coughed.

He stood before me, my chain in his hand, and squatted. His grip on my cheeks felt like claws digging in. As I snarled at him, he looked at me with pity. "No, I'm not."

My heart skipped a beat.

"Don't worry though, I got revenge for you." Seeing my confusion, he continued, "You didn't think it strange that Sally Brown managed to plant a bomb so close to our borders without anyone noticing?"

Red settled around us, clinging to him as my vision blurred. I head-butted him. He fell backward and I was on him. I hit him over and over until he grabbed my chain and pulled so hard, it cut me. I screamed. My back was wet with blood. He bucked me off and the color was suddenly gone from my vision, the adrenaline that had been sustaining me rushing out of me like a wave on the shore. I tumbled, feeling suddenly exhausted.

A loud *bang* sounded out before Robert could continue his assault. The partially closed door flew from its hinges, hitting the opposite wall and clattering to the ground. My friends rushed in.

"You sick bastard!" Kyle said as he saw the state I was in on the ground. Hayley was bent, panting beside him, her eyes wide as she took stock of the room. Shan's eyes were storming as they spotted me.

With a cry, Kyle pulled a sword from his hip, advancing on Robert.

Robert spun. He dodged as Kyle tried to hit him. Grabbing the fallen broom, he blocked the next one. The wood splintered but didn't break.

I blinked and Shan was beside me.

"Oh Loran..." his soft voice called.

I strained to sit up. The cry that sounded in the room wasn't my own. I turned in time to see Robert going down, a large gash across his face, slicing through his right eye.

Kyle kicked out as he tried to stand. Robert's leg gave way with a *snap*.

"We need to get you out of here," Shan said over Robert's screaming, putting his hands under me and helping me to sit. "Can you stand?"

I shook my head, the chain rattling. He looked at it, his eyes almost black.

Another *snap* filled the room, and I relished in Robert's screech as the world shifted before me. I was somewhere else again.

The surrounding room was dark, lights flickering above, dozens of children surrounded me.

Then I was back, Shan scooping me and the box up and carrying me out.

I turned my head in time to see Kyle swipe down, cutting Robert's crying off with a hit to the head.

Give in.

I felt suddenly sick.

"Shan?"

He looked down at me. "Hang in there. We're going to the hospital," he murmured.

Such an angelic voice, a male voice whispered like a memory.

"I'm so sorry," I said, tears streaming down my cheeks.

"You have nothing to be sorry for," he countered gently.

I groaned in pain as I bumped against him. Shadows disappeared as light shone over him; we were outside. The cool winter breeze blew along my exposed skin, my shivering intensifying my agony.

"Let's hurry," said Hayley, coming beside us.

Trees rushed by, and I closed my eyes to prevent dizziness.

"Let us through!" yelled Shan.

I heard whispers and felt the chilly air conditioning of the hospital. I opened my eyes to see we were in the athletic sector.

Someone gasped as nurses spotted me.

The pain flooded back when a light caught my eyes, and I closed them with a groan.

"We'll take her from here," said a woman's voice.

I was laid down on a bed. Opening my eyes, I grabbed Shan's hand. "Don't leave me," I whispered.

He nodded, following the gurney along. His hand was firm, my anchor to life.

"What happened?" a doctor asked, inspecting me as he approached.

"Someone attacked her," said Shan, acid dripping in his voice.

The doctor nodded and didn't ask any more questions. Instead, he pushed me into a room with enormous lights hanging from the ceiling. "Everyone out," he said and shuffled them away.

But Shan stayed strong like a rock.

A mask was strapped around my head, and I breathed in the oxygen hungrily. I watched the doctor's masks wave, then I blacked out.

Chapter 46

The world around me was black. I blinked a few times, concern gripping me when nothing changed.

"Hello," I called, my voice echoing into the void.

I sat in the emptiness, waiting for a reply. When none came, I began to worry. I was disassociated from my body as I tried to wander around. It felt like forever before I heard the faint sound of voices.

"Hello!" I ran toward them as fast as I could. The voices grew louder as I drew closer. "Hello?" I called again, slowing as I made out the words.

"I told you, Brutus, I told you! But no, you didn't listen. You just had to give her the second serum and right before her tournament, no less!" a feminine voice snapped. The anger shocked me, the voice somehow familiar.

"Ella, you know it's good. All our test subjects so far show signs of increased strength and endurance. It's just the thing we've been looking for. The tournament was the perfect test," a male voice replied with a whisper in what I assumed he thought was a soothing tone.

"Yes, but all those subjects had been relatively clean. They weren't genetically enhanced, and full of at least three other serums! I swear, *if this 'brief' experiment of yours costs us another heir, I'm done. I don't care what you say. I can't go through this again." Ella's voice broke at the end, the pain bringing back a memory.*

"Mother?" I called out to the woman, somehow knowing she was mine.

"I promise, Ella, she will be fine. I admit, her body reacted more severely than I thought it would, but I know she will pull through. Number Fifteen has always been strong even before she was born."

I recognized the other voice as Father's.

"Father! Mother! Where are you? Please help!" I cried out, tears falling down my face as I panicked.

"She's five years old now. Use her name, for God's sake. After all, you were the one who chose it." Mother huffed in annoyance. "Just look, you've made her cry."

"I'm sorry, my love. I didn't mean to."

I suddenly felt a hand upon my cheek wiping away my tears.

"It looks like she might be coming to. Loran, sweety, it's time to wake up."

The darkness faded around me.

I woke to the sound of a heart monitor in my ear, the sterile smell of the hospital filling my nose. My strange dream played alongside memories of what Robert had done. I saw lights dancing and felt hands everywhere. There was blood, so much blood; my world was tainted with red. I wanted to let out a scream, but something was stopping me. Panic encompassed me, but a voice pulled me to reality.

"She's awake." Shan's face appeared. "Hey, calm down, it's all right. You're safe now." He grabbed my hand gently. Instantly, the blood and images stopped. "Go get the doctor, please."

I saw Hayley rush off.

"How are you feeling?" He brushed a strand of hair out of my face. My heart calmed as the shadows disappeared.

"Like I got hit by a train." I groaned as my body flared in pain.

"Don't move, please. The doctor will be here soon. Oh, and don't talk, your vocal cords were bruised. That was my bad, asking you..." Shan put his hand on my shoulder, pushing me down.

My memory was splotchy now that I was calm. The last thing I remembered was Robert standing before me in the woods. The red tint returned to my vision.

"It's been two days since we found you. When Mike took you, everything fell apart. Sally Brown was lying in wait for him. It took a while to fight them back. Once we did, we couldn't find you." Shan stopped, and I saw his hands clench. "We thought they had taken you, spent two days searching for them to get you back. Then Jaz got your message. It took a while to find out where Robert was hiding you. He..." Shan gently touched the side of my arm, his hand tracing a line down my bandages. "I don't want to think about what would've happened if we had been too late."

"Shan, I'm so sorry," I apologized, my voice a husk.

"Please don't talk. Here, take this." He passed me an old whiteboard and marker. "If you need to, write it out."

*It is all my fault. If I hadn't gotten so close to Mike, he wouldn't have been able to use me against you all. Then Robert wouldn't have been able to...*My hand shook.

Shan placed a gentle hand on mine. "All of this." He gestured to my injuries, stopping me. "The attack it was on him, not you. It's not your fault." Those four simple words broke me. Slowly, tears fell, but Shan's hands kept me together, holding mine. He rubbed them absently as I cried, whispering soft encouragements until I ran dry.

The door opened not too long after, Kyle, Hayley, and the nurse walking through.

"Hello there. I wasn't expecting you to be up for at least another day. How do you feel?" the nurse asked, smiling down at me.

Not that great, I wrote, and she chuckled.

"That's to be expected. You were in pretty bad shape. We don't know what happened, but some of your injuries were delayed in their healing."

He took off my PortMed. I shook as the memories flooded me and the script was barely legible. As the room read, I watched each and every face fall into disbelief.

"That would explain it." The nurse hesitated. "You should know now. Due to that and whatever weapon he used on you, some of your injuries will never heal fully."

Kyle was beside me, his hand joining Shan in comfort on my arm.

*I see—*A sharp pain shot up my hand as I wrote, dropping the pen with a hiss. I felt a squeeze.

"Oh dear, I'll go get you some more pain medicine, alright?"

I nodded and she left. Kyle took center stage as Shan got up from the chair beside my bed, allowing him to sit down.

"I'm glad you're awake," he said, stroking my cheek, his eyes soft.

So am I...I need to know what happened after Shan took me away. Where's Robert?

Kyle exchanged a look with Hayley. She nodded, and he looked back at me. The emotion on his face took me by surprise. Anger couldn't describe it, even fury was too meek a word. It twisted his face into an unrecognizable mask.

"Let's just say he won't be bugging us anymore."

Kyle, what did you do? My heart sped up, fear pumping through my veins.

"Officially, nothing. See, the building you were in caught fire when Sally Brown attacked. I barely escaped, but sadly, Robert didn't make it out. It was kind of hard for him to run with two broken legs." Kyle's eyes gleamed as he hissed out the words.

You didn't. I was both revolted and comforted by the notion.

"I did and would willingly do it again." Kyle grabbed my hand and looked into my eyes, begging me to understand.

But he was burned alive. My hands shook as I tried to reason the whirlwind of joy and disgust in me.

"I'm not a monster. I knocked him out before I left. He didn't feel a thing." I tried to take some assurance in his words. "Please, don't be mad. I just wanted to protect you. Make sure he could never come back for you." He lifted my chin.

I couldn't resist his sad face when I felt so weary already. *I can't stay mad at you.* I allowed the matter to drop. I'd enough horrors to face; adding him to the list wasn't what I needed. I'd reevaluate us and him when I was through it.

"Thank you," he said, kissing me lightly on the brow.

The nurse walked back in. Gently she grabbed my wrist, inserting a disk into my PortMed. My body relaxed, and the pain was gone.

"It's time for you all to leave," she told my friends.

Kyle nodded. He and Shan followed the nurse out, but Hayley stopped, hesitating at the door.

"He really cares for you, in his own way. Like, I know what he did was wrong and, like, disturbing, but this is war. It's official now. After that attack, things are only going to get worse. More people are going to die. We are going to have to deal with it, but we couldn't let an enemy inside our ranks live. We have enough to deal with without, like, watching our backs…" Her growing bravado died as her eyes landed on me. "I'm sorry for what you have been through. Jaz, the girls, and I are totally here if you need to talk," she said to the door, her hand on the frame shaking. After a few calming breaths, she turned to me, tears in her eyes. "I'm glad you're alright." I heard her voice crack.

Quickly, she left, shutting it before I could respond. I sighed and sank into my pillow. So many thoughts buzzed through my head as I drifted off. I never wanted this. But it was bigger than me. Everyone wanted to be the top dog at the top school and apparently, they were willing to kill for it. I knew it wouldn't just stop with Sally Brown. Soon everyone would be involved.

"Beg, princess, beg."

"No, you're dead," I cried, scampering back from the claws reaching for me.

"I will never die," the monster that slunk from the shadows said. "I will always be here, inside you." A single claw pointed to my head.

Tears flooded around me, mixing with a dull red as the room filled. "No, please, no."

The monster grabbed me by the neck, drawing me close, keeping my head just above the rising waters.

"Did you really think you could escape me?" it hissed, a forked tongue snaking out and wrapping along my face. "This is just the beginning. And this time you will choose."

I felt like I was wasting away in the hospital. I was allowed to present my finals from my bed, ignoring the way the teachers watched me with concern from the screens before me. My nightmares followed me into my days and nights, no relief from the horrors I'd faced.

After the third day, I felt good enough to leave my bed on my own. During one of the rare moments that I was left alone, I stumbled out of it and to the bathroom. Locking the door behind me, I turned to the mirror above the sink. The image of a broken girl greeted me, looking worse with the hospital gown. My skin was unusually pale. My wavy hair was tattered and matted. Large bags sat under my eyes despite the constant flow of MEDs, making them look sunken. Lines littered my neck, almost making a jagged ring. I traced the slowly fading line down my cheek, the small slash separating two clusters of freckles. The bandages around my hand caught my eye, and I stared at it.

Taking a deep breath, I reached for it, gently unwrapping it. It fell to the floor.

My twisted finger, bent from the break, was surrounded by tiny scars. Up and down my arm they weaved. Shakily, I unwrapped the rest. The bandages hit the ground, not making a sound. I pulled the gown off, continuing, and I didn't look up till the last strip of gauze was in my hand. Trembling, I stared at the mirror.

My hand flew to my mouth as tears formed in my dim green-gray eyes. I couldn't find a spot Robert hadn't touched in some way. Various shapes, lengths, and designs littered my body. But the one that almost broke me sat on my stomach, next to the one from Jaz. A twisted, jagged R flowed into a lopsided O, the B and second R were clunky, the E and T the cleanest of cuts. My world tilted as I softly traced the lines. I felt...hollow.

Give in.

All alone in the room, there was no way to ignore the voice inside me.

Give in and get revenge.

I staggered back, hitting the door as my eyes flashed red in the mirror. My world crumbled around me as I fell to the floor and cried.

Chapter 47

The world kept on spinning, snow covered the land, and before I knew what was happening, Christmas came and went. I'd passed term finals and it was New Year's Eve.

Walking the campus on that sunny day felt wrong. My friends chatted around me. Everyone was smiling and laughing, excited for the New Year's party that night, but their eyes remained guarded, their motions rigid.

As people passed me, they stared. I pulled my hoody closer, hiding away in its depths. The two burly boys next to me, my new bodyguards, stiffened as a group got close, whispering into their hands.

I left my friends at the lobby of our dorm and headed up to my room, taking off my jacket, the meat walls on my flank. The hall was eerily quiet, putting me on edge, but I ignored the feeling.

As we stepped into my room, the hair on my neck stood. I barely dodged the bat coming for my head. Two grunts and my guards fell. I moved too late as my door shut and locked in front of me.

"Hey Lightning, what's up?"

I froze. Slowly, I turned to see my intruder.

Chris stood before me, smirking as I stared into his bright eyes. Months flew by in a second, nothing seemed to matter but the love in his gaze.

"Chris?" My voice came out in a raspy whisper. On his right stood Mike and his left Alex, watching me warily.

"That's my name. Don't wear it out," Chris said, the grin on his face bigger than before.

I blinked, taking stock of my trashed room. He stood in the middle of it, comfortable in my space. I felt strangely violated.

"Wha-what are you doing here?" I stammered as I put my hands behind my back to message my friends.

He watched my movements with a tilted smile. "You won't be able to get to them," he said and I froze. "Kathy has hacked into the system. All security cameras are down and communications."

I started to tremble.

He watched me, concerned. "Loran?"

"Why are you here?" I was confused, scared, and yet for some reason, I was longing for him to come closer, to love me like he used to. *I thought I was over him.*

"Loran, listen, I..." He started. I saw the love in his eyes, and I broke.

"No, you listen. Do you know what you did to me? You Browner." I spat the insult, satisfaction filling me at the hurt in his eyes. "You left me. You hurt me more than anything else in this godforsaken war. I was lost without you, Chris. I had to go through hell. Because of you, I had to let go of everything, everyone. I was left alone here with strangers. I—" The weight of everything hit me and I fell to the ground crying.

I heard Chris's footsteps, but didn't look at him as he put his hand on my shoulder, stroking it. I calmed. It bothered me that he still had that effect on me.

"I'm so sorry you had to go through that. I really am. I was wrong." His voice was soft, his blue eyes kind. "We should have faced this war together, hand in hand. I see that now. Will you forgive me?"

I couldn't find my voice to answer, so I nodded. Even after all the time and pain, I couldn't hold a grudge against him.

"Come here."

I could hear the smirk in his voice as he lifted me up onto his lap and I didn't resist.

"You know, I sent for you. Many times, in fact, but every time someone got near, you were taken away from me."

"Did you ever come for me?" I asked through sobs.

"I did once. But it didn't work out well. I almost found you, but then...there were complications." He glanced back at Mike and Alex.

He was always weak. Robert's voice was taunting.

"He said I was your bait," I confessed, shivering at the memories.

"What? Who are you talking about?"

I felt the world begin to change around me. "Robert. He took me. It was to bait you. He was...unstable." I found myself tracing my stomach and forced myself to stop.

"Loran..." Chris traced my scars and somehow the world rightened. "Mike told me about his imprisonment. He told me you said they weren't abusing you, but look at you." His hand came up, tracing the now faint scar on my lower cheek then along my arm where the much more obvious scars were. It was hard not to lean into his familiar embrace. His voice was melodic. "They let this happen to you. If you had come with him, none of this would have happened."

I didn't know it was possible to love and hate someone at the same time. "I didn't come because I didn't want to Chris. I miss you, that's true, but I live here now. I have friends here, have a life and I have..." I hesitated on telling him about Kyle. "It doesn't matter because I didn't—I don't want to leave. I understand it's hard to believe, but I belong here at Kent Wood now."

I felt Chris's hands tighten on my back, grabbing my shirt. "So, he was telling the truth," I heard him say to himself. Looking into his eyes, I was met with cold, hard anger. They were the eyes of a stranger, eyes that chilled my soul.

Run.

"Chris, what are you talking about?"

He let me go suddenly and swiftly stood. I tumbled to the ground as he hovered over me.

Run.

"I'm sorry for doubting you, Mike." His voice softened as he looked toward his friend.

"It's all good, dude, I understand. Besides, I still don't want to believe it," said Mike, his face solemn. There was an underlined meaning in their words I didn't understand.

"Chris, what's going on?" I demanded, rising. I was on my feet seconds before I hit the floor again, my cheek stinging. I lifted my hand to my face, surprised. *He punched me.*

My world tilted. I looked up at him and saw shock cross his face. He stared at his fist in wonder. His eyes softened, and he looked down at me, sad and pleading.

"How could you?" he said, as if he hadn't just hit me. He squatted down, reaching out to me.

I flinched. For a moment, Robert was before me.

Chris dropped his hand. We stared at each other as I braced myself on my palms. "Tell me it's not true."

"What are you talking about?" I asked, my voice wavering. I could barely breathe.

"Mike told me about that boy!" His tone turned to hysteria.

"What boy?" I searched Mike's concerned face.

"The boy. The one that was there when Mike was captured! Loran, please tell me that he misunderstood the situation. That that boy wasn't a—" Chris stopped, his face scrunched as if the next words were sour on his tongue.

"Wasn't a what?" I snapped, rising in anger. I stood over him, glaring down as my breathing slowed.

"Boyfriend!" Chris spat out, rising as well, yet his eyes were still pleading.

I looked away, answering his question.

"How could you?" He raged.

I took a step back.

"How could you do that to me?"

My fear quickly turned to rage, and I advanced on him. "What do you mean do this to you?" I spat back. I felt in control as fury pushed down my spinning rosy world.

"How could you betray me like that?"

I couldn't help the shrill laugh that escaped me.

"Betray you, please. What did you think? That after our breakup, you still had some sick claim on me?" The look in his eyes told me he did. "You were wrong. I moved on, Chris. You hurt me, and I moved on. Kyle is a great guy, and I like him."

"Kyle..." he trailed off. The room grew cold.

"Yes, Kyle. Kyle. James. Patson." I sait each word at his face. A sick pleasure filled me at the lost look in his eyes.

"You didn't," I heard Alex say, surprised. I turned to him with vengeful glee.

"I didn't what? Date him? Yeah. I'm still dating him," I sang, feeling hysterical. My world was tilting again.

"You're dating Chris's biggest rival?" Alex advanced on me, but Mike stopped him with a hand and a sharp look.

"So, you're just a whore then," spat Chris, and I stumbled back, feeling as if he punched me again.

"What?" I croaked. *Was breathing always this hard?*

"You heard me! He's the boy you cheated on me with when we were still dating." Chris advanced. We met in the middle of the entryway.

"No, I didn't. He kissed me and I told you about it; I wasn't cheating on you." If looks could kill, I'd be dead, but I didn't care.

Chris's eyes flickered with different emotions as he watched me glare at him. "Why him?" His voice was a quiet whisper then. The world started to return to white, the feeling of falling fading.

"Because he cares for me. He's willing to look over the fact that I'm from Sally Brown. He accepts me," I said just as quietly. "So few have after you exposed me."

Chris's eyes widened, and I watched as he fought an internal battle with himself. "I'm sorry," he said, stepping forward and I shoved his hand away.

"Don't touch me." I wasn't pleased I had shared that with him. Somehow, it just slipped out. I didn't want to be weak in front of him, especially with his current violent nature. The rose color filled my vision.

"Loran, listen. I've come for you and I'm not leaving without you." Chris's voice was soft, but his words were not.

He has that tone he uses when we argued, the one that always allowed him to win. It worked back then, but now it just bothered me.

"We will be together again. With us united, we could win this war."

It always comes back to the stupid war.

"No." I suddenly knew that single word would change my life forever in more ways than I could ever imagine.

"No?" He stepped back to look me over, his gaze manic.

"Yes, no, I won't go with you. I'm staying here," I said calmly.

He began to pace. "Why? What could be holding you back?"

I saw recognition flash across his face and the angry snarl was back as he spun on me.

"Do you love him?" he demanded.

I didn't flinch or step back as he got into my face. I couldn't understand how I could fall and yet stand in one spot at the same time as my grip on reality slipped.

Chris isn't Robert. I had to remind myself.

Are you sure? The voice was back.

"That's none of your business," I said, watching him fume.

He isn't Robert!

Still, as I observed him standing above me, his anger pouring from him in waves, I wondered who he truly was.

"Tell me!" he shouted in my face.

I shook my head. Suddenly, the pain was back, gripping my arms and tearing into my flesh with sharp nails. *Beg.*

"Chris, stop, you're hurting me!" I cried out, trying to wiggle from his grasp.

Give in, the voice called.

I need my pills now!

"Fine, then. I will fix this problem." He turned to Alex, not letting me go. "Find him."

Alex's fingers flew on his screen.

"What are you doing?" I asked. Strange reflections hit my eyes, like mirrors to another life, and the room seemed to shift before correcting.

"Like I said, you're coming back with me. Nothing is going to prevent that. If this boy is stopping you, then I will make sure he's out of the equation."

Realization hit me like a wave, and I started to struggle in his grasp, clawing at him to let me go.

"Stop that!" he smacked me hard.

I raised my fist to punch him.

His hand caught my wrist, spinning me so it was pegged behind my back.

You have to choose, Robert's voice whispered in my ear.

"Chris stop! Don't do this. I'll come with you. Please, just don't hurt him," I begged him, his fingers dug into my skin as a panic attack took over.

I looked to my right to see Mike and Alex exchange nervous glances, waiting for his reply.

"I can't find him," Alex said hesitantly. "And no one has eyes on them."

"Tell me, Loran. Tell me where they are!" Chris hissed, shaking me. His breath ghosted the back of my neck.

I felt a small trickle of blood rolling down my hands from his grip. In his anger, Chris didn't see it, but Mike did.

"I think I know where." Mike stepped up and Chris immediately stopped, releasing me.

I stumbled forward from the motion, catching myself on the wall. Mike was trying to defuse the situation, but my heart plummeted.

I spun to him, pleading. "Mike."

He crossed his arms in defiance, watching my face.

"Where?" Chris said.

You never had a choice.

I staggered forward, unable to move properly as I kept flashing between location, a dimly lit room made of concrete exchanging itself with my dorm every other breath.

"There was discussion of a party. Somewhere in the woods near where they held me, at a cabin. I could find it if we can get to my cell."

A gasp escaped my mouth, my hands flying up to cover it, but I didn't move fast enough.

Chris turned to me in one fast, fluid movement and looked me over. His eyes flared in rage. "...I see. Well then, it looks like we will be going man-hunting after all, boys," said Chris, backing away from me. His face was blank and ice cold. There was a red shadow over his form. It flashed, and for a moment I swear I saw Father standing over me.

You're such a disappointment, he hissed.

Alex and Mike moved to leave. I stepped in front to stop them.

"Don't do this, please. They mean nothing to me." Ignoring the way the world swam, I shoved them back. They staggered, and I pushed through, advancing on Chris. "I'll come with you."

His gaze was speculative. Finally, he spoke, his words sending chills to my bones. "It's not enough. If you come now, your heart will still be here. I will not have that. He and all the others must go."

I felt an eerie sense of calm settle in as the red in my vision solidified, settling around Chris like a second skin.

Give in.

"I won't let you," I said, dropping into a fighting stance.

"You won't be able to stop me."

I felt a sharp pain in my neck. The red faded as my world dimmed.

Chapter 48

"Beg, princess, beg."

The world around me felt disconnected.

"You know you're dead, right?" I was more weary than scared as I looked at my attacker.

Robert grinned down at me. His smile twisted. "You don't know that," he countered, coming to stand before me. A surprisingly gentle claw traced my cheek. "He could have just told you I was dead."

I batted his hand away. Standing, I crossed the stage, the stands suspiciously silent. As I stopped center stage, I looked out into the bright lights.

"Give in." The voice floated across the room.

"I don't think Kyle would do that," I countered. My feet felt warm and wet, I looked down. Gold flowed around me, twisting and swirling as it passed my ankles.

"He doesn't trust you, you know." Robert's wings fluttered as he encircled me. I watched the black feathers fall below, dissolving into the liquid. "Why would you give him the privilege of trusting him in return?"

"Give in."

The flow below increased; the gold tinting red as it hit my knees.

Robert watched it rise with curiosity. "You're not afraid any-more?" he asked as a claw came up to grip my neck.

I blinked. "I'm terrified."

"Give in."

"But you're not the only monster in here."

Red eyes glowed from the stadium seats, peering into my soul.

I awoke in a daze, searching around, trying to get my bearings. My vision was hazy with a pink, rosy fog floating in and out. As the world cleared and a headache set in, I realized I was in the back of a car. The vehicle was empty.

I struggled to sit up, my hands tied behind my back, making it difficult to move. My heart raced. The dull screams in my ears didn't fade without my golden pills.

I scooted my way to the window, looking out. I let out a sigh at the sight of the familiar red trees around me barely visible in the sliver of moonlight.

I'm still at Kent Wood.

I wiggled about, trying to turn so I could grab the handle of the car. It didn't budge. With a frustrated shout, I flopped down, my face hitting the leather under me.

As my mind whirled, I breathed it in. I needed to escape and find my friends. I didn't know how long I had been out for, but if Chris wasn't back, then it probably meant he hadn't succeeded with his mission yet.

Thinking of his name filled me with rage. Red seeped around me. I flipped over and with a roar, kicked at the door. It gave way slightly. Wide-eyed, I inspected the small gap in the side where it had separated from the car.

I took a deep breath and kicked again. A screeching sound filled the space. The lock gave way. The door flopped open, the cool winter air hitting me.

With a distorted laugh, I push myself up again and started scooting toward the exit. The ragged corner cut me on the way, and I tried not to cry out as my arm started to bleed.

Inspecting the jutting piece of metal, I had an idea. Turning, I raised my hands behind me and threw them down. The tie on my wrists gave way as sharp shards tore my palms.

"That's what you get for using basic ties!" I cried out, whipping around to search my surroundings. I recognized our location as I saw the old shack Mike had been kept in.

I took off toward the small cabin where my friends were supposed to be. *Please be alive,* I begged. *Please don't let Chris have found them yet.* Adrenaline pumping through my body kept me going even when my legs started to protest.

I stumbled into a clearing. Beyond the small lake before me, a wooden A-frame cabin sat peacefully, soft yellow lights illuminating from its bay windows, a tiny porch surrounding it. I sighed in relief.

Laser fire rang through the night with a *bang.*

My heart skipped a beat, and I ran. Water splashed as the lake ice broke. I ignored the sting. As I drew closer, I could make out people fighting on the front porch.

Halfway across the lake, I spotted Shan's shaggy brown hair over the rest of the bodies. I heard shouting and saw shoving as a glass door slammed, trapping my friends inside. I stumbled onto the grass in front of the porch as it did.

Kathy stood tall above me with a bat in her right hand, her eye bruised, cradling her left arm as she assessed me. Her gaze was hard. Sarah stood next to her, her right arm bleeding, a wrench in the other hand. The rest of the boys and girls I once called friends stood beside them, each holding a weapon pointed at the cabin and nursing their wounds.

Across the porch, the sight of Kyle slumped over in the arms of Alex and Mike made my heart break. His face was swollen and bleeding, his shoulders shuddering as he tried to breathe.

Across from him, a clear glass door separated my new friends and my old. Sally was cradled against Garret, unmoving. Zack held Jaz as she cried, blood seeping from her hair. I couldn't see Hayley, but I caught sight of bright blonde hair from behind Dee. Dum comforted Bee and Dorothy.

The sight that stopped my heart was the face of Shan, battered and bruised, standing tall next to Zack. His eyes were colder than I had ever seen as he glared out the window. I followed his gaze to see Chris holding an L-gun. The model was older than the ones I had seen before, and I knew it had duller and slower laser bullets that didn't explode inside on impact. It sent chills down my spine all the same.

He held it like an expert, cocking it with a flick of his wrist, then pointing it toward the window as five red lines skittered across the barrel, a small sick smile on his face. "I'll take care of you first. You can watch your best friend die." Chris's voice sounded strange and sickly.

I felt my body move. It was as if I was watching from a distance as I ran up the steps. In the back of my mind, I saw the shocked faces of my old friends as I dodged Kathy's outstretched hand. Sarah's anger turned to fury. Mike and Alex were surprised to see me, and Chris, well, I chose not to look his way. I stopped in front of the window, my arms outstretched, and my head slumped over as I caught my breath.

"No," I said, loud enough for everyone to hear. Time froze. The only sound mine and Kyle's heavy breathing.

"Loran, what are you doing? Move. Now!" I heard Chris in the distance, like listening through a door. His voice was icy but filled with hurt.

I slowly straightened and looked right into his eyes. They didn't belong to the boy I loved. No, they were cold, the eyes of a killer. Chris was gone. With him, a piece of my heart, the last connection to my old life. I felt it *snap*.

"No. I won't let you do it," I said again, glaring at him. I saw regret flicker over his face, but it was gone too quickly. Slowly, Chris straightened and his hand holding the gun moved.

"Move or I'll shoot you," he said, pointing it right at my heart.

"Never." I squared my shoulders.

"Fine, then have it your way," he hissed.

I searched his eyes one last time, but they were like ice, no emotions visible past their shining, rigid exterior.

"Do it." I challenged. My life didn't flash before me but gradually played, like watching a silent movie. I took a moment to be thankful. Laughing faces and loving kisses, I was lucky to know them.

In the distance, the sound of laser fire filled the air. Fire consumed me as he hit my left shoulder. I had never felt pain like that, not even when Robert tortured me. Knowing Chris had caused it made it ten times worse.

"Loran." Kyle's strangled cry accompanied me as I staggered forward, gripping my shoulder.

The world moved in slow motion; all sounds muted as I pulled away my hand. It was covered in blood. I glanced up to Chris, my surprise mirrored on his face. Red covered my vision, sticking to everything like a second skin.

Give in.

That part of me that had never healed, the part that haunted my nightmares, the one I thought I buried long ago, shattered as I saw Chris's love.

My scream of rage filled the air. In seconds, I was before Chris. His head snapped back at the force of my punch. The gun flew away. He tumbled backward, and I followed him down.

Over and over, I struck. Bones cracked, blood flew. Somewhere, someone wailed, hands grabbed at me, trying to pry me from him. They were enough of a distraction that he was able to buck me off.

We rolled apart, and I swept my leg under Sarah as she tried to restrain me. She tumbled. Mike and Alex helped Chris up and he wiped his face, blood smearing as we made eye contact.

Kathy tried to come at me, her weapon raised, but I dodged the blow, watching it as if it was in slow motion. The red shifted. A smaller version of her stood before me for just a moment. Then I was back. My hit sent her crashing into the rail. Before Alex and Mike could advance on me, Chris stopped them.

"No! You know I'm the only one who can take her like this. Get the others out of here. I won't lose anyone else today."

They hesitated, exchanging nervous glances before they nodded and stepped back.

Panting, I ignored them, my eyes locked on Chris. "This has been a long time coming," he said, straightening. He flipped a few switches on his PortMed and something changed.

Kill him.

I wanted his blood.

"I will enjoy this," I spat, feeling as each of my muscles flexed, years of training taking over my base instincts.

Chris rushed me.

I met him halfway, hooking a punch into his gut at the same time his hand connected with my head. It snapped to the right. I kept moving despite the pain.

I dodged his next blow. Stepping around him, I spun, kicking him hard in the back. A cracking noise accompanied my hit as I contacted his spine.

I turned to him, expecting to see an incapacitated enemy. Instead, he stood hunched over, panting. I could literally see his back popping and clicking back into place. It was ungodly fast.

I've never seen the MEDs kick in like this.

The world shifted. I was no longer in the woods. A room filled with monitors was before me.

"What are you?" I asked, my voice full of fear. The world fell back.

Chris's head snapped back, looking at me over his shoulder. I staggered as his eyes flashed an unhuman red.

Run.

He spun and launched at me. I barely twisted away from his hit.

"The question you should be asking is, who are you? Do you remember yet?"

I dodged his punches as they flew around me. It was almost like a shadow followed him, echoing a memory deeply repressed, putting my nerves on edge. I blocked a hit.

A *snapping* sound rang in my ear as I felt my arm give out. I fell to the ground with a howl, holding my limp arm.

Chris stood over me, panting. Then, as if it had a mind of its own, I watched my arm twitch. My fingers spazzed, my arm jolted, and it snapped back into place with a crack. A scream ripped from my throat in fear and pain.

The world bled.

Chapter 49

Logically, I knew we were moving at inhuman speeds as the world around me passed in a blur, but each hit, each throw and flip, felt so normal, so natural, as if I was born to be that fast. I disconnected from my body as Chris landed a hit so jarring; my ribs cracked and reformed.

Welcome back.

The world around me shifted. We were somewhere else as we fought. The room was cold, the mat below us bouncing slightly.

I dodged a round kick and slammed my shoulder into his solar plexus as I came up.

He went flying, hitting the mat, then falling from the porch.

Finish him.

I advanced on him.

He skittered back to his feet and his eyes flashed with fear for just a moment. A sick satisfaction filled me as I blocked his hit, delivering one of my own.

As he staggered backward, I bent over, picking up a discarded knife. I twirled it in my hand as I approached.

No, stop!

I wanted to bawl. To cry out and stop myself, but I kept moving forward.

"Robert was right." My voice it sounded wrong—off. I knew I was speaking. I knew it was me, but I felt like I was hearing and seeing everything through a wall, and I didn't want to stop myself anymore.

I thrust forward with the knife, digging it into Chris's gut. "You were always weak."

No!

A red fog disappeared from my view as if I was waking from a dream. But I wasn't in my bed, and it wasn't tears my hands and face were wet with.

Before me, Chris stood, his hand covering a slowly closing hole in his stomach. Shaking, I looked up, our eyes connecting. The fear in his was clear.

"What am I—"

"Chris!" Sarah's scream cut me off as she came running toward us. "We need to go. Now!" She pulled on his arm as others retreated, running into the woods.

But Chris couldn't break eye contact with me. My other friends crowded him, helping him up and making to leave.

"Help me," I called out to them. *They have to help me.* I knew they had helped before.

They stopped. A chill filled the air.

"Please." I staggered forward. "Help me."

"How?" Chris croaked as he pushed against Sarah.

I didn't know what to say to the question in his gaze.

"Chris, come on." Mike pulled at him, but he didn't budge.

"You have to help me!" I cried out. I felt so lost and all I knew was that the people before me could make it go away.

"We don't have to do anything," Kathy snapped, advancing on me.

I staggered back onto the porch.

"I helped you kill once before. I won't do it again."

Tears sprang to my eyes, and I began to hyperventilate.

"You are a monster!" she spat.

Alex grabbed her hand before she could get closer. "Not now. We have to leave," he said.

Sarah succeeded in moving Chris at the same time, and as if breaking from a trance, he looked around. Panic flooded his face, and he allowed her to drag him away.

"Come back!" I cried. *They have abandoned you.* I hit my head with my fists. "No. No!" Tears fell down my cheeks, hitting the wood below, mingling with the brown and red. "Please come back." I felt so small, like a child. My knees hit the porch with a *bang* as I collapsed in on myself.

A *shattering* of glass sounded out around me. I whipped my head back to the cabin.

Kyle stood with a wrench in hand, the glass door scattered around him. We made eye contact, and he froze.

"Please?" I pleaded.

He glanced to his right, and I followed his gaze to my other friends. They were in relatively the same spots as before, each watching me with wide eyes.

They will abandon me as well.

"Loran?" My eyes snapped to Jaz. She was pushing herself up, staggering a bit under her wounds as she did. Hope flared in me. She made to move toward me, but Zack stopped her.

"Don't," he said.

My heart broke.

She turned to him, a gentle smile on her face. "Let me go, please. It's still her. I can see her in there." Reluctantly, he did as she asked.

Kill her! The voice snarled as she stumbled her way toward me. *Kill her before she can leave us like the others!*

"Loran." Jaz's soft voice broke through the rising red.

My eyes snapped to hers, searching.

"It's okay." She fell clumsily to her knees before me. "We're here," she said as she reached for me.

I flinched at the approaching hand.

She stopped. "I won't hurt you. I won't ever hurt you again."

I relaxed at the sincerity in her eyes.

"I'm scared," I choked out as I sobbed.

She pulled me into her arms as I fell apart. "I know," she murmured, stroking my hair. "I know."

"You should leave before I hurt you too."

She put a gentle hand under my chin.

I allowed her to direct my gaze to hers. "I'm a monster."

"I know you, Loran." Her voice was full of conviction. "I have known you for years. Yes, you are capable of inflicting great pain upon me."

I looked to her missing ear. Guilt flooded me.

"But—" she stopped me before I could spiral, "—you are also capable of great kindness."

"How do you know?"

The sound of feet hitting wood drew my attention past her. My eyes widened as I saw all my friends standing behind her. Their faces were tired, but their eyes were kind.

"Because ya have shown us that kindness," Dorothy said. Bee leaned on her, nodding.

"You were willing to look past the person the world saw me as and just see me," Kyle said as he stepped forward and knelt next to me. My heart warmed at his caring gaze.

"You were willing to take a bullet for me," Shan sounded broken as he looked down with deep storming eyes.

"They might see a monster. But we see a girl who, despite her school—" Hayley stepped forward, "—despite our history—" she gestured to Kyle and Jaz, "—welcomed each of us with open arms." She placed a gentle hand on my head.

"And that is not the actions of a monster," Sally said.

My tilting world calmed, and my vision cleared. Everything had an almost white glow to it.

Fine, then. The voice sounded resigned.

With surprising strength, Jaz pulled me up. I stabilized myself against her as I reorientated. Pulling back, I saw I'd stained her clothes with blood. "I'm so—"

"If you say you're sorry, I'm going to drop-kick you," she said, with mirth in her eyes.

I couldn't help but laugh. "I have a feeling that won't affect me like it used to." My smile dropped. Everyone watched me with worried expressions. "I don't think I can keep it down anymore." My voice was hollow.

Garret stepped forward, putting a large, gentle hand on my shoulder. "Then you don't have to."

I searched his eyes.

"We will help you learn to control it. Together." The resolve in his gaze strengthened mine.

I stood, taking stock of the damages around me. The area was a mess, broken glass, wood, and blood scattered about.

"We should, like, probably clean this up," Hayley said, mirroring my thoughts.

Dee pulled up his PortMed and began to type. He let out a breath as his message went through. "The signal is back. I've contacted HQ," he said.

Relief flooded me as I realized back-up would be coming to help.

"What should we say about..." Dum trailed off, gesturing to me and the space lamely. There was a beat of silence.

"We tell them the truth," Jaz spoke up with conviction. I searched her eyes, feeling on edge. "We were preparing for the party, waiting for Loran to join us when we were attacked. The only reason we made it out alive is because she came just in time. If it weren't for her, we wouldn't be standing here now."

Warmth filled me as everyone nodded. "Thank you," I said, past grateful tears.

Kyle wiped them away. "I said once before, you might be a Browner, but you are *our* Browner." He gave me a gentle smile, which I returned.

"She's not a Browner anymore," Shan spoke up. He stepped forward, passion in his eyes as they looked at me. "Now she is a true Knight."

Chapter 50

"And you're sure that's what happened?" Blake asked, looking around at the group.

My friends stood by my side the next morning, covered in bandages, unwavering.

"Yep, that's our story and we are sticking to it," Jaz said with a wide smile.

My heart warmed.

He looked at her, an unknown expression in his eyes. "And the security footage?"

I didn't look up to the monitor where a paused image of me gutting Chris was displayed.

He deserved it.

I shoved the voice away.

"Planted by Sally Brown when they hacked the system." Shan shrugged. "It's not that hard to fake such a thing."

Blake eyed each of us.

I tried not to fidget under his gaze. Kyle grabbed my hand, squeezing it in comfort.

After a beat, Blake smiled. "Well then, welcome to the team, Agent Wolf."

I felt the needle leave my arm and watched as the wound cleared quickly.

"Alright, I think that's all we need today." Karen, the lab head, said as she pulled back. A small vial of blood swirled in her hand as she handed it off to Lin.

The pale, yellowing boy gave me a kind, sickly smile. "Thank you for helping us," he said, his s's hissing as he did.

"No, thank you," I replied as I rolled my long sleeve back down. "I really appreciate all you have done the last few days. Hopefully, this will help you figure out what is going on with me."

A burly hand rested on my shoulder. "We will do our best," said Aaron.

I sat down for my first day of the winter term, looking around at the other students in my Marine Biology class. Word was spreading about the night at the cabin. Rumors abounded, and I didn't miss the cautious gazes sent my way.

"—eard she slaughtered them—"

I ignored the whisper that passed as someone took their seat behind me. I felt their eyes burning holes in the back of my head and tried not to reach back and scratch at my left shoulder.

Despite the rapid healing from my L-gun wound, a small scar had managed to form right at the heart of my raven tattoo, leaving a cruel reminder of that night.

They don't trust you.

It was a little easier to push Robert's voice from my head as I saw a set of familiar faces walking into the room.

"Sorry, got held up in HQ," Kyle said with a kiss on my forehead as he took the seat next to me.

Hayley gave me a small smile, her eyes sad as she looked down at Kyle's hand in mine as he settled beside me.

"I understand. I hope everything is okay."

Hayley nodded as she pulled up her Holo-screen.

"We, like, totally have Trident in the bag. Blake is sending a party out to sign the treaty tomorrow."

The room was full of laughter and a soft white light. I looked around at my friends from my chair as they milled about my dorm room. The Tweedle brothers and Sally sat on my couch, debating the finer points of our new strategy class. Bee was in my kitchen, making a mess as she cooked our dinner. Dorothy stood beside her, catching items she dropped and working to contain her sister to one spot.

"No, I'm telling you, white is totally better," Hayley argued with Jaz as they flipped the colors on the panel of my wall.

"No, she needs something soothing, not a reminder of the hospital," Jaz countered as she landed on a midnight blue. The walls in the room shifted colors as she hit it.

I smiled slightly.

"See!"

Hayley *humphed* at Jaz's triumphant smirk. "She'll grow tired of it, you'll see," she mumbled.

I laughed quietly as she pouted.

"What's so funny?" A gentle voice whispered in my ear, and I turned with a bright smile to Kyle.

"Nothing." I pecked him on the lips and enjoyed the way he brightened. He shifted under me as I sat on his lap, wrapping his arms around me.

A knock at my door resounded through the room. I turned to my PortMed and pulled up the new cameras outside. Shan's smiling face appeared before me. My heart fluttered as I flipped the switch and the door opened, letting him in.

He stomped his feet, dusting the remainder of the snow from his clothes.

"Hey, not on my carpet," I called.

Shan looked up from his boots. He smiled with a bright blush. "Sorry," he said, turning to the panel near my door. The carpet cleared with a flick. "It's freezing out there. I almost skipped my hiking class today."

"Why didn't you?" Garret asked as he came up behind Shan. "I skipped my Forensics, and it was inside."

Shan gave him a lopsided grin as an embarrassed blush grew. "I-I'm going to be gone for two weeks." The room quieted and everyone turned to Shan. He was beet-red as he continued. "Blake has a mission for me. It's pretty covert, so I'll be going alone...but, well, he wants me to spy on Sally Brown."

I felt the room tilt as fear and concern gripped me. "Why?" I couldn't finish my question as a mild panic attack set in. Kyle's hands rubbed the back of my neck as I worked to control my breathing.

"Rumor is Sandy Village and Michel Thomas are going to be signing a treaty with them." Shan shrugged, putting a hand to his neck and rubbing it uncomfortably. "Turns out I'm pretty good at going unnoticed."

I felt a twinge of guilt over the adrenaline pumping. Kyle passed me a golden pill, and I slipped it into my band. No one commented as the *snapping* of the lid filled the room.

"Well, come in and stop dilly-dallying in the doorway," Dorothy instructed, and the boys did as she commanded.

The Tweedles and Sally made room for Garret on the couch as he flopped down, placing a kiss on her brow. Bee finished with dinner as Shan took a seat at one of my new chairs.

We thanked her as she passed out the plates. Sally picked a movie from the selection on my HTV and we settled in to watch.

As the action scenes grew more intense, screams began to fill my ears. I tried to fight them off, not wanting to take another golden pill so soon. The sounds of gunshots made my world turn red.

Hello.

Suddenly all the white in my world was gone as it mixed with blood red. I could feel my heart race as I watched Chris walk onto the screen.

"No, you're not real," I whispered to myself.

Do you really believe that? He smirked that smirk I used to love, and I fell into a world all my own.

"If you think for one moment, I will allow you to come here and infiltrate my life and my new family, then you're wrong."

The concerned looks my friends were giving me made something in the back of my mind tingle, but as Chris laughed, it was shoved aside.

What are you going to do to stop me? You're powerless, after all. To afraid of the monster, you believe lives within, not realizing it's really just you.

His voice was taunting, and I shook my head, angry tears streaming down my face as the voice whispered, *Give in.*

Seeing my distress, his smile grew. *I'm coming for them, and there is nothing you can do.*

Our eyes locked. Hate. I felt hate so strong that it burned. Chris's blond hair disappeared as a car passed by on screen, leaving behind a silent street.

I watched as the fires burned and ash danced in the spot where he once was, determination and anger growing with each breath. Silently, I prayed for the opportunity to see his face again.

Because I knew that no matter what, I'd have my revenge.

Book 2

An icy wind blew against the left side of my half-covered face, sending shivers down my spine and spinning my brown, gold-tipped hair in front of me. The moon was full, casting an eerie glow over the land as I stared into the vast valley below the hill I stood on, overlooking the Sally Brown campus. The snow-laden ground around me gave off the smell of wet earth and the shuffling of my team behind me filled the air with a soft crunching. Lights flickered below and I could see people moving around with the enhanced vision in my mask. The sight ignited the fire of anger inside of me.

Give in. I shoved away the small voice in my head, taking a deep breath to calm myself before the pink settled in. My right hand shook on the hilt of my Katana, strapped to my hip, the cool metal grounding me as I forced down the urge to pop a pill.

"The contact should be here in a few moments," said a voice behind me and I turned to the figure, my anger and fear depleting as I stared at my friend.

"Thank you, Fox," I said, and Garret nodded, pulling his standard-issue black jacket around himself. The red and black fox Kabuki mask on his face shifted slightly, his single gold earring peeking out from under his black cap that covered his short black hair.

I turned back to the valley, my back facing the rest of my team and the vast wood behind us. From the corner of my eye, I could see Garret watching me cautiously, his light brown eyes shining with concern. His towering height and large muscles to anyone else would be deadly, but I knew the gentle giant beneath. One that sat quietly with me on long, lonely days and listened for hours without complaint, adding just the right words at the right time. I heard my other friends turn to me when they heard me sigh.

"He'll be like fine," said Hayley to my right.

I turned to see her bright smile as she slipped her mask off to sit on top of her head. The red and brown hawk glinted with the movement. Her platinum blond hair fell around her, Emerald green eyes shone in the moonlight. Sally stood behind her, looking small and innocent with her gray and gold otter mask firmly in place. Her usual gold bangles with green studs were gone, replaced by a black long-sleeved shirt and standard-issue pants. She caught my eye, her soft light brown ones squinting as she smiled, nodding in agreement with Hayley.

As the wind picked up again, I nodded to thank her, pulling my jacket closer. I was tempted to cover up the exposed part of my face, but pushed the feeling aside. *I can't show weakness.*

"Time?" I asked, turning to my left, where Jaz and Zack stood.

His arm hung protectively over her shoulder as she looked at her PortMed. Her green eyes turned to slits behind her black and white horse mask. Her gold and green earrings atop her right ear made two distinct bumps on her black cap, her flaming auburn hair swirling in the wind despite it.

Zack looked down at her, love and protectiveness shining in his dark green eyes. His artistic blue and green dragonfly mask glinted as he pushed a piece of Jaz's auburn hair out of her face. The movement showed part of his green and gold sword tattoo behind his ear.

I wondered if he felt the night chill across his blond buzz-cut head. His cap, like my mask, was damaged on our way to Sally Brown in an ambush. I cursed myself once again for not taking our high-tech gear instead. If we had, then maybe there wouldn't be a small gash on the side of his head.

"Five till midnight," Jaz said.

I nodded in acknowledgment as my heartbeat speed up. *He should arrive any moment.*

"I'm excited to see him, too." The weight of Kyle's hand on my shoulder was familiar and comforting, grounding me. I turned to my boyfriend, giving him a small smile as my stomach constricted.

Gold and brown eagle wings crossed his mask, highlighting his deep brown eyes. He squeezed my shoulder in reassurance, aware of my unease.

I forced a smile, feeling the sting of the chilly wind on my exposed, cut lip. The sound of footsteps in the crisp snow broke through the air, making everyone turn, weapons in hand. I tensed as a figure emerged from the trees, pushing a branch out of the way. A brown and white owl mask looked up at me as I made eye contact with stormy silver-blue eyes. I couldn't hide my smile as I saw Shan.

"Report," I said, the joy in my voice obvious. Every muscle screamed to run to him, but I held back. *Not yet. Complete the mission first.*

"Everything is as we expected," replied Shan, his voice like music to my ears. "They are preparing for war. Sandy Village signed the treaty yesterday." I nodded, feeling suddenly grim. "Michel Thomas has also chosen to ally itself with Sally Brown."

"Trident is with us, and The Florida Falcons are already discussing a treaty," Zack informed him. "The biggest problem will be Water High. We need their numbers. If Sally Brown gains their alliance, then we will lose the advantage."

"That's true, but these are matters best left for later," I said, looking at the group.

They turned to me, watching. The wind no longer bothered me as Kyle stepped up behind me, blocking it.

"What's the plan, captain?" he whispered in my ear, sending new shivers down my spine. I ignored the way Shan's eyes glinted behind his mask as he watched us, focusing instead on the peace Kyle brought me.

"It's time we moved out," I commanded to the group.

They nodded, and we turned to the woods, leaving Sally Brown in the dust. Our cars sat where we left them as we pushed through to the next clearing, the green and golden lines along the sides faint and chipped from the last few months of abuse.

Shan followed me, sliding in beside Kyle and me as Garret took the wheel, Sally beside him in shotgun. The car started up with an almost imperceptible purr and we were off. Despite the unnecessary gesture due to its advanced AI, Garret kept his hands on the wheel as we flew by landmarks at breathtaking speeds.

It wasn't until we passed the borders of Sally Brown around four hours later that I let out a breath. Sinking into Kyle's shoulder as he pulled me close, I traced the lines of his sword tattoo on his wide shoulder as I stared up at Shan, admiring his eyes. They watched me behind shaggy bark brown hair, reminding me of storm clouds over a rough ocean bank.

"We missed you, brother," Kyle said, and I could hear his smile as he leaned his head on mine.

"It's not been the same since you left," I agreed. Shan rubbed the back of his neck, and I knew his signature blush was in place even if his mask blocked it.

"I missed you too," he said, refusing to look at either of us.

"You've gotten bigger," Kyle noted.

I nodded, pretending it was the first I took notice of how Shan's once slim, defined muscles, were now bulked up, though nothing like Kyle's.

"Yeah, I had little to do other than reading and training between the treaty talks. I finished two of my term projects already."

I shouldn't have been surprised he was so far ahead of the pack. Shan was always brilliant, a true Kent Wood genius.

"That's good. You missed the first two weeks of lectures and I know the teachers will be less upset at your absence if you have work to show for it," I said, watching the tension leave his shoulders. As the boys continued to talk, I glanced at Garret and Sally, watching as he reached over the armrest to grab her hand, turning to pay attention to her. I smiled at the sight, then turned back to Shan, listening as he filled us in on the minor details of his two-week stay in the mountains of Sally Brown.

The surrounding desert gave way to rolling foothills.

"We just passed checkpoint three. We should be home soon," said Garret from the front as we passed by a guard tower on the right.

I watched a group of five students turn as we passed, waving as they loaded into their ATV. After the night I was taken by Robert, Kent Wood had stepped up our patrols. It became an impossible task on foot, so cars and ATVs were essential and a major target for our enemies. Ambush and death often came hand in hand when driving, as my team learned the hard way.

The loss of Sam and Lucy still stung.

Though we were safe past the second border, my team stayed alert till the third. The remaining tension in the car gave way as the tower disappeared.

I checked us in with my PortMed. "Ghost will want to see us as soon as possible," I said, my voice business-like even with my head resting in the crock of Kyle's shoulder. "Tell the others to meet us at HQ for debriefing."

Garret nodded and Sally pulled out her PortMed. She pressed the newly installed button on the side and spoke into it. "Wolf said to rendezvous at HQ, you will receive further instruction when we get there."

"Roger that," replied a voice that sounded like Zack. Our speed increased once we were in safe territory.

A black square building, five stories high and seven stories deep, peeked over the last hill seventy-five minutes later. There wasn't a single window and the three visible doors were heavily guarded, access to most of the building outside the lobby restricted. We passed by the lobby doors, looping around to the back and parking on a turned-down lawn.

I crawled out of the car, stretching my legs, as the morning rays broke through the cloudy sky.

Kyle followed me, wrapping his arms around my waist and resting his chin on my head. A gentle hand tugged a few stray strands of my hair over my left side, reminding me I was partially exposed. I pulled my hood up, covering my face in shadow and hair before the guards at the door in front of us could notice.

"Thanks," I whispered to him, grateful for his mindfulness as people started to look our way. A simple bump on the back of my head, like a kiss through his mask was his reply.

Shan stepped out with Sally and Garret, looking around at the new HQ with wide eyes.

I led the team to the doors before us, tossing the car keys to Reed, the guard at the door. The cars were technically school property, and we shouldn't have been using them, but for unknown reasons, the school system had turned a blind eye to the war. Reed stepped aside as he caught them, revealing the small Holo-panel on the wall. I pressed my hand into the image, watching as light ran over every curve, a needle appearing to take my blood. I winced slightly, watching as the small hole closed as if never there.

The door opened with a click and beep, and we piled into the mostly empty back hall. Navigating through the many twists and turns of the ground level, we made our way to the debriefing room. At an inconspicuous white door, I scanned my hand again and entered the small, dark room. When everyone was inside, the door shut automatically with a click, telling us it was locked, darkness consuming us.

"Welcome back, alpha one SHS. I trust that the mission was successful," said a voice in front of me. A small light clicked on, revealing the shadow of a man sitting behind a large desk. At the sight, we all stood at attention. His vibrant red eyes, the only defining feature in the light, were piercing in the darkness as he scanned us. "At ease," his powerful voice commanded. We relaxed, and I looped my fingers together behind my back as I spoke.

"Ghost, sir. The mission went off as planned. Agent Owl is back with us and has brought valuable information."

Shan stepped up next to me, and I ignored the heat of his body as his familiar scent settled around me. He unzipped his jacket to reveal a bulletproof vest and reached into the pocket, pulling out a thick file zipped tight in a life-proof case. He tossed the file into the darkness and Ghost caught it expertly. Opening the case, his eyes skimmed the papers, his red tear-drop tattoos bright against his snow-white skin catching the light as his face turned.

I followed them down to his collarbone before he looked back up, making eye contact with me.

"Good job, alpha one SHS. You will have a two-day leave before you need to report back. Oh, also the hall to the lockers is under construction. An accident in the weapons lab led to a cave-in. You'll need to take the long way around."

"Understood," I said with a small bow, making to file out with my team before Ghost stopped me.

"Agent Wolf, I need you to stay behind," he commanded. I turned back to the desk, Shan catching my eye. I motioned for him to go on. He cast a worried glance my way, then left me alone with the most feared strategist in Kent Wood.

KRISTIN SATTERFIELD IS AN engineer by day and an author at night. In all she does, whether it's working on satellites or writing about new worlds, she enjoys exploring and creating the future. Her passion for writing started young in an eighth-grade writing course and has only grown. In her debut novel Lightning Rising, book one of The Shadow Wars series, she invites you to see the future she's made in a dangerous world of tomorrow.